© Copyright 2020 Sarah Bingham

All rights reserved worldwide. No part of this publication may be copied, reproduced or transmitted in any form whatsoever without written permission of the author and publisher.

Disclaimer: All characters and events in this book are a creation of fiction by the author. Any similarities to real people or events are purely coincidental.

# Angel of Rome

By

Sarah Bingham

To my parents who have supported me unfailingly and Melanie Bell, my former English teacher who took a passion for writing and nurtured it into a skill.

**Chapter 1**

Daniele awoke to find himself spread-eagled on top of his bed. It appeared that he had walked through the door, fallen onto the covers and dozed off immediately. Despite how drained he usually felt after a long day at work, that had never happened before. A glance at the clock told him that it was 11.30pm and he had been asleep for around an hour and a half. He sat up and finally became aware that the ringing wasn't his alarm, but his phone. He couldn't help groaning. The number wasn't recognisable which could only mean one thing.

"Hello?" he said, trying to cover a yawn.
"Hello, is this Daniele Caruso?" The voice on the other end was brisk and imperious, that of a man who has no time for nonsense.
"It is."
"My name is Massimo Ferrero. Are you the support worker for Isabella Moretti?"

That got his attention. Isabella was one of his favourite clients, a seventy-nine year old widow that he'd been working with for the past three months. Her husband, who had died suddenly last year, had looked after all of the bills and she'd struggled to stay on top of them. She'd been staying on a friend's sofa for six months before she was referred to Daniele, and after he had managed to find accommodation for her, she'd been making good progress.

"That's me. What's happened?" he asked, sitting up too fast and feeling momentarily dizzy.

"There has been a fire at Ms Moretti's home address. She has been taken to San Giovanni's for smoke inhalation and the Vigili del Fuoco are at work trying to save the property. You were listed as her emergency contact."

"I am. Thank you for calling, sir."

Grateful that he was dressed, to the point of still wearing his coat, he ran out of the apartment and then doubled back to lock the door. His fingers beat an anxious tattoo on the steering wheel and he wondered whether the police would accept his excuse to get out of a speeding ticket.

*She's already gone to hospital,* he told himself sternly. *Driving fast won't change anything.*

He reached San Giovanni's and barrelled through the emergency department, up to the front desk, and almost slammed into it.

"I'm looking for Isabella Moretti. I'm her support worker" he told the surprised looking receptionist. He dug around in his coat pocket and flashed the card which proved it. She looked at it, at him and tapped at the computer.

"Room 10" she said.

"Thank you" he called, already taking off. When he opened the door, he found Isabella lying in bed. A doctor was by her side, taking notes.

"How is she?" Daniele asked.

"A few minor injuries, but she's going to be alright."

He nodded gratefully and approached the bed. "Hello Isabella."

"Daniele!" Her wrinkled face lit up with joy. "You didn't have to come, although I'm pleased to see you."

"You look well," he said, sitting on the edge of the bed. "That's a relief."

"They tell me I'll make a full recovery. How's the apartment? I heard the bedroom was bad. Did they save it?"

"I haven't seen it yet. Isabella, what happened?"

She sighed and folded her arms on top of the blanket, reminding him of his mother when she was trying to avoid a difficult question. "My new Jacuzzi caught fire."

For a second, he didn't think he'd heard her correctly. "Jacuzzi? When did you get a Jacuzzi?"

"A few weeks ago. It's perfectly good. I don't know why it was thrown out."

"Did you plug it into the mains?"

"I think it overloaded the socket. I'm sorry, Daniele."

She did look genuinely contrite and that softened his incredulity. She wasn't the first client to do something moronic - only last Thursday, another one had fallen asleep while cooking and compounded the problem by throwing water on a grease fire - but still, a Jacuzzi was a new one.

"You're not supposed to plug a Jacuzzi into the mains. You need special generators for it."

He wasn't wholly confident in that statement, but Jacuzzis definitely didn't seem like the kind of thing that could be safely installed in a residential building, never mind by an old woman who wasn't capable of reading numbers on a spreadsheet.

"Excuse me?"

Both he and Isabella turned their heads. A young man in a police uniform had poked his head through the curtain. A stone sank into Daniele's stomach at the sight.

Hopefully this was just standard protocol and not a sign that Isabella would be charged with anything.

"Sorry to interrupt. I need to take a statement from Ms Moretti about the fire," the officer said, stepping inside with a notebook already in hand. "My name is Alessandro. Do you feel able to talk?"

"I'm not in trouble, am I?" she asked fearfully.

"No, it's simply normal procedure. It shouldn't take long" Alessandro said reassuringly. He shuffled past the doctor and took a seat on Isabella's far side.

Daniele listened as she repeated her story about the Jacuzzi, occasionally breaking off to cough or apologise. Alessandro gave no response to any part of her tale, simply writing as she spoke before asking her to sign the bottom of the statement.

"Thank you, Ms Moretti. I'll let you rest now" the young man said, standing up.

"Is there any news about the apartment?" Isabella asked. "Were the Vigili del Fuoco able to save it?"

Alessandro paused and released a long breath before speaking. "Fortunately there were no injuries," he said. "Your neighbours have been moved into a hotel for the time being."

Her dark eyes filled with sorrow as she watched him leave. "It's gone, isn't it?" she said quietly.

"I'm sorry, Isabella" Daniele said.

He didn't bother to say anything reassuring about how she was alive and only possessions had been lost. They weren't only possessions. They were the photos of her husband, the food she couldn't afford to replace, the few luxury items she'd saved up for and was so proud of buying. Most of all, the apartment was gone. Daniele had been so proud to present her with that decently sized one-bed, with its reasonable rent and proximity to her best friend. He wouldn't find anything like it again and they both knew it.

"I'm sorry" she said again. Part of him wanted to shake her, tell her that yes, she should be sorry and how could she be so foolish? And yet he knew from experience that only the cruellest person would display anger towards someone who had already been brought so low by the world.

"Don't worry. I'll look for another apartment. You'll get a rent voucher since you don't do drugs, so it won't be so bad."

"Thank you, Daniele. I'm sorry. I'm so stupid."

"You're doing well, Isabella. You've come so far since we met. This is a setback, but we'll work through it."

\*\*

The next few hours were spent sitting with Isabella, keeping her company as the doctors decided whether to discharge her. At last their tests came through and they announced their decision to keep her overnight. She had overcome her shock and upset now, and assured Daniele that she was comfortable and able to sleep. He bid her goodnight before heading home through empty streets. It was past 2am when he opened his front door.

His apartment was on the ground floor of what had once been an impressive house, but had now been converted into four small boxes. The living room contained a dark green leather sofa and armchair that he'd got from a skip, a TV which didn't work and a coffee table where his silver laptop sat proudly. A corridor led to the back of the apartment, passing the galley kitchen with room for only one person inside, the bathroom large enough for him to lean his back against the bath and touch the door with his feet, and the door to the communal garden with the washing machine tucked into a nook beside it. Finally there was the other main room in the apartment, his favourite room, a bedroom overtaken by a soft double bed which left only enough room for an antique chest of drawers. His most precious photos were lined up in silver frames on top of it.

What would he do if he lost these photos? He couldn't imagine it. They were all he had to cling to.

He sat on the bed, intending to dial the familiar number, but then saw that he already had a missed call. For a second he experienced a feeling like leaving his body, until he saw the name. *Pietro*. Oh, okay. He took a deep breath and dialled.

*You have one new message.*

"Hey Lele, what are you doing on Saturday night? I've got a ticket to a Triplemania concert at the Palalottomatica, but I've just found that I have a prior engagement and can't go. Do you want it? Let me know tomorrow."

Daniele deleted the message and then dialled another number.
"Hi." Cristina's voice was soft with tiredness.
"Did I wake you?"

"No, I was taking advantage of a quiet house to work. Thank you for the reminder to go to sleep" she said. He heard the quiet sound of a chair scraping across the floor.

"Sorry for calling so late. It was another hard day at work."

"Aren't they all?" she said. "The kids are good. Matteo's match went well. His team won 3-2 and he scored two of those goals."

She didn't say it, but he knew that Matteo would have wanted to tell him about it and he'd missed the call. If it was mentioned tomorrow at all, it would be with the dismissive tone of describing something that no longer mattered. He'd missed his chance to hear his boy chat excitedly about his achievement and he hated himself for it, but Cristina never judged or made him feel even worse about himself for not being there.

"Sofia isn't friends with Chiara anymore" she added, changing the subject quickly. There was a smile in her voice as she spoke. Sofia's friendship with Chiara was like a long-running soap opera. They fell out and made up with alarming frequency, for no reason as far as Daniele could see. He sometimes worried that it was unhealthy for his daughter to have such an unreliable friendship.

"I'm sure they'll be friends again in time for her birthday," Cristina continued. "She's really looking forward to seeing you. They're both asleep right now, but I'll put the phone next to Sofia and you can listen."

There was a crackle followed by silence, and then he heard the slow, steady breaths of a soundly sleeping child. Tears began to run down his face and he put a hand over his mouth to muffle the sobs.

**Chapter 2**

The next morning, Daniele dragged himself out of bed at 6am. Between the Roman traffic and all the stops it made en-route, the bus took two hours to reach the office. He could drive to work in less time, but that would deny him the opportunity to sleep, so public transport it was.

His workplace was on the first floor of an imposing six-storey building in Esquilino. The double doors leading inside had been covered in graffiti of six different colours, and the grills of the now defunct businesses that had once shared the space had been similarly adopted as canvases for the neighbourhood artists. Once the visitor had passed through the dimly lit corridor and stepped into the interior office, however, they found a bright and clean space which offered a pleasant welcome to the person seeking their assistance.

Daniele had spent fifteen years here, first arriving as a client when he was referred after eleven months in prison for stealing a car, and later as a volunteer at the shelter where rough sleepers went for a hot meal, a bed and access to a doctor. When Riccardo left to work at a bank and earn three times more than his colleagues could dream of, Daniele was recommended for the newly vacant full-time position and couldn't bring himself to say no.
"Did you get my message?" Pietro asked as soon as he walked in.
Pietro was the one in charge of finances, more specifically donations since the centre was entirely reliant on charity to stay open. He was the one who met with investors and local government representatives, explained how their money would be spent and why the centre was

a worthy cause, and then kept up gentle pressure until they'd agreed to put some of their money into the pot. He was charming, but terrifying if people tried to mess him about, and very good at his job.

"I did," Daniele confirmed, removing his jacket and putting it over the back of the chair. "Who are Triplemania?"

"They're a Europop group from Sweden," Gianni piped up. "He asked me if I wanted it too, but I said no. I will be busy on Saturday attending the album signing of Shady Oaks, who are a real band."

Gianni was their administrator. He dealt with paperwork, queries and complaints, and was often the first point of contact for new clients. Carlo had once held that job, until he left to work in the back office of a museum. The centre had quite a high turnover of staff due to the stress and low pay. Daniele and Pietro were the longest serving staff members and Daniele quietly lived in fear of Pietro leaving too. He couldn't imagine ever leaving this job, and the thought made his chest tighten.

"Shady Oaks wear bed sheets and sing in a made-up language" Pietro said.

Gianni scoffed in response. "Triplemania throw paint at each other" he retorted.

"Children," Daniele interrupted, making them both laugh. "Both of those sound like fun in different ways. So why can't you go to the concert?"

Pietro immediately turned to him. "I'm going to the cinema with Giorgia" he declared proudly.

Giorgia worked in an employment agency. They often had reason to deal with her or her colleagues, since the people they housed needed a way to make money which didn't involve a return to crime or sex work. Pietro had been trying to ask her out for five months, but she remained blissfully oblivious. It had become a source of both entertainment and frustration in the office, but this was a very welcome development, if only because it might stop him from looking so forlorn upon returning from yet another failed attempt.

"Congratulations" Daniele said. Gianni concurred with a thumbs-up. Pietro smiled, basking in his victory for a moment, and then looked again at Daniele.
"Do you want the ticket?"
He thought about this Saturday, as empty as the one before and after it. It had been months since he went out and did anything, and hearing his friends talk of album signings and movies had momentarily made him wonder what they would say if they knew he spent every Saturday locked in the house watching YouTube. Maybe it would be fun. Even if he didn't know or care about Triplemania, the atmosphere of a concert could be enjoyable. He used to love attending live shows.
"Yeah, I'll take it."

The rest of the day was spent trying to find a new apartment for Isabella, which meant dealing with estate agents. Daniele hated estate agents. They were all about twenty years old and in each other's pockets, humming and hawing as they tried to squeeze people for money, allowing their clients to pull out of deals on a whim and for the most ridiculous reasons. The stereotype was that lawyers were the most morally bereft profession, but Daniele begged to differ.

Between the agent's calls to his clients and three hour lunch break, and Daniele's calls to Isabella, the bank and the management company for the block, it was ten to five before he managed to lock down the apartment. It was smaller, more expensive and a few miles away, as the estate agent delighted in telling him, but it was all that was available.

The management company had refused to give any kind of compensation to help Isabella find a place that she could afford without a rent voucher, and not only because the fire was her fault. Apparently they weren't offering financial assistance to anyone, the heartless bastards. Isabella had told him about the mandatory monthly payments they demanded to look after the gardens, a task their tenants could do with a rota, and yet the overseers wouldn't stump up in their time of need. Daniele felt drained and like a total failure as he turned off his computer to go home.

\*\*

Isabella was released from hospital the following day and spent a few days at her friend's house. Daniele picked her up on Friday and his heart broke to see her standing alone on the pavement. When he ferried clients to their new homes, they were often carrying bags filled with clothes and pictures, but Isabella had nothing. He squeezed her hand when she climbed into the front seat of the car and she smiled back.

"I can't wait to see the new place," she said, apparently sincerely eager. "I think Laura was getting tired of me staying on her sofa. We're not the greatest of flatmates, with her bad hearing and my bad hip. Even when we were young, she needed her space. She was always telling me to go out and do something back then, just to get me out of the house. Is this your car? It's very small."

Daniele laughed. "It is, but it lets me park anywhere."

"I hope your colleagues don't drive around in Maseratis and make you feel bad" she replied, smiling.

"Oh no, I'd love it if they did. My little Fiat would always be safe from thieves" he said.

Isabella burst out laughing.

The new apartment was in a building that looked older and more unkempt than Daniele would have liked. It didn't have parking space, which wouldn't inconvenience Isabella too much, or a lift which was more of a problem. The area, to its credit, was pleasant to look at with only cracked tar and uneven paving stones as indications of disrepair. Daniele's research indicated that it had a very low crime rate. It was clear as they walked towards the building that Isabella was overjoyed with it and her enthusiasm was infectious, until Daniele slotted the key into the door and discovered that it didn't work.

One quick conversation on the phone, conducted almost entirely in furious whispers as Isabella sheltered in the doorway a few metres away, and Daniele had established that the landlord was currently in Florence. He promised to return as soon as possible with the correct key, which meant Daniele had no choice except to return to Isabella and admit that they were going to have to go looking for the nearest café and wait.

The café was crowded and they were fortunate to find a table outside, next to a chalkboard where the prices were written. Daniele bought a slice of cake and some tea for Isabella. She ate the bottom layer of sponge, but found the buttercream too rich and urged him to finish it.

"I'll try to find time next week to visit and go over the bills with you" he said. She smiled gratefully.

"That would be great, Daniele. Thank you so much. Could you…?" She paused and looked down, playing with the napkin. "Never mind."

"What is it?"

"This online banking thing that everyone talks about," she admitted. "I don't understand how it all works, but it might be useful if this hip gets worse."

He nodded. "I'll help you with it. Actually, Isabella, I think I might make a doctor's appointment for you as well."

She looked up, startled. "Oh no, that won't be necessary."

"Are you sure? You're finding it more difficult to walk."

"I can still walk," she insisted. "It just takes a little bit of time to click my bones into position these days."

"Maybe it's worth having it looked at, in case there's something that can be done to ease it."

"I know what it is," She pierced him with her glare. "I have arthritis. It's what happens when you get to my age. Thank you for your concern, but a doctor's appointment will not be necessary. There's no sense in making a fuss when there's nothing they can do."

Daniele thought about arguing, and then decided to drop it. This was a fight for another time.

It was after 7pm before they finally gained access to the apartment, and closer to 9pm by the time Daniele had shown her how everything worked and made sure she was settled. He held his breath as she silently looked around the living room, taking in the rough carpet with the hideous psychedelic swirls of purple and red, and the vertically striped pink and cream wallpaper. It was a nightmare from the 1970s and Daniele wished he could take her to Ikea in order to make it a little more homely, but he lacked the time and money, and she lacked the health for redecoration.

Finally she turned to him and he saw tears glistening in her eyes. She swallowed.
"I love it" she said.

**Chapter 3**

Throughout the rest of the week, he drove people to their respective addiction meetings, spoke to a new client whom he'd found sofa surfing at an existing client's house, did some shopping for Isabella and brought five ready meals over to her new apartment to see her through the week, spent three hours on two separate days talking down a suicidal client while frantically Googling and urging them to see a real therapist, and finally visited the hospital again to see a coke addicted client who'd relapsed and overdosed spectacularly.

He could never say that his job was boring. Exhausting, difficult, but never monotonous.

He slept until 1pm on Saturday, ate a late lunch from the deli while watching Triplemania on YouTube - their songs were decent, but he wouldn't spend money on them - and then prepared to go out to the show. He wasn't sure whether to wear his sleeveless top and ripped jeans, or a shirt and trousers, but he went for comfort over fashion. He took his old coat, the one his mother threatened to steal and burn every time she saw it, to protect against the chilly night.

Triplemania's fans numbered ten women to every man, and none of them were over 35.
Daniele had a sudden fear that he wouldn't be allowed inside, but he was. The woman at the door ripped his ticket unnecessarily viciously and let him pass. He looked at the card, barely held together now, and hoped Pietro hadn't wanted it for a souvenir.

His seat was in the sixth row, next to the aisle, surprisingly close to the stage and with an excellent view. Well, it had an excellent view for a few minutes until a woman with an afro sat in front of him. Still, it wasn't necessary to see the stage in order to enjoy the music, although he confessed he was a little curious about Gianni's talk of throwing paint. Pietro would have been furious to have paid for what was surely an expensive ticket and then been forced to crane his neck throughout the show. The thought brought a smile to Daniele's lips.

The band arrived ten minutes after their scheduled start time. Daniele admired their punctuality. The crowd around him cheered wildly as they began the first song, and he smiled and sat back in his seat, relaxing as those around him danced and sang. It was fine. Not at all his kind of music and he didn't understand a word, but he was enjoying himself.

Three songs had passed. The current track was some loud, upbeat dance track with a bass that shook the floor and hurt Daniele's ears. The lead singer came to the edge of the stage and held the microphone out to the crowd. Above the loud, tuneless singing in response, Daniele heard a shriek.

It came from close by and he turned in surprise. His eyes picked the man out quickly. He looked out-of-place among the bright T-shirts and jackets, wearing black jeans and a black sweatshirt with the hood pulled up. The bang was not lost among the drums. It was an unnatural, horrifying sound that reverberated around the enclosed space. Those further away looked around, confused.

Daniele was frozen, staring at the man and the shape in his hand. And then he saw the girl.

She was lying face down. She had blonde hair that spilled into the aisle. The gunman stepped on it as he passed her. People were starting to notice, scream, and try to run.

Daniele stepped into the aisle, feeling numb, as if some otherworldly entity had taken control of his body. The gunman wasn't looking at him. He was taking aim at the crowd by the exit.

"Hey!"

Daniele charged as the man turned. The gun wasn't lifted in time and they collided, both of them falling to the floor. Daniele instinctively put his hands around the man's neck, but something hard hit him in the skull and he was knocked sideways. His vision briefly shorted out and when the world faded back into focus, he saw the man standing up, pointing the gun at him. Daniele immediately grabbed his ankles and pulled his legs from under him, just like he'd done when he was wrestling with his brother as children.

There was a crack as the man's head struck the floor and then Daniele was on top of him, trying to pin his arms with his knees, except they weren't where he expected. He felt something small, round and metallic press against his chest. The adrenaline faded, replaced by gut-wrenching terror as he realised that this was his death.

He didn't feel anything else.

## Chapter 4

He didn't know he'd fallen asleep until he woke up, not in his bed as he expected to, but in a dark abyss. There was nothing above or below him. He felt as if he was floating in space.

"Hello?"

His voice was muffled. He could hear other voices, speaking quietly somewhere in the distance, but their words were impossible to understand.

"Hello?"

He was lying horizontally on nothing and tried to sit up, to stand, but his waving arms didn't push against anything. This really was like space. It was odd, but he didn't feel frightened. It was peaceful in this abyss, more peaceful than he could remember feeling for a long time. If he could float here forever in the quiet, that would be okay.

The light began small, just a pinprick on the edge of his vision, and then growing larger and brighter until he had to turn away from the 100 watt shine.
"It's time to go!" a booming voice echoed through the darkness.
Out of nowhere, Daniele felt joy. So all of those stories were real. There truly was a light that invited you to enter the next life.
"I'm ready" he said.
He reached out, but something was happening. Something was going wrong. The light was starting to fade.

"Wait..."

The light got dimmer and dimmer, until it was gone entirely, and Daniele was plunged back into darkness. The abyss suddenly seemed much less welcoming than before. The voices in his head were back, clearer now. He could hear his mother, his father, his sister, an unidentified woman...

"Stay with us, Daniele."

They were no longer in his head. They were above him. He looked up and saw the edge of the abyss wavering. He wasn't in space, he realised. He was underwater, in the ocean, and the waves were breaking above him. He moved his arms and this time they met resistance, pushing him up and up, closer to the surface, until he broke through...

He gasped for air and then realised that he didn't have to. An oxygen mask covered his face. He ripped it off and looked around. He was in a hospital room. There was a TV in front of him, a small table with a few Get Well cards and a bunch of flowers next to him, and a drip on his other side. He looked down at his arm and saw the tube leading to a blood bag, and the electrodes on his chest connected to a heart monitor. An uncomfortable tug on his nether regions indicated the presence of a catheter as well. How long had he been out? What had happened? Who else had been hurt? Before he could call for help, the door opened and a pretty dark-haired nurse walked into the room.

"Oh! Mr Caruso, it's so nice to see you awake."
"What happened?" he asked. His voice sounded weak and croaked from lack of use.

"We almost lost you for a moment. You're lucky to be here. Your family will be delighted."

There was a gentle knock at the door and a man poked his head inside. "Excuse me, is this the room of Daniele Caruso?" he asked.

The nurse turned and smiled at him. "It is. Mr Caruso just woke up" she reported.

"Good timing." The man came inside, holding a bunch of yellow flowers. "Hi Daniele."

"I've never seen that man before" Daniele declared quickly. He would certainly remember someone with such striking green eyes.

The man's face fell and Daniele almost felt guilty for denying that they knew each other, as insane as that was.

"Don't you remember me?" he asked. "I'm…I'm Marco."

"I don't know anyone called Marco."

The nurse was frowning, looking between them. The man took a shaky breath and then pulled out his phone. "We're best friends, Lele."

"My best friend is Pietro. I don't know you."

Nevertheless the man came over to the bed and turned his phone screen towards Daniele. Unbelievably, he saw himself and this same green-eyed man with their arms around each other's shoulders, smiling.

"Wh…Who are you?" he demanded.

The man turned to the nurse, pulling an anguished face. "Did the bullet do any damage to his brain? This is so worrying."

She looked between them once more, but the photo seemed to convince her. "I'll ask the doctor to run another few tests" she said, and hurried out of the room. Daniele was struck dumb by her ineptitude. She had just abandoned him, bedridden, to the mercy of a stranger who somehow had a photo of them together! He started looking around for anything he could use as a weapon.

"Well, that could have gone better" the stranger remarked. He dumped the flowers on the bedside table.
"I don't have memory loss" Daniele said.
The man glanced at him dismissively. "I know."
"Who are you?"
He smiled slightly and bowed, spreading his arms on either side like a second-rate magician. "I am your guardian angel."
"What?" Daniele reached for the call button. The man grabbed it before he could. "Don't do that" he said politely.
"Nurse!"
The man's amused expression vanished in an instant. "Are you serious?" he demanded. "Like this job isn't hard enough as it is. Alright," He set the call button aside and sat down heavily, barely missing Daniele's legs. "Listen and I'll try to explain in a way that even you can understand. So you died…"
"Died?"

"That was not the best way to open, I grant you that," the man said smoothly. "You didn't really die. Your heart stopped, but heavenly intervention brought you back. The people in the clouds beyond thought you deserved a second chance, because you're a hero."
"I'm not a hero" Daniele replied at once. The man cocked his head to the side.
"You saved a lot of lives."
"What about the girl with blonde hair? Did she die?"

"Well..." He paused, obviously uncomfortable. "Yeah, but no-one else did."

"That's no comfort to her family" Daniele sighed, looking away.

"Most people would be celebrating that they survived, and that they did it in such style."

"Why would I?" he demanded furiously. "She was young. She had her whole life ahead of her."

"So do you," the man said without hesitation. He lifted his legs and extended them to rest on the chair beside the bed, looking utterly relaxed. "I have been assigned to keep you safe from further harm so that you may reach the end of your natural lifespan. Included in this is providing, within reason, anything that could improve your quality of life. This is the reward for your sacrifice. In essence, I am both your bodyguard and your butler from now until the time of your death. So what do you want from me?"

"You're crazy. Nurse!"

"Okay, so we're doing this."

The man stood up and walked to the end of the bed so Daniele couldn't avoid looking at him. His skin began to glow gently, like moonlight, and a pair of enormous feathered wings unfurled on either side of him. Daniele screamed and tried to shuffle away, but his legs wouldn't move and he only managed to pull painfully at the wire in his arm.

"Wow, he runs towards a man with a gun, but a pair of wings makes him have a breakdown. Humans never cease to surprise."

Daniele kept his face averted, terrified of seeing those wings again. Once he could discount as a hallucination, but twice would probably make him lose his mind. Several seconds passed in utter silence, and though he could hardly bring himself to look, finally the need to know where the stranger was and what he was doing became overpowering. He turned slowly and was astonished by the sight. The man - the *angel* - was sitting on the windowsill and staring at him anxiously, wings gone. In the next second, the door flew open and the dark-haired nurse rushed in.

"What happened?" she gasped, looking around frantically.

"He's having flashbacks," the man replied. He sounded genuinely afraid and Daniele had to admire his acting skills. "He seems so confused and distressed, poor man."

The nurse released a sigh of relief and smiled at Daniele. "Everything is alright now," she said, in the same tone that he used when his children had a nightmare. "We'll have you well in no time."

Physically well, Daniele thought, although even that was doubtful when he remembered his numb legs. The mental injuries would take longer to go. He thought of that girl's long hair spilling across the floor, the cold determination in the man's eyes, the terror that had taken him outside his body. He never wanted to experience anything like that again.

"I'll call and see you tomorrow" Marco said, hopping off the windowsill and leaning over the bed as if he was about to kiss Daniele's forehead. From this angle, his eyes were blue.

"Don't tell anyone," he whispered. "They'll think you're crazy."

He straightened up, smiled and walked out.

## Chapter 5

His parents were the first people to visit. His mother ran into the room and almost climbed into the bed with him.

"Daniele! You're alive! I was so worried!"

"Mama, I'm fine. It's okay."

He raised one arm to hug her while trying to shift his body out from under her weight.

"Eleonora, get off him. You'll pull out his wires," his father admonished. He stood off to the side, arms folded, uncomfortable. "How are you, son? What did the doctor say?"

"I haven't seen him yet. No brain damage, but I'm finding it difficult to move my legs."

His mother promptly wailed in distress.

"We'll wait to see what the doctor says," his father said pragmatically. "I'm sure it won't be so bad."

The door opened and his siblings joined them, Antonio coming straight over to the bed while Stefania hung back.

"There are reporters outside" his brother said.

"What? Why?" Daniele demanded.

"They want to talk to you. You're front page news."

"Is nothing else happening in the world?"

Antonio chuckled at that. "I don't think there's anything more interesting than you at the moment" he said.

Daniele opened his mouth to say that he didn't want to talk to reporters, and he didn't want his family speaking to them either, when a more alarming thought popped into his head.

"Wait, how big is this story? Does Cristina know? Do the kids know?" he asked frantically. His mother looked down at her hands.

"Cristina heard," she admitted. "She called us when she couldn't get hold of you. I told her that you were alive and to wait until you were feeling better."

"Well, now I am," Daniele retorted, automatically trying to get out of bed and forgetting about his useless legs. He groaned and lay back on the pillows. "I need to talk to her. I need to tell her everything's okay. I don't want the kids worrying."

"Daniele, don't get stressed. It's not good for you. We're keeping her updated, don't worry" his father replied.

"I'll bring a phone in for you tomorrow," Antonio said. He sat on the end of the bed. "Why were you at that concert anyway?"

"Pietro gave me the ticket."

"Bad luck, or maybe good luck," he remarked. "You saved lots of people."

"I don't know whether to hug you or scold you," Stefania interjected, coming forward. "That was such a stupid thing to do."

She bent down and gently hugged him, taking care not to disturb the wires.

"Stefania, it worked! He's alive, everyone's alive" Antonio insisted.

Not everyone, Daniele thought, feeling a dark cloud slide over his head once more.

"He's paralysed" his mother said. Antonio turned sharply, horror written across his face for the first time.

"What?"

"The doctor hasn't confirmed that" his father said.

"Oh my God." Stefania put a hand over her mouth.

Daniele felt a headache coming on. He rolled over and closed his eyes, trying to block them out for a moment.

"No!" his mother shrieked, grabbing his shoulder and shaking frantically. "Don't leave again!"

He was relieved when his friends arrived, not least because his family cleared out to make space for them. He loved his family, but his head was being pulled from side to side trying to listen to them, and he was exhausted.

His friends were laden down with treats. Each one of them carried food in his arms. "I can never eat all this" Daniele said, staring as they piled their snacks like offerings on an altar.

"I know," Riccardo replied. "This is mostly for us. Take what you want."

Daniele looked at the selection of sweets, crisps, fruit, pastries, chocolate, water, alcohol, books and magazines laid before him. He took some grapes and a bottle of water before settling back against the pillows. Riccardo took up a position on the windowsill, Carlo on the chair in the corner, Gianni at the bottom of the bed, and Pietro on the chair closest to Daniele.

For a few moments, no-one spoke. The silence was filled by the gentle crunch of crisps and munches of sweets as they attempted to create an atmosphere of normality. In the end, it was Daniele who took the first step.

"How was your weekend?"

It almost seemed as if his friends froze, glancing at each other. "Is that what you want to talk about?" Pietro asked.

"What else are we going to talk about?" he inquired. He sounded sharper than he'd intended, he noted ruefully. They looked at each other, and then Pietro reached out and put a hand on his arm.

"Are you doing okay, Lele?"

"Yes, I'm fine. I'm alive, aren't I?"

He definitely sounded defensive now.

"As long as you're okay," Pietro insisted. "You can talk to us if there's anything you want to say, alright?"

"Alright."

"Alright." Pietro sighed, but dropped the line of questioning, and reclined in his chair. "Well, the movie was fine and the date was not in fact a date."

"No way!" Daniele stared. "How did that happen?"

"Giorgia's friend cancelled on her and she wanted someone at short notice. She thought it was just a friend thing."

"What happened? How did you find out?"

"I held her hand the whole time and she didn't complain, but then after the movie, I tried to kiss her and she recoiled. It was so embarrassing!"

"Sorry Pier."

Now it was Daniele's turn to reach out. The wires and Pietro's position prevented him from making contact, so his sympathy was expressed via some foolish waves in the air. His best friend shrugged nonchalantly.

"Oh well, I didn't have the worst weekend in the team."

Once again, awkward silence descended on them. Daniele could see eyes glancing around, searching for the person who would start another topic of conversation, hoping it didn't have to be them. Gianni was the next volunteer.

"The signing was cancelled" he declared. All heads turned gratefully in his direction.

"Why?" Daniele asked.

Gianni snorted unhappily. "The lead singer broke his leg," he said. "As I said to Carlo, he doesn't need two legs to sit behind a table and sign some albums, but no. So I was stuck in Empoli with nothing to do for the whole day."

"It was in Empoli? You didn't say that. Oh, I'm sorry."

Gianni shrugged. "It doesn't matter. There will be another opportunity" he said, with more equanimity than Daniele was sure he would have displayed if not for the current situation.

"I walked under the automatic barrier in a car park," Riccardo blurted out, not giving silence a chance to creep over them again. "I didn't even see it. It came down on my head. I've still got a huge lump. So yeah, none of us had a great weekend, I guess."

"Pietro," Carlo said. "Tell us about the movie anyway."

Somehow half an hour passed with Pietro regaling them with the exact plot of the movie, plus his overall impressions of the story, soundtrack, casting and cinematography. The in-depth review only ended because a nurse told them to leave so Daniele could sleep. He did feel quite weary, actually, and he felt his mind empty within several minutes of their departure.

When he woke up, he had already been joined by another visitor. Marco, if that was his real name. He was sitting on the windowsill, and if Daniele's eyes weren't deceiving him, was engaged in making a very neat row of paper figures.

"How are you feeling?" he asked without looking up. Daniele didn't bother to question how the angel knew he was awake.

"Something's wrong with my legs" he said.

Marco nodded as if that was reasonable and expected. "Yeah, probably a spinal cord injury."

"Can you help me walk again?" Daniele asked.

"No, you have to do physiotherapy for that" he replied quickly.

"I thought so."

They lapsed back into silence. Daniele looked at his legs and tried to lift one. It was so strange to feel his muscles clenching and to know how much effort was going into the attempt, and yet see no response. This was going to be so difficult, he realised. He always knew physiotherapy was hard, but he had thought it was a matter of building up strength and learning how to walk again. If his legs weren't moving at all, he had no starting point and nothing to build on. Panic sparked in his chest.

"I might be able to speed up the process a bit" Marco said suddenly.

Daniele looked at him curiously. It seemed like he had been receiving so much information in such a short space of time that he hadn't even considered that some kind of supernatural entity was in his room. The memory of those wings was the only thing which assured him that he wasn't losing his mind and Marco was not just a delusional stranger. That did not make him any less suspicious of the other man's intentions, but now he wondered if it would be worth exploring what having a guardian angel actually involved.

"Can you do that? I mean, what are your powers?" he asked.

Marco put down his paper and placed his hand thoughtfully on his chin. "That's a good question," he said. "I can function well without sleep. I can eat any kind of food and it seems that isn't a common skill. I can run over rough terrain without twisting my ankle, which I think you'll agree is impressive. Oh, I can do a proper dive. I'm very proud of that one. And I can fly."

He finished the list with a satisfied grin which clearly told Daniele that he would not get a straight answer out of this guy.

"You're not what I expected an angel to be" he remarked.

"What did you expect?"

"I don't know, perhaps a blonde woman in a long white dress."

"Didn't you ever learn not to stereotype people?"

"You're right, I'm sorry."

Daniele pulled the blanket up to his chin, feeling cold. "What happened to the gunman? Do you know?"

"I'm sure he's been arrested by now," Marco replied, and suddenly giggled. "You cracked his skull when you knocked him down."

Daniele thought about it for a moment, waiting to feel some modicum of guilt for causing such a large injury. There was nothing.

"Are there still reporters outside?"

Marco turned to look out of the window. "Yes."

"Can you get rid of them?"

"They're here to praise you."

"I don't want them here," Daniele retorted. "It's all about making a good story for them, but they don't care about the real lives that were affected by this. They'll poke around in my private life and then they'll leave with their columns, and meanwhile I'm paralysed, a family is grieving and who knows how many other people will feel nervous in a public space for the rest of their lives?"

He could feel how heavy his breathing had become. His blood pressure was probably through the roof and the doctors would raise their eyebrows at the readouts for the heart monitor. He glared at Marco, suddenly wanting to fight someone, anyone, and the angel was the only person in the room and the only one available to take out all of his frustration and hatred on. Marco was looking at him silently with an expression that Daniele couldn't read.

"You care a lot about people, don't you?" he remarked. Daniele couldn't figure out his tone.
"I'm a housing support worker. I deal with the people who fall through the cracks. Caring is part of the job," he snapped. His own words suddenly reminded him of yet another horror that he had to deal with. "Oh God, how am I supposed to go back to work now?"

He bent forward and hid his face in his hands. His breathing was growing shallow and rapid now as the full implications of the situation became clear. If he was paralysed, he wouldn't be able to drive. He wouldn't be able to go up all of those steps in apartment buildings with no lifts. He could take Gianni's desk job...But no, the light was extinguished as soon as it was lit. He wouldn't be able to negotiate a wheelchair up and down the steps outside his building. He'd be housebound. He'd need a carer. How would he wash himself, or cook, or move around his tiny flat?

"I'll see what I can do about the reporters" Marco said, drawing him out of his spiralling thoughts. He was already gone when Daniele looked up.

## Chapter 6

The next day, Rome was furiously battered by storms. Daniele was woken by the sound of thunder and stared, open-mouthed, at grey-skied Armageddon outside his window. When he grabbed for the remote control, he found that the TV wasn't working. He pushed the call button and a harassed-looking nurse poked her head into his room. He immediately felt awful about calling her.

"What's happened? Has the power gone out?"
She nodded. "Don't worry. The hospital has emergency generators."
"Do you have a phone so I can call my family? I don't want them travelling in this weather."
"The official advice is to stay inside unless your journey is absolutely essential" she replied.
"My parents will still try to visit me. Do you have a phone?"
He could see the impatience on her face, but to her credit, she remained helpful. "I'll look in the nurses' station, but it might take some time."

He nodded and she left the room. He sat back on the pillows and looked out of the window. Lightning cracked across the sky. It was only mid-morning and it looked like evening outside.
"Isn't it amazing? There's nothing better than watching a storm when you're safe indoors."
"Did you do this?" Daniele asked without turning his head.
"They're gone," Marco replied, answering a different question than the one he was asked. "I imagine that this

freakish unseasonable weather will replace you in the column inches. You're welcome."

He turned to face the angel, scowling angrily. "Do you know how dangerous this is? You could cause a car accident. You could destroy a house. If you bring down power cables…"

"And yet I haven't," Marco interrupted. "What would you have preferred, an earthquake in the centre of Rome? I had to do something spectacular. I mean, they would have got bored of you if you'd just given them enough time. You're not very interesting, after all, but you did insist that they left immediately and so…" He spread his arms out once again. "I am doing my job. Anyway," He came forward and dug into a brown leather satchel on his shoulder, the kind once carried by paperboys. "I'm not staying. I don't think anything will be happening today. Since the TV isn't working and you won't be getting any visitors, I brought this so you have something to amuse yourself with."

He tossed something on the bed and Daniele leaned forward. It was a comic book. *Batman* was written boldly on the front and every one of the caped crusader's muscles was lovingly rendered, as he grimaced furiously in the middle of driving rain. He looked up and the room was empty. The door opened a second later and the same nurse appeared, holding a phone.

As promised, he called his mother first and told her not to even think about going outside. She surprised him by replying that she had no intention of going out in such unsafe weather, not even for grocery shopping, and her husband was in agreement. He didn't bother to call his siblings or friends. If his parents weren't willing to step through their front door, they certainly wouldn't be. Nevertheless he held onto the phone, glancing at the door and listening for footsteps outside to check whether the nurse was coming back for it any time soon. After a minute, he realised that he was wasting time with his indecision and simply dialled.

Cristina picked up on the fourth ring. "Hello?"
She sounded harassed, like she was in a rush. Maybe this wasn't a good time, he thought guiltily.
"Cristina, sorry, I just…"
She spoke over him. "Hi Daniele, how are you? Are you alright?"
"I'm fine. Still in hospital, but I'm going to be okay."
"Well, thank goodness. I was so worried when I heard you were involved. Your mother said you were in the hospital, but I didn't know how bad it was."
"Are the kids with you?" he asked.
"Sofia's at a sleepover, but Matteo is here. I'll put him on."
There was a crackle and he heard her walking away, her distant voice saying something, and then footsteps getting closer and the phone being lifted.
"Dad?"

It felt like too long since he'd heard his son's voice and suddenly he wanted to cry. The whole thing seemed so real now. For the first time, he realised how easily he could have died. How could he have been so stupid? He'd already abandoned them once and to risk doing it again, this time forever, was unforgivable.
"Hi Teo" he said, trying to keep his voice strong and calm.

"Are you okay, Dad?" his son asked immediately.

That was always the first question out of his mouth whenever they spoke. He was a remarkably sensitive kid, probably a little too much for his own good. Daniele still remembered the worry on his face when he heard about his parents' split. There had been tears for the loss of the family unit, but almost immediately following that had been an unexpected series of questions about where his father would live and whether he would be lonely without them. Ever since then, he asked after Daniele's health during every conversation. On one hand, he admired his son's caring nature, but on the other he hated to see him worry so much about things that were out of his control.

"I'm fine" he answered.

"Mum said you were in the hospital" Matteo remarked.

"I am, but it's nothing to worry about, just a few scratches."

"How long will you be there?"

"I don't know, probably only a few days."

"Can we come and see you?"

"No, it's too far and you'd be so bored here. I know I am." He'd hoped to raise a chuckle with that, and fortunately he did, albeit a quiet one. "How is school?" he probed, trying to change the subject.

"It's fine," Matteo replied immediately, and then sighed. "It's boring. Our science teacher just makes us write everything off the board. We don't do any experiments or anything."

"That sounds very boring," Daniele agreed sympathetically. "How did your last match go?"

"We lost."

"Oh, I'm sorry" Daniele said, unsure of how to respond. It wasn't his fault that he was behind the times, after a busy week and then the horror that had followed, but Matteo was very impatient about discussing old news. If he'd told one parent, he expected the other to be informed by telepathy.

"When can you come and see us?" his son asked, now taking his turn to change the subject.

"I'll be there for Sofi's birthday. We can spend some time together."

"Do you promise?"

That hurt. Even though he knew where it was coming from, he hated to think that his son felt neglected in any way. In a way he was, but every time Daniele had the thought that it was ridiculous not to be with his family, the practical implications would immediately come to mind and he'd be frightened into staying in the same miserable position that he was already in.

"I promise," he said. "We'll go wherever you want."

"Okay."

"I love you, Matteo." He never said that enough. He preferred to demonstrate love, but now that he was no longer in a position to do that, he found himself forcing the words out more often. He was sure that Matteo could see through him, and sure enough, his son was quiet for a fraction too long.

"Yeah," he said. "Can we come and see you for Christmas?"

"Um, I'll ask your mother. I could come up to see you..."

"No, I want to come down to you," Matteo interrupted. "I don't like Milan."

"We'll sort something out" he promised.

"Okay. I have to go now, Dad. I have football training, but I'm glad you're okay."

"Keep me up to date on any news" Daniele said quickly, knowing from that tone of voice that the phone was about to be hung up immediately.

"I will" Matteo said. The line went dead. Daniele sighed deeply and pressed the call button to bring the nurse in.

## Chapter 7

The storm cleared after only one day, but Marco was right. The journalists didn't return. Daniele was bed-bound for another four days, visited religiously by his parents and three times by his siblings. His friends came to see him on a rota basis, one each day. And always, always, Marco would come. He had a freaky ability to simply appear, so that Daniele would close his eyes for a moment and open them to find the green-eyed man in the room.

The angel was supremely disinterested. Often he only spoke to ask Daniele how he was and if he wanted anything, and when the answer was invariably no, he would sit on the windowsill and draw glasses and moustaches on people in magazines. Daniele spent these visits reading the books that Pietro brought in for him. He asked once why Marco hung around so much, and the angel replied "Staying ready for action" without looking up. For the most part, though, they pretended the other wasn't there.

On the fifth day, he was transferred to a new care team and spent all afternoon meeting a never-ending stream of people who planned to help him get better. No less than three physical therapists – all of them purporting to have different aims, although since the only goal was to get him walking again, they all melded together in Daniele's mind – plus a specialist doctor and some nurses passed through his room. Marco complained about having his activities constantly interrupted by yet another knock at the door and Daniele was sympathetic. It was impossible to settle when doctors kept looking in on him.

He didn't realise how fortunate he was when they only looked.

That weekend, the nurses came for him. Marco was there at the time, fashioning paper planes and throwing them out of the window to see how far they went. He looked up from his latest design when the door opened.

"It's time for your physiotherapy to begin, Mr Caruso" the nurse in front said, with a bright smile that did nothing to hide the steel in her eyes. She pulled off the blanket while another nurse presented him with a wheelchair.

"I don't feel strong enough to try walking yet" he protested.

"All the more reason to begin," she insisted. "Any longer in bed and your muscles could atrophy."

"That would be a shame," Marco remarked. He jumped off the windowsill. "Come on, Lele. I can come as moral support, right?"

The nurses eyed each other, but didn't refuse. Daniele couldn't think of a reason to say no either, although his head was still reeling a bit from the casual address. Pietro was the only person who ever called him by a nickname. It was a sign of familiarity and long-standing friendship, and it felt odd to hear Marco use it after a week's acquaintance. Then again, everything about this situation was already so odd.

**

"I can't" Daniele insisted. He couldn't believe how difficult it was. He knew exactly what he wanted to do and willed his legs to move, but somehow the signal wasn't getting through. They felt numb and tingly, and when he told the doctor, her eyes lit up.

"They tingle? So you can feel them?"

"They really hurt. I can't stand up."

"Hold onto the bars," she insisted. "Put down one foot and use it as support to shuffle the other one forward."

He was already holding onto the bars and bit his tongue to avoid snapping at her. The bars weren't helping. Yes, they were keeping him upright, but at what cost? His legs were shaking and his nerves were shrieking with pain. He had to look down constantly to make sure his feet were flat and he hadn't turned onto his ankle, because his joints seemed so disconnected from each other that it would be an easy mistake to make. He pushed his weight onto one foot and immediately cried out in pain, tightening his grip on the bars and almost bending double. He heard a sob escape his throat and hated himself for his weakness.

"I can't! I can't do it! Please…Please don't make me do it."

"You have to, Mr Caruso," she said. "It's the only way to regain use of your legs. I know it's difficult, but you have to try."

"Come on" Marco urged.

To Daniele's surprise, he came forward and offered his hands. He did so with an impatient sigh, but at least the invite was there. Daniele grasped them both and moved forward with the gait of an arthritic penguin, Marco moving back step by step to encourage him. At one point the angel moved too fast and Daniele nearly fell. He released one hand and clung on to the wooden bar. He was walking, he thought. He was hunched over and unable to lift his feet, only to push them along the floor, but he was moving already. He reached the end of the line and Marco released him. He grabbed the bars gratefully and held himself upright, terrified of crashing to the ground if he let go.

"Now again."

Daniele was sweating from pain and exhaustion. "No, not again. I can't."

They did it again, of course, and again until Daniele was permitted to return to his wheelchair. From then on, he had physiotherapy every day and Marco was remarkably engaged with it. His 'guardian angel' preferred to read under normal circumstances - stealing the books that Pietro had brought, whether or not Daniele had finished with them - but when it came time for physiotherapy, he was more dedicated than the doctor herself.

Not only did Marco support him physically and offer advice, he also made him practice outside therapy. It became a routine that Daniele would complete physiotherapy for the day and rest until after visiting hours, at which point the angel would come to hurt him further.

"Please no" he begged, seeing the dreaded silhouette framed against the window.

"The more you practice, the easier it will become" Marco replied mercilessly.

Daniele would end up aching, sweating with pain and sometimes trying to hold back tears before he was allowed to go to bed. Marco was a hard taskmaster at first, but over time he seemed to realise just how difficult the sessions were on Daniele, and began to ease up.

"Just a little bit," he urged, leading Daniele around the perimeter of the bed. "Now we'll go back the way we came."

Physiotherapy was agonising no matter where it came from, Daniele soon realised, his secret hope of finding a painless way through swiftly extinguished. However he came to find it marginally easier when Marco was in charge. His aims were smaller – to the door and back, around the bed two or three or four times – and unlike the doctor, he listened when Daniele asked to stop. Ironically that made him more inclined to push forward, to try to meet Marco's goal for the evening. The pain was inevitable. If he could complete the exercises, at least it would be worthwhile.

When he complained of the pain in his tingling nerves at night, Marco would even give him massages. He would firmly rub along Daniele's back, his hips and down the length of his legs to his feet. It was uncomfortable, but not painful, and his nerves would stop screaming within minutes of Marco touching him. He was starting to think that the angel had lied, and he did have some form of magic.
"Why are you doing this?" he dared to ask one night. He'd almost done so a couple of times already, but fear of offending the angel and losing his admittedly effective help had stilled his tongue. Eventually, though, Marco's contradictory behaviour had gotten the better of him.
"Why wouldn't I?" the angel replied, pressing his thumbs into the back of Daniele's knees.
"You don't seem to like me."
"You've given me no reason to dislike you. Besides, I wouldn't leave someone paralysed because I disliked them. That's just evil."
"You said you couldn't help me" Daniele pointed out.
"I said you needed to do physio. I didn't say I couldn't speed up the process. I'm not a miracle worker."

"You're an angel, aren't you? You should be able to work miracles."

He cried out as Marco pushed down hard on a sensitive spot. "Sorry," he said. "You need to rethink what you know about angels."

"I don't know anything about them. Tell me."

Once again, he heard that unhappy sigh that had become so familiar over the past few weeks. The hands moved to his back, which was secretly Daniele's favourite place to be massaged. He knew he wasn't supposed to have a favourite place or gain any enjoyment from something that was meant for a purely medicinal purpose, but Marco had a delicate touch when he wanted to employ it, and he was very gentle with Daniele's spine. It was quite relaxing.

"We don't have any power over humans," he replied. "All we can do is guide them, give them a bit of luck when they need it, and the rest is up to them."

"You've helped me a lot already, with the physio and getting rid of those reporters," Daniele said, closing his eyes and sighing as Marco rubbed his shoulder blades. "Thank you."

"You're welcome. Do you think you can sleep now?"

"Yes. Thank..." He turned, but the room was already empty.

## Chapter 8

Time passed. His family continued to visit him every day, although increasingly they would simply sit there and be with him. All topics of conversation had been exhausted long ago. When his friends came, twice and then once a week, they would talk non-stop about everything that had happened since their last visit. Daniele suspected that they saved up every event that could possibly be called interesting for these visits. He appreciated their effort, albeit it was sometimes a struggle to remain engaged. Carlo had accidentally spilled coffee over a barista, but she wasn't going to make him pay for cleaning? On one hand, how unfortunate, but on the other, that was good. Gianni had saved some woman from missing the train by sticking his foot in the door? That was nice, hopefully he hadn't been hurt. Riccardo had left the bar and found a taxi right outside, and how lucky was that? Very lucky.

To his surprise, he found that his preferred visitor was Marco. Not because Marco cheered him up, quite the opposite, because Marco didn't even try. He arrived after normal visiting hours to help with walking practice before bed and he would be there in the early morning, reading books he'd taken from the patient library, before visiting hours would begin and he'd vanish again. He was so unobtrusive. With him, there was silence and no beady eyes watching Daniele's reactions. With him, he could process his thoughts and cry without anyone begging him to stop because it made them uncomfortable. Marco simply acted like it wasn't happening and Daniele appreciated that more than he could say. He just wanted to be invisible.

Physiotherapy continued daily. The doctors lauded his progress. They stopped short of calling him a medical miracle, because apparently his spinal cord hadn't been damaged severely enough that permanent paralysis was a certainty, but they had expected him to need a wheelchair for the first six months. Instead, in half that time, he was regarded as well enough to go home. When pushed by an anxious mother, the doctor admitted that he would still need a stick to walk until his muscles regained strength, and he shouldn't drive for the foreseeable future. Physiotherapy appointments and check-ups would continue to be arranged, but she couldn't see any further reason to keep him in residential care.

"He is going to need some practical assistance for a while," she warned. "Things like housework, cooking and getting around."

"Don't worry, son," his mother told him later. "Your family will rally around. Your bedroom is already made up for you."

"What?" Daniele looked up from tying his shoes. They were somewhat redundant since he would be leaving hospital in a chair, but it felt good not to be wearing slippers. His feet immediately felt much warmer. "No, I'd rather just go back to my own house."

"You're in no fit state to live alone. Your father and I will take care of you until you're better."

"I really think..."

He broke off as the door opened, and his mouth fell open when Marco stepped into the room, wearing a nurse's scrubs.

"Mr and Mrs Caruso?" he said, approaching with his hand outstretched. "My name is Marco De Laurentis. I am

Daniele's nurse. I've been assigned to do home visits until he's well enough to live independently again."

"I don't think that's necessary. He can stay with us while he gathers his strength" his mother replied.

"I think Daniele's case warrants some professional assistance. The road to recovery will be long and hard."

"We can manage. We're his parents."

Marco paused and gave a tight smile, evidently unhappy with the resistance. "So you'll be able to manage supporting him to the bathroom, washing him and helping him use the toilet?" he queried.

Daniele noticed his father's eyes widen with alarm. "Things aren't as bad as that. The physiotherapy has been progressing well."

Marco looked at him and smiled reassuringly. "Yes, but he's still unsteady on his feet and stairs would be too much to handle in his condition. I understand he lives in a ground floor flat. We believe that would be much better suited to his needs."

His parents hesitated, looking at each other, and Daniele watched them make two different decisions. His father's face became resigned, his mother's became stony.

"Alright, if you say so, but we'll still be the ones taking care of him" she declared.

"Eleonora, he lives on the other side of the city" her husband said.

"And you can't drive," Daniele interjected. "I need someone to take me to work."

His mother looked horrified. "You're not thinking of going back to work so soon?"

"I have to. I need to pay my bills and there are clients who need me. I've neglected them long enough, I've put extra burdens on Pietro and Gianni while I've been in here, and I need to get back on track."

"Could Pietro move in with you again?" she asked. "He did such a good job last time. I would feel more comfortable knowing you had someone familiar around you."

"This situation is nothing like last time," Daniele retorted. "Pietro stayed with me for three days. He didn't move in, and he didn't need to do anything. I need actual medical assistance, and…and Marco is a qualified nurse. I'm sure he knows what he's doing."

The lie tripped slightly on his tongue and he hoped no-one had noticed. He met the fake nurse's eye and received a secret wink in response. At last, his mother sighed resignedly.

"I suppose you're right. We'll come home with you today," she said quickly. "I'll cook some meals for you and tidy the place up at least. I'm sure Marco would appreciate the assistance."

She looked at Marco sternly, clearly giving him no option but to accept.

"If you're offering, I won't say no," he replied easily. "Daniele, I'll let you get settled in and then I'll come and see you. Is that okay?"

"Yeah, sure."

"Let me call you a taxi."

With one more beaming and utterly fake smile, he withdrew.

\*\*

Daniele felt like a child sandwiched in between his parents in the taxi. In fact, it gave him flashbacks to his younger days when they would collect him from the police station and the three of them would ride home in silence, neither of his parents looking at him and all of them afraid to speak in case the tension in the car exploded into full-blown fury. The silence was now caused by concern rather than disappointment, but Daniele hated the feeling anyway.

"Oh, Daniele, I've suddenly realised that you don't have food in the house," his mother said suddenly, and leaned forward to tap the taxi driver's shoulder. "Excuse me, can you stop at the nearest butcher?"

"I'm not really hungry" Daniele said.

"You need to eat, love. How about a leg of lamb? You love that."

He hadn't eaten lamb for months, but her maternal drive to feed was a powerful force and the trio in the taxi were soon joined by a smelly package of raw meat. They arrived back at his flat and his father helped him out, holding his arm until he felt confident enough to move his feet, supporting him as he limped across the courtyard. When he reached the side door leading directly into the flat, he came up against his first issue, mainly the three steps that separated his home from the garden. Once again his father had to hold his arm and Daniele felt like a toddler learning how to walk. He fumbled for his keys and managed to unlock the door. His mother took charge as soon as they were inside.

"You sit down there. I'll make you some food" she instructed, as his father hurried him into the living room and directed him to the armchair.

"You really don't have to..." he insisted.

"Sweetheart, you've lived on that hospital food for long enough. Look at you, skin and bones. A mother's home cooking is what you need."

"I can just order a pizza in."

"A pizza?" She appeared in the living room, having somehow gotten hold of a wooden spoon, and shook it disapprovingly. "That's not a dinner, Daniele. You need to keep your strength up."

"Mama, that's really not necessary" he called, but she'd already gone back to the kitchen.

"Let her do her thing, son," his father said. "Do you mind if I turn your heating on? It's freezing in here."

"Yeah" Daniele agreed, crossing his arms and trying to surreptitiously rub them.

His father went over to the electric meter, pondered it for a moment and turned a dial, then went over to the airing cupboard. He returned with a tartan woollen blanket, bearing it shyly in front of him, and put it over Daniele. He had never used this blanket for its intended purpose before. Typically it was the setting for Sofia's toy picnics, but he had to admit it was a good insulator. He looked down at the red and black checked pattern and thought that his transformation into an old man was almost complete. He even had a stick resting beside his chair, for God's sake. All he needed now was a stove pipe and he would have become his grandfather. The thought was depressing.

His father lowered himself onto the sofa with a grunt, as his mother returned from the kitchen. "Daniele, where's your tinfoil?" she asked.

"I don't have any."

"No tinfoil? How do you cook your Sunday roast?"

"I don't have a Sunday roast."

She looked as scandalised as if he'd said he didn't go to Mass, which he didn't. He hoped she wouldn't find that out as well. "How long has it been since you stopped eating properly?" she asked.

He shrugged carelessly. "I don't know, probably since I stopped having a reason to cook. Why would I make a whole leg of lamb just for me?"

His mother actually leaned sideways and held onto the doorframe. It was hard to know if she was genuinely so shocked or simply being dramatic. She'd always had a tendency to exaggerate.

"I can come over on Sunday…" she began.

"I'd prefer if you didn't. I hadn't thought this needed to be said, but just in case, I am forty-two years old and I do not need my mother cooking for me."

The silence which followed was the real deal, sincere horror. Nobody spoke to Eleonora Caruso like that without suffering the consequences, the consequences being a guilt trip so prolonged that they would rather have cut out their own tongue than voice their unedited opinion by the end.

"I'm sorry, Mama. I don't mean to be so harsh. I just…"

"It's okay, darling," she interrupted. "You've been through a lot. If you don't feel like eating right now, that's okay. Would you like to rest?"

"No, I'm fine."

She nodded and then gestured for her husband to stand, coming over to Daniele to give him a hug. "Make sure you tell that nurse to cook you something if you're hungry," she said quietly. "Please don't eat a pizza and nothing else. And make sure that you rest."

"I will" he promised. He had nothing else to do.
"See you soon, love."
"Bye."

And then, with a sad look and a wave, they were gone and he was alone once more. He would have to call her in the next few days to offer a proper apology, he thought. He should call Cristina to tell her he was home too, so she could tell the kids. How soon would he be expected back at work? If the decision was up to Pietro and Gianni, he wouldn't have to worry. They were his friends, they'd have his back, but the city council were always looking for ways to save money and if his job was vacant for too long, they would jump on the opportunity to downsize the centre. He should have asked for the phone before his parents left.

He looked down at his stick and wondered if he could make it to the phone and back. If he fell, it might be a long time before someone came to help. Being found sprawled on the floor would be the final humiliation.
He glanced up and shrieked. Marco had materialised in the centre of the room.

"I wish you wouldn't do that" Daniele snapped, pressing a hand to his chest. The walls in the building were thin enough that he could hear arguments, children crying, the person above him walking around their room at 3am and the music tastes of the students across the hall. If anyone was home, they would certainly have heard him yelp at nothing.
"I was saving you from having to get up and open the door," Marco replied. "I saw your parents leaving. I didn't want to come in while they were here because, you know,

logically it would make more sense for me to be here when they're not. So when they do turn up, you can say it's a visit. It might be a bit weird if they knew I was living here. See, I've thought this through."

"You're going to live here?"

"Yeah. Guardian angel, here for all your needs, which means I have to remain by your side."

"I only have one bed" Daniele pointed out. Frankly this flat was so small that two people sharing the space would get tiresome after a few hours, never mind however long Marco planned to stay, but the bed problem seemed like the most immediate issue.

"Oh. Well, it's not the first time" the angel replied casually.

"No! I...You can sleep on the sofa if you have to. I just need to get blankets..."

He started to lift himself from the chair, but to his surprise and consternation, Marco pushed him back.

"Stay down and tell me where they are" he ordered.

"In the cupboard outside the bathroom. Do angels even sleep?" he added as Marco went over to the airing cupboard.

"It's an option. We can stay awake as long as we have to, but it's nice to lie on a soft surface and dream."

"Okay. Did you get the pillows too?"

"Pillows...Yes. Hey, you don't have any bedclothes for them."

"Sorry about that, I threw them away. I'll order something off Amazon tomorrow."

"It's fine, I don't need them."

Marco came back and dumped the pillows and duvet in an untidy pile on the sofa, sitting down and spreading his arms out on either side of him.

"Where did you get that uniform?" Daniele asked. "Did you steal it?"

Marco looked at him sideways and smiled, and then clicked his fingers. The nurse's uniform immediately became a blue three-piece suit. Daniele lifted his eyebrows, surprised and impressed. Marco pointedly looked him over and then clicked his fingers again. At once he was dressed in the same outfit as Daniele, even including the slogan on his T-shirt.

"It must be easy for you to get dressed in the mornings" Daniele remarked.

"You'd be surprised" Marco replied, tossing his head. His reddish-brown hair, forming a neat pile of curls on top of his head, was the only thing about him which matched the classic image of an angel. As he moved, the sunlight caused them to gleam like fire. He could lose his hand in there, Daniele thought, not that he would want to put his hand in a virtual stranger's hair. He didn't know why he'd let that thought cross his mind.

"Can you get me the phone?" he asked. Marco stood up, retrieved it and handed it over. Alright, so who should he call first?

"I'm going to order a pizza. Do you want anything?"

Marco looked at him in surprise. "Me?"

"Yes. Do angels eat?"

"We don't have to, but it's nice."

"So do you want something?"

The angel narrowed his eyes as if Daniele had somehow caused offence, although he wasn't sure how he'd managed that. "I like Margherita" he said at last.

"Classic. Me too. We can share then."

Daniele dialled through to Capri Pizza, which was right at the bottom of the road and would only take about six minutes to walk to, if he felt able to do that. He hoped Cesare wouldn't think he was lazy for asking a delivery bike to come up here.

"Hi Cesare, can I order a twelve inch Margherita? Yes, that's all. Um…Do you want garlic bread?" he asked Marco. The angel shrugged and Daniele barely resisted the urge to roll his eyes. How helpful. "No bread then. Can I have it delivered? Thanks so much. See you soon."

He hung up the phone and saw Marco looking at him like he had three heads. "Why are you looking at me like that?" he asked.

"Most people don't offer me food."

"Why not? Is that a bad thing to do?"

"No, they just assume I don't eat."

"Without asking?"

Marco nodded.

"Well, that's very rude, especially to a guest. I won't do that, I promise."

"You're not what I expected either" the angel said.

Daniele looked at him and Marco swiftly averted his eyes, as if he'd let a secret slip. There was something intriguing about him. It was strange to realise that they'd met each other months ago, and yet Daniele knew hardly anything about him. Marco didn't seem like the sort who was inclined to open up to strangers, but it felt like an oversight that they should still be strangers after spending so much time together. It seemed like an especially untenable position if Marco planned to live with him.

"Marco, can I ask you something?"

The angel looked back at him, surprised. "Sure."
"What kind of people do you normally look after?"
"People like you, heroes" he answered with a shrug.
"I'm not..."
"Shh," he interrupted impatiently, waving his arm. "I mean people who've saved others at the expense of their own lives. It's a shorthand term. I've had one guy save a girl from a burning building, one guy who dived into a river to save a bus full of children, a girl who saved twenty people from a fire at a university...It turned out that she'd set the fire for the glory."

"No!" Daniele gasped.

"Yeah, hardly anyone becomes a hero for a selfless reason. Most of them end up losing their angels eventually. I've started to look for clues whenever I'm assigned a new job."

"What's my clue?" he asked.

Marco paused for slightly longer than was comfortable. "You don't have one yet, but there's still time."

"If you dislike humans so much, why do you keep doing this job?" Daniele queried.

"I have bills to pay" Marco said dismissively.

"You absolutely do not."

"How do you know?" he demanded. "Do you think the heating bill for an endless expanse of sky is cheap?"

He smiled as he spoke, however, and his whole face changed. The closed-off and grumpy expression, demanding to know why the person in front of him was using up his valuable time, softened into something much more youthful and friendly. Daniele found himself smiling back.

The moment was broken by the sound of the doorbell and both of them looked towards the window.

"Will I...?"

"I can do it," Daniele assured him, levering himself up and trying not to show how difficult it was. "I've got to practice with these legs anyway."

He waddled out of the flat and down the hall to the front door, almost throwing himself into the pizza boy's arms. He paid by card and was glad not to have ordered the garlic bread. One hot box, balanced on his palm as he turned back to the flat, was difficult enough. He kicked the door gently and Marco opened it, removing the pizza box from his hand and placing it on the coffee table, and then went over to the fireplace.

"Is this yours?" he asked. Daniele moved across the room to see what he was looking at, and his blood chilled in an instant. Marco had found the cardboard box shoved in the corner, filled with junk he'd never unpacked.

"Oh. Yes, that's mine."

"Did you sing professionally? That's impressive" Marco said, smirking over his shoulder.

"It was a long time ago." Daniele turned away and sat down heavily on the sofa, leaning over to open the pizza box, and hoped that the food would draw Marco away. It didn't. When he looked up, the angel was actually holding one of the plaques.

"I can tell," he said cheerfully. "These are from the last century. How old were you?"

"I started shortly before I turned twelve and finished shortly before I turned thirteen."

"Wow," He glanced at Daniele and grinned. "You must have been good, judging by these awards."

"I was lucky. I wrote a song for a music class at school and my teacher passed it to the radio station."

"You should put these up on the mantelpiece."

"That's not necessary."

Marco was suddenly sitting next to him, still holding the plaque. Daniele's eyes fell on the silver frame and he couldn't stop himself from reaching out for it. Why had he kept these? He never looked at them unless some visitor brought his attention to them, an event that was increasingly rare these days, and they only ever made him feel sad. He thought of his younger self, writing lyrics in school when he was supposed to be paying attention to the teacher, staying up late to play guitar and suffering for it the next morning, the combination of nervousness and excitement every time he got the chance to perform. He had been so happy back then. The sun had been so bright and warm, or at least it seemed to be in his memories, and he'd been so certain that the future would be equally golden.

"Are you okay?" Marco asked, looking at him with concern.
"I was just remembering. That was the last time I was on stage."
"Why did you stop?"
"I had to."
Marco looked confused for a moment, before his expression cleared. "Was it puberty?" he asked. "I know that can do damage to young singers' voices. You know," he added conversationally. "They used to castrate boys to stop that happening. It's a big sacrifice for a high voice though. Fortunately they don't do it anymore."
"That wasn't the reason."
Marco deliberately shifted closer and put his chin in his hands, like a child awaiting a bedtime story. It was almost

enough to raise a smile. Daniele looked down at the photo as he spoke, carefully picking his way through the words.

"I was asked to sing at the Palazzo Senatorio. There was some event going on, I don't remember, but it was a weekday. I asked if I could skip school to go and my father was furious. He said I was too old to keep messing around, that I was wasting all of our money and depriving Stefania and Antonio of attention because our mother was so busy rushing around after me. He said I needed to focus on school or get a job, and stop being a burden on the whole family. I didn't attend the event, of course. I regretted it, but I couldn't...I never knew that he resented my singing. I always thought my family supported me. I realised that I had it all wrong then."

The memory was back in full force and it was ridiculous that it could still sting even now. He could remember his excitement when his mother said yes, seeing his father approach and expecting to receive a message of encouragement, and instead hearing those bitter words that had sucked all the joy out of him. He could never look at his guitar without hearing those words. He hadn't picked it up again until Matteo was four.

"Bastard."

Daniele flinched in shock, staring at the angel, unsure if he'd heard correctly. "Excuse me?"
"Your father, he's a bastard," Marco enunciated carefully. "Fucking humans."
"Don't talk about my father like that."
"Why are you defending him? He crushed your dreams."

"He didn't crush my dreams. He was right. I was never going to make it professionally..."

"*How do you know that?*"

Suddenly Marco was on his feet, looking furious. He swung his arm to point at the box of trophies. "This is what you did! This is what you could have done, and your father took that away for spite!"

"He didn't force me to quit. It was my choice."

"Oh, sure," Marco retorted contemptuously. "Am I talking to the same man who grieved the death of a stranger and completely disregarded his own survival? You made food for me."

"I ordered pizza. It's not a big deal."

"Yes it is! Do you think your father didn't know you'd quit music if he made you feel bad about it? Honestly, the depth of humans' selfishness amazes me every time. As soon as your kind gets any power over someone else, it goes straight to their heads. Do you know why nearly everyone who's assigned a guardian angel eventually loses them? It's because they can't resist the temptation to hurt others. They have a heaven-sent gift and they use it to carry out petty plots for revenge or advancement. As for the way they treat their own families, it's shocking. I'm convinced that nearly everyone who has children is doing it so they can have control over someone."

He was pacing around the room, shouting and spitting. In the back of his head, Daniele worried about the neighbours hearing all of this, but he was more immediately concerned with his own safety. Marco was terrifying. He hated humans, Daniele realised. And now they were trapped in this tiny space together.

"I wish I hadn't said anything now" he said. Marco stopped moving and turned slowly towards him. The sight of Daniele pressed back against the sofa, holding a cushion as if it might act as a shield, seemed to surprise him.

"No, Lele," he said, his voice suddenly calm and emotionless. "Don't be afraid. I'm delighted that you did."

## Chapter 9

For the rest of the evening, a tentative peace was restored by observing hospital rules, in other words ignoring each other. Marco lay on the sofa and read while Daniele listened to music on the laptop. He did not have a pair of headphones, never having need of them while living alone, so he turned the music down to its lowest setting. Nevertheless he glanced up to see Marco bobbing his head slightly.

"Is it disturbing you?"

"No, it's okay" the angel replied.

"If there's anything you'd like to listen to, tell me."

There was a long silence and Daniele looked again. Marco had sat up from his horizontal position and was holding onto his toes, wearing the same suspicious expression as he had when pizza had been offered.

"Do you have anything…classical?" he asked after a moment. "Piano, violin, something like that?"

Daniele nodded and turned back to YouTube. He typed 'classical music' into the search bar and scrolled briefly through the suggested options. "There are a lot of old symphonies if you have a favourite."

"No, I like songs, just not the ones you hear on the radio all the time. You know, those dum-dum-dum heavy beats. I don't like those" Marco explained.

Daniele considered the problem, and then a brainwave struck. He typed a few suggestions into the search bar and one option kept reappearing.

"I think you might like this" he said, and clicked on a song at random.

It began as a vaguely familiar symphony, an upbeat cheery tune led by the violin and cello, accompanied by a soft guitar. Marco was smiling slightly as he listened. Nearly three minutes in, it abruptly changed to the opening bars of *Enter Sandman* and instrumental supremacy switched to the piano and guitar. The cello became faster and more frantic to keep up. The violin was replaced by a saxophone. Marco's eyes widened in surprise and appreciation. By the five minute mark, he was tapping his foot on the floor with a huge grin.

"What's that?" he asked.

Daniele looked down at the video. "They're called Stelis Ornata. They're a fusion of classic and rock" he reported.

"They're good."

"Come here."

Marco obediently stood and came over to the armchair. Daniele pointed to the screen. "This is their playlist. You can pick and choose the songs, or you can let them play in order." He got up then and gestured for Marco to sit in his place.

"Where are you going?" the angel asked.

"You may not need to sleep, but I do. Don't put the volume up too high."

It was strange to be back in his room. The bed felt too soft now. He was alarmed at how much the mattress sank to accommodate him, and how far his head was absorbed by the pillows. The duvet felt thick and heavy, and the bed itself was so big. He could roll from one side to the other without falling out. That was ridiculous. He didn't like it, much to his surprise, after so long spent lying in a bed that felt too small for him. It was lonely. All of the space was unnecessary.

For a second, only a second, he considered asking Marco if he wanted to share after all. That idea was swiftly discarded. A stranger in his bed? Not a chance. He wouldn't mind if Marco wanted to move into a sleeping bag on the floor though, he admitted. He'd rather not be alone, but wanting someone in the room while keeping the bed for himself was self-absorbed and exactly the kind of request that would earn him a vicious tongue lashing.

He forced his eyes to close. All beds were alike in sleep. He only had to empty his mind and allow himself to drop off. That proved easier said than done. His brain was fully alert and crammed full of thoughts that refused to let him rest.

He should have called Cristina and his work. Why had he forgotten that? Marco took up so much of his headspace that it had entirely slipped his mind. That was another problem to consider, how they were going to tolerate each other when neither of them wanted to be in this situation.

What if he couldn't work anymore? What if he lost his job? He glanced in the direction of the photos. At least he could go and be bankrupt in Milan if it came down to that. What a great father figure he would make then. Okay, sleep now, really. He closed his eyes again, but without the power of sight, his hearing sharpened. He could hear cars outside, faint music playing, thumps...Loud thumps, very close by, coming from inside the room.

BANG! BANG! BANG!

He jolted upright, turning his head wildly from side to side. In the darkness he saw him, the silhouette of a man standing in the corner. Frozen in fear, he stared and stared until more than a full minute had gone by and he slowly realised that the man wasn't moving at all. He blinked and the silhouette vanished, revealing itself to be an empty patch of darkness between the doorframe and the wall.

BANG! BANG! BANG!

He looked up and finally identified the thumps, not as gunshots, but as his upstairs neighbour doing his usual mindless circuit of his flat. God knew what the man was trying to achieve by pacing in the middle of the night, but Daniele wished that he wouldn't walk as if he was trying to break through the floor. He fell back against the pillow, breathing deeply and rubbing his eyes. Everything was okay. He was home, he was safe, nothing was going to happen. If that guy upstairs would be kind enough to shut up and go to bed like a decent person in the next hour, Daniele still had a chance of some rest.

Everything was not okay. Long after everyone else in the building had gone to bed, including the man walking his horse up there, Daniele was still awake. He tossed and turned, unable to get comfortable. His mind was wide awake now, not necessarily thinking of anything, just simply awake. It wanted to get out of bed and do something, but it was the middle of the night and Daniele couldn't even take a walk around the flat because of his newly acquired guest. He rolled over once more and watched as blue light began to show against the curtains, indicating that night was drawing to a close. It couldn't happen fast enough.

"Please let morning come soon," he prayed desperately. "Please let morning come soon."

"Daniele…" He turned towards the door and saw Marco, leaning against the frame and rubbing his forehead. "I can hear you whispering in here. It's keeping me awake."

"Sorry." He took a deep breath and rubbed his eyes. "I was…I couldn't get to sleep."

Marco hummed and came over to the bed. Without hesitating, he climbed on and leaned against the headboard. "Do you want to talk about it?"

Daniele shook his head. "I don't want to think about it anymore."

He heard his voice breaking and lowered his head, covering his face with his hands, desperately trying not to let his mind overwhelm him again. He felt something touch the side of his head and looked up, just in time to see Marco's hand moving away. The angel folded his arms and faced the wall straight ahead.

"You need your sleep," he said matter-of-factly. "I know what humans are like. You need to eat every few hours, you need to go unconscious every night, you need to pee so much that it's almost not worth the inconvenience of leaving the house. It seems like a very inefficient method of survival, but I don't make the rules."

"I don't know if I can go to sleep. My head is…" Daniele waved a hand vaguely and then slowly allowed his head to fall back against the wall, closing his eyes.

"I could make you have nice dreams, chase the bad stuff out."

Daniele opened his eyes and frowned at the angel. "Can you do that?"

Marco nodded. "What kind of thing do you like?"

"Um...I suppose I..." He was hesitating and he didn't know why. The answer was clear. Was he worried about giving this piece of himself to Marco? It wasn't as if it was a closely guarded secret, but his earlier words were circling Daniele's head.

*I'm convinced that nearly everyone who has children is doing it so they can have control over someone.*

He assumed that Marco was speaking from past experience, but that prejudice might bring scorn against Daniele or even his children. He wouldn't be able to stand that.
"My kids" he said simply, and waited for the hammer to fall.
"I didn't know you had kids" Marco remarked, not sounding judgemental to Daniele's ears, merely surprised.
"Two, a boy and a girl. Matteo and Sofia."
Marco looked around the room and his gaze landed on the photos. "Is that them?"
"Yeah."
The angel stood up and walked over to the drawers, selecting one frame and lifting it close to his face. Daniele could only make out his profile, but his teeth shone white when he smiled.
"Your little girl is as cute as a button."
His voice was definitely gentle, even fond, and Daniele finally relaxed. "Yeah, and she knows it" he remarked.
Marco laughed slightly, squinted at the photo again, and then replaced it to return to the bed. He leaned against the headboard once more and patted Daniele's pillow, indicating he should place his head upon it. He did so and closed his eyes.

He was on the beach. The air was warm and the sea made a gentle rushing sound as the tide struck the shore. Brightly coloured towels lay on the sand, familiar towels; thick blue and yellow stripes on one, another pale orange, the third bearing an enormous image of Winnie the Pooh. None of them were occupied now though. He saw Matteo first, sitting in the wooden cabana with a glass of lemonade in his hand, watching his little sister create pillars of sand with her bucket. She looked up at Daniele and then jumped to her feet, running towards him. His heart melted at the sight of her. She was so small, barely more than a baby. When she stood in front of him, she only came up to his knees. She clung onto his leg and pulled, pointing out to sea. When he looked, he could determine what she was asking. Jet skis sped across the waves and parasailers soared in the sky above them.

"No, baby. You're too small."

She pouted, deploying her lethal puppy eyes, which won her nothing except a big hug. Matteo had noticed him by now, and came running over. His son too was smaller than he remembered, and so cute. His face was still round with baby fat, no sign of the sharper angles that were developing as he grew up. Daniele lifted one arm to pull him into the embrace, savouring the warmth of their little bodies. It had been too long since he held them like this.

"Papa, can we go in the sea?" Matteo asked. Daniele duly stood up, lifting Sofia and holding Matteo's hand, and paddled into the shallows with them. The water was shockingly cold against his legs, but it felt clean and fresh after the heat on the beach. He leaned over, keeping hold of Sofia, so that she could skim her fingers across the surface. After a few minutes, the sea started to feel too cold to bear, so they returned to the cabana and ate gelato at a table on the deck. For just a moment, it seemed like the world was in perfect balance and Daniele felt true happiness.

**Chapter 10**

He opened his eyes to a room bathed in soft yellow light, the sun now long since risen, and the bed beside him empty. He sat up and rubbed his eyes, taking the easiest breath he'd had in weeks. Even if it was only a dream, the warmth and happiness it brought clung to him, as did the vague taste of ice-cream in his mouth.

    He remembered that day. It hadn't happened exactly as it had in the dream. For a start, Cristina had been there. It was one of the last times they'd been out as a family of four. They had sat on the beach for hours, with Matteo occasionally paddling in the sea, but mostly they had done nothing except rest in the sun and build sandcastles. Sofia had tried to bury him in the sand, he recalled, grinning at the memory.

    He limped over to the photos and immediately found the right one, which had been replaced at a slight angle. The three of them were clearly shown on their distinctively patterned towels, Sofia on his lap and Matteo next to him. That explained a lot about how Marco had gotten the details right. They looked so happy. He supposed that they had been. It was hard to remember now, it felt like so long ago, but he had undoubtedly been satisfied with his life. He took another breath, marvelling at the champagne bubbles that arose in his stomach when his lungs expanded, and headed for the bedroom door. Immediately he tripped as one of his legs seized up and he grabbed the bedframe, glaring at his traitorous limbs. Not everything had changed overnight then.

Stick in hand, he attempted the journey a second time. He heard the sound of moving crockery in the kitchen when he opened the door, and immediately felt an urge for breakfast. It was very nice of the angel to prepare food, he thought. What was he making?

"Marco?"

He walked into the kitchen and stopped dead, staring in horror at the sheet of crumbs strewn across the worktop. A loaf of bread sat there, which was a miracle considering he hadn't been shopping yesterday, and it seemed that every plate he owned now hosted a slice. They had been roughly cut in a variety of shapes and were spread with strawberry jam, butter, Nutella, blackberry jam, cheese, cold chicken, mayonnaise...Was that ketchup?

"What are you doing?"

"I'm making breakfast," the angel replied. "I didn't know what you liked, so I made it all. I can eat whatever you don't."

Daniele advanced and picked up the strawberry jam offering. The bread had split and jam was visible through the crack, resembling an open wound. His stomach turned at the sight.

"It doesn't matter what it looks like," Marco said. "It's jam. If you like jam, it'll taste nice."

"I appreciate it, Marco, but...I usually just go to the deli."

"You don't want any of this?"

"I don't mean to seem ungrateful," he said, carefully replacing the sandwich and licking jam off his fingers. "Why don't you come with me and you can choose a sandwich too? Something that you really like, not only someone else's leftovers."

Marco narrowed his eyes. "It doesn't matter what I eat, and I already made this" he insisted.

"I know, and we can have it for a snack later, but I need a proper breakfast" Daniele said. That defence seemed to work. The angel nodded and stuck the knife into the jam jar. Daniele winced. He was pretty sure there had already been butter on that.

"Let me get dressed and we can go," he said, beginning to turn before he remembered. "Oh, and thanks for last night."

"Don't mention it, really."

To Daniele's chagrin, it took twenty minutes to get dressed, and that was without showering first. He would need to adjust the time he woke up for work if this was a long-term problem, unless...No, he was not thinking about that again, not right now. Marco was waiting in the living room when he emerged.

"What are you wearing?"

Daniele looked down at himself, confused. "A shirt and jeans?"

"That's not a shirt, it's a vest, and is that paint?" Marco took a step closer, peering at his trousers.

"It's bleach. I was cleaning the shower and it splashed. Anyway, it doesn't matter what I look like. We're going to a sandwich shop. What about you?" Daniele asked. "It's twenty-six degrees outside. You don't need a jacket."

Marco pulled his jacket around himself as if Daniele would try to take it away. "I don't feel the changes in temperature and this is nice" he retorted.

"Alright, so we're both making questionable fashion choices..."

Marco pulled a face to indicate he did not agree. "I would tell you to get changed if you didn't take so long in the first place" he remarked.

Daniele barked with laughter. "You could try!"

"Well, you are a reflection on me," the angel said. "However, you have to be fed. Shall we go?"

He held the front door open and allowed Daniele to precede him. Once they were outside, Marco linked their arms together and then laughed.

"What is it?" Daniele asked.

"I just feel like we should be skipping" the angel remarked.

"Let's not."

"Maybe when you don't need the stick anymore."

"Probably not even then."

Marco pouted at him, but said no more about it. They walked in comfortable silence down the street until they'd reached the main road.

"This is one of the most annoying things" Marco muttered suddenly.

"What is?"

"Walking. It's so convenient being able to fly."

"Or using your teleporting thing" Daniele suggested.

"What? Oh, that only works on me. I would end up a hundred metres down the road and you would still be here."

"Well, it was worth a try" Daniele sighed. His legs were already aching and the idea of being able to move without having to walk had appealed tremendously to him.

"I could fly us there" Marco volunteered.

Daniele looked at him, testing how sincere he was, and chuckled. "I don't think so. I think showing your wings in the middle of a city would cause more trouble than a sandwich is worth."

Marco's shoulders slumped. "It was worth a try" he muttered.

They were second in line to order their sandwiches. Daniele moaned quietly at the sight, and felt Marco's hand move to his back and gently rub a circle at the base of his spine.

"What do they serve?" the angel asked.

Daniele looked up at the menu board. "Tuna, smoked salmon, cheese and ham, chicken and lettuce, beef…"

"What do you recommend?"

"I don't know, I usually have cheese or chicken."

"I'll have whatever you don't have."

They were called forward and the man behind the counter looked to Marco for his order first. "Can I have a cheese and ham sandwich?" he requested.

"Would you like it toasted?"

His eyes lit up. "Toasted? Yes please!"

The bread was duly put on the grill, where it was turned and poked for a good five minutes before it was declared ready to be served. It was wrapped in brown paper and handed to Marco, and then Daniele was asked for his order.

"Chicken, please."

"Toasted?"

Daniele raised his head to shake it. He was now leaning against the counter with his head down, trying to bear the pain, and the thought of waiting for two more slices to go through the grill was too much.

They sat down on a bench in the square outside - Daniele didn't feel ready to walk all the way home right now - and unwrapped their sandwiches. Marco took a huge bite from his and then smiled, his cheeks blowing out like a squirrel's. "This is delicious" he declared.

"I'm glad you like it." Daniele took a smaller bite from his and immediately regretted that he hadn't chosen to have it toasted.

"By the way, you got some calls last night" Marco said. Daniele frowned at him and dug into his pocket. The screen of his phone was blank, no missed calls and no messages.

"Why do your clients call you so late at night? I thought you were a nine to five worker."

"I'm a whatever time I'm needed worker. Where are the calls?"

"I listened to them for you."

"You went through my phone?" Daniele asked incredulously. Marco shrugged, pointing to his mouth to indicate there was sandwich in it right now.

"It was ringing and you were asleep," he mumbled, and then swallowed. "Jacopo called to say he needs to reschedule his appointment because he's going to see a DJ. Michele also wants to reschedule because he's going to a football match. Jessica wants you to look after her kids next Friday while she's on a date. I'm dubious of that one. You're a support worker, not a babysitter. Luciana has a job interview and wants you to go shopping with her to choose some new clothes. Elena's message was the same. And finally, Francesco wants you to come over to help him write a CV and fill in some application forms."

Despite the invasion of privacy, Daniele couldn't fault his delivery of the messages. "Alright, thanks."

"Do these people know that you've just been in hospital?"

"My work is never done. Pietro and Gianni have done a lot, I'm sure, but clients get quite attached to their assigned support worker."

"Why would you call someone at midnight though?" Marco insisted.

"People feel scared and lonely at night. They often don't have anyone else so they turn to the person they know will listen. Are you saying that the situation in Heaven isn't similar?" he inquired, smirking.

Marco raised an eyebrow. "I wouldn't know. The call centre deals with prayers."

"Call centre?" Daniele squinted at him, unsure if he was being serious. Marco looked back with wide-eyed sincerity.

"How else would you deal with 7 billion people trying to speak at once?" he queried. He formed a phone with his fingers and held it to his ear. "Hello, you're through to Heaven, my name is Michael and you are currently number 4 billion and eleven in the queue. Please hold, your prayer is important to us."

Daniele snorted with laughter at his saccharine tone of voice. "Tell me they use hymns for the music while you're holding."

"Of course. In fact, they sing down the phone."

"Good. That's the level of customer service I expect."

They grinned at each other, and then Daniele turned back to the phone, opening his reminders. "Did Luciana and Elena say when their interviews are?"

"No, but..."

"I should do that first. I can go out with one today and the other tomorrow. I can go over to Francesco on Monday and spend the whole afternoon with him. He'll probably need it. Oh, but how can I do that if I don't drive? I might need your help."

He turned and found that every trace of amusement had vanished from Marco's face. "You won't have it" the angel said.

"Excuse me?"

"You're supposed to be resting, not looking after other people's children and buying their clothes."

"They're vulnerable people. It's my job to look after them. You couldn't neglect your job because you're tired, right?"

That earned him a derisive scoff. "That's different."

"How?"

"Because you have a choice," he snapped. "Daniele, don't you think these people are taking advantage of you a little? Why do Luciana and Elena need you to go shopping with them? They're going for an interview. A black dress and shoes is all they need. And why can't Jessica..." He broke off suddenly and the light of epiphany came over his face. "Oh, I understand!"

"What?"

"They're women! All the stupid requests come from women! They don't need you to do this stuff, they just want you around to look at you. It makes sense!" Marco yelled, far too loudly for a public street.

Daniele looked around quickly in case anyone had been close enough to hear, feeling his face burning.

"No, it doesn't," he retorted. "Jessica got out of an abusive relationship two years ago and she's hardly been out of the house since. Luciana has an anxiety disorder and she needs someone to go to the cash desk for her. To be honest, I'm not sure about Elena," he conceded. "I think she just wants a second opinion. She's very fashion-conscious."

"And she's asking you to advise her on fashion?" Marco queried, and threw his head back. "Ha! She has the hots for you."

"She doesn't!"

"How old is she?"

"Twenty-seven."

"She has the hots for you," Marco asserted confidently. "Don't worry, you're going to give this stuff to Pietro or Gianni, and tell them to film her face when they turn up. You'll see I'm right."

Daniele felt anger spark and shook his head forcefully. "Whatever your problem is, you don't have to be nasty about people," he said. "Are you finished your sandwich? Let's go home then. We'll get the papers on the way past."

He grabbed his stick and pulled himself to his feet.

"Are you annoyed at me?" Marco called. "Hey, are you annoyed at me? I was joking, Daniele! Oh, for God's sake!"

Daniele went into the newsagent, browsed the selections for a moment, and then picked up a newspaper and two magazines. That should keep them occupied for the afternoon. Marco was still on the bench when he came out, and stood up only as Daniele passed him. They walked home in silence, about six inches apart from each other. Daniele looked at the angel only once, to find that he was still eating his sandwich on the move. When they got into the flat, he lowered himself onto the armchair and opened his paper, blocking out the view of Marco on the sofa.

"So what are we doing today?" the other man asked, after several minutes of silence had elapsed.

"I have no plans."

"Is there anything you want to do?"

"No."

More silence reigned. Daniele turned the page and finally, unable to keep ignoring Marco any longer, looked up. The angel was hanging upside down on the sofa, hands folded neatly on his stomach.

"Is there anything you want to do?" Daniele inquired politely.

"I don't know. I don't want to sit in this room all day. Don't you get bored?"

"No. I run around so much for work that it's a relief to spend the weekend relaxing. You can go out if you want" he added.

Marco grimaced at him. "I'm supposed to stay with you though" he said.

"Does being a guardian angel mean you have to shadow me at all times?"

Marco remained thoughtfully silent. "Not necessarily, but the paperwork will be a nightmare if you get hurt while I'm gone" he declared at last.

"I promise I won't move from this chair."

As soon as the words were spoken, Marco kicked his legs up and executed an admittedly impressive backflip to return to a standing position. "I'll wash the dishes before I go" he volunteered, already walking away. Daniele felt his annoyance dissipate then. It was nice of Marco not to leave that huge mess to be dealt with by someone else. He might be able to live with his sharp tongue, he thought cautiously, if he turned out to be a considerate kind of flatmate.

He read a few more articles in the paper, until the back of his mind registered that the water was no longer running in the kitchen. He lifted his head and listened. There was utter silence from the next room.

"Did you put them away?" he called. There was no response. "Marco?"

Daniele sighed and put the paper aside. He couldn't stand dishes left in the sink. There was every chance that Marco had done the job properly, but he needed to make sure. He stood and immediately regretted it, feeling his legs groan in protest, and he had to grip onto the arm of the chair to stay on his feet. Slowly, throwing himself from chair to sofa to wall, he made his way to the kitchen.

The dishes were still stacked on the draining board, washed and now waiting to be dried and put away. Daniele rolled his eyes and lifted a plate. It was still covered in soap and slipped from his fingers, smashing against the floor. Groaning, he sank to his knees and tried to lift the pieces. A sudden sharp pain informed him of the jagged edge he'd missed and he pulled his hand back, too late. A seam had opened in the skin across his palm, filling with red, and he felt nauseous with horror at the sight of it. The nearest available item with which to staunch the blood was a tea towel and he grabbed for it.

"You weren't going to leave the chair, huh?"

"Jesus!" Daniele screamed, recoiling backwards and knocking his elbow painfully against the cupboard under the sink.

"You may call me Marco" the angel retorted dryly, advancing towards him.

"We…We need to come up with a rule about you using the front door," Daniele gasped. "You can't just appear like that. You're going to give me a heart attack."

Marco sighed and shook his head as if Daniele was a moron. "Where's your First Aid kit?"

"That box there."

Marco knelt down and opened the box, taking out a little brown bottle and pulling Daniele's palm towards him to check the size of the cut, before selecting a bandage.

"I guess you don't have healing powers then" Daniele said.

"Oh, I totally forgot I had those. Why am I wasting time with a First Aid kit?"

"Alright, smartass," he muttered. "How did you know I was injured anyway?"

Marco glared at him and then lifted his palm to show the thin red line running across it.

"Oh. I didn't know that happened."

"Can you please be more careful from now on? I didn't even make it to the museum."

Daniele started to smile, and then the cotton pad of antiseptic touched his palm and he hissed, looking away. It lasted only a few seconds before the pleasantly dry sensation of a bandage replaced it. He looked back and watched Marco expertly wrap it around his hand and secure it.

"Out of all the things you could do in Rome, you decided to go to a museum first?" he queried.

Marco frowned at him. "Rome has a lot of history. It's interesting."

Daniele nodded. "I used to go to museums all the time," he admitted. "My son loves them. It doesn't matter if it's art, history or science. He just loves learning."

Marco moved away and sat with his back against the fridge. "There are no signs of children around here."

"They don't live with me, obviously."

"Obviously," the angel retorted. "You seemed close in the photos."

Daniele tried to smile, suddenly finding the floor very interesting. "We used to be," he agreed. "I used to have them every second weekend. We'd go to museums, the beach, eat a pizza and watch a movie. It was great. There were never enough hours in the day. And I used to pick them up from school two days a week and cook their dinner."

"And now?"

"Now I don't do any of that."

"What happened?"

Out of nowhere, he was struck by the memory of that day. He remembered going over to the house with his arms filled with games and books, and seeing the *Sold* sign outside. He tried to act as if it was an exciting adventure for the kids' sakes, and it worked well enough on Sofia, but Matteo sat there with his arms folded and kept repeating that he didn't want to go. He refused to look at Daniele. Cristina gave him a hug when she locked the house up and said they'd organise visits when they were settled in. The last thing he saw was his kids in the backseat, being driven away from him. Everything else was a bit of a blur. Apparently he'd walked around in a daze for days.

"Their mother, my ex, met someone else" he answered.

"Oh. He doesn't want you around?"

"That's not the problem. They live in Milan. He comes from there and Cristina moved with the kids to be with him."

"Why didn't you go?" Marco asked innocently, and Daniele closed his eyes. That was always the million euro question. That was what everyone asked, so well-meaning, as if no-one had asked before. His son, his friends, his sister. Some of them understood the reason, others not so much.

"I didn't want to leave my job."

"It means that much to you?"

Daniele silently awarded him a four out of ten on the tactfulness scale. "Of course it doesn't," he sighed. "I was just scared. I don't know how I would get another job. I don't have any qualifications and I have a criminal record. How do I go to an interview and say that? I only have my current job because Riccardo recommended me for it."

"But you miss them?"

"Of course I miss them," he snapped, offended at the implication that it wasn't written across his face. "I hardly see them anymore and Matteo doesn't understand why I won't move."

Marco bit his lip sadly. "It's a difficult situation" he said. His tactfulness marking was moved up to six for that.

"Yeah," Daniele said shortly. He placed his hand on the floor and turned onto his knees. "I'm going to lie down, okay?"

"Sure. Need help getting up?"

Marco was already starting to move, but Daniele shooed him away. "I'm fine" he insisted.

He expected Marco to go back to being a tourist, his duty done, but when he woke up three hours later, he found the angel sitting on the sofa and colouring his fingernails with a black marker. He looked up when Daniele walked into the room.

"Who decorated this house?" he queried.

"Um…the previous tenants, maybe. Why?"

"It's so ugly. I feel like I'm waiting to be digested. Haven't you ever thought about redecorating the place?"

"No," Daniele sighed, lowering himself into the armchair. "I don't have time or money, and it doesn't bother anyone. I thought you were going out" he added, before Marco could reply.

"I'll go tomorrow. It's too late now" the angel said, returning to his makeshift manicure. That didn't wholly explain why he hadn't gone this afternoon, but Daniele couldn't be bothered to push the issue.

## Chapter 11

The following morning, Daniele awoke to find two perfectly made sandwiches sitting in the kitchen, one cheese and one chicken. Both were toasted.

"Eat up," Marco said. "Do you want to stay with your chicken or try cheese today?"

Daniele picked up the chicken, feeling how crisp the bread was. "How did you know that I preferred toasted sandwiches?" he asked, wondering if the angel was a mind reader as well as everything else.

"You grimaced when you bit it yesterday," Marco explained. "I figured it wasn't the filling because you said you'd had chicken before, so…Anyway, how do I get to Villa Borghese from here?"

"The buses go every hour. Why?"

"I'm going back to the art gallery today and we can take a walk around the park while we're there."

Daniele turned to look at him, sensing trouble. "We?"

"You're coming with me." Marco smiled cheerfully at him, as if daring him to argue.

"Says who?" Daniele demanded.

"Says me."

"I still need a walking stick to get around."

"I know," Marco said, grimacing. "I'm not mean. A gentle walk through the park won't kill you, and I'll put you on the benches in the gallery while I'm looking at the paintings."

"Your generosity is overwhelming" Daniele remarked sarcastically. Marco replied with a sunny grin.

"Thank you. Now eat your breakfast. I'll get your outfit ready. I'm so helpful."

He walked out of the kitchen, swinging his arms. If he was asked, Daniele would wholeheartedly deny that he smiled.

They rode the bus in silence. Daniele sighed at the realisation that he looked just like the sign next to his seat, a rendering of an elderly person with a walking stick. Marco was standing next to him and, as soon as the bus stopped, extended his palm.

"Need a hand?" he offered.

Daniele accepted the assistance and swiftly regretted it, as Marco pushed his way to the front and he nearly lost his footing in the effort to keep up. Once they were on the street, Daniele shook him off and started to move as quickly as possible. Marco fell into step alongside him, at a pace so casual and deliberately slow that it was insulting. Daniele attempted to go faster and the angel sped up with him, until he started to go too fast and Daniele fell behind, at which point Marco slowed almost to a standstill. In this uncomfortably choppy way, they progressed to the entrance of Villa Borghese.

"Can we please sit down?" Daniele asked almost as soon as they were among the greenery.

Marco looked at him incredulously. "You cannot possibly be tired already."

"I'm not," Daniele retorted. "I'm worried about making it home if we go too far."

Marco scoffed. "I can fly you home if you need."

Daniele tried to turn too fast and needed to lean heavily on his stick. "We are in Rome!" he retorted, too loudly. "Do you really think people won't notice?"

"No," Marco replied immediately. "People never notice things. They'd think it was a bird or a plane or something."

"Listen..." Daniele's retort was cut off as his knee buckled, and Marco quickly grabbed his arm to hold him up. They made their way to the nearest bench. Daniele sat down heavily and lowered his head, taking a few deep breaths. When he looked up, Marco was sitting beside him.

"Okay. How far does the walk extend?" he asked.

"Um..." Daniele squinted up the path, trying to walk it in his mind. "It goes straight, then around the corner and there's another path...A very long path and...Yeah, I'm pretty sure there's another lane that takes you to the top of the park then."

"You mean that's not it? This place is bigger than I thought it was going to be" Marco remarked.

"If you want to see the art gallery, there's a train that goes from the viewing platform up there. It'll take you there. I really don't think I can walk it."

Marco nodded, and then looked around and laughed at something behind them. Daniele turned and saw a group of children messing around in the play area. Two of them were clinging onto the roundabout while four others ran around it, spinning it faster and faster, trying to make their friends fall off.

"That looks like fun, doesn't it?" Marco said. "Do you want to be the one sitting or pushing?"

"I think we're too old for that game."

"You're only as old as you feel."

"I feel eighty-two."

The angel sighed deeply then, looked at Daniele as if he was a disappointment, and patted his knee. "You rest," he muttered. "Let me know when you're ready to keep walking."

A high-pitched scream made Daniele flinch and gasp out loud. He looked around frantically. Where was the danger? What was happening? He couldn't see any indication of unrest. A family having a picnic, a couple walking their dog, two teenagers playing Frisbee, no sign of anyone being hurt or anyone with the intention to hurt. He heard the scream again and looked back. One of the kids had fallen off the roundabout and was lying on the ground, wailing. Daniele's shoulders slumped and he put a hand on his chest, waiting for his heart rate to slow. That had been frightening in more than one way. This had happened twice now and what if it happened again? He hated the thought of becoming a nervous wreck.

When he turned, Marco was gone. He looked around and spotted him already standing at the gate of the play area. The injured child was still on the ground, showing no signs of getting back up, while her friends had stopped spinning and were looking at her with concern. Daniele scanned the lawn area for any sign of a parent, but no-one was rushing to her aid. By the time he twisted his body to look again, Marco was inside the play area and bending down to speak to the little girl. He lifted her onto her feet and brushed a hand over her hair. She pointed towards the lawn area and Marco walked with her towards the gate.

Daniele struggled to get up, hunched over the bench as he urged his spine to let him stand up straight, gripping the stick and taking a moment to remind himself of his instructions. *Right foot down, left foot move*, he recited. The problem was not walking - that invariably happened within a few steps - but the fear of the pain when he put pressure on his leg. He stumbled one step, then two, managing to intercept them as they came down the slope. The little girl was limping and had a red gash on her knee. Marco was keeping up a steady stream of reassurances.

"You're okay. It's not far to go now," he said, putting a hand out as the little girl stumbled. "Will I call your mother?"

She sniffed and nodded

"Excuse me, Alice's mother!" Marco called. "Is Alice's mother here?"

The woman who had been part of the picnicking family rose to her feet and rushed forward. Marco stayed with Alice until she reached the edge of the grass, and then moved back as her mother wrapped an arm around her shoulders.

"She fell off the roundabout and couldn't get back up" Marco explained.

"Thank you for helping her" the woman said, already turning to assist her daughter down the hill.

Marco watched until she was on flat ground and then returned to Daniele. The sun caught his eyes and caused them to glow with an astonishing green hue. "Hey, are you ready to keep moving?" he asked.

Daniele nodded, feeling his legs shake as he realised that he'd been standing still for almost a minute. Marco linked their arms together once more.

"This is my life now, a living crutch" he said jokingly as they walked.

"That was a kind thing you did" Daniele said.

"I can't stand seeing kids in pain," he admitted. He glanced back over his shoulder. "I gave her a little blessing while I had the chance, so hopefully she'll have a long and happy life ahead of her."

They made it to the viewing platform, where Marco parked Daniele on the wall until the train arrived, and helped him get into the last carriage. The movement of the rickety train sent mild shots of pain up his back, but it was nevertheless a relief to be off his feet. They arrived at the art gallery and the driver had some choice words to say about his delayed departure, as Marco took his sweet time ensuring that Daniele could disembark with some dignity.

"Sorry" Daniele said. He doubted that the driver heard him, as he peeled out as fast as one could in a toy train. Marco stuck up his middle finger. Fortunately the driver didn't notice that either.

As promised, Daniele was permitted to sit on a bench while Marco walked around the rooms of the gallery, all of his attention focused on the artwork. After each circuit, he would sit down and tell Daniele about the sculptures and paintings before moving on.

They had been here for ninety minutes and only seen three rooms. Daniele looked at his watch and knew they wouldn't have time to go through the whole gallery. Besides that, he felt exhausted and desperately hungry. As they entered the fourth room, he was waiting for an opportunity to ask Marco if they could go and buy a sandwich on the way home.

"I like the Titian paintings" the angel remarked.

"I suppose you would," Daniele said. "They're all very religious."

"That's not the reason," Marco snapped. "They have bright colours and they're gentle. Bernini has nice sculptures if you don't read the cards. I feel so guilty about laughing at the one with the woman sticking her hand in the man's face. And Caravaggio is so dark and gruesome. I don't like him. He paints too much death."

Daniele smiled at him and moved over to one of the benches. "Look at this one" he suggested, pointing to the painting right in front of him. It depicted two cherubs with dark red wings looking either thoughtful or bored, depending on the viewer's interpretation, and the card said that it was a work by Raphael.

"Oh yes, this is a very famous painting," Marco said, sitting beside him. "I've seen this one before."

"Is it accurate?" Daniele asked.

"It could be, although I'm not sure how the artist met such young angels. The little ones aren't sent back to Earth, unless they escape themselves or they have a black mark that needs to be atoned for. Those two are babies. Heaven would never reject them. Maybe they went looking for their parents. They're so young…What must have happened to them that they died together? Their poor family…"

Daniele looked at him, surprised. "Why do you think they died?"

"That's how angels are born," Marco replied matter-of-factly. "Only an innocent can become one, so they are typically children."

Daniele paused, processing that information, and looked at Marco again. Did that mean…? He'd never thought about it, he'd just assumed that angels were an entirely different species that were begotten fully formed.

"Is that what happened to you?" he queried.

Marco smiled. It was a wide, toothy, unpleasant smile. "Not exactly," he said. "In fact, you could argue I'm here because I'm not innocent."

"What happened?"

Marco hadn't looked away from the painting throughout the conversation, but now he slowly turned his head towards Daniele. "Do you really want to know?"

"You don't have to tell me if you don't want to."

"I was ten years old," Marco said at once, with an unnervingly blank expression in his eyes. "I felt unwell that morning and didn't make outside in time before I threw up. My father locked me in a coal bunker as punishment for making a mess and wasting food. He'd done it before, but this time he left me in there for…I don't know how long. Days, I'm sure."

He spoke so quickly and plainly that Daniele didn't initially understand what he'd actually said. It struck him like a punch to the face. "Oh my God. I'm so sorry" he blurted out, ridiculously, but his brain had short-circuited from sheer horror and there didn't seem to be any adequate words.

"It was so cold in there," Marco said. "I can still remember it. My mother snuck out to talk to me whenever his back was turned. When I stopped responding, she forced him to open the bunker. I wish she hadn't been there when…when my body was found."

His bland tone of voice broke then. There were tears bubbling very close to the surface and Daniele regretted ever asking, regretted that he could never forget this information. For just a second, he thought of his kids. He put himself in the shoes of that poor woman and then had to physically shake the thought out of his head before it made him sick. He would lose his mind, he knew that. They would have to put him in a straitjacket for the rest of his life. There could be no coming back from a sight like that.

"Did you try to go back to them?" he asked, hearing his voice come out like a whisper.

"I did," Marco said, and when he smiled, it was melancholy tinged with pride. "I couldn't let them see me, I knew it would terrify them, but I did appear to my father. He had a heart attack and I watched."

Once more, Daniele was taken aback by his deadpan delivery of such terrible information, and the shock must have shown on his face.

"Don't look at me like that," Marco snapped. "He was a very cruel man. My mother and siblings were much happier after he was buried. I watched them when I could. I saw their weddings, the births of their children, their happy lives, and then I saw them go up to Heaven. I'm happy they're safe."

"But you can't see them again?"

"No, at least not until I atone for killing my father. Apparently his penance is paid," he said with undisguised resentment. "As far as I'm concerned, it was justice, but the powers that be see no difference between us. I guess I'll be stuck on this plane for the rest of eternity because I will never regret what I did."

He looked at Daniele so stubbornly that he suddenly wanted to pull the angel into a hug. No wonder he was so unhappy. Perhaps it was a different time and he was right to spare his family from an apparently deadly shock, but Daniele thought of his own children again. God forbid anything ever happened to them, but if they had the power to come back and assure him that they were well and happy in a place he couldn't see, it might ease the suffering even slightly.

"I can see you judging me" Marco said, interrupting his thoughts.

Daniele quickly shook his head. It would do no good to share what he was thinking. Marco must have had this conversation with many people before, and Daniele couldn't be the first to have considered that novel suggestion. It was too late to be anything but another source of regret to someone who must have too much of that already.

"I'm just thinking that I have a little more understanding of why you act this way. You do this job because you have no choice, but you resent it the whole time. Is that right?"

Marco said nothing for a moment, and the defiant look on his face slowly softened. He rubbed the back of his neck and moved his head as if it was stiff.

"I do my best, but there's no light at the end of this tunnel. So why would I do more than the bare minimum if I have nothing to hope for?" he said, and Daniele felt that finally the angel was being completely honest with him. This felt like progress.

"What's the bare minimum?" he probed.

"Keeping you alive." Marco started to get up, as if trying to escape the conversation, but Daniele grabbed his hand before he got out of reach and pinned it to the bench.

"Marco...I know that for an immortal creature, a human lifespan is nothing, but I still have decades of life ahead of me and that's a long time to be around someone who hates me."

Marco turned towards him and the look on his face was the same as the one Daniele had seen when he'd first appeared in the hospital. It was hard, frustrated, and almost angry. So this was not progress after all.

"We've been over this, Daniele," he said icily. "I don't hate you. I wish you would go outside more, but that's not enough to say that I hate you. I'm just doing a job, and remember, you have an eternity in the clouds to look forward to. All I have in my future is an endless line of people who show me pictures of angels to ask if they're accurate."

He pulled his hand away sharply and looked down on Daniele as if he could crush him. "Now let's move on before the guards think we're plotting to steal one of the paintings."

He walked away and by the time Daniele had struggled to his feet, the angel had moved on to the next room. Daniele found him thoughtfully gazing at a series of charcoal sketches that, although he didn't claim to have a great understanding of art, looked a bit ugly. Marco turned towards him and smiled brightly, as if the previous conversation had never happened.

**Chapter 12**

Daniele was off work for another week, but that didn't mean he wasn't busy. For a start, he used the spare time to make all the calls he needed to. He called Pietro to tell him that he wasn't ready to return yet, but he'd try to come back as soon as possible. His friend assured him that he should take all the time he needed to recover, kind words which they both knew had no meaning. He added that nobody except himself and Gianni knew that Daniele hadn't returned on Monday and he intended to keep it that way for as long as possible, which nearly brought tears of gratitude to Daniele's eyes.

"If you really need me to come back, call me and I'll be there the next morning" he said.
"I will, but seriously don't rush yourself. You need to get better. Do you want me to do anything for you?"
"It's okay, Pier. I'm getting a lot of support from the hospital."
"Alright, but the offer stands. You call me if you need anything and I'll be there."

He was a great friend, Daniele thought after the conversation ended. He always had been from Daniele's first week at the centre when Pietro brought his lunch over and asked if they could eat together, later explaining that he'd seen Daniele eating alone for days and thought it would be nice to find out if he wanted company. When Cristina and the kids left for Milan, mere weeks before Christmas, Pietro had shown up at his door on the 24th and invited him out for a Christmas dinner. It was only a meal at a pizzeria, not the usual turkey and trimmings, but it got him out of the house and Pietro had stayed with him until the 27<sup>th</sup> so that he didn't spend the worst days of the season alone. He'd never figured out how to adequately express his thanks for that.

He also called Cristina to let her know he was home, but got a pleasant surprise when the phone was picked up by Sofia.
"Hello!"
He grinned at his daughter's loud, cheerful voice. "Hi piccola, how are you? Why aren't you at nursery?"
"Papa! Hi Papa! I'm sick! Mama said you were in the hospital. Did you get hurt?"
"Just a few scratches, nothing to worry about."
"And you're fixed?" she asked. He laughed quietly. There was truly no better mood enhancer than Sofia's simple view of the world.
"Yes, I'm fixed. What's this sickness you have? You don't sound very unwell to me."
"I was" she declared stubbornly.
"You should be in bed then."
"Bed is boring."
He chuckled. "I agree with you there."
"I miss you" she said, and he wished he could reach all the way across the country to wrap her in a big hug.
"I miss you too. Do you know what you're doing for your birthday?"
"Yes, we're going to Dreamland because Chiara's been there before and it's really amazing. Papa, can I have Alice from Tubby Teddies for my birthday? She's the green one."
"Okay, I'll see what I can do. Is Chiara coming to your party?" he asked.
"Yes."

He would never, in a million years, understand the way this friendship worked. "I thought you'd fallen out with each other."

"We had, but now we're not" she replied simply. He supposed he couldn't argue with that logic.

"Will you tell Mama that I called to let her know I'm home?"

"Okay!" She ran off, leaving the phone off the hook. Cristina picked it up, he passed on the message, and she wished him a speedy recovery.

The other reason that he was busy was because of work. Officially he was on leave, but clients' issues didn't magically vanish simply because it was inconvenient for him. He discussed it with Marco and they were able to agree on a compromise, which was essentially made of Marco giving him orders and then backing down on anything Daniele argued back about, which admittedly wasn't much. He gave the shopping expeditions and the rescheduled appointments over to his colleagues, but kept hold of Jessica and Francesco because his involvement was essential in those cases.

On Monday, as promised, he went over to Francesco's place and quickly discovered that he had not actually been called to help with a CV. Francesco admitted that the long, hopeless quest for employment had got on top of him. He'd done something stupid, handing his money over to an online course that had frightened him with screaming declarations of *Only One Place Left*, *Pay Now to Get a Discounted Price*. He didn't even want to work in that particular industry. He was just getting so desperate, and burst into tears as he explained.

"What if I'm completely unemployable?" he asked. "What if I can never get a job?"

"You will get a job. Something will turn up if we give it enough time, but you need to be calmer. Don't rush into things."

"I feel like a failure!" the man cried, and Daniele couldn't stop himself from giving him a hug. How well he knew that feeling.

He spent three hours making phone calls and sending emails, and thank God that the company was actually legitimate, for all their cheap scare tactics. Francesco was still within the time frame for a refund and the whole thing was sorted with no long-term repercussions, except for a better understanding of the consequences of rushing a major financial decision. Daniele looked through his CV and suggested some edits, went through the jobs listings to find out what Francesco was interested in, and finally referred him to the employment agency for some additional support. He was in much greater spirits when Daniele departed, feeling drained despite the fact that he'd only seen one client today.

Marco was sitting in the stairwell outside, playing *Angry Birds* on Daniele's phone. In some ways, the angel's need to be constantly active reminded him of his children and he couldn't help finding it slightly endearing. That didn't mean that it wasn't exhausting to be stuck with someone who was so easily bored. He didn't know how he was going to handle this in the long-term.

"You look tired" Marco said, looking over his shoulder. Daniele was bracing one hand against the wall and was forced to nod in agreement.

"I might need a bit of help getting back downstairs."

Marco immediately jumped up, pocketing the phone and putting an arm around Daniele's waist. He threw his arm over the angel's shoulders and began the descent. Fortunately Francesco lived on the first floor of his building so there was only one flight to handle, but Daniele was still growing lopsided and leaning heavily on Marco as they emerged onto the street.

"I'm good now, I'm good," he said, stepping away and pressing his stick into the ground. "I can make it on my own."

"Maybe you're trying to run before you can walk, pun intended," Marco said, hovering close by. "You're not even getting paid for this."

"You sound like my father" Daniele said, in between heaving deep breaths.

"Ugh!" Marco's face screwed up in horror. "Listen, the Spanish Steps aren't far from here. Let's take a rest. We can have a gelato."

Daniele smiled slightly at the hopeful note in his voice. "Now you sound like my kids."

"That's better."

There was no gelateria in Piazza di Spagna, but Marco had evidently used the time to do some research. "There's a shop up there and down there," he said, pointing like he was bringing a plane in to land. "They're about equal distance. Do you know what flavour you want?"

"Biscotti," Daniele said, sitting on the edge of the Barcaccia Fountain. "Can you get back here before it melts?"

"I can do anything" Marco said. He turned and started to run up the street.

"Marco!"

"Yeah?"

"Money."

"Oh," Marco hurried back to his side and took the proffered coins. "I always forget about that."

He ran off again, leaving Daniele to enjoy the panoramic view of the piazza and the Steps, and the feeling of the sun absorbing through his trousers which was just on the right side of uncomfortable. At 3pm on a Monday, it was likely that most of the people milling around were tourists, and it was easy to spot them by the cameras held high. He watched them take photos of the buildings, the horses, the fountain, as if they'd never seen such things before. It was one thing to admire Rome's unique history, another to snap photos of an apartment building as if it was the most fascinating sight. Their priorities confused him, but he supposed they would also think he was strange if he went to their countries.

"Delivery" Marco announced, having appeared without a sound. He presented a sandwich of gelato between two pieces of biscotti, and turned his attention to a bowl of three scoops topped with caramel. Daniele could see that it was swimming in a pool of vanilla and a dribble was running down the side of the bowl. Even angels couldn't prevent some things.

"What did you get?" he asked.

"Panna cotta, although I expected it to have strawberries."

Marco pulled an exaggerated sad face and then stuck his spoon in, happily eating his treat. Daniele did the same, glad for the napkin as the cream made a bid for freedom.

"I haven't had gelato for a while. This was a great idea" he said when the dessert was done.

"I'm glad you think so," Marco smiled and pulled nervously on his fingers. "Do you feel better now?"

"My back still aches, but less stressed, yeah.

"We can stay here for a little longer. I suppose I should tell you..." Marco reached into his pocket and pulled out Daniele's phone. "You missed a call."

"What?"

He grabbed the phone and tapped the screen. The caller ID flashed up as Luca and he swore.

"Did I do the wrong thing? I didn't want you to start running after someone else..."

"For f...Marco!"

It wasn't his fault, Daniele had to remind himself. He didn't know. His fingers shook as he redialled, already imagining what he would say to the emergency services.

"Hello? Daniele?" Luca answered, sounding confused. Daniele too was confused. Luca was alive? And didn't sound in any particular distress?

"Hi," he gasped. "Did you call me? I'm sorry I missed it. Is everything okay?"

"Today? Yeah, everything's okay today. Just muddling through, you know," Luca remarked semi-brightly. "Sorry, I must have sat on my phone and it called the last number on the log. I'll let you know if I need anything."

"Do that," Daniele agreed. "Bye Luca. Take care of yourself."

He hung up and immediately second-guessed his response. What if that had been too abrupt? What if Luca felt that Daniele was eager to get off the phone – which he was – and it sent him into another blue mood, which wouldn't have happened if he hadn't called back? Why did everything have to be so hard?

"All good?" Marco asked hopefully.

"Yeah, it was just a mistake" Daniele muttered.

"Who's Luca? Another client?"

"Former client," he admitted. "He thinks he has depression, and maybe he does, but he's never been diagnosed. He's been using me as an out-of-hours therapist for about nine months. I've never missed a call from him before. Sorry that I shouted at you."

"Why doesn't he go to a real therapist?" Marco asked.

Daniele looked at him and smiled ruefully, shrugging. "They cost money."

Marco frowned deeply and Daniele sighed, lacking the energy to deal with this anymore. "Let's just go home," he said. "I need to lie down after that."

\*\*

He didn't work again for the rest of the week. He did, however, attend his first outpatient appointment with the physiotherapist. Marco came in to assist for the first few rounds, and then retired to let Daniele try it on his own. It was harder without some support from a hand or a stick, but he managed to get around without falling. The doctor let him sit down after an hour, tapped his knees with a little hammer and noted his responses.

"How is the stick working out?" she asked.

"It's good. It really helps," he said. "When do you think I can stop using it?"

She hummed thoughtfully, consulting her notes. "It's hard to say, although I must admit that I've been very pleased with your progress. I would urge you to keep attending physiotherapy and I can prescribe pills to ease the pain, but there are medical trials you could sign up for if you were interested in exploring alternative treatments."

"What kind of treatments?" he queried nervously.

"Inducing hypothermia is currently being tested as a way to lessen inflammation and encourage nerve regeneration."

"Hypothermia?"

"It is better suited for people in the very early stages of recovery," she conceded. "I doubt your mobility would see a great improvement regardless of the outcome. Volunteers are also being sought for the trial of a new intravenous injection if that was an option you were willing to explore."

"What would that involve?"

"It's quite simple," she said. "The medicine would increase the strength in your legs and take pressure off the spinal cord. I can't promise it will be a miracle cure, but it will improve your mobility."

He thought about it. There was no reason to say no, every option was worth trying, but the idea of having drugs in his body put him off. It also sounded like quite an experimental treatment and whether that made him a coward, he didn't wholly trust experimental treatments. He didn't even like being seen by student dentists, regardless of the discount or supervision, and this was a much more important problem to solve correctly.

"And it will definitely work? It won't make things worse?" he queried nervously.

"In the short-term, you will feel worse. An injection into the spine will leave you unable to walk at all at first, and you will have to rest as much as possible for a few days afterwards, but there is a chance of noticeable long-term benefits."

That sounded far too wishy-washy, but nothing ventured, nothing gained. "I'll try it" he said quickly, seizing onto one second of courage before he could talk himself out of it. The doctor nodded and wrote something down.

"Do you have someone who will be able to help you for the few days afterwards?" she asked.

"Yes" he said, and looked over to see his help swinging on the parallel bars like a gymnast.

\*\*

So it was that on Friday, after pulling out of his scheduled babysitting appointment with regrets, he found himself lying on a table with his pants pulled down and staring at the far wall. All of a sudden, this didn't seem like such a good idea. He'd had injections before, but none that required him to sign a release form listing such potential side effects as blood clots and pneumonia. These nurses were also taking their sweet time about getting prepared and with every second that passed, the fear increased. What would an injection into bone be like? Painful, of course, but how bad? As bad as getting a tattoo or...?

"We're almost ready, Mr Caruso. Just keep looking at the wall."

He was rapidly running out of time to call a halt to this. He knew that he didn't have to go through with it, but he thought of all the times that he'd braved pain for the greater good - when he'd had braces, when Rico had practiced tattoos on him, when he'd had a tetanus injection in the sole of his foot after idiotically playing on a building site and stepping on a nail. He could do it again. This would help him. However much it hurt, it would be worth it.

It was like having his bone broken. They forced the needle into his back and left it there for ten minutes. He coped atrociously. He cried, he writhed, he completely lost all sense of where he was and how much time had passed. If one of his children had behaved as he did, he would have been embarrassed, but the agony was so overwhelming that he didn't realise the needle was gone until a nurse put her hand on his arm.
"Is it over?" he asked.
"Yes" she said. Through the tears he realised that the nurses were packing up their equipment and no-one was near him anymore, and only then did he realise that the burning pain had turned to a manageable ache.

They sat him up and helped him into a wheelchair. His legs felt fine, or at least no different than before. His head, however, was light and woozy from crying. He was brought to the waiting room. Marco was sitting out there, or rather lying across three chairs with his teeth gritted.
"Are you okay?" Daniele asked, remembering that particular part of the arrangement too late.
"I'm fine, how are you?" Marco retorted, grimacing and rubbing his back.
"I'll be fine. It really hurt though."
"Did it? I had no idea. Tell me more."

Marco stood up, took the handles of the wheelchair and pushed Daniele out of the surgery. They'd barely gone halfway down the street when the first twinges of pain wrapped around his thigh. Alarmed, Daniele tried to stand and was forced to sit back down.

"They're seizing up. I need to walk" he insisted.

"They told you this would happen."

By the end of the road, his legs had entirely seized up. The muscles felt too heavy to move and he couldn't even try. His legs felt like they were being crushed in a vice, as if metal plates were tightening more and more around them, breaking the bones and twisting the muscles. He was paralysed again, and now in chronic pain as well. The realisation made him start crying anew. He should never have agreed to the stupid treatment. He'd been doing just fine and now all the progress was gone.

"Daniele, calm down. It's okay. They told you this was a short-term thing. You're going to be fine. We just have to get back to the flat."

Every jolt of the wheelchair went straight to his spine and made him whimper. "If you keep whining, I'm just going to pick you up and fly" Marco muttered.

"I wouldn't mind if you did."

The chair was pulled to a halt and two arms slipped under his, crossing over his chest. "No!" he called.

"What? You asked me to!" Marco let go of him and started pushing again. "I should just do it anyway," he added quietly. "Like I have time for this."

At last, he saw his building and the torture was nearly over, or so he presumed. Marco pushed him right up to the steps and then stopped. Both of them looked at the small, but insurmountable problem. Marco opened the door first and then attempted to push the wheelchair up, but it tipped backwards and Daniele gripped onto the armrests for dear life, making unintelligible panicked noises.

"Can you walk at all?" Marco asked. Daniele attempted to move his legs as if anything would have changed, and shook his head.

"Can you crawl?"

Obligingly he slipped out of the chair and then draped himself over the steps, managing to drag himself commando-style up one step, and then collapsing with the edge digging into his ribs.

"I can't do it. My legs won't move at all."

"Oh, nuts, what am I going to do?"

Marco ran to the top of the steps and then looked down at Daniele. For a second, it seemed that the angel would actually take his arms and drag him over concrete. He looked around the courtyard.

"I'd lift you, but my wings aren't going to fit through the door."

"Take your time" Daniele said, trying to move positions to relieve the pressure on his chest.

Marco sighed, looking in all directions as if inspiration might be found anywhere, and then glanced back into the flat. He suddenly froze, squinting thoughtfully, and walked inside. He returned pulling Daniele's duvet after him, which he lay out on the ground. Daniele raised his head and frowned incredulously. Marco pulled him onto the duvet and wrapped the sides around him, and then started to drag him inside. He felt the ground and the steps below him, but there was no pain through the thick cushioning. The surface changed to the smooth wooden floor of the flat and then Marco was hauling him, not too gently, onto the bed. He positioned Daniele's head on the pillow and straightened his body. Daniele was left looking like an Egyptian mummy crossed with a sushi roll.

    Marco stepped back to look at him, and stifled a laugh.
    "I'm glad you find this so amusing" Daniele said acerbically.
    "Can I do anything for you?" the angel asked, ignoring the remark.
    "Can you unroll me?"
    "I don't want to move you any more than I have to. How about some pleasant dreams?"
    "If you want to."
    "What else am I going to do, sit and stare at your kidney-coloured walls?"
    "How about you bring the laptop in here and I can watch a movie?"

    Marco left the room and returned with the computer in his arms, the plug draped over his arm and the wires trailing behind him. He placed it on the bed and lifted Daniele into an upright position, removing some layers of duvet so he could move his arms, and put the laptop into his hands.
    "Do you want to join me?" Daniele offered.
    Marco looked at the laptop dubiously. "Am I supposed to lean over your shoulder?"
    "Well…" Daniele considered. "I suppose you would. There isn't anywhere else to put it, unless we move to the living room, but you don't like my kidney-coloured walls, right?"

    Marco eyed him and then sat down on the bed. Daniele opened the lid of the computer and glanced at Marco as he started moving through the list of genres. "What do you like? I have cartoons, action-adventure, classics, documentaries…"

"Anything except romance" Marco said.

"You don't like romance?"

"I don't like movie romance. The protagonist inevitably falls in love with the first person of the opposite sex who appears on screen, and those relationships are nearly always toxic. There's always some element of miscommunication, stalking or jealousy. My…An old client used to love that sappy crap, and I used to ask what was so romantic about forcing someone to love you through a campaign of attrition."

Daniele couldn't help grinning at him. He was starting to find that he enjoyed how deadly serious Marco was about such trivial things, the way he would yell at the newspaper and couldn't abide fictional characters in books being cruel to each other, berating them as if they were real people.

"What?" Marco demanded. "Why are you looking at me like that?"

"We're definitely watching a romance now" Daniele declared.

The angel's eyes widened in horror. "No!"

"I don't like them either. If we find a good one, maybe we'll have our minds changed. What about this one? It's got rave reviews."

Within ten minutes of the movie's start, Marco's commentary began. "I guarantee that it'll be the guy in the lift…What did I tell you? And he's her boss! The big businessman taking advantage of his secretary, how clichéd…A dream sequence? Really?"

They were now twenty minutes into the film and the two lovebirds were the only people in the office at night, flirting shamelessly from either side of a conference table.

"Do you think he knows that he looks like a serial killer?" Marco asked. He put on an exaggerated feminine voice. "Oh, my new boss is so sexy. Every time our eyes meet, I feel like he wants to push me in front of a car."

Daniele burst out laughing, stopping after several seconds to find Marco grinning at him triumphantly. For the rest of the movie, Marco took it upon himself to act as the thoughts of the male lead. At a stroke, the hero was turned from Mr Darcy to Patrick Bateman, and the burgeoning love story became a farce about a serial killer continually foiled by bad luck. Daniele found the angel's version of the screenplay vastly more enjoyable than the actual movie. He was repeatedly made breathless from laughter, and that seemed to spur Marco on to make more and more jokes.

As time wore on, he started to become quieter and Daniele looked at him, wondering where his quick wit had gone. Marco looked back. "I'm bored" he said.

"We can stop if you want" Daniele offered, already hovering the mouse over the Pause button.

Marco grimaced indecisively and looked at the screen. "And then what?" he asked.

"I don't know. You can go and do something else."

Marco sighed. "No, I can't be bothered. Can I just sleep on your shoulder?"

"Um…Okay, but I don't know if it'd be very comfortable…"

Marco had already placed his head on Daniele's shoulder, shifting a bit to get comfortable. His hair tickled Daniele's face and he tried unsuccessfully to move away without disturbing the laptop.

"Can you move your head a bit?" he requested.

Marco obediently shuffled down so that his head was pressed against Daniele's upper arm. "Better?" he asked.

"Very much so."

"You have a very comfortable shoulder."

"Thank you. I've often been complimented on it."

For several minutes, he heard nothing from the angel by his side. The movie was much less fun to watch without him. The two leads were now in a hotel room, admiring the view of Paris. It was the perfect moment for a quick shove, in Marco's version of the story, but instead they only began another sex scene and Daniele sighed. He rolled his mouse over the screen to see how long was left, and his spirits nosedived upon discovering that forty-five interminable minutes still lay ahead.

"Did it hurt?" Marco asked suddenly.

Daniele turned, grateful for a distraction. "Did what hurt?"

The angel pressed a finger onto Daniele's arm and he looked down, lifting his elbow for a better view. "The tattoos? Maybe a little."

"It must not have hurt much if you kept doing it" Marco remarked. He didn't take his finger away, but started tracing the shape of the tattoo. It tickled a bit, but Daniele found that he didn't mind. He watched Marco finish the outline of one and move onto the next.

"One of my old friends did them. He wanted to work in the industry and I was his canvas. Do you like them?" he asked.

"Some of them," Marco moved his finger to Daniele's wrist, and his arm tingled slightly from the sudden removal of the angel's touch. "This heart is nice. I don't know what this is trying to be."

He gripped Daniele's lower arm and pulled it towards him, squinting at the image.

"It's an owl" Daniele said.

"Is it? It's not very good."

"What's wrong with it?"

"The eyes are too big. They're staring into my soul" Marco said, trying to point, but Daniele pulled his arm away. "It was one of his early works. It's very good for an amateur" he insisted.

"Did you pay him for it?"

Daniele shot him a look and turned away, refusing to engage any further.

"You can always get it fixed," Marco said after a moment. "I'm sure it would look nice if it was more in proportion. The rest are okay. I like the red bird and the little ship. They're pretty."

"Did it hurt when you got your wings?" Daniele asked.

Marco raised a small, sad smile. "Yes, but not as much as it did for others. I'd been through worse."

An awkward silence settled over them again. Daniele looked back at the screen, unsure of how to respond, but the movie was so uninteresting and he wondered if perhaps this was an opportunity to know Marco a little better.

"Do you…I mean, if you wanted to…talk about it, I'd be willing to listen."

"What is there to talk about? It's not something I like to dwell on."

That told him, but there was something else. "What about the rest of your family? Were they nice?"

"They were great" Marco said, his voice immediately becoming warmer.

"Yeah?" Daniele probed cautiously, not asking any leading questions, simply encouraging him to talk. It was the same tactic he used on reticent clients.

"Yeah," Marco said immediately. "I had two siblings, Tommaso and Caterina, and my mother. She was amazing. Our neighbours used to say that all of us kids had a piece of her. You know, my sister had her looks, my brother had her sense of humour and I had her intelligence. So you can imagine what a great person she was, with all of those traits together."

He spoke of his mother with so much love that Daniele felt his heart ache a little. "I can imagine. Were you close to your siblings?" he asked.

"Very close, especially to my brother. We weren't too far apart in age and we did everything together. Caterina was a bit younger than us, but she was the boss. Have you ever seen an old dog being chased by a puppy, just because the puppy is too young to know its place? That was Caterina."

Marco chuckled, no doubt at some fond memory, and Daniele felt a wave of envy. They sounded like such a close family, father not included. The relationship Marco described having with his siblings was exactly what Daniele had dreamed of having with his own brother and sister, and never quite managed to achieve.

"That sounds lovely. I was never very close to my siblings," he admitted. "Well, to my sister, I suppose. She's the closest to me in age and...for a long time, she was my only friend. I was really shy throughout school. I could never talk to people, so I just used to hang around when Stefania had her friends over and sometimes they would include me. Sometimes it was just about being around other people so I didn't look alone. My mother always hated the fact that I didn't have friends. It's never left her. Even now, she sometimes asks how often I talk to people."

"She's concerned about you" Marco remarked.

Daniele scoffed dismissively. "It's annoying. It's like she still sees me as a twelve year old and doesn't recognise the progress I've made."

"What progress is that? You spend all of your time in this burrow."

The angel's bluntness took him aback, although at this point, perhaps it shouldn't have. Even his parents would never be so direct. "I hardly have a choice at the moment" he retorted.

"I grant you that, but it doesn't seem like you have a great social life anyway" Marco insisted.

"How would you know? You know nothing about me."

"You're a good-looking man and you don't date. You don't want your family or friends to come over and see you. You just want to be on your own. I bet you quietly resent me being around all the time."

"I don't, actually," Daniele replied. "I'm glad not to be alone. I don't want my friends and family coming over because they'll just worry about me."

Marco was quiet for a moment. "Someone once said to me," he remarked slowly, as if he was picking his way through the words. "You might think it's annoying to feel like people are checking up on you, but when you don't have anyone who cares enough to do it, you miss it. Food for thought."

He placed his head back on Daniele's shoulder and neither of them spoke for the rest of the movie.

## Chapter 13

He was woken by the high-pitched whine of a vacuum cleaner. Confused, he lifted his head and listened. The sound definitely came from the living room.

"Marco?"

The vacuum droned on. Daniele experimentally tried to move his legs and, finding that he could, rolled out of bed and grabbed his stick. He shuffled down to the living room and stopped in the doorway, looking at the scene in disbelief. Marco was nowhere in sight, but his parents were here. His mother was using all of her strength to push the vacuum across the floor while his father sat on the sofa with a cup of coffee. He had coffee? How long had they been here?

"Hi" he said.
His mother saw him and turned the vacuum off. "Hello, love. How are you feeling?"
"I'm fine. I didn't know you were coming over."
"We knocked, but you were still asleep, so we just came in. I thought you might appreciate some help with the house."
"Of course I do. I'm a bit surprised, that's all."
His legs were shaking, he noticed. He'd been standing up for too long and swiftly moved to the armchair.
"Take it easy, sweetheart. I'll take care of this."
"Marco can do that" he said without thinking.
"He isn't here."
"No, but..." Actually, would Marco appear later? Would he rather stay away while Daniele's parents were here? He didn't feel confident enough to make a prediction.

"Oh, I brought you some food. It's in the kitchen. I'll unpack it for you."

His mother headed for the corridor and Daniele stood to follow. "I'll help."

"No need" she called back.

The external doorbell rang before he could take a step. A second later, his front door rattled as the lock was turned, and Marco pushed it open. He had two sandwich bags in his hand and startled when he saw Daniele's father.

"Mr Caruso, hello! I was just getting some breakfast for Daniele. I would have bought something for you if I'd known you were visiting."

"That's alright," his father said. "I'm happy with my coffee."

Marco smiled at him and turned to Daniele. "What are you doing? You need to rest or the injection won't work. Sit down."

Daniele obediently returned to the chair. "What injection are you talking about?" his father queried, looking between the two.

"I had an injection yesterday to help my walking" Daniele replied.

"How does that work?"

"It strengthens the muscles and takes pressure off the spine so it doesn't hurt so much and……" He broke off as Marco pushed a sandwich into his hands.

"Eat first," the angel said. "Is your mother here too? I should say hello to her."

He marched off to the kitchen and Daniele tried to lean around the chair, listening to what he might say.

"Did the injection help?" his father asked, bringing his attention round.

"It's hard to tell at the moment," he said. "I hope it did."

The older man nodded thoughtfully. "Painful?"

"Very painful."

The small talk was once again interrupted by Marco, returning to the living room after a conversation that couldn't have lasted longer than thirty seconds.

"It looks like it's going to be a busy day, Daniele," he declared. "Your mother is doing the ironing and I have to finish vacuuming in here. Mr Caruso, what are you going to do?"

Daniele's father looked astonished to have the spotlight turned on him. "Oh! Um..."

"There is some washing in the machine that needs to go out," Marco said smoothly. "I'll help you if you like. Would you prefer to be in charge of clothes or pegs?"

"Um...The pegs then, I'll do the pegs."

Daniele watched his father stand up and precede Marco outside, looking bewildered, and couldn't help smirking. That angel was a remarkable manipulator, he thought. He was so skilled at getting people to do what he wanted simply by making them feel that they couldn't refuse. It probably wasn't a trait to be admired, but for Daniele, who hated confrontation and bent over backwards to avoid troubling people, Marco's confidence and no-nonsense attitude was a breath of fresh air. He was exactly the kind of person that Daniele wished he could be.

He heard his mother humming in the kitchen, opening cupboards and drawers, and then her footsteps approached the living room. "I've brought you cereal, milk, bread, cheese, spaghetti, a roast chicken, some potatoes and carrots," she said, listing them off with impressive speed. "That should cover all of your mealtimes, right?"

"Yes, thank you. You didn't have to do that."

"It's no trouble. You can pay me back when you're able. Is Marco cooking for you?"

Daniele thought of Marco's attempts to cook since his arrival. Pots bubbling over, spilled oil and egg yolk, incinerated vegetables, yelps as he burned his hand, recipe books thrown in a rage across the kitchen. They had lived on takeaway food and microwave meals, and Daniele looked forward to the day when he would be able to stand upright for long enough to cook again. His diet hadn't changed all that much from before the attack, but now that the option of some freshly cooked meals wasn't there, he was suddenly desperate for them.

"Yes," he answered quickly, before his mother noticed his hesitation. "He shouldn't have to do it for much longer. My legs have improved a lot."

She put a hand on his arm as if he would attempt to leap from the chair at once. "Don't rush yourself, sweetheart."

"Why does everyone say that? I want to rush myself. I hate sitting around."

She smiled sympathetically. "As you said, it won't be for much longer. By the way, I should buy you a new ironing board. That one must be older than you are."

Daniele opened his mouth to refute the suggestion and then paused. Actually, he really did need a new ironing board. The current one had creaking, rusty legs and the cover was torn. He needed a new vacuum as well, but all of the good ones were ridiculously expensive and he had no chance of upgrading.

"I'm going to buy one," he promised. "It's on the list."

"Maybe I'll get you one for Christmas" his mother suggested, but the twinkle in her eye suggested that she was joking. He honestly wouldn't mind if he did get an ironing board for Christmas. That was definitely one of the signs of middle age.

She went to the airing cupboard and lifted a pile of T-shirts and jeans. "Can I do something?" he requested. "I can't sit here while people are cleaning my house around me."

"You can dust if you want. Where are your cloths and polish?"

"Under the sink."

She brought the supplies to him and left him to it, telling him to call if he needed help. He had no intention of doing that. He got to his feet, moved the few steps to the coffee table, and then sank to his knees to rub it down. The loud metallic squeaks of the ironing board sounded clearly from down the hall. He finished his first job and pressed his stick into the ground, using it like a staff to haul himself to his feet. Now it was time for the mantelpiece, and all of those trophies and frames. That was not going to be an easy job. He'd probably have to take them to the armchair to polish them and then put them back one by one. It would take forever.

"Daniele, what are you doing? I told you to rest."

He hadn't noticed Marco return, and before he could respond, the angel was manoeuvring him across the room.

Sharp pressure on his shoulders caused his legs to buckle neatly and he landed in the armchair. Marco loomed over him.

"You can't have that injection again, so we have to make sure this works as well as it can. The doctor said you need to rest for 48 hours and you're going to, even if I have to strap you down to do it."

He smiled sweetly and then went to the vacuum cleaner. Daniele opened his mouth, but the loud howl of the suction drowned him out.

Daniele's father arrived a moment later and took his seat on the sofa, hands clasped and staring at the ground. He recognised that hunched-up posture from his childhood. It meant that something had offended his father and he was waiting for someone to ask what was wrong. He hated that deadly silence. It was like watching storm clouds gathering on the horizon, knowing there was nothing he could say to clear them. They could last for days sometimes.

Marco went around the living room quickly and then packed the vacuum cleaner up. "Okay," he said, with a nervous bounce that Daniele couldn't understand. "I guess I'll see if there's anything else to do. Oh, I can strip and make your bed if you want."

"Thanks," Daniele said. "That would be nice."

Marco gave him a thumbs-up and hurried out of the room. Daniele looked at his father, now staring silently out of the window. "Papa?" he ventured. His father turned slowly to look at him, his expression blank. "Is everything okay? You're very quiet."

"Were you really so upset about what I said?" his father asked.

"What?" Daniele frowned.

"That day I told you to go to school instead of performing at the Palazzo Senatorio. Your nurse said you were telling him about it and you made me sound like a villain."

"I didn't..." Shock momentarily stole his voice. "What? No, I didn't mean to. I can't believe he said that! He saw the trophies and asked about them, so I told him about the last time I was on stage."

"You obviously told him that you quit because of what I said. Was that the reason?"

Daniele said nothing. The lie required to soothe the older man didn't come in time.

"I really thought that you were planning to give it up anyway," his father said unhappily. "Was everything that happened afterwards my fault then?"

His voice was accusatory and Daniele felt his stomach drop with fear. In an instant he was back to being a teenager, picking his way through a conversation, terrified to say the wrong thing and cause the storm clouds to turn black.

"What do you mean?"

"The drugs, the petty crime, the prison sentence, the inability to hold down a job. Was that my fault?" his father demanded.

"Of course it wasn't, you were right. I was never going to be a professional singer. You did not derail my life, okay?"

He desperately hoped that would be the end of it, but his father would not be dissuaded. "You were never like that before" he remarked.

"I was a difficult teenager! We've established this!"

"Do not shout at me" he snapped. The storm clouds were getting darker and the first flashes of lightning could be seen.

"It was so long ago. It doesn't matter" Daniele insisted distraughtly.

"It obviously does if you've been telling people."

"I told one person and that was because he asked. I just...Why did you have to say that? Why did you have to be cruel about something that made me happy?"

He hadn't meant to say that and he was horrified to hear the words come out of him. They were the questions of a child and he knew how pathetic they sounded from the mouth of a grown man. His father looked away and moved his jaw.

"Your mother and I had a fight that morning," he said. "I was bitter and I took it out on you, and perhaps I shouldn't have done that. We had so little money, Daniele. I was working my fingers to the bone and you were out playing at this ridiculous hobby that was never going to turn into a career. I apologise if you felt that I was cruel, however."

Daniele felt his eyes sting and looked away, taking deep breaths to hold himself together, and biting his fist when that didn't work. Why was he getting upset so easily these days? Was this something else related to his attack and if so, when was it going to stop? He couldn't stand looking weak, especially in front of someone like his father.

"Are you crying? Why are you crying?" he demanded, sounding confused and insulted.

"I can't believe he told you."

Daniele heard his voice pitch upwards and suddenly all he wanted was to grab Marco and scream at him, hurt his throat and make his voice hoarse, punch a wall…He'd never hurt Marco, he'd never do that to anyone, but he wanted to do something!

"I thought it was out of line too" his father said.

No more was said about it. The storm clouds lightened in colour and Daniele suspected that his father was content to believe some wicked usurper had stirred up the past in an attempt to disrupt their relationship, but had been happily foiled in his schemes. Daniele himself bided his time, making sure to ignore Marco and speak only to his parents when his mother made lunch for them all, until the washing machine clicked to indicate the cycle had finished and he saw his chance.

"Need help putting the bedclothes out?" he offered.

Marco frowned at him. "No, I'm fine. You need your rest."

Daniele was already standing up. "The duvet cover is huge. I'm happy to help, even if it's only to peg."

The angel sighed, but nodded. "We'll be as quick as we can" he said, more of an order than a promise, as he piled the bedclothes out of the machine and into the basket. He offered his hand to help Daniele down the steps, but he managed it using only his stick and the careful two-footed descent of a toddler. Seeing that he didn't need help, Marco strode across the grass to the washing line and was hanging up pillowcases when Daniele reached him.

"Why did you talk to my father?" he asked immediately. Marco stopped and looked around a pillowcase at him. He looked surprised, but not rueful.

"I hoped he would apologise."

"Oh, he did," Daniele retorted. Sarcasm truly didn't sound good, he thought, hearing his own voice. His sister always said that he was too nice to do it properly. You try, she said, but you clearly don't mean it. "He said he was sorry that I thought he was cruel. He already thinks I'm hyper-sensitive. Can you imagine what he thinks of me now, a man in his forties whining about something that happened decades ago?"

"I was trying to help," Marco said. "I thought if he atoned, you'd be able to look at the trophies without feeling sad, or talk to your father without swallowing bitterness."

"He didn't need to atone for anything!"

"Yes, he did! He hurt you badly enough that you still get upset thinking about it!"

"You don't have to stick your nose into every aspect of my life," Daniele snapped. "I never asked for a guardian angel and I never asked you to dredge up the past. You've just made everything worse. I wouldn't have said anything if I'd known you were going to use it as a weapon."

Marco looked stunned. He reached down and grabbed another pillowcase from the basket, and tossed it over the line. "I had to try," he said suddenly. "I'm sorry that it didn't work out as I planned, but I was only trying to help."

"Is that what you call it?" Daniele muttered. He turned and walked back to the flat, and only when he was inside did he realise that Marco hadn't called him back about the pegs. When he returned to the living room, his parents were already wearing their coats.

"We were about to say goodbye," his mother said, coming over and giving him a hug. "We're on babysitting duty for Stefania today. Do you think you'll be able to come over for Sunday lunch tomorrow?"

She stepped back and looked at him hopefully.

"Uh, I don't know. Maybe…" He avoided looking in his father's direction.

"Well, if you can, please join us. We've missed you over the past few months."

"I'll call you" he promised. She hugged him again, squeezing him tightly as she had when he was small, and then stepped back. His father took her place and Daniele held his breath.

"Daniele…I am sorry if…No, I'm sorry that I hurt you so much." It seemed like the words didn't come easily, but he forced them out and Daniele couldn't doubt his sincerity. "You and I existed in very different worlds when you were young. I hope you can understand me a little better now."

"I do."

"Do you forgive me?"

He almost said it. 'There's nothing to forgive.' The words were on the tip of his tongue, but they got stuck there. It had never been about the music. It had been about his father's dismissiveness and anger towards something that made him happy, and he could forgive that, but he didn't think he would be able to forget it. Words like that were impossible to take back, and he doubted that he would ever stop holding a vague sadness about the incident, but he wasn't going to let the past interfere with future interactions between him and his father.

"I forgive you."

His father smiled and hugged him, and Daniele felt that warm glow of affection that had been so long absent between them. He held on for a few seconds to soak it in before letting him go.

"Don't be a stranger" his father said, his meaning clear, and then he opened the front door and followed his wife outside. Daniele watched them go through the living room window with a strange sense of wellbeing, as if a barb had been pulled out of his chest. The apology didn't mean half as much as the simple acknowledgement that he'd been hurt. He'd never known that that was all he needed.

**Chapter 14**

Marco hadn't come back from hanging the bedclothes out yesterday. Daniele had waited for ten minutes before opening the side door and finding his bedclothes neatly placed along the line, securely pegged, and no sign of Marco. He'd apologised to the air for being unduly harsh, in case the angel was waiting for something like that before returning, but the flat had still been empty when he gave up and went to bed. He was surprised to realise how unsettled that made him feel, and it wasn't only for the selfish reason of having no-one to keep his nightmares at bay. Rain had started to pour outside and he wondered where Marco was, if he'd found a dry place to stay. He hated the thought of the poor angel being soaked because Daniele had made him feel that he wasn't wanted. It took him a long time to fall asleep due to worry.

When he woke the next morning and rolled over, he saw a bright red envelope beside the bed. Opening it, he found a card, one with statements and tick boxes on the front to make a message.

**Dearest**...*Daniele.*
Marco had written his name in round, sloping letters.
**I want to**...*say I'm sorry*...
**in regards to the**...*stupid*...**thing I did. (Please don't make me say it.)**

Daniele had to raise a smile at that, although he noted that Marco hadn't ticked the 'beg for forgiveness' box. He supposed he couldn't expect that much contrition.

**I promise**...*I will make it up to you.*

**Let's move forward. I hope that you**...*don't hate me...forgive me...get amnesia and forget what happened.* **Sincerely**...*Marco.*

He opened the card and found a simple message written inside. *I'm sorry I told your father things that I should have kept inside my head.*

He felt much better today. The nurse had said that the injection worked instantaneously for some people, and for others it took a little longer to kick in. Daniele was one of those who needed a bit of time, but now he could definitely feel it working. For the first time, he was able to stand up like a normal person without hunching over or grabbing onto a support.

Marco was sitting on the kitchen worktop, his long legs almost reaching the floor. His eyes widened when he saw Daniele. They looked at each other for several seconds, waiting for the other to speak first.
"Where did you go last night?" Daniele finally asked.
"Nowhere. I was on the roof watching the city lights."
He nodded, feeling a small spark of annoyance for the night he'd spent worrying, before quelling it. He had been the one who made Marco feel that he couldn't come inside, after all. "I got your note" he said.
"And what did you think of it?"
"I appreciate it, and I do know that you were trying to help."
Marco released a deep breath and rubbed his arm. "I didn't go about it in the right way. I realise that" he said.
"Actually," Daniele admitted. "It did help. He apologised, like you hoped he would."
"It wasn't about what I wanted" Marco retorted.

"I know. He's not used to people being that honest with him. I guess he just needed some time to get over the shock. I should thank you, and I should apologise if I upset you with my attitude."

The angel shrugged and gave him a slight smile. "I'm hard and you're soft. I guess we both have to get used to that."

"I think it's admirable," Daniele said. "The way you stand up for yourself and others. I'd like to have that much courage."

"Well," Marco shrugged again. "It's in my nature to face things head-on, but sometimes I want to run away from it all." He looked down, rubbing his palms together. "I know you hate it, but I look at the way other people take charge and look after you, and I think it'd be nice to be taken care of sometimes."

"We could come up with a more equal arrangement," Daniele said at once. "I could take care of you sometimes. I'm pretty good at that."

He smiled and Marco smiled back. "That wouldn't work. This is my job."

"It's my job too."

Marco's smile widened, causing his eyes to crinkle up adorably. "I wish I could be like you, connecting with people, making them happy" he said.

"You could be."

He shook his head. "I can't."

Daniele came forward and extended his hand. "Will we try working together?" he asked. Marco, after a second, shook on it. Daniele smiled at him, happy to be back on an even keel. He hated conflict.

"Daniele..." Marco said slowly. "Where's your stick?"

"What?" He looked down quickly, observing his legs and his distinctly empty hands. "Oh my God! Oh my God, where's my stick?"

He put both hands on the worktop to steady himself. Marco jumped onto the floor to make room for him. "You don't look like you need it" he remarked.

"That's impossible! I've only been home for two weeks!"

"Maybe the injection really helped, or I did."

Daniele threw his arms around the angel, hugging him delightedly, only realising his error when Marco stood there like a piece of cardboard instead of returning the embrace. He swiftly let go and moved back. He didn't stumble, he noted. He started to pace around the kitchen, taking care over every step, testing how much strain his legs could handle. His spine had a dull ache, but it didn't translate further than his waist. His knees could hold him up. His feet didn't cry out in protest. After three circuits of the tiny space, he turned to Marco and felt a grin spread across his face.

"I can go back to work!" he declared.

"Yes..." Marco said, his small smile conflicting with the confusion in his eyes. "Really, this is your first thought? This is what fills you with joy?"

"I don't have to live on my savings anymore. That fills me with joy. Oh..." He suddenly remembered and stopped short. "My parents want me to come over for Sunday lunch today."

Marco nodded. "Okay."

"I don't think...um..."

"That I would be welcome? Probably true. The cover story is that I'm a nurse, after all, and you clearly don't need me to follow you into the bosom of your family. I think today will be a history day. I might go to the Roman Forum, the Colosseum, the Sistine Chapel..."

"The ancient part of Rome and the Vatican City are quite spaced apart, just so you know."

Marco answered him with a mischievous grin.

"Don't," Daniele warned. "Do not dare to try flying. I do not want to come back from lunch and find reporters besieging me again."

"I didn't say anything."

"No, but I can hear you thinking."

Marco laughed. "Have a nice time with your parents. I'm happy you like me again. It makes life easier." He headed for the kitchen door.

"Please don't do anything like that again" Daniele requested.

Marco stopped and turned to him. "You're scolding me and yet you're smiling."

"Just because it worked does not mean it was the right thing to do."

"It was the only thing to do. Now you're happy. You are welcome."

The angel blew a kiss and walked out, leaving Daniele dumbfounded. Had he really just done that? God, he was unbelievable! How could anybody be such an asshole and yet be so cute? How was it possible to be driven mad with frustration and still want to smile?

\*\*

He had once enjoyed Sunday lunches with his family. They were large-scale affairs, involving not only his parents and siblings, but aunts, uncles, cousins, partners, ex-partners, children and sometimes even friends. As a child, they had provided abundant company to play with.

Hosting duties were passed around on a weekly basis as no-one could be expected to regularly provide such a feast, but since his family had all lived within a few streets of each other while he was growing up, he had attended every Sunday for most of his childhood.

As a teenager, his attendance had dwindled from every week to whenever his mother was hosting and he couldn't escape, and then he stopped going at all. He became one of the cousins who were spoken about with shame and concern. Even when he turned his life around, he hadn't felt able to show his face until Matteo was born. It felt like his son was a gift he was bringing to gain admission. Even if his parents didn't want to see him, he hoped that perhaps they would want see their grandchild. His kids had formed a bridge across the chasm between him and his parents, giving them something to reconnect over. When they moved away, he'd stopped coming again, unable to face the questions and being surrounded by people when he was so alone. Today was only his third visit in the past six months.

Within ten minutes of arrival, Daniele found out that he couldn't stand crowds. He'd never been fond of being crammed into a small space with lots of other people, but it was something he'd had to get used to, growing up in a big family. His dislike had been pragmatic - how hot it was, how difficult it was to move without bumping into someone - but now he felt genuinely claustrophobic, as if his chest was being crushed. He checked every room in the flat and the hallway of the building in search of some breathing space, and eventually found himself hiding in the bathroom, sucking in air from the open window.

Stefania forced him to come out to help with the dinner. His mother was taking care of the bruschetta, his brother was cooking the lamb chops and his sister was chopping garlic for the seasoning, so he was handed the easy job of drinks. White wine for the adults and lemonade for the children was a simple order, but the heat in the kitchen was extraordinary, and the smell of oil and vinegar and garlic was unexpectedly nauseating. That was surely a sign that he'd gone too long without a home-cooked meal, he thought, as he attempted not to keel over while pouring.

There were two pieces of news dominating the afternoon. The first was discussion about one of Daniele's many cousins, who had left his wife and child last Thursday to go travelling for a year, claiming that he'd given up too much time to work and family, and wanted to live a little before he was dead. The response from the women was scathing, and from some of the men too, although a few uncles dared to voice their envy that the man could have the best of both worlds - a bit of freedom before he returned to his welcoming family. The aunts howled with laughter.

"If he thinks he can take up where he left off, he will be sorely disappointed" Zia Beatrice declared, to loud cries of agreement.

The other piece of news was Daniele himself. People kept reaching over to touch his hand or shoulder, praising him or asking him how he was doing, ignoring it when his shoulders began to draw up defensively.
"Your mother was very worried that you would be paralysed, but I see you're doing well" his aunt said.

"I'm attending physiotherapy and my doctor is going to write a prescription for painkillers, so yeah, I'm fine."

"I hope they're not addictive" his uncle remarked.

"I don't think so. It would show up on my medical record" Daniele replied, a little bitingly, which shut down conversation for a few seconds. It swiftly restarted with talk of children, exchanging stories of new babies or impressive feats at school, and that was something he could definitely join in with. On this subject, he could talk for days.

Dessert was a cheesecake that his mother had prepared and refrigerated ahead of time, made with ricotta and flavoured with lemons. More wine was poured and conversation became louder, more nonsensical and more hilarious. In the middle of the afternoon, no-one would call them drunk, but they were certainly tipsy. Anyone who remained stone-cold sober at a Caruso family gathering was unlikely to have a good time.

Daniele checked his watch. It was coming up to 4pm. "I think I'd better go."

His mother turned away from the conversation, waving a hand at him. "No, darling, stay a little while longer."

"I can't drink too much. I have to drive."

Her eyes popped. "Drive? You can't drive. You told us so. It's not safe."

"Oh. Well, I drove here so I have to take the car back. I'm sure it'll be..."

"It's not safe, Daniele," she said again. "Why don't you stay here tonight? We'll take you home in the morning."

"Or that nurse can come and get your car, if you haven't fired him yet" his father suggested.

He was suddenly struck by desperate cabin fever and the desire to get out of here as soon as possible. "Um..."

"So it's settled," his mother said, taking advantage of his hesitation. "You stay here and call him tomorrow to pick you up."

"That's not how it works. He's not a taxi. Besides, he has other patients to attend to." He stood up and pushed his chair in. "I'm sorry, I know I shouldn't have driven so soon, but I did and I really need to get home. I want to start work again tomorrow and I'll need to go home for a change of clothes anyway."

His mother turned away and put a hand to her forehead. He saw her face crumple with the onset of tears. "You're always running away from us."

"Mama, I'm not. I have to go," he insisted, feeling so horribly guilty that he almost sat down again. "Besides, I can't sleep on that old bed right now. I need support for my back."

"I know," she sighed, wiping her fingers under her eyes. "Call us as soon as you're back to let us know you're safe."

"I will," Daniele leaned over and kissed the top of her head. "Thanks for a lovely meal."

She held onto his hand for a moment, patting it affectionately, before she let him go. "Thank you for coming. We've missed your face around here."

He was a little embarrassed to be the first to leave, mainly because he knew they would talk about him. "Oh, poor Daniele, that whole incident must have really messed up his head. Why else would he leave his warm and helpful family to go back to an empty flat?"

Except his flat wasn't empty, and he couldn't explain the little jump of excitement he felt at that thought. He was sharing his home with a prickly hedgehog of a person, but one who was starting to show a softer side, and whom Daniele cautiously hoped could be a friend. They'd left things on a good note this morning. He only hoped their agreement would stand the test of time.

## Chapter 15

The next morning, Daniele woke at 5.30am. That was early even for him, who preferred to aim for a 6am start, but he had been chased out of slumber by a vivid sensation of something sitting on his chest, crushing his lungs, and knowing that he had to wake up if he was to avoid death. He barely managed it, and sat up straight in the bed, gasping for breath until he was certain that he was safe. He knew he couldn't go back to sleep. The fear was waiting for him. It would kill him if he went back there.

He got up and tried to move towards the kitchen as quietly as possible, an ambition soon rendered fruitless when his leg fell to one side and he knocked his shoulder against the partition wall. Marco was inside the room within a second.

"What are you doing? Did you have a nightmare?" he asked.

"No. Well, yes, but I'm going to work now."

"Now?" The angel squinted at him, as if wondering whether Daniele had lost his mind.

"I might as well go since I'm awake," he explained. "It'll let me get home earlier."

"What time will you be home?"

Daniele tried to ignore the brief, but powerful sense of deja-vu that washed over him. He'd been asked that question so many times by Cristina. It was a strange and unsettling feeling to hear the words in a different voice.

"I don't know. It depends. I'll try to be home before seven."

Marco closed his eyes and released a sigh, and then walked over to the wardrobe. "What are you wearing?" he asked.

"You decide" Daniele replied. It would save him from having to choose something, and it would save him from having to get changed if Marco didn't like his choice. The angel flicked through the hangers for a moment and then threw a pair of black jeans onto the bed. A moment later, they were joined by a black shirt that Cristina had bought for him, and which was too formal for everyday use.

"You can't go wrong with black" Marco said, moving to the drawers.
"What about a T-shirt?" Daniele suggested.
"Oh my..." Marco pulled out a monstrous white hoodie and turned in askance. Daniele stared at it and grinned.
"I forgot I had that," he said, coming over and taking it away. "Matteo bought it for Father's Day. The poor kid wanted it to be a surprise so he didn't ask what size I was. He just assumed XL was the default for men."
He wrapped his arms around the hoodie, hoping that he didn't look like he was giving a hug to a piece of clothing, even though he was.
"And what about this?"
He looked up to see Marco holding another hoodie, this one bright pink with *Papa* written in glittering black letters across the back, and burst out laughing. "That's from Sofia."
Marco laughed too. "Well, it fits you, so..."
He tried to hand it over and Daniele pushed it away. "Not a chance" he squeaked, speaking through the giggles.

Marco sighed good-humouredly and put the pink hoodie away, delving into the drawer and emerging triumphantly with a simple black zip-up. A white crest in the corner was the only decoration.
"This seems more your style" he said, handing it over.

"It is" Daniele agreed. He gave the white hoodie to Marco and the angel promptly pulled it over his head, emerging with his curls draped over his eyes, and pushed them back so he could see. The hoodie swamped him, reaching past his thighs and covering his hands, the sleeves hanging down like a pair of tentacles.

"You look good" Daniele said politely.

"I feel cosy" the angel replied, looking down at himself with satisfaction.

"Alright," Daniele thumbed over his shoulder. "Be gone so I can get dressed."

Marco obediently shuffled out, having to take small bouncing steps due to the restrictions around his legs. As soon as the bedroom door closed behind him, Daniele bent over and muffled his laughter in the duvet. Well, at least he was wide awake and ready for the day now. His cheeks ached from smiling so much and his heart was buoyant. He'd forgotten how much fun it was to simply be silly and laugh about nothing. How long had it been since he'd done that?

He dressed quickly, replacing the formal black shirt with an old comfy T-shirt, and hiding it under the jacket. Marco was standing in the middle of the living room when he emerged, no longer clad in the white hoodie, but now in slim black trousers and a white shirt covered in small purple dots.

"Can I come with you?" he asked as soon as he saw Daniele.

He stopped short and frowned in surprise. "You want to come to work with me?"

"Yeah. Is that a problem?"

"I guess not. Why though?"

Marco smiled as if he'd been waiting for this question. "Because I feel like I'm sitting inside a giant liver, and your TV doesn't work."

Daniele gave him a dry look. "You could have just said that you were bored."

There was a small scuffle over the keys - Marco insisting that he could drive, albeit not legally, and Daniele threatening not to let him come if he didn't get in the passenger seat - before they were able to head onto the road. Marco was not a good passenger, wincing when Daniele took corners too fast or drove a little too close to the pavement, yelping in horror if he met another car on the narrow streets. Finally, at 6am, they pulled up outside the centre. Marco took a moment to stare up at the building. Through fresh eyes, Daniele supposed that it looked a little grim, with its industrial façade and the graffiti on the walls.

"So what do you do here? Shelter for the homeless?" Marco asked, following him to the door.

"No, we're not a shelter," Daniele explained as he stepped inside. "We help former addicts and convicts kick their old habits, get into accommodation, turn their lives around. I guess it's not so different from what you do."

He glanced back to make sure Marco was following, seeing the angel looking around the entrance hall with a slight frown. "I know it doesn't look great" he said apologetically.

"What?" Marco's frown deepened.

"It doesn't pay well, and it's not easy, but it's fulfilling."

"Who are you defending yourself to? It's not me."

Daniele turned away, feeling a sudden urge for a cigarette. After a second, he turned back. "My father wanted me to work on a construction site or train as a mechanic like him. They're better-paid and more skilled according to him" he admitted.

"Looking after people is a skill in itself" Marco said.

"I think he believes I only have that skill because..." Daniele cut himself off quickly and started walking again.

Marco was by his side in an instant. "Oh, a dark past?" he probed, half-teasing. Daniele smiled reluctantly.

"That's my clue," he said. "I'm not doing this for selfless reasons either. I used to be one of these people and now I'm trying to help them escape like I did."

Marco was silent for a moment, nodding thoughtfully. "It's a big improvement from arson," he declared. "In fact, I think it's quite noble."

Daniele glanced at him. "Are you messing with me?"

"No," the angel retorted, sounding offended. "Contrary to what you might think, I am capable of sincerity."

"I'll believe that when I see it."

He opened the door to the office to find that he wasn't the first to arrive. Gianni's head popped up from behind the computer, and he scrambled to his feet. "Daniele! You didn't say you were coming in today!"

"Oh! I'm sorry, I didn't know I had to call ahead. I thought because it's Monday..."

"It's fine, it's fine," Gianni waved his concerns away, pulling him into a hug. "It's so good to see you." He squeezed affectionately and then stepped back, looking at Marco. "Hello."

"Hi, I'm Marco."

"This is my...uh, I suppose my support worker," Daniele said. "He drives me and helps me with practical things while I'm recovering."

"That's good service," Gianni remarked. "I didn't get anything like that when I broke my leg."

"You have a desk job, Gianni. You don't need one."

His friend grinned at him and headed back to his desk. "Do you want Isabella's file?" he asked. "I've been taking care of her while you were gone. Actually, no, you sit down and rest. I'll do the running about."

"I'd rather get back on visits. I hate the idea of unfinished business."

"Daniele?"

He turned towards the new voice and saw Pietro in the doorway, looking like he'd seen a ghost. "I didn't know you were coming back today. Did you know, Gianni?" he demanded, faintly accusatory, as he came towards them. "We would have got you a cake."

"That's really not necessary" Daniele assured him.

"Pietro, this is Marco," Gianni said. "He's going to assist Daniele with work, aren't you?"

"That's right."

"It's good to meet you," Pietro smiled at him briefly. "Daniele, Gianni has been taking care of the visits while you were gone. It'd probably be better for you to rest and he can finish up the current cases. The clients like consistency."

"I see. I understand."

That didn't mean that he liked it. Telephony was his most hated part of the job. He liked to visit clients and talk to them in person. Sitting at a desk and arguing with service providers or, even worse, dealing with client complaints was a nightmare. He didn't know how he would make it through the day if they didn't let him leave the office.

"This one came in today though," Gianni piped up, coming to the rescue. "You can go to her if you want. It'll just be talking, the usual."

Daniele looked at the folder that he'd been handed. The name on the front was Carlotta Russo, and he barely restrained a sigh. Of course Gianni would leap at the opportunity to get rid of her. Still, beggars couldn't be choosers. "Thanks" he said.

"Oh, Pietro, tell him the story" Gianni said excitedly.

"Which one?"

"The five thousand euros."

"Thank you for spoiling the end," Pietro smiled. "Yes, you remember that we've had six meetings with the local council? Six meetings with three different people, no less, and not a cent. Well, they had their budget meeting two weeks ago and I went over there to persuade them to add an amendment for us."

"He ambushed them" Gianni interjected.

"They had money to spare for an arts exhibition and not for us? I believe they were overdue a visit," Pietro replied with dignity. "Anyway, I was very respectful. I gave them some information to help them make a decision and they awarded us five thousand euros. I did not ambush anyone."

"That's really impressive, Pietro. Well done" Daniele said. His friend grinned proudly.

"I've been thinking...Well, credit where it's due, *we* have been thinking of creating some events," he said. "It would be a good way to let the clients network, have a bit of fun and fundraise for the centre. I was thinking of a sponsored fitness challenge."

"My idea was portraits," Gianni piped up. "It would give them an excuse to gather their loved ones together and have a picture taken. It might serve as motivation to keep going with the programme."

"It's a good idea," Daniele said, as Pietro nodded his agreement. "I'm sorry I missed out on the planning stage."

"It's still very early days," Pietro assured him. "If you have any ideas to put in the hat, please do."

"A sale?" Marco suggested, speaking up for the first time. All three of them looked at him, surprised. "You could bake pastries or buy flowers and sell them. It would be a good way to boost their spirits."

"Maybe," Pietro remarked. "Food is always popular. It's a matter of whether we would have enough time to bake. Trying to guess the level of demand beforehand is tricky."

Marco shrugged. "You run this ship" he said.

Pietro chuckled. "Is that what Daniele has told you? He's very kind, but I doubt this operation would come crashing to the ground if I left."

Daniele felt a chill of fear run through him and quickly disguised it with a laugh. "Pietro, don't even say that. You're irreplaceable," he said lightly. "Alright, Marco, will we go and take care of the morning's business?"

"Sounds great, lovely to meet you guys," Marco said cheerfully, hurrying after his companion. "So who are we visiting today?"

"Carlotta. I got her an apartment some time ago, but she's missed a few doctors' appointments and her attendance at the mandated counselling sessions is becoming irregular, so a follow-up is in order. Hey…" Daniele began and then stopped, shaking his head. "No."

"What?"

"Nothing. I was going to take advantage of you for a second, sorry."

Marco grinned and briefly rested his head against Daniele's shoulder, an impressive feat since they were walking. "Were you going to ask for angelic intervention in this case?"

"Nothing too dramatic, maybe just giving her enough energy to go to the bus stop for the addiction meetings" he admitted.

"Is that her excuse?"

"Yes, and it is an excuse. She's afraid of what her life will become without drugs. I know…" He nearly finished the sentence, saying 'I used to feel the same way', but stopped in time. The trust between them was still tentative, an infant taking its first steps, and not ready for admissions of that magnitude yet.

Carlotta lived on the top floor of her building, and Daniele had been able to handle the five flights with only slight breathlessness on his last visit. By the time he reached her floor today, he was clinging onto the banister for dear life. Carlotta took a step back in surprise when she opened the door.

"I didn't know you were coming," she said, standing back to let him enter. "Did you call me?"

"I did," he lied. "Don't worry about it, we can talk face to face."

"Hello, you're a new face" she said.

"This is Marco. He's on work experience."

The flat was pristine. Curtains had appeared to cover the view into her neighbour's living room, and bright cushions now replaced the drab grey furnishings that were present on Carlotta's first day. Photos of her children and grandchildren were dotted around every available surface and had been joined by an impressively large collection of plants.

"The place looks nice" Daniele remarked.
"Do you like what I've done with it?"
"I do."
She beamed with pride. "Thank you. I think there's nothing more depressing than walking into a bare room. It never feels like home until you've put your own mark on it."

She sat on the sofa and wrapped a blanket around her shoulders. Daniele sat on the armchair and Marco, after casting about for a place to sit, perched on the arm of the sofa between them. Daniele talked pleasantries for a few moments, asking about her latest knitting project, if she'd seen her son recently, if she was ever planning to go to the doctor about that persistent cough, and finally got to the subject he really wanted to discuss.

"Did you go to your meeting last week?" he asked casually, looking through his notes as if the question was of no consequence.

"Oh…Did I? My memory isn't so good anymore. I'm sure I did."

Daniele looked up at her. "It's simply that the meeting coordinator didn't recall seeing you there" he said.

She refused to make eye contact. "I remember…" she said slowly. "I did mean to go, but I met Viola on the stairs. Her husband is dead now and she's planning to go on a cruise to Greece this summer. She always wanted to do that. And her granddaughter is doing so well. She showed me pictures. It's such a shame that they moved so far. Viola can't go all the way to Trento often so she never sees the baby. I understand why from their point of view, but…"

"Carlotta, we're here to talk about you" Daniele interrupted gently.

"Oh, of course." She nodded and reached for a pack of cigarettes, lighting one and offering the box to the two men. They both accepted. "I haven't seen Viola in a while since she was so busy nursing her poor husband, and I don't often get the chance to share news with visitors. My daughters are so busy with their own families and my son..."

"Carlotta."

"Anyway, by the time I got to the bus stop, it had gone and the meeting would have started before the next one came, so I went back home."

She looked pleased with her airtight alibi. Daniele set his notes aside and leaned forward. "Carlotta, do you want to go to rehab?"

"Of course!" she complained, launching into another violent coughing fit. "Frankly I don't understand why you haven't got me a place yet."

"I'm sure Gianni has gone over this with you, but you won't be accepted until you've demonstrated commitment to the programme. That's why you need to attend these meetings."

"What about all of those celebrities who can go in and out as they please?" she demanded. He sighed, wondering if the real answer would make things better or worse.

"They're wealthy," he answered simply. "I'm sorry to be harsh, but the facilities won't accept people if they don't believe they can complete rehab successfully."

"I have a much better chance of getting sober if I'm locked away where the drugs can't get to me" she retorted.

"I know, but that's not how the system works," Daniele said apologetically. "You have to take the first few steps under your own power. If there's anything I can do to help, if you'd like me to accompany you to the meetings…"

"I've never even missed a doctor's appointment," she insisted. "I would never waste someone's time."

Daniele nodded. "So will you attend the next one?"

"Absolutely," she declared. "When is it? Wednesday?"

"It's tomorrow."

"Okay, tomorrow. I'll be there. You'll have no reason to complain about me."

There was little more that could be said then, and Daniele told her to call if she needed anything. He knew she wouldn't. She never picked up her phone and used it even less. He worried constantly about her reconnecting with old friends who were still using, but there was nothing he could do. He'd learned his lesson about frog-marching clients to meetings. Contrary to what they believed, maintaining sobriety was more difficult than gaining it, and completing a rehab programme in perfect isolation was no preparation for returning to the real world and relearning how to function. There was a reason why addicts were forced to take their first steps alone. Short-term fixes only brought about long-term suffering and he would never do that to his clients.

As they left, Marco turned in the doorway.

"It was such a pleasure to meet you, Carlotta. This job is so interesting. I'm learning more and more each day" he said, and extended his hand. She shook it and he tugged her slightly towards him, putting a light kiss on her cheek.

"Oh!"

She pulled back and put a hand on her chest like a fairytale maiden, a gesture which Daniele hadn't known people performed in real life. He could have sworn that Marco winked at her before turning away. He quickly bid Carlotta farewell and hurried down the stairs after him.

"What was that?" he demanded.

Marco turned and smirked at him, almost unbearably smug. "That was a little gift to you. I gather she's a difficult client."

"She's not difficult," Daniele retorted defensively. "She's a great client in a lot of ways. Her reluctance around the meetings is the only thing we're having trouble with."

"You don't have to defend her to me," Marco replied. "I can tell from the way you talk to her that you've been going around in circles, and I do believe that she genuinely wants to get better, which is why I helped. She will go to the meeting this week, I promise."

"How do you know that?"

He grinned. "A little bit of angel power. The touch of an angel is good luck, you see, and the kiss of an angel is *great* luck."

"Oh," Daniele nodded. "Well, I have a lot of paperwork to do back at the office, so do you think a little bit of luck would help me get it done by 6pm?"

Marco wordlessly lifted his palm and Daniele pressed his against it, holding it there. He felt like he was engaging in some kind of devious plot with a partner-in-crime, and the thought made him grin. Marco smiled back. He really did have a lovely smile. Daniele wondered why he'd never noticed that before.

## Chapter 16

The next day, he slept in, waking at 8am and nearly falling out of bed in his haste. There was only time for a shower or breakfast, not both, so he elected to wash and get food later. Throughout all of his rushing around, tripping over his own feet, Marco was lying on the sofa with his face covered by a magazine. Finally Daniele was dressed and ready to go, and tapped the angel on the shoulder.

"I'm going to work now" he said.
"Have fun."
"Are you coming?"
"I don't think so. It's not for me. Too much walking."
"Alright," Daniele was surprised at the little pang he felt. It had been nice to have company yesterday. After Carlotta, he'd been abandoned on telephones while Gianni and Pietro did their rounds. With someone to talk to, and Marco employing his usual amusing distractions, the day had seemed to fly. "Um...If you..."
Marco lowered the magazine slightly to look at him over the page.
"If you're staying home, would you mind cooking dinner?" Daniele said quickly, internally flinching.
"I'll try," Marco said shortly, lifting the magazine in front of his face and shaking the pages. It was a clear sign of dismissal. "See you later."
"See you."

His day was suspiciously sedentary. He wouldn't accuse his colleagues of leaving insultingly small tasks on his desk yet, but if it continued in this manner, he might have to. His only opportunity to get out of the office was to have a cup of tea with a newly relocated client who was feeling isolated in a neighbourhood full of strangers. Daniele was unable to offer anything except some company for a morning and encouragement to talk to her neighbours. The visit had no long-term benefits, but her spirits were improved when he left, no matter how temporarily. The rest of the afternoon was spent on the phone, discussing with a landlord whether a tenant was in fact still dealing drugs from their new apartment, and having to hear from a probation officer that their mutual client was nowhere to be found at any of his known addresses.

He filled the day in another manner. There were advantages to being out of Marco's sight and away from his interference. It allowed Daniele the freedom to visit some of his most difficult clients under the radar. Even his colleagues didn't know that he did this. He suspected they would disapprove of his extra activities, so he could only imagine the reaction that a touchy angel would have. At lunch time, he went shopping and swept through the bargain section of the supermarket. He bought water, milk, bread, tins of spaghetti, some frozen dinners, sausages, bacon, cheese, eggs, fruit at 50% off and vegetables that had been reduced to cents because of their deformed shape, along with some biscuits and sweets as a treat.

After making his purchases, he called to see how Luca was, and the lunch hour turned into two as he sat on a park bench, listening to his former client pour out his negative feelings. There was a lot that could affect Luca's mood, from daytime charity advertisements about abused donkeys to a stranger who had looked at him with apparent anger. Sometimes it just seemed to happen if he hadn't spoken to anyone for a while. Daniele suspected that he didn't need counselling so much as someone who was willing to listen. It was occasionally frustrating to go through the same script again and again, but he had come to realise that Luca's problems were the kind that required managing, not solving.

He succeeded in getting off the phone by asking if Luca had searched for any jobs this week, and sucked in a deep breath. Even though the task was arduous, he must be doing something right. They were now on three years and ten months without a suicide threat.

After work, he went over to Valentina's house. He hadn't worked with her for months, but he visited occasionally for her three children. It was a difficult situation because from the outside, she seemed to be doing everything right. She now worked three jobs, but somehow they didn't seem to pay enough to keep her children fed and clothed. Daniele had never been able to work out why. The money didn't seem to be going anywhere else. He'd tried to convince her to give up one of the jobs, which would qualify her for state assistance and let her stay home with the kids more often, but she'd flat-out refused. The stigma of taking money from the government apparently took precedence over sending her children to school with breakfast. Daniele found it incredibly difficult not to get frustrated with her.

He'd deliberately gone in the early evening, when her cleaning job had finished and her job at the bar hadn't started yet, in hopes of catching her. She was home, and scowled when she opened the door to him. He knew that she hated him and thought he was an interfering nuisance, hurting her pride with his silent insinuation that she wasn't looking after her kids properly. He didn't care. He handed the shopping bags over to her.

"There are apples and raspberries, and I know the kids love raspberries. You can make apple pie as well. I've got carrots and potatoes, and there are sausages, bacon and eggs in there too if you have time for a meal in the evening. If you don't have time, you can make cheese on toast or spaghetti. I got a few frozen meals…"

She closed the door in his face. He'd long ago stopped being offended. He'd done what he could for now.

He drove back home and entered a curiously empty flat. No Marco in the living room, no Marco in the kitchen, no Marco in the bedroom. He tried the bathroom door and found that unlocked and also devoid of life.

"Marco?"

He cast his mind back over recent events. They hadn't fought. In fact, they'd had fun yesterday. Marco had seemed to be in a bit of a mood this morning, but Daniele wasn't sure why. It couldn't have been caused by anything he did, right? Of course not. There was no logical reason to worry. The angel had the freedom to come and go, and he'd probably be back soon. Daniele had no idea why he was fretting, when Marco wasn't a child and could certainly look after himself. He was going too far in his attempts to be caring, he thought. If he wasn't cautious, he risked becoming a genuine nuisance.

He opened the side door just to check the garden, and stared in disbelief at the scene. Marco was lying on the grass, wearing only sunglasses and a pair of shorts, looking as if he was sunbathing even though the sun had set hours ago. Daniele leaned against the doorframe and waited for the angel to acknowledge his presence. He didn't. He was completely still, and without being able to see his eyes, it was hard to tell whether he was asleep or not.

"I see you had a tough day" Daniele remarked conversationally.

"I would like to inform you that I vacuumed the floors and cleaned your trophies," Marco replied immediately. "I haven't been here all day."

Daniele turned to hide a smirk. "I see. Just long enough that you're wearing sunglasses at night."

Marco lifted his sunglasses to look at him. "Envy is one of the seven deadly sins" he remarked.

"So is sloth. I've been on my feet for eleven hours while you've been sunning yourself, so forgive me if I need a moment."

"There is enough lawn for two if you'd like to join me," the angel said acerbically. "What kept you anyway? I made food and you weren't here. I had to bin it."

"Thanks for that. I'll order a pizza. Do you want to share?"

Marco climbed to his feet. "No need." He walked briskly across the grass and past Daniele. "I'm bored enough to cook again. I know I complain about the humans who treat me like a servant, but they are usually grateful and it keeps me busy. With you, I can't do anything."

"What a hard life you lead," Daniele retorted, following him into the kitchen. "If you're really so bored, you should come to work with me, or maybe look for a little part-time job to get you out of the house."

"Volunteer to run around after people that it's not my job to run around after? No thank you." Marco turned on the stove and pulled a saucepan out of the bottom drawer, along with a thin pink recipe book from the 1950s.

"Did you have a good day?" Daniele asked, leaning against the worktop to watch him.

"The best part was enjoying the sun in your garden," Marco replied. He grabbed his curls in both hands and pulled them back, tucking them behind his ears. Daniele felt his mouth hang open for a second. "Where can you buy a bath mat? You need one."

The added information brought him back to reality. "Why do you want to buy a bath mat?" he asked.

"If you slip in the shower, I'm the one who'll have to pick you up, and I'm not doing that." Marco grabbed pasta from the cupboard and poured it into the saucepan.

"It's a thoughtful idea, thank you, although you've been here for a while and I've never slipped. Where does this sudden concern come from?"

There was a hesitation. Marco moved away, filled the kettle with water and turned it on before answering. "I slipped" he said quietly.

"Did you? Oh no! What happened?"

"I was listening to the radio and tried to dance."

Daniele snorted before he could stop himself. Marco spun around, his embarrassment exploding into indignation. "Don't laugh!"

"I'm sorry! Really, I'm sorry. Were you hurt?"

"No."

"I..." He reached out to touch Marco's shoulder, and then had to turn and hurry out of the kitchen before he started laughing again. The image of this elegant creature trying to dance to some 80s disco track and going head over heels was too funny. He had never been immune to some slapstick humour.

"I don't even have to do this, you know!" Marco yelled after him. "This isn't in my job description. You can cook your own damn food if that's your attitude."

"I'm sorry" Daniele called again, still chuckling as he sat down on the sofa. The magazine that Marco had been reading this morning was still on the coffee table, open on a quiz called *How Attractive Are You Really?* Marco had filled it out, he noted, and gotten 41%. Obviously the quiz had no idea what it was talking about. To fill the time, Daniele went through the questions himself. He got 86% and scoffed derisively as he closed the magazine and tossed it into the junk pile. His chest and stomach felt light with amusement and happiness, just like yesterday morning, the heavy stress of the day simply vanished.

That heavy feeling had once followed him around all evening, he thought. He'd worked all day, come home to his empty flat, and waited for the next day's work to start. What was different now? He had someone to talk to, someone to come home to, something to look forward to? Something to fill the weekends, someone else to think about? He'd missed living with someone, he realised.

"Here's your food." Marco appeared with one plate of spaghetti, only one, and set it in front of him.
"Aren't you eating?"
"No."
He soon discovered why. The pasta was what he would charitably call al dente, which really meant cold and chewy. If it hadn't been covered in water, he wouldn't have believed that it had been cooked at all.
"I don't mean to be a bother, but is there any sauce?" he asked.

Marco went to the kitchen and returned with a bottle of ketchup. Not tomato sauce, but ketchup. "Are you good?" he asked. "Okay, I'm going back out to stargaze. You're welcome to join me."

Daniele stayed in the living room for another ten minutes, working his way determinedly through the pasta, as what little heat it contained escaped and left him feeling like he was chewing plastic. Soon he would start cooking again, he swore, soon. When the plate was cleared, he left it in the sink and went out to the garden. Marco was sitting on the grass, legs outstretched in front of him, and gave Daniele a smile as he lowered himself onto the ground beside him.

"How are your legs?" he asked.
"They're working well, although I don't know if I'll be able to get up from here" Daniele admitted ruefully.
"That's why you have me."
Daniele smiled at him and looked up at the sky. "I don't see many stars."
"You can see them if you squint," Marco said. "If you want, I can fly you to the roof and we can see the lights of Rome instead."
"I'll pass. I'm not a big fan of city lights. They always make me feel very alone."
Marco looked at him curiously. "It makes me think of all the people who are at home with their families" Daniele explained.
The angel nodded and momentarily put a hand on his shoulder, and then lay on his back and looked up at the sky. A peaceful silence reigned for several minutes. Marco looked deep in thought, so Daniele decided not to disturb

him and simply sat there until the cold started to get to him.

"I have to go in now" he said. He tried to stand, failed, tried again and made it halfway. A hand on his back gave him the extra push required to find his feet.

"Can I have your phone number?" Marco asked.

"Excuse me?" Daniele looked down at him. "Why do you want it?"

Marco looked away. "Forget about it, it's fine."

"No, I'm curious now," Daniele insisted, bending as far as his knees would let him. "You don't even have a phone, do you?"

"There are public phones" Marco muttered, not meeting his eye.

"Why would you need my phone number? We're living together. Do you want to call me at work?"

"No, just..." Marco closed his eyes as if he was in pain and then sat up. "I thought you had an accident, okay? I thought you'd be back by seven and it's almost ten now, and...Humans are so stupidly fragile. Anything could have happened. I want to call you so you can tell me if you're working late."

Daniele stared at him. It had never occurred to him that Marco would worry about him. A few hours surely weren't a big deal. His friends would worry about him if he hadn't been seen for a day or two, but nobody would think anything of him working late. Even Cristina had been used to it. He must have truly gotten used to living alone, not having to take other people into account.

"I didn't think. I'm sorry" he said finally.

"It's fine. You're one of the good ones, that's all," Marco said dismissively. "You don't yell at me, or tell me

I'm not allowed to use your shower or eat your food, or make me sleep on the floor, or make me do petty stuff. I don't want to be reassigned so you have to look after yourself."

He looked at Marco and it was as if he was seeing him for the first time. *You lied to me*, he thought. *You lied when you said you do nothing except what you're compelled to. You care*. Out of nowhere, he felt a rush of fierce protectiveness for this angel.

"Okay, I will. And I'll give you my phone number so you never have to worry."

It seemed the most natural thing in the world to kneel and put his hand over Marco's. The angel glanced down and then turned it over to put their palms together.

"You're warm" he remarked.

"You're cold" Daniele replied.

"Cold hand, warm heart," Marco smiled at him. "That's what my mother always said. I don't know if it's true. Look at how tanned you are compared to me."

He grinned down at their hands and Daniele looked too. Marco's skin, already pale in daylight, now glowed gently. His hand looked like a doll's, smooth skin and long fingers next to Daniele's darker hand with lines that indicated how many years it had lived and how much it had done. He thought about that magazine quiz and wanted to ask why Marco had done it, how he had taken the result, did he know that result was completely wrong? He wanted to say that Marco didn't need a magazine to tell him he was pretty when a mirror could do the job just as well, but to speak those words aloud would start a conversation that he didn't know how to finish, and so he said nothing at all.

**Chapter 17**

Over the next few weeks, they began to fall into a smooth routine. Marco didn't come to work again, but he would always be awake first and Daniele would always come into the kitchen to find two deli sandwiches waiting for him. On one morning, he dared to ask whether it would be possible to have something different, perhaps a fruit smoothie. The next day, he was served a glass of mashed fruit that was so thick, it was undrinkable.

"What's in this?" he asked.

Marco counted off on his fingers. "Raspberries, blueberries, bananas and apple juice."

"How much apple juice?" Daniele took a spoon and tried to stir it. The spoon got stuck in the mixture and wouldn't move.

"Just a little bit, I didn't want to make it too watery."

It warmed his heart to see what an effort the angel made to be accommodating. He was starting to realise that if Marco saw an opportunity to assist, he would throw himself head-first into it. The notion of admitting that he didn't know how to do something had never occurred to him. Daniele determined not to rock the boat again on culinary issues, but nevertheless he found that he liked his constant companion. It was hard not to be cheered by a bright smile in the morning and coming home in the evening to questions about his day. He'd gotten used to being alone, but always having someone in the flat had swiftly turned to something very pleasant.

They would eat their breakfast together, and on weekends, Marco would have newspapers waiting on the coffee table. Daniele was allowed to choose which section to read first. He was very predictable in his choices, always going for the sports section followed by the general news and the classified ads. Marco was equally unsurprising, reading the reviews first and then the Lonely Hearts. They got into the habit of passing the papers around without even needing to speak. Daniele found it amusing to have the section he wanted handed to him as soon as he opened his mouth, as if he and the angel had developed a telepathic connection.

When he left for work, Marco would give him a high-five for luck and he didn't know how much could be attributed to the angel and how much to coincidence, but life did seem to be going like clockwork these days. Carlotta not only attended a meeting, but her son unexpectedly came to visit after months of refusal. She was over the moon and still talking about it when Daniele next visited. Francesco got a job, a mere two weeks after Daniele had spoken to him. It was menial work, but remarkably well-paid. He couldn't quite believe his good fortune. On a more personal level, Daniele's bus hadn't been late for weeks and he was making it into work five or even ten minutes early on a daily basis.

His health was also going well. He attended another physiotherapy appointment, but then backed off. The appointments took too long, sometimes nearly two hours, and he didn't have time for that now that he was working again. Group sessions on Saturdays were suggested as an alternative. He went to one and spent an hour listening, aghast, as one of his fellow patients shrieked and moaned as if under torture, making sure to inform the whole group of her life story in between. That had confirmed to him that he was not unwell enough to belong here.

Hydrotherapy was the next idea and Marco had been quite enthusiastic about it. Daniele had been less so. The idea of bouncing up and down in a public pool, looking like an idiot, did not appeal. Instead pills had been offered to fill the gap. They were essentially glorified painkillers, but that was really all he needed. The ability to walk properly was within him, and all he needed was something to ease the strain of actually doing it.

In truth, the pills were no less evil. They were so strong that he had to start taking other pills to prevent an upset stomach, and he hated putting chemicals into his body. The fear of becoming addicted was never far away. Marco held a different attitude. In his mind, medicines were invented for a reason and were the first line of defence against any ailment. He nagged Daniele about them as much as any mother, eyes sharp for any stumble or hesitation, at which point he would pounce.
"Did you take your pills today?"
When the answer was no, he would sigh and roll his eyes, and Daniele would feel like a naughty child.
"Do you need me to take responsibility for your medicine?" the angel would ask.
"I'm going to take them now" Daniele would reply, and Marco would then follow him and watch as he did so. It was an argument that repeated itself endlessly, a tug-of-war between Daniele's preference to use the pills as a treatment and Marco's preference to use them as a preventative measure, with neither of them willing to soften their stance.

The nightmares continued for six more weeks. Marco tried to wean him off needing angelic intervention in his sleep schedule, with the result that Daniele didn't sleep through the night for a full week. He would feel the stomach-plunging terror of being seconds away from death and scramble awake, visceral pain and fear clinging to him, feeling like he'd barely escaped a dark force that was within seconds of killing him outright. He often ended up locking himself in the bathroom, the one place that Marco wouldn't follow him, and crying in front of the mirror. His fear of going back to sleep was so great that sometimes he wouldn't even let the angel replace his dreams.

On one particularly bad night, he had seen the blonde girl. She was only metres away from him, face hidden by her hair as she hunched over a bleeding wound. He called to her, but she didn't respond. He couldn't move to help her. The nightmare had followed him into the waking world, leaving him unsure of what was real. He'd stumbled around the flat looking for her, shaking Marco and telling him to get up and help. It had taken several minutes before he woke up properly and was surprised to find himself in the living room, with no-one who needed his help. Marco had taken control of his dreams again after that. On the first night that he was able to sleep without dreaming of anything, good or bad, Marco turned off his alarm to let him take advantage of the undisturbed slumber and it was 11am before Daniele woke up. He couldn't decide whether to be annoyed or grateful.

His last panic attack came two weeks after that. He loathed them in particular because, unlike the nightmares which could be papered over, there was almost nothing that could be done to stop them. The romantic comedies that had started as a joke became the only films he could watch. The gut-churning suspense of thrillers, the blood and screaming of horrors, and the large number of big things exploding loudly in action-adventure movies stole his breath and caused his heart to start thumping so fast that he was afraid he would go into cardiac arrest, which did nothing to quell his panic. At night, as happened often in a large city, he would hear loud yelling and screams from somewhere in the distance and would sit to attention. His logical side figured that they were drunken teenagers on their way home from a night out, but his emotional side heard only the sounds of someone being murdered.

The last panic attack was the result of a wedding. Someone had decided that the communal garden would be an excellent place to hold the reception, and they had really gone all out on the entertainment, hiring a rock band followed by a comedian. Daniele and Marco had settled themselves on the steps outside the side door, enjoying the music and the jokes with some drinks. Daniele had gone inside to refill their glasses when he heard the first bang and tensed up, followed by another and another and another.

His heartbeat immediately began to race and his skin prickled with adrenaline, the fight or flight response kicking in. He fell into a sitting position against the wall, making himself a smaller and less easily seen target, and turned his head frantically in search of the danger. His entire body shook with panic and he struggled to breathe, and when he opened his mouth to call for Marco, his voice refused to work. He began to cry silently, realising that he was about to die and there was no-one who could help him. And then, he didn't know how, some spark of a thought managed to make itself known through the paralysing terror. With more force than elegance, he flung his arm out and slammed the back of his hand against the cupboard handle.

Marco was there in a second. "Lele...Oh!" He knelt down and held Daniele's arms. "Breathe. You're okay. In through the nose, out through the mouth. That's good. They're just fireworks, Lele, they're not going to hurt you. You're okay, you're safe. Keep breathing."
Daniele inhaled and exhaled wheezily, squeezing his eyes shut as yet more explosions erupted around him.
"Just keep breathing, okay?" Marco said. "I'm going to be five minutes."
"No." Daniele's voice sounded like a dying old man. He tried to reach out, but he couldn't grip properly.
"One minute."
Marco pulled away and for thirty awful seconds, Daniele watched the world around him take on an unreal aspect, as if he had fallen into a painting and was the only real thing in an imaginary world. He had a terrible pain in his stomach and he knew that this was his death. It felt like he blacked out for only a second, but Marco was beside him when he woke and the first thing he heard was the angel calling his name.

"I'm okay" he insisted, trying to stand up, and then fell down again. Marco handed him some water and he drank greedily, grateful to feel himself being grounded in reality again. He handed the bottle back and promptly burst into tears. "I don't know how to make it stop."
"It's stopped," Marco put an arm around his shoulders. "I told them to stop the fireworks."
"I can't avoid fireworks for my whole life."

"Really? I wouldn't have thought they were an essential part of everyday life, but what do I know?" Marco smiled and nudged him slightly, evidently trying to cheer him up. "Anyway, it won't be for your whole life. Nothing is ever permanent. Time heals everything."

"Yeah, that's what my father says," Daniele sighed. "I know it's true, but the problem with time healing things is that it takes forever. And I just want this to end."

Marco moved his hand down Daniele's arm, rubbing the heart tattoo comfortingly. Out of nowhere, he leaned in and kissed Daniele's cheek, earning a startled look.

"Maybe that will help" he suggested, shrugging.

Maybe it did.

They were approaching the halfway point of summer and the mercury was climbing steadily. It wasn't yet at the hellish heights it would reach in August, but 29 degrees was now regarded as a mild day. Marco wasn't wilting under the sun like most of Rome. He happily walked around in long-sleeved jackets even as his curls started to lose their bounce, and while Daniele had half his buttons undone to let the air at his skin, Marco's only acknowledgement of the weather was "it's nicely warm."

The temperature had fallen unusually low for the time of year today, down to 26 degrees, a perfect opportunity for Daniele to walk his angel. They meandered down the street, going in no particularly direction, simply enjoying the day and the company until Daniele asked to stop on a bench under a shaded tree. They sat there for a few minutes, watching the cars go by, until there was a metallic screech and a loud roar behind them, like a bull preparing to charge. Both of them turned. Two cars had stopped in the middle of the street and two men, one out of his car and one inside, were having an aggressive discussion about some rule of the road.

Daniele felt Marco's hand grab onto his. "Are you okay?" he asked.
He nodded. The initial surprise had dissipated and left behind…nothing. No panic, maybe a momentary speeding-up of his heart rate, but he hadn't missed a breath and his muscles were already relaxing.
"I think I'm getting over it," he said cautiously. "At least I think I'm starting to get over it."

Emboldened by that sign of progress, two days later, Daniele decided to make a detour on his way home from work and visit the supermarket. When he arrived home, he found Marco already in front of the microwave.
"There's no need for that," he said before the angel could go any further. "I'll cook dinner tonight."
Marco turned and his eyes landed on the shopping bags. He moved over to watch as Daniele unpacked his supplies.
"I bought fresh ingredients," he explained eagerly, handing a bag of tagliatelle to Marco. "This is absolutely delicious, so much better than the dried stuff. Believe me, you'll never go back once you've tasted it."
He set out the rest of his shopping, gathering the ingredients required for the pesto sauce. Marco picked up the bag of fresh parsley leaves, frowning suspiciously, and then put his finger in and placed a leaf on his tongue.
"This doesn't taste of anything" he reported.
"It isn't supposed to."
"What's the point of it if it doesn't taste of anything?"
"It makes the food look nice."

Marco grimaced dubiously. Daniele took the bag from him and started to chop the basil. "This is going to make the pesto sauce for the pasta," he said. "Come over here, watch me."

Marco moved to his side and gazed at the preparations in silence, nodding along as Daniele added verbal instructions to each step. Olive oil was added to the chopped basil, followed by crushed pine nuts. Garlic was then included in the mix and finally Parmesan cheese topped it off. The sauce was stirred in with a pot of spaghetti and split between two plates. Daniele proudly carried them out to the living room and placed one in front of the armchair, the other in front of the sofa where Marco had taken a seat. The angel's curiosity turned to confusion as he looked at his dinner.
"Why is the sauce green?" he asked.
"Because of the basil," Daniele replied patiently. "It's very nice. Eat up."
Marco hesitated for a second more before lifting his fork and digging out some pasta.

**

"I didn't know you liked cooking" Marco said later, picking off the last pieces of Parmesan.
"I haven't done it for a while," Daniele admitted. "I guess I've rediscovered the love of it."
"Yeah, it's pretty good when that happens, isn't it? Does that mean you want to be the chef from now on?"
"I think so. You don't mind, do you? I know I eat late…"
"It doesn't matter," Marco waved the concern away. "You know food is optional for me. Anyway, I don't like

cooking. I only did it because most people don't want to do chores if they have a servant to do it for them."

Daniele rolled his eyes and immediately regretted it. "You're not a servant," he said. "I know I haven't been pulling my weight on the housework front and I'm sorry about that."

"Don't be ridiculous."

"Did you like it?" He tried and failed to keep the hope out of his voice.

"The food? Yeah, it was good. Once you get past the green sauce" Marco added, smiling impishly.

Daniele scoffed and waved a fork at him. "You need to expand your palate, that's your problem."

"Lele, I can eat anything," he said proudly. "I've had people tell me that I don't have taste buds, so if you cook something that I don't like, it's really a reflection on you."

"You…" Daniele stood up and collected the plates. "You are so annoying."

Marco burst out laughing. He had a bright, unreserved chortle for a laugh and it was utterly infectious. "I know you love me. Stop pretending you don't."

"I wish I loved you. It'd make life much easier." He headed towards the kitchen, grinning. Over the sound of the tap, he thought he heard Marco's voice, and turned it off. "What did you say?"

"Are you doing anything on Saturday?"

"Why, are you asking me on a date?"

He wished he hadn't said that. There was a line in their teasing and he worried that he might have crossed it. He waited for a couple of seconds and heard no reply. Panic began to set in.

"No, I'm free on Saturday. Is there something you want to do?" He hoped moving on swiftly would prevent any potential awkwardness.

"No," came the response from the living room. "I was just curious."

**Chapter 18**

It had been a hard day. Daniele had been called upon to find apartments for no less than twelve clients, most of whom had children, and some of whom had come from rehab. Even the more generous landlords were reluctant to let to people who hadn't been sober for at least a year. Daniele had succeeded in getting accommodation for five families in the space of ten hours, and of that number, only one had been happy with what they were given. Marco had taken one look at him as he shambled through the door, and ordered him to take a nap.

"I'll take care of dinner" he promised. Daniele was so shattered that he agreed. Tasteless, chewy pasta was a price worth paying for a chance to lie down, close his eyes and let the pain in his head subside.

"Daniele…Lele? Wake up."

Daniele turned his head from where it was buried in the pillow and found the room empty. Was that a dream? No, apparently not, as he heard a very real thump on the bedroom door.

"I can't open the door, Lele."

He rubbed his eye, smiling at the petulant tone, and got up. The sight that greeted him was unexpected, to say the least.

"Surprise!" Marco declared. He was holding a plastic McDonald's tray with several plain white plates and cutlery. Daniele stared at it, initially uncomprehending, and then felt his face split into a grin.

"Is this for me?"

Marco nodded delightedly. "I come bearing dinner!"

He started to come forward and Daniele swiftly moved back to let him in. Marco headed over to the bed and brought the tray down a little quickly, causing the cutlery to clang.

"Sorry, it's heavy."

"Wow!" Daniele climbed onto the bed, careful not to disturb the tray, and ran his eyes over the dishes. "This is so nice."

"I didn't make it. I got it from a catering company," Marco said proudly. "Your mother said you love spaghetti and meatballs. Was she right?"

"She was."

"Good," Marco applauded himself. "It looked better on the website, but it still looks nice. I got strawberries for dessert, and also some bread and minestrone in case you want a lighter meal. I'll eat whatever you don't."

"You didn't need to go to so much effort" Daniele said.

"I wanted to," Marco said, sitting down beside him. "And I am also trying to soften you up."

"Why?" Daniele queried warily.

Marco giggled and pecked his cheek. "I have a plan for tonight."

"I'm very tired. I'm staying in bed."

Marco gave a discontented hum and grabbed one of the meatballs. "You've just woken up. I thought that would get rid of the tiredness" he said.

Daniele shrugged and Marco smiled, reaching out to ruffle his hair. "Old man," he said fondly. "I promise you'll like it."

"Where are we going?" Daniele asked, muffling a yawn. Marco simply smirked enigmatically.

"That's the surprise."

\*\*

"Where are we going?" Daniele asked again.

"Repeatedly asking will not get you a different answer. Next exit, please" Marco replied, consulting the directions on his knee.

Daniele shook his head and took the exit as instructed. Marco directed him towards a roundabout and ordered him to take the first turn-off. He caught sight of a gleaming white building coming towards them, as tall as it was wide and looking like a piece of concrete wedding cake. The building was the only thing in this area, so this had to be their destination.

"Is this a hotel?" Daniele asked, driving into the car park and turning the engine off.

Marco shrugged and opened the door. "Maybe" he said.

"Well, you must have some idea of what we're doing here. Is it swimming?"

The idea suddenly came to him, remembering how much Marco had enjoyed playing around in the pool during the short-lived hydrotherapy, and how disappointed he had been when they quit. It would be just like the angel to ambush him. He went to the back of the car to check whether he had smuggled a swimming costume in.

"Well…It takes place near the pool." Marco had his hands clasped behind his back, swaying from side to side and grinning. He looked adorable, but that didn't stop Daniele from feeling nervous. Neither did the angel's next comment.

"Would you mind closing your eyes? I'll guide you."

"Are we going swimming, Marco?" he asked again, nevertheless closing his eyes without waiting for an answer. Two warm hands pressed over his eyelids.

"No peeking," Marco said cheerfully. "Okay, now walk. I'll tell you when to turn."

Daniele was sure that there must be no greater fool than him. He started to move cautiously across the ground, taking tiny steps.

"Keep going, keep going, keep going, stop!" Marco halted him sharply. He heard the sound of a car driving past.

"Is it really necessary to do this now?"

"We're nearly there. Keep going, keep going, stop, lift your leg, there we are. Turn left, keep going...Oops, sorry, they really need to pave that properly. Stop, turn right."

Marco let go of him and Daniele blinked, seeing a gate in front of him. Marco pulled it open and he caught a glimpse of terracotta paving stones before the angel's hands covered his eyes again. He could hear the sound of music blaring through a bad sound system and was reminded of the awful parties he'd attended in his twenties. There was no way Marco had brought him to such a gathering.

"Forward! Now left."

Marco released him and Daniele blinked, focusing on the strings of fairy lights first of all, before noticing the blue glistening water of the pool beyond. He saw white plastic tables, people dressed in vests and shorts sitting at them, the booming sound of an old speaker...

"Ta-da!" Marco declared, spreading his hands. "I know it's not what you're used to, but it's the best I can offer considering the season."

Daniele stared in disbelief. They were at a karaoke night, one that he would presume was meant for the guests of this hotel, but the sheer amount of people in attendance suggested that it was open to the public. The place was crowded with both singers and spectators. One man in a Hawaiian shirt was already on stage and murdering *Super Trouper*. He suddenly felt panicked.

"Marco, I can't sing."

"Your trophies beg to differ."

"Did you see the years on those trophies?" he demanded. "I'm far too out of practice and far too old to even attempt it."

"How do you know? Haven't you ever sung to your kids?"

"That's a low blow. Of course I have. I don't think lullabies count."

"So you have been practicing. See how good you are when you don't have to keep your voice low."

Daniele shook his head vehemently. Marco was absolutely correct to say that he wasn't used to this. There were so many people here! He couldn't go out in front of them all. He wasn't that boy anymore. He was old and nervous and stiff, and the stage was no longer his friend.

"Lele," Marco said, loudly enough to stop him in his tracks as he turned to go. "Don't take something you loved and twist it into something bitter."

He took Daniele's hand and squeezed reassuringly. "I'm not asking you to do anything spectacular," he said. "I can see how much you used to love singing. I just want you to see whether it's a love that can be revived."

"What if I fail? What if I make a fool of myself?"

"You won't," Marco said. "No-one will judge you. Look at the standard in this place. If you really don't want to, we can go, but why not give it a try since we're here?"

"Are you coming?" Daniele asked. It wouldn't be so frightening if he had someone beside him.

Marco pulled a face at the stage. "I don't think that would be a good idea. This is your moment. Go on, have fun."

Daniele looked back at the stage. The welcoming glow of the lights and the beat of the music pulled him towards it, and Marco's encouragement was like a gentle hand at his back, urging him not to resist. He felt his reasons for refusal begin to melt away.

"Alright then," he said at last. "I'll do it."

The compere laughed as he thanked the latest performer, directing him off the stage and not quite hiding his relief that it was over. "Who is next?" he called in English. Marco nudged Daniele and he put his hand up. The man in the sparkly jacket pointed to him and then beckoned.

"Come up here, sir. Do you have any particular song in mind?" he asked as Daniele reached the top of the steps.

As a matter of fact, he did, and knowing which song he wanted to perform was the only reason that he'd agreed. *"Non sono una signora"* he requested. He and the kids used to sing it at the top of their lungs whenever it came on the radio. Even out of practice, he felt confident that his voice could handle it.

"Oh, Italian. Welcome" the compere said, sounding delighted for a chance to slip back into his native tongue for a moment. He gestured for Daniele to move to the microphone and stepped away, speaking to the girl in charge of music.

Daniele was left alone, exposed to the disinterested eyes of sunburned tourists who had already been treated to all the tone-deaf performances they wished to hear tonight, and just wanted to play some bingo. He fixed his eyes on Marco, who had slipped into an empty plastic chair near the front and gave him an encouraging nod when their eyes met.

And then the music started.

As soon as he heard the opening bars burst from the tinny old speakers, Daniele felt a smile spread across his face, and was a little surprised by his own reaction. Marco was clapping along and he couldn't help laughing. Suddenly the fear was gone and he leaned into the microphone, starting to sing on cue.

He made it through the first four lines before anyone began to pay attention to him. Some members of the audience started to turn away from their drinks, surprised to hear someone who could hold a note. As the first "volo a planare" loomed into view, Daniele took a quiet breath for courage before letting his voice free of the cautious whisper he had kept it in. There was only the slightest waver, but not enough to send him off-key. Emboldened, he let the second fly with even more confidence.

They were approaching the chorus and he let his voice build in volume and confidence with each line, until he reached the "ora" and let rip. That was the best thing about this song – there was no such thing as holding back and that chorus could bring even the most self-conscious singer out of their shell. He could see the compere mouthing along in the wings. Marco was dancing in his seat. The audience had all turned to watch, some with expressions of open-mouthed astonishment. Daniele felt so light, so happy.

The second verse went easily and when it was time for the chorus again, he heard Marco yell "ora" alongside him in support, and managed to give him a quick thumbs-up. He closed his eyes and shut out everyone else – the audience, the compere, Marco – and let himself get lost in the music and the joy of performing again. Thirty years later and it was like no time had passed.

As the music faded away, he couldn't help finishing it off with the last "una con pochi segni nella vita." It was a habit from the days of singing in the car or the kitchen, but his eyes opened and he felt exposed, letting his voice float out alone without any music to mask it.

The brief second of silence felt awful, but then his audience was applauding and he smiled, incredulous and euphoric. He hadn't expected such a response and for a moment he stood there, basking in it.

It felt amazing.

He made a little bow to the crowd and walked off, unable to wipe the ecstatic smile from his face. As he reached the bottom of the steps, he looked around for Marco and saw him wearing such a large, triumphant grin that it must have hurt his cheeks. Daniele met his eye and they both started giggling.

"Won't you come back and give us another?" the compere called. A few of the audience were also looking hopefully at Daniele. He chuckled and shook his head.
"Maybe another night."
"I'll hold you to that" the compere warned, but let him go.

He grabbed another free plastic chair and joined Marco at his table. The angel smiled at him when he sat down.

"Well, that was better than I was expecting" he said.

"That wasn't you, was it?" Daniele asked breathlessly. "You didn't use some angel power to..."

Marco shook his head before he'd even finished. "That's not how angel power works. That was all you."

Daniele burst into almost delirious laughter. It must be a result of the adrenalin or the surreal glow of long-awaited victory that made him want to reach over and hug Marco tight. "I can't believe I did that! Oh, at my age...I'm so happy!"

"I'm glad for you, Lele."

Daniele smiled at him. He was starting to associate that name with Marco more than Pietro now. He'd supposed that he'd gotten used to hearing it in a particular voice, but he had to admit that Marco's accent – pitching up the first syllable and drawing out the last – made it sound especially soft and sweet.

"You look lovely when you smile" Marco said unexpectedly.

Daniele blinked, his brain momentarily short-circuiting and leaving him lost for a response. Marco seemed equally alarmed by his words.

"I didn't say that" he added quickly, looking down.

"So do you."

Marco lifted his head and slowly smiled. They looked into each other's eyes for slightly too long to be appropriate. Daniele felt his body temperature rise suddenly and the sounds of the karaoke machine seemed to fade away. Marco's smile was starting to disappear, he noted. He looked serious, too serious.

"And I've decided you are capable of sincerity after all" he blurted out.

Marco cackled loudly and the strange tension was broken in an instant. "Thank you!" he declared dramatically, stood up, and then bent down to put the lightest butterfly kiss on Daniele's cheek. "Do you want to stay and play bingo?"

"Why not?"

"I'll go and get our cards."

He walked away jauntily. Daniele stayed on the chair for a moment longer, waiting for his head to stop spinning before he attempted to stand up. He was still shaking from the adrenalin high, he thought. That was surely the only reason why he felt dizzy.

**Chapter 19**

The crowd looked like red seaweed ahead of him, waving gently in the breeze. There were a lot of them today, far more family members than could be accounted for by all the boys on the team. Something else was strange. The pitch looked larger and greener than usual, and much further away. Why couldn't he see properly?

    He looked down for the line that normally went around the boundary of the pitch, and realised that he was sitting rather than standing. He looked up and saw the grey stadium roof above him, and when he looked around, he was surrounded by people on every side. Those closest to him were wearing blue like him, the colour of Matteo's team, but there were too many. Where was he? He was supposed to be on the side of a playing field on the outskirts of Rome, not in a stadium. How had he ended up here? He needed to go. Matteo would be so disappointed if he wasn't there.

    He started to get up, just as the stadium burst into loud cheers and the players took the field. Most of them were shapeless, skin-coloured blobs, but he recognised one even from 40 metres away. Matteo was there, wearing his blue shirt with the white school badge, alongside his teammates on the pitch of an enormous stadium. Daniele sat down quickly, heart swelling with pride. This was his son's greatest dream and it was actually happening, and he was here to witness it. He needed to get a photo of this.

    He fumbled for his camera, as the floodlights on the pitch began to move over the crowd, more like strobe lighting at a concert. One hit him in the face and he turned away, squeezing his eyes shut and waiting for it to move on. It didn't. It continued to shine directly into his eyes, blinding him.

Wait, where were the other team? Who were they supposed to be playing?

He twisted away from the light and knocked into the man sitting next to him, his head sinking into his neighbour's shoulder.

Why was Matteo wearing his old school shirt? He didn't go there anymore. What did his new school shirt even look like?

Finally he jolted awake, feeling bereft at the realisation that it had been a dream, and noticed that his room wasn't as dark as it should be. The window was entirely illuminated as if a spaceship had landed in the garden, and as Daniele stared at it in bemusement, the light moved. Oh God, that was a torch! Someone was outside the window with a torch! He threw the covers over his head, operating under the tried-and-tested method of *You can't see me if I can't see you.*

There was a knock at the window and he put a hand over his mouth to quell a scream of terror. A hard bang came at the side door, and the light at the window hadn't moved, which meant there were two of them. His side door was a useless piece of crap. A few good kicks would break it, and what would happen then? Even though this area wasn't the safest part of the city, it wasn't the worst either and he'd never considered becoming a victim of crime. He had so little. What could they possibly want to rob him of? What if they killed him? He didn't want to die. His heart beat rapidly, threatening to break free of his ribs, and his chest tightened with the onset of a panic attack. Having his head covered with a thick duvet didn't make it any easier to breathe.

The bedroom door opened. Silent tears began to scroll down his face. *Please go away, please don't hurt me, please...*
"You can come out" Marco said.
*Oh, thank God! Thank God, thank God, thank God!*
Daniele struggled out from the cushioned maze. The room was dark now, except for Marco gently glowing.
"Are they gone?" he asked.
"Not yet, but they will be. They're looking for your upstairs neighbour."
"What? How do you know?"
"I spend a lot of time in this house when you're not here. I hear them all the time, going up and down."
"Who?"
"The immigrants." Seeing Daniele's confusion, Marco elaborated. "They're the ones who live there. The owner hardly ever visits. He's just providing them with a place to squat."
"And you never thought to tell me?"
"I assumed you knew. It's pretty clear that something weird was happening up there. Don't you hear them walking about at ungodly hours? They sound like a herd of wildebeest."
"I would never..." Daniele began, and then another thought came to mind. "Have they tried to break in before?"

Marco glanced at a random piece of wall, shrugging and swinging his arms like a child caught on a lie. "That's why I stopped coming to work with you."

"For God's sake," Daniele muttered. "Thank you."

Marco nodded. "You should still carry your passport around with you from now on. Identity documents are as valuable as money, and I don't believe that they'd investigate a ground floor flat by accident when they should know their squat is on an upper level."

He came over and sat on the bed, putting an arm around Daniele's shoulders. It was a gesture that was no doubt meant to calm and relax, but instead it made him suddenly very alert. "Go back to sleep. I'll sort it out."

"What are you going to do?"

"I think I'll call the police." For the first time, his bland and reassuring tone cracked, and something much harder became audible. It sounded almost like anger. "I was willing to let it lie as long as they minded their own business, but now they've scared you and my job description says I have to do something about that."

\*\*

A loud thump woke him with a start. When he sat up, the only light in the room was courtesy of the sun, and the bedroom door was open. He sat up and grimaced as his back informed him of the awkward position he'd dozed off in last night. There was another thump at the door and he saw Marco going towards it.

"What's going on?"

The angel turned and sighed. "They woke you? The police are here and I suspect your neighbour just found out why. Stay there and be quiet."

Daniele sat up and listened as the door of the flat was opened.

"Hey!" His neighbour's voice yelled immediately, and then a surprised pause. "Who the hell are you?"

"Your neighbour's live-in support worker. I don't know if you remember that he's recovering from a severe injury, but..."

"Which one of you called the police?"

"Neither of us," Marco replied. "There are more than two flats in this building and your tenants have been causing problems for everyone. In fact, how do you know it was someone in the building? Do you think those people across the road are happy to have their house prices dragged down by a squat?"

Daniele wondered if everyone else could hear the faux-innocence in the angel's voice as clearly as he could. The man upstairs was not the right person to antagonise with that act. There was another pause as, presumably, he tried to figure out if he was actually being mocked or if it was just his imagination.

"Tell Daniele to keep his nose out of other people's business, and make sure you do the same" he said at last.

"Good day to you too." The door closed and Marco came into the bedroom. "What an asshole."

Daniele nodded ruefully. "I made a complaint to the landlord about him once. He's had my number since then."

Marco moved his jaw unhappily. "We're going to write that down and start making a case for intimidation. If it's not safe for you to be here, you need to move."

"I tried to. I applied to the housing authority and they promised me a house in Fiumicino, and then put it on the private market behind my back."

"You couldn't afford it?"

"Way beyond my price range. It was a little far out of the city, but it would have been worth it to have my own place. Half of the development was meant to be public housing, but they decided they'd make more money from making the whole thing private."

The angel folded his arms, glared at the wall, hummed. "Then if you can't move, he has to go."

"That sounds vaguely threatening," Daniele remarked, smiling slightly. "Can you do that? Is it within your angelic abilities to make someone disappear?"

Marco frowned at him. "Who said anything about angelic abilities? I can certainly make someone disappear if I tell the police he's trafficking illegal immigrants."

\*\*

Daniele hadn't seen or heard his upstairs neighbour for three weeks. At first he thought that Marco had told the police as he'd promised, and the neighbour had been arrested, but he soon discovered that wasn't the case. Two officers had come to his door and asked if he knew anything about Vittorio Perin - he'd never even known the man's name before then - and explained that they were looking for him, but he seemed to have abandoned his address. As soon as they were gone, Daniele had summoned his angel.

"I thought you were going to tell the police" he said.
"I did, but I also told him" was the unrepentant reply.
"Why?"
"Because the point was to get him out of here," Marco replied. "The police aren't going to charge him on the

basis of one anonymous tip. They'll arrest him and then let him come back here, and he'll make trouble for you. If he knows they're looking for him, he'll go far away and never come back."

Daniele had to take a moment to think over that statement. "I'm pretty sure that's obstruction of justice."

"I'm pretty sure that human justice has no bearing on how I do my job, which is to look after one person."

The methods involved prevented Daniele from giving an outright thank-you, but he whispered it in the dark on that first silent night, and he wondered if Marco had heard it.

Today he heard noise above his head again, heavy things scraping across the floor and footsteps, indicating that someone new was moving in. Marco had done a little victory dance. His triumph had quickly soured as afternoon turned to evening, and the new resident revealed themselves to be a fan of music, or rather of one particular song.

They were ensconced in the living room as usual, Marco reading a book and Daniele watching YouTube videos, squashed into one corner of the sofa. Why were they sitting like this? Daniele couldn't have explained. He was here first and Marco had decided that, of all the places on the mostly empty sofa where he could sit, the one he wanted was with his back pressed against Daniele's ribs. He had to put his arm around the angel simply because there was nowhere else for it to go, but he wasn't complaining, not at all.

"I suppose it was too much to hope for peace and quiet" Daniele remarked, as the track began for the twenty-eighth time.

"I wouldn't care if they'd play another song. How can anybody stand to listen to the same music over and over again?" Marco asked.

"It's their favourite, I suppose."

"I used to like this song," Marco said mournfully. "At least I didn't mind it. I don't think I'll be able to hear those opening bars again without breaking the radio."

"Don't be dramatic." Daniele casually ran a hand over the curls on the back of his head, realising a second too late what he was doing. Marco flinched slightly, but then leaned his head into the touch, making a contented humming sound.

"Do you like that?"

"It's okay."

Cautiously, ready to pull back if necessary, Daniele continued to stroke his hair. Marco closed his eyes and his face relaxed. He moved only to direct Daniele's hand around his head, twice shivering when the hand got too close to the nape of his neck, and every so often made a hum of disapproval if he felt Daniele was slowing his ministrations.

"My arm hurts" the masseuse complained.

"Change arms" his client retorted.

Daniele grinned at him. "You're like a little cat."

"Meow."

Daniele chuckled. If he'd been a braver person, he would have put a kiss in the other man's hair, but he hesitated and let the moment pass. Marco suddenly shook his head, tossing the curls like a shampoo model, to indicate that permission to touch had been rescinded. Daniele obediently removed his hand and let his arm fall across Marco's shoulders instead.

"We have to go shopping this weekend" he said.

"I know. We always get the food for the week on Sundays."

"No, we're doing that on Saturday. On Sunday we're going to the market to find the toy that my daughter wants for her birthday."

He hadn't appreciated how popular the Tubby Teddies were. Every child in Italy wanted them, and the shops didn't have enough to keep up with demand. Online sellers were buying them in bulk and trying to resell them at ridiculous prices. At the end of the day, it was just a teddy with colourful fur, certainly not worth 80 euros. Daniele still hoped that Porto Portese would have a few at a decent price. It was possible to get almost anything there, if you visited on an auspicious day and were willing to spend some time browsing.

"These are the little bears that are sold out of all the shops?"

Marco had assisted him in his search. For two weekends in a row, they had split up in the centre of Rome to cover more ground, before reuniting with empty hands.

"Will you give me some luck before I go?" Daniele requested.

Marco twisted around to look at him. "I will, but you should know that luck only increases the likelihood of something happening if the possibility is there. If there are no Tubby Teddies available, then a multiplication of zero is still zero."

"Then let me find something else she'd like."
"I can do that."

## Chapter 20

Daniele's plan was to find the toy stand, pick up his daughter's bear, and leave quickly. Unfortunately that proved more difficult than expected with Marco in tow.

"Lele, look at this! Isn't it the ugliest thing you've ever seen in your life?" he called, pointing to a plastic torso that was emitting a soft yellow glow.

"Marco, you don't have to yell" Daniele urged, shooting an apologetic look at the insulted stall owner.

"All of these lamps are my own design" the man declared irritably.

"Why did you decide to put a lamp inside a mannequin? It's horrifying. Imagine waking up in the middle of the night and seeing that."

"Alright," Daniele grabbed his elbow and pulled him onwards. "That's enough now. Keep an eye out for anyone selling soft toys."

Less than a minute later, Marco escaped him again, running over to a stall selling jewellery. "What do you think of these pendants? I like this one. Look, it's got wings! How much is it?"

"Twelve euros" the woman answered, as Daniele stared in horror.

"Marco, we're here for Sofia. We're not on a shopping spree."

"It's only one thing and it's so nice," Marco pleaded, and Daniele wished that he didn't find it so adorable when Marco looked at him with sad puppy eyes. "I've never seen anything like it. Look, we can still get something for Sofia here. How much are these?"

He held up a pair of silver drop earrings with a blue gem embedded in each. "Four hundred" the woman said. Daniele baulked. Even Marco looked unsure.

"Four hundred? Are they real sapphires?" he asked, half-joking.

"Synthetic sapphires. That's why the price is so good."

Daniele removed the earrings from Marco's hands and placed them back on the tray. "I will not be buying sapphires for my five year old, thank you."

He grabbed Marco's wrist and pulled him away. "I bet she would have liked them" the angel remarked impishly.

"Oh, she definitely would have liked them. Her mother would not have liked me, however."

"Hey, Lele, there's a vintage clothing stall. Do you want to look at that?"

He didn't, but Marco was already dragging them in that direction and he had no choice but to follow. "Do you have any stuff for kids, little girls about five or six?" the angel asked.

The owner pointed them to the relevant rack and Marco once more led the way. Daniele looked at their conjoined hands with amusement. "You can let go now, or are you afraid to lose me?"

Marco glanced down, seemed surprised to find them still holding onto each other, and swiftly let go. He turned and started going through the clothes with efficient speed, coming up in about six seconds with a blue and white T-shirt and matching tennis skirt.

"This looks really cute. It's the right age for her" he suggested.

"Yes, but it's not made for a child who loves chocolate ice-cream. It's not safe to dress her in white."

Marco's shoulders slumped and he put the outfit away. Daniele looked around and finally saw what he was looking for, a stall devoted entirely to teddies and plush toys, right next door. Leaving Marco to it, and trusting he would follow, he went over there.

"Excuse me, I'm looking for one of the Tubby Teddies for my daughter," he said. "Do you have a green one?"

The stall owner glanced behind and then shrugged. "Sorry, they're all sold. We've got orange."

"The green one is her favourite."

"Yeah, it's everyone else's favourite too. There's always one that takes off."

Daniele looked across the selection of bears on the shelf at the back of the stall. There were plentiful orange versions, one yellow and one pink. As far as choice went, it wasn't extensive. "I'll be back" he said politely, and took his phone from his pocket as he walked away.

"Hey" a man's voice answered the call.

"Hi, can I speak to Cristina, please?" he requested lightly. He had nothing against his children's stepfather, but he'd never felt the need to speak to him. Both of them were adept at tolerating the other's existence without acknowledging it.

"She's making lunch, but I'll get her."

"It'll only take a minute."

Cristina was there in a second and he launched straight into business. "Cristina, does Sofia like any Tubby Teddies besides the green one?"

She laughed incredulously. "Did she ask you for that too? Lorenzo and I have been running around Milan like headless chickens looking for that bear. He asked all of his friends at work to keep an eye out, but no joy. I found second-hand sellers online, but they're all ridiculously expensive. I guess you haven't had much luck either."

"There's a stall selling them at Porto Portese, but the green is all gone," he explained. "I don't know what the best colours are, but there's orange, yellow and pink."

A silence immediately followed which he didn't like.

"Daniele...I'm sorry," Cristina said, sounding genuinely contrite. "I've already bought her a blue one. She likes that one too."

There was a privilege to being the parent who saw her every day and knew every detail of her likes and dislikes, and Daniele tried not to be bitter about that. It had been his choice after all.

"Oh. It's alright," he said casually. "I can get her something else. Cristina, while I'm speaking to you, do you mind if I bring a friend with me?"

"A friend? Pietro?"

"No, his name is Marco. He's...my neighbour. He moved in while I was in hospital and he's been calling in on me, checking that I'm okay. I told him I was going to Milan for my daughter's birthday and he asked if we could use an extra pair of hands."

"I see. And you trust him?"

"Completely."

"I suppose if you trust him, I'll go along with it. Every pair of hands is welcome. Bring him to the house with you when you arrive."

"Okay. Thanks, Cristina. I'll let you go. Tell them I love them."

"I will."

He turned to look for Marco, finding the angel gone from the spot where Daniele left him. It wasn't difficult to relocate him even in the sprawling market. He was at a stall selling butterflies, berating the owner.

"You murder innocent creatures just so people can hang them on their wall! How can you sleep at night? How can you stand to look at them knowing that they're dead because of you?"

"I don't kill them."

"You don't feel any guilt?"

"Alright, Marco, let's go." Daniele put an arm around his shoulders and pulled him along.

"God will pay you back!" the angel yelled, before turning around and falling into step with Daniele.

"I hope you never meet a taxidermist" he remarked, grinning at the other man.

"Taxidermy is okay as long as the animal was dead to start with."

Daniele opened his mouth to mention hunters who went looking for wolves and deer to mount their heads on walls, and then closed it again. "Would you like to come to Milan with me?" he asked instead.

Marco looked at him curiously. "In what capacity? Do I stay in the hotel room or wander around while you're at the birthday or...?"

"Come to the birthday with me." His hand was still on Marco's shoulder and he squeezed it gently, hoping to encourage an affirmative answer.

"Really?" Marco's face lit up and he quickly attempted to conceal his delight.

"I warn you, there'll be at least twenty little kids there. It'll be all babysitting."

"I can do that" he said immediately.

"Great. Cristina wants to meet you before we go to the party, but it shouldn't be a problem."

"Of course, I would expect that. Oh, that means I have to get a present for Sofia!"

"You don't have to..." Daniele began.

"No, I want to."

Marco was already pulling away, picking up speed as he disappeared between the stalls. Daniele attempted to give chase, but Marco was too fast, so he gave up and went looking for his replacement present. After browsing a few stalls, which were mostly selling sculptures that a little girl was unlikely to appreciate, he found himself back at the jewellery stall and looking over the wares with fresh eyes.

His attention was caught by a necklace with a long chain made of plastic beads and a green butterfly at the end. It reminded him of the pink necklace that Sofia used to love. The owner informed him that it was a mere seven euros, but the clear plastic resembled a silver chain and he was sure that Sofia would be delighted with it. He bought it and was about to return to the open piazza near the beginning of the market when he paused. Seven euros for a plastic necklace made twelve euros for a stainless steel pendant seem quite reasonable, and Marco had seemed to like it so much. The thought of being able to make two people he cared for smile was irresistible.

Marco was waiting for him in the piazza, clutching a bag close to his chest. "What did you get?" Daniele asked.

"I got shoes, but I think she'll like them. I really liked them anyway. What did you get?"

"I got her a necklace," Daniele took the box out to show him. "And I got this too."

He handed the second box to Marco and waited. The angel opened the longer box first and grinned. "That's lovely. And you got her two things?"

The ring box was opened and his eyes seemed to dilate with shock. He looked questioningly at Daniele. "That's for you" he confirmed.

"You bought it for me? Why?"

"You said you liked it."

Marco smiled and took one step forward, lifting his arms as if he was coming in for a hug.

"DANIELE!"

They both turned towards the voice and Daniele saw a young man in an oversized black T-shirt breaking through the crowd, sprinting towards them. He skidded to a halt right next to Daniele, mere seconds away from colliding with him.

"Daniele, OH MY GOD!" he yelled, far too loudly considering that Daniele was right next to him. "It's been ages."

"Dom?" He had the same unreal feeling that one might have when meeting a celebrity. "Wow...How are you?"

"I'm good" the boy replied, grinning.

"What are you doing these days?"

"I've gone back to school."

"Seriously?"

"Yeah! Who would have guessed it? I'm going to be a vet! Maybe. To be honest, I like the idea of specialising in big animals, and I don't mean dogs and horses. I mean snakes and crocodiles! Wouldn't it be cool to be one of those people who travel the world and film animals in their natural habitats? I could even write a book, a conservation book, ideas about how to save the lions and rhinos. But I probably have to be a vet first to do all of that, so I'm studying and I'm going to get an internship next year."

Daniele was pretty sure that Domenico hadn't breathed in the past fifteen seconds. "Where are you living now?" he asked, feeling a bump in his shoulder as someone passed him, sending a scowl in his direction. He gestured for his companions to walk with him towards the exit.

"In a flat with three other guys," Domenico replied. "I love it. How are you?"

"I'm fine."

"I heard about you on the news."

Daniele sucked in a deep breath, surprised yet again. Nobody ever talked about that anymore. It had long been forgotten and to have it brought up so suddenly made his heart skip a beat.

"I'd rather not talk about that" he said.

"Okay," Domenico agreed easily. "I just want to say that it was a really cool thing you did. Not many people would have."

"Yeah, and for good reason."

"Hi, I'm Domenico." The boy's attention turned to the third person in the group, and he reached across Daniele to shake his hand, nearly tripping him up.

"I'm Marco. I work with Daniele now."

"Cool. Is it going well?"

"Yeah," Marco said thoughtfully. Daniele glanced at him and wished he hadn't, because Marco was smiling at him. "Yeah, it's better than I thought it was going to be."

"You're lucky to be working with him. He's the best" Domenico declared.

"Dom..." he sighed, embarrassed, which did nothing to end the torment. Domenico simply returned his full attention to Daniele.

"Do you still play guitar?" he asked. Daniele felt his cheeks turning red. He didn't dare to look to his left. "No, I gave that up a while ago" he said casually.
"Why? You were good."
After all this time, he still remembered how curious Domenico was. Once he had a loose thread in hand, he would pull and pull until the whole thing unravelled. "No time" he replied.
"Not even at the weekend?"
"Yeah, not even at the weekend?" Marco echoed. "I know you're busy, but..."
Daniele shot an annoyed look at him and got an infuriating smirk in response. Marco's eyebrows shot up and even if he didn't know how, Daniele knew that this wasn't going to end well for him.

"Well, listen," Domenico called his attention back and he was grateful to give it. "There's a really great bar called La Baia where I go on Saturdays. They have a big piano there. It'd be cool if you came to listen some time, if you wanted to."
"You learned in the end?" he queried.
"Yeah, I did. I remember you saying that the worst part of quitting was how much time was left on your hands, so I made this list of things I wanted to do when I didn't have an addiction anymore, and that was one of them. I'm going to cooking classes now."

Daniele stopped walking, never minding the crowds of shoppers around him, and gazed at the boy. His hair was cut, his weight was healthy and he looked so energetic and happy. A lump came into his throat.

"I can't tell you how proud I am of you."

He grinned from ear to ear. "To be honest, Daniele...I don't know what I would have done without you."

There was a moment when they just looked at each other, basking in their success, before the sentimentality became too much.

"Okay, so practice your guitar this week so you can come to La Baia and accompany me," Domenico ordered. "That's your homework. You got it?"

"I got it."

"It's so brilliant to see you, Daniele."

He came forward and hugged him, tucking his head into Daniele's chest like a little boy, which brought with it a powerful flash of memory. It seemed too soon when he moved back.

"I have to go and finish an essay for tomorrow, but I hope you have a good day."

"You too, Dom."

He watched the boy walk away with a bounce in his shoulders, and felt so many warm emotions in his chest that he thought he might cry.

"He seems nice."

He had forgotten that Marco was here. "I haven't seen him for two years. I'm amazed he remembers me" he said.

"Why wouldn't he? To him, you were the most important person in his life for a time. I'm more amazed that you remember him. To you, he was probably client number six that day."

"No..." Daniele smiled and shook his head. "I could never forget him. He was a twenty year old with a heroin addiction when we met. I saw myself every time I looked at him. He was so determined to get better, even on the days when he was angry or scared or unwell. He did everything right, went to all the meetings and got through rehab, and I stopped working with him when he'd been clean for a year. It makes me realise what a pity it is that I only see people at their worst. It's great to see him doing so well."

**Chapter 21**

"I'm going to use the shower now! Go if you need to!" Marco called.

"I'm good" Daniele called back. A second later, he heard the bathroom door close. In all the time they'd lived together, there had never been a problem with the bathroom, and that was remarkable considering Marco could stay in there for an hour and leave it like a sauna. Still he always gave fair warning and it was one of those small, insignificant gestures that made living with him so easy.

He looked at his watch and opened the laptop, clicking on the little green phone in the corner of his Skype screen, listening to the muffled ringtone as he waited to be connected. He both loved and hated that sound. Today, or rather yesterday, had been a very important day. Matteo had turned ten years old and Daniele hadn't been there. It had been agreed months ago that he couldn't come up to Milan twice in such a short space of time, but guilt had still niggled at him all day. Ten was a significant birthday, perhaps not on par with 13 or 18 or 21, but not unimportant either.

A gift had been sent in his place, the best material compensation that Daniele could give. It had been far easier to get Matteo's present than Sofia's. His son was so simple to buy for, any football related merchandise and he would be happy. Daniele had bought a Fifa video game from the second-hand store. He was quite proud of managing to find a completed game that would allow

Matteo to play however he wanted, rather than wasting hours grafting for achievements.

    The little bubble sound popped as the phone symbol turned to a grainy screen, and there was Matteo in the centre of the laptop. "Hi" he said.
    "Hi little man, how was your birthday?"
    "It was good. We went to a concert."
    He felt strangely proud to hear Matteo expressing an interest in music. It felt like something they could share in the same way as football, albeit nothing could ever replace the beautiful game in his son's affections.
    "Did you? Who did you go to see?" Daniele asked interestedly.
    "Red Squirrel."
    Perhaps the apple fell a little further from the tree after all. Who on earth was Red Squirrel? Was it a band, a solo artist? What genre did he/she/they play? And who had chosen the name?
    "Okay. I'm not too familiar with them" Daniele admitted, giving a light chuckle that meant *go easy on me*.
    "He's a rapper. He did Grey Lady, remember?" Matteo probed, as if this was (a song, an album, a tour, a movie?) something that everyone should be aware of.
    "Absolutely." Sounded awful if you asked him, but Matteo didn't. "Did you get your present?" he asked, moving on swiftly.
    "The game? Yeah, I did. It's the best present I got."
    "Don't let your mother hear that" Daniele chided jokingly, while glowing with delight on the inside.
    "She bought the concert tickets, so she's in a different category from you. You both won your categories" Matteo assured him.

"Well, that's good to hear." He paused before forcing himself to open the can of worms. "I'm sorry I wasn't there."

"It's okay," Matteo said at once. "You can't talk during a concert so there's no point. Are you definitely still coming for Sofia's birthday?"

"Definitely."

Matteo's head lifted to look at something beyond the screen. A moment later, a bob of brown hair, two lovely eyes and a pair of nostrils suddenly appeared in the video, blocking out half of Matteo's face.

"Hi Papa!"

He grinned. "Hello, my love."

"I watched a movie yesterday!"

"What movie?"

"Godzilla!"

"Aren't you a bit young for that?"

"No, I'm not!" Sofia insisted.

"We wanted to watch Godzilla" Matteo said defensively. Daniele sympathised. It wasn't fair to make him watch Disney princesses on his birthday.

"Did you like it?"

Matteo shrugged while Sofia nodded vigorously. "It's got dinosaurs in it" she declared, as if this was all the explanation required. Daniele felt a rush of love for both of them and sorely wished that the next three weeks would fly.

"Dad, why is your shower running?" Matteo asked suddenly. For an instant Daniele didn't know what he was talking about, he was so caught up in his warm feelings.

"Oh, that's my friend."

"What friend?" his son queried suspiciously.

"His name is Marco."

"His? It's a man?"

"Yes, it's a man" he answered.

"Mum said you were bringing a friend to Milan," Matteo remarked. "I thought it was a girlfriend."

"No, I don't have a girlfriend."

"Good" his son replied, not even attempting to hide the warning in his voice.

He had asked – no, ordered – Daniele to remain single five years ago. He remembered Matteo screaming and crying, only calming down when the promise had been made enough times that he believed it. It broke his heart to see his son still so anxious after all this time.

"Did you see the match?" Matteo asked, moving the conversation on as if he'd said nothing of any importance.

Sofia sighed deeply and dramatically. "I'm going now" she declared, climbing off the bed.

"Bye, sweetheart..."

She was already gone, the gentle clunk of a door indicating her departure. How self-assured she was, Daniele thought, taking others' affection as her due and leaving them whenever she pleased in the knowledge that they would still be waiting for her when she deigned to give them attention again. She was unlike himself at that age, clinging desperately onto the few people he trusted and painfully shy with anyone else. He was so proud of her.

He turned his attention back to Matteo. "Was this Lazio v. Roma? Yes, I did."

"It was an awful match, wasn't it?"

"I don't know about that. They scored in the end" Daniele remarked.

"Yes, in the final ten seconds and that was brilliant, but my heart!" Matteo pressed a palm against his chest and his father chuckled. "Mum told me off for yelling at the TV."

"What kind of things were you yelling?"

Matteo gave a shy smile and looked away. "They kept doing stupid moves like they were ballerinas instead of just kicking it, and jumping over the ball, plus possession was really bad" he said.

"27%, wasn't it?"

"In the first half, it was 33% in the second, which still isn't great. Oh, and the best player got a red card."

"Was that the best player? I was just amazed. I've never seen a red card before."

"Yeah…" He looked as if he was about to say more, but there was a creak from off-screen and he broke off.

"Matteo, Mama says dinner is ready" Sofia's voice ordered.

He nodded and turned back to the computer. "I have to go."

"Talk to you soon."

"See you soon. Bye Dad."

Daniele unthinkingly blew a kiss at the screen and was very glad that Matteo had already hung up. His son wasn't one for sentimental displays and that would have been too much.

"Are you done?" Marco asked, and he jumped slightly, not realising the angel had been there.

"Yeah, I'm done. Did you want…?"

Daniele turned and did a double-take at the sight of him. He was wearing tight black leather trousers, which was the first thing Daniele noticed and took some time to look away from, with a belt sporting a large silver buckle.

His black T-shirt was equally fitted, and then there was a sparkly silver jacket to add some colour and glitz to the ensemble. It was an outfit that called for attention, and in fact, the jacket was the least eye-catching part. The shirt clung tightly to his chest and flat stomach, offering a tantalising promise of what might lie underneath. The smooth shiny fabric of the trousers invited hands to stroke them. The belt asked to be opened and pulled free in one smooth motion. He looked sexy, Daniele admitted. Even if the clothes made the man, it was still unnerving to realise how much he liked the view.

"You look nice. Are you going somewhere?" he asked.

"We are going to La Baia to accompany Domenico" Marco declared, emphasising 'we' so it was impossible to misunderstand.

"What? When was this decided?"

"When he mentioned it last Sunday."

"You didn't say anything to me."

"I knew you'd try to get out of it."

Daniele took a deep breath and counted to ten in his head. "Marco, he was being polite. He wasn't actually inviting me to come."

"Why would he say something he didn't mean?" Marco retorted. He crossed the room in a single bound and leaned over the back of the sofa. "Daniele, you've been given a great opportunity to see the difference you've made to someone's life, to see the effects of your good work, and most importantly to spend a night outside this burrow. I don't know how you stand it. I feel like the walls are advancing on me. Now come on, put on a nice shirt and pick up your guitar."

"I don't have my guitar anymore. I sold it to cover the first month's rent on this place."

Marco looked disappointed, but even that didn't deter him from his mission. "Won't it be nice just to see him and listen to him play?" he insisted, and Daniele couldn't deny that.

"Alright, but I'm not changing my shirt" he warned.

"Why not?"

"I'm not going on the stage, end of discussion."

"Fine," A warm-looking beige coat appeared on Marco and he immediately removed it, holding it open for Daniele. "Then you're wearing this. It's too cold to go out without sleeves."

"I thought you didn't feel temperature" Daniele said.

"I don't, but you do, and you have to stay warm."

"It's 24 degrees outside." Nevertheless, he put his arms into the coat, knowing that he would be condemned to carry it for at least half of the evening.

They took the metro. Daniele bought his ticket quickly, but Marco clearly had no idea what any of the buttons did, and gained the attention of a few beggars who offered to assist him for payment. Daniele dismissed them quickly and offered his own help.

"How have you been getting around if you don't know how to use the metro?" he asked, putting money into the machine.

"I have been using the metro. I just haven't bought a ticket before."

Daniele briefly closed his eyes, pondering whether to ask. "How did you manage that?"

"It's a busy station. If you walk really close behind someone, you can get through the barrier with them and they never notice."

"Oh my God, Marco" he muttered, handing the ticket over.

La Baia was found after wandering up and down three streets, and was immediately distinguishable by the blue neon crotchet at the top of the steps. Inside they found a warm, crowded, but surprisingly peaceful bar. The blue theme continued within. Walls, carpets and lights were in a range of shades from light blue to indigo. It was like being in a fish tank. In the centre of the room was a raised stage with a gleaming black piano. No-one was currently playing, preferring to drink or contribute to the rumble of conversation. Daniele, who had already accepted that he was old enough to prefer bars where he could hear his companions, liked the place immediately.

He swept his eye across the room, and then did it again. There was no sign of Domenico. He started to do a short circuit of the bar, before realising that he was peering at strangers and stopped. The disappointment was unexpectedly crushing.

"Dom isn't here," he said, returning to Marco. "Let's go."

His arm was captured before he'd managed to take one step. "Not so fast," the angel warned. "Do you know who is here? Me."

"Can you play the piano?" Daniele asked, following him across the room.

"Of course," Marco looked over his shoulder to answer. "I also play cello. I favour the classical instruments."

He went straight towards the piano and sat down, flexing his fingers over the keys as if he was about to launch into a full symphony. "Any requests?" he asked.

Daniele shrugged. "Whatever you can play."

Marco grinned at him. "I can play anything. Angels have a natural affinity for music and I've had a long time to practice."

That sounded like a challenge to Daniele. "Something people can sing along to" he suggested.

Marco smiled again, took a deep breath, and put his hands on the keys of the piano. Daniele leaned against a pillar as the opening bars of the song began, not recognising it until Marco leaned into the microphone and started to sing.

"Penso che un sogno cosi non ritorni mai piu…"

His voice cut through the bar and people began to turn towards him almost immediately. Daniele smiled and Marco looked at him, winking before closing his eyes and concentrating on the music.

"Volare, oh oh! Cantare, oh oh…"

His voice was high and clear, with a naturally echoing quality that reminded Daniele of a choir in church. He could hardly take his eyes off him, until he became aware of movement around him and realised that a crowd was gathering. Swaying, clicking their fingers, mouthing along and all together launching into the chorus. Even accompanied by a crowd, Marco's voice soared above all others, as distinct and captivating as ever.

In that moment, Daniele knew that things had changed. He had always developed feelings spontaneously, like petrol-soaked wood set ablaze. There was always a moment when his view of someone changed and there was no way back. With Cristina, it had been the very first moment he saw her across the bar. Discovering that she also had a great personality was a pleasant surprise. This had been softer and more unconscious. He'd always felt drawn to Marco, but without knowing exactly why until this moment.

It vaguely occurred to him that this might be another angelic trick, especially given the mass of people who had joined him, but somehow he didn't think that wholly explained it.

The song reached its gentle ending and the bar erupted into applause. Marco looked around the crowd, and as their eyes met, he smiled at Daniele. "This is my favourite song" he murmured into the microphone.
Daniele felt tears sting his eyes as he applauded, spontaneously blowing a kiss. He wasn't alone – many of the women around him were showing their appreciation similarly. Marco wasn't looking at them though. He felt an elbow dig into his ribs and stepped aside, a pair of young women grabbing his front row seat. He waved at Marco and headed towards the bar.

"Encore! Encore!"

Apparently Marco had amassed a fan club similar to that of Andrea Bocelli, Daniele thought. He perched on a stool and ordered a drink, sitting back to enjoy the sights and sounds of this unexpectedly successful night out. Domenico wasn't here and that was the whole point of the visit, but perhaps this was better.

He was surprised that Marco chose *Nessun Dorma* for his encore. Such a song was typically chosen to close a show, and indeed, Daniele thought the crescendo would take the roof off the bar. The applause that followed almost did.

He thought he might understand the choice when the audience called for another encore, and Marco cast him a resigned look. He grinned and nodded. The angel wasn't getting away from his adoring audience so easily. Marco grimaced at him and accepted his fate, beginning the jaunty *La donna e mobile*. That was followed by the beautiful *Torna a Surriento*, the cheerful *O Sole mio*, and the melancholy *E lucevan le stelle*.

Daniele felt a shiver up his back as he listened to the latest song. Marco was facing away, but he could see how the angel was hunched over the piano, as if the weight of the song was too heavy. Or perhaps he was just tired of playing non-stop. A change had come over the bar's patrons too. They were still, listening intently, looking more like mourners at a funeral than an audience at a concert.

The last song was *Con te partiro*, which left no doubt that this was the finale. Marco looked over his shoulder and Daniele tapped his watch, pointing at the door to indicate his imminent departure. The words of Andrea Bocelli answered in agreement.

As the song began to build to its conclusion, Daniele drained his glass and went to locate his coat, ready to be gone as soon as it was an option. Applause rang in his ears and he turned, watching as Marco almost fled the piano stool, making his way through the crowd and nodding his thanks in response to their compliments. A girl climbed up to take his place and began to play a simple refrain. The majority turned their attention to her, but a few gravitated after Marco as he crossed the bar.

The first to reach them was a man with dark brown hair, already holding a card between his fingers as he smoothly appeared from the shadows.

"That was superb," he said. "The kid who normally plays for us on Saturdays is sick tonight and I want to thank you for taking his place. You're welcome to have your name put on the roster if you'd like to be paid for it next time."

Marco laughed and shook his head. "No, thanks. I don't want to steal someone's job."

"It's shift work," the man said. "Take my card in case you change your mind."

Marco took the card and shoved it into his pocket.

"It also has my personal number on it," the man added meaningfully. "Feel free to call at any time."

Daniele felt a sudden urge to step in front of Marco and guide him to the door, away from all of these people. He'd never noticed his lack of competition for the angel's attention before, and it was unpleasant to discover how jealous he felt now that he had some.

"Hey!" His attention was caught by the arrival of a pretty blonde girl who almost leaped on Marco. "That was fantastic. You are so talented!" she said, stroking his arm in a manner that made Daniele want to lift her hand and replace it by her side.

"Oh...Thank you. I practice a lot" Marco said, backing away.

"Are you leaving now? Hang on, can I give you my number? My name is Margherita..."

They finally made it through the door and onto the street. It was startlingly cold after the warm bar, and completely empty. The atmosphere of levity and warmth vanished as the door closed and Daniele suddenly felt silence wrap around them like the wind.

"Wasn't that unbelievable?" Marco asked, giggling. "They wouldn't let me go."

"You weren't exactly fighting to escape" Daniele remarked.

Marco leaned against the wall and closed his eyes, smiling. "That has to be one of the best things I've ever done."

"The people in there certainly enjoyed it."

"Oh yeah," Marco giggled. "I'm probably going to get in trouble for entrancing a whole crowd of people."

"What do you mean?"

"Well…" Marco opened his eyes and a small furrow appeared on his brow. "Our voices are meant to make humans fixate on us, for the delivery of important messages and such. I don't think I'm supposed to hypnotise people just to give a concert of Neapolitan songs in a piano bar in Rome. But whatever, it was fun!"

"Oh," Daniele frowned, hugging himself against the chill. "So it's just a temporary thing? It'll wear off?"

"Yep," Marco stood up and started to walk away. "It's so nice to be out in the fresh air. Hey, will you be okay getting home on your own? I want to stay out and stretch my wings while there are no people on the streets."

"Yeah…Yeah, I'm sure I'll be fine. Can I ask you something?"

"Of course."

"The song you chose…*Nel blu dipinto di blu*? Did it mean anything?"

Marco inclined his head curiously. "You asked me to choose something that people could sing along to. Even people who've never visited Italy know Volare."

"Right…"

"What did you think it meant?"

"Nothing," Daniele said quickly. "Just let yourself in when you're ready to come back."

Before Marco had a chance to answer, he charged away down the street.

Half an hour later, Daniele rushed through his front door. He was grateful for the coat that Marco had made him wear now because the temperature outside had dropped with alarming speed. He idly wondered if all of Rome felt the same conditions or if this was another way that Marco was able to affect the environment around him. He climbed into bed and closed his eyes, but his mind refused to stop thinking. Instead it replayed images of Marco; his smile illuminated by the bar's lights, his fingers running over the keys, the piercing blue of his eyes when they looked at Daniele… What had happened back there? Had it all been just a trick of the light, or an effect of the music? He wasn't even sure whether or not he wanted it to be. Sighing, he gave up and opened his eyes, rolling over to face the wall. Sleep would be a long time coming tonight.

He jolted awake in darkness, briefly disoriented before hearing the scuffles of another person moving inside the apartment. He reached blindly for his phone, squinting at the piercing light of the screen. It was 2.26am. He pulled the duvet over his shoulders and tried to fall asleep in the five seconds allotted before the bedroom door opened.

"Lele?"

Even the affectionate nickname was painful now.

"What time do you call this?" he demanded roughly. Marco chuckled in a sheepish way that didn't sound remotely apologetic.

"Sorry, I lost track of time. It's been so long since I've had a chance to soar above the city lights. Maybe the song put me in the mood for it" he suggested cheekily.

"You were flying for three hours? I'm sure" Daniele muttered.

There was a slight pause. "Are you okay, Lele?"

The second use of the nickname was too much. Daniele sat up. "Do I need to move onto the sofa? Is that why you woke me? Did you bring a companion back and you need the bed?"

"Why would I have a companion?" Marco retorted.

"You made a whole bar full of people fall in love with you. Why wouldn't you?"

They looked at each other in the darkness. Daniele could see him so clearly. He seemed to absorb the moonlight and glowed gently, looking every inch like the angel he was. He was even more beautiful now than he had been at the bar, the bastard.

Marco walked backwards out of the room and closed the door quietly. Daniele lay down again and punched his pillow, burying his face in it and fighting the urge to scream.

**Chapter 22**

He was rudely awoken by Marco shaking him. "Alright, rise and shine. Get up."

"Why?" Daniele moaned, trying to hide in the pillow.

"We're going out today."

"Where?"

"I don't know. Let's go to the beach."

Daniele turned to face the window. He could hear raindrops outside. "It's raining" he said, and lay down again.

"Well, it's going to be raining in here anyway," Marco retorted. He pulled the duvet off, exposing Daniele all the way to his toes, and folded it at the bottom of the bed. "For whatever reason, you were in a bad mood last night and that means you're going to be moping around all day. I'm not sitting on the sofa and watching the walls get closer again. Let's go."

Daniele attempted to resist, but the angel would not be dissuaded, and that was how they ended up trapped in Roman traffic with the windscreen wipers at full speed. Marco was hanging out of the window, blowing cigarette smoke.

"I can't believe you smoke," Daniele remarked. "It doesn't seem very angelic."

"You're stereotyping again," Marco sighed. "Besides, it won't hurt me. What's your excuse?" Nevertheless he threw the cigarette out of the window and sat back in his seat. His arm remained out of the window, fingers playing with the raindrops.

"Let's play a game" he said suddenly.

"What game?"

"I Spy."

"I Spy?" Daniele took his eyes off the car in front to grimace at him. "Really?"

"Not the typical I Spy. You say what the thing reminds you of, and then your partner has to guess what you're looking at. I'll start. I spy with my little eye...A rainbow."

Daniele looked through the windshield. They'd been sitting at a junction for several minutes now and there was very little to see. "The traffic lights, by any chance?"

"Yes!" Marco clapped cheerfully and Daniele couldn't help smiling.

"Okay," he agreed. "I spy with my little eye...Um... Strawberries."

"Ooh, the red car!"

"That's correct."

"Yay!" Marco threw his arms up victoriously and, fortunately, Daniele was distracted by the traffic finally beginning to move. After spending so long struggling to sleep last night, staring at the wall as his stomach tied itself in knots, it seemed almost unfair that Marco should be capable of making him smile and yet it was so difficult to stay in a bad mood when he was around.

The game continued all the way out of the city and towards the coast.

"I spy with my little eye...Um...Your pills."
"Where...Oh, the quarry, right?"
"Uh-huh."

"I spy with my little eye...Chocolate."
"That muddy field."

"I spy with my little eye...Wool!"

"The clouds."
"No, it's more obvious than that."
"The sheep?"
"Yes."

"I spy with my little eye...Swiss rolls."
"I don't know. I give up."
"It's the hay bales."
"That's cheating. Swiss rolls are chocolate."
"Okay, I spy with my little eye...Barrels?"
"Is it the hay bales?"
"It is."
"Yes!"

"I spy with my little eye...A postcard!"
"Those are the cliffs. We're nearly there."

Daniele pulled into a gravel car park, surrounded by metal fences that hadn't been maintained in a while, judging from their peeling white paint. "We should have stopped for lunch. I have food on the brain" he remarked as he casually parked in two spaces.
"How many points did I get?"
"I don't know. Were we meant to be keeping track?" Daniele queried, smirking.
"Lele!" Marco admonished. The nickname didn't hurt now. "Now we're going to have to play again on the way home."
He smiled and Daniele smiled back. Against all odds, his mood really did feel lifted.

The weather, however, remained glum. The rain and cool temperatures had followed them from the city and, if anything, were even worse on the coast. Unsurprisingly the beach was empty. Daniele suggested that they simply drive somewhere for lunch, but Marco was insistent on stretching his legs. With their jackets pulled up around their necks, they walked along the damp sand until they reached the edge of the water, and sat down. The sky was grey and the sea reflected its colour.

Daniele felt the gentle raindrops on his head disappear and lifted his eyes to see a large feathered wing over him, acting like an umbrella. He looked at Marco and saw that the other wing was covering the angel's head.
"Are they always there?" he asked, slowly reaching up.
"Yes, of course. They're not a jacket I can take off."
Daniele carefully touched the feathers, prepared to take his hand away if Marco wanted him to. He gave no indication of discomfort. Daniele held one feather between his fingers and then stroked his palm over the mass. They were soft, albeit not as soft as he'd expected, and already felt wet.
"They look beautiful in the rain" he said.
"You should see them in the snow. It gathers on the edges and doesn't melt. Pretty, but inconvenient."
The wings abruptly shook, feathers ruffling violently, chasing Daniele's hand away. He placed it on his lap. "So what do we do now?" he queried.
"We look at the sea."
"And that's it?"
"It's relaxing."
"Okay."

Silence descended again. Daniele watched the sea for as long as he could stand it, and then glanced sideways at Marco. He was still sitting ramrod straight, eyes fixed on the water and sucking in deep breaths of salty air.

"I didn't tell you this last night," Daniele said. "And I should have done, but you have an amazing voice."

Marco looked at him, surprised, and then shrugged nonchalantly. "Oh. Well, like I said, angels have a natural affinity for music."

"Next time you have a client and you want to prove who you are, try singing instead of showing your wings" Daniele suggested.

Marco smiled, but it didn't reach his eyes, and he looked melancholy as he returned his attention to the waves.

"Can I ask you something?" Daniele ventured. Marco looked at him. "When...When do you get a new client? I mean, when is the mission considered finished?"

"When you die" the angel replied at once.

"Oh!"

"That's what guardian angel means," Marco said testily. "You guard them for their whole life."

"I see."

"Is that a problem?"

"No," Daniele shook his head quickly, losing the ability to make eye contact and rubbing his finger in the sand. "I was just thinking that maybe I should look for a bigger apartment if you're going to be staying permanently."

"I could live next door."

He tried to quell the stab of panic in his heart, resisting the impulse to grab Marco's hand, as if he was planning to leave at this very second.

"Is that what you want? I'm sorry for last night, I didn't mean..."

"I'm not saying you're a bad person to live with," Marco interrupted. "Far from it, you're very easy. I just thought you might consider it, so that we won't be stepping on each other's toes if we come back with *companions*."

The vitriol in his voice made 'companions' sound like a euphemism for something sordid. Daniele tried not to take it to heart, not to ask whether being with a human was really such a disgusting idea. He didn't want Marco to know how much that had stung.

"Have you ever...wanted something like that?" he ventured nervously, already bracing himself for the response. It didn't come immediately. Marco kept staring at the water, and Daniele wasn't sure whether he hadn't heard the question or was just ignoring it. He was about to move on when the angel spoke.

"I had something like that once."

Daniele hadn't expected that reply. He stared impolitely, lost for words. Fortunately Marco didn't stop talking.

"It was a client, before I really knew what it all meant. She was a good person," he said quietly, the simple description hiding none of the emotion behind it. "I loved her very much, and then she died, and I learned not to do that again."

"Not to...get involved with clients?" Daniele probed.

"Not to get close to them, because in the end they always die, and a part of me dies with them."

"What happened to her?" Daniele asked after a moment.

Marco shrugged. "Medicine wasn't as good as it is now, and they don't let you come back twice."

"What was she like?"

He didn't know if he really wanted to know anything about this woman, and at the same time, he wanted to know everything. What did she look like? What was her personality? Was she anything like him?

"Different," Marco said. "People in general were different back then. I suppose you could call them God-fearing. If you said you were an angel, they didn't question you, and they really tried to prove themselves worthy of the gift. It was only later when I got the doubters and the petty ones. But even by the standards of then, she was different. She was the first one who treated me like a person and not some creature."

"Do you still miss her?"

He didn't want to know. He couldn't bear to hear him say yes, that all of the progress their relationship had made was limited, and it would never go beyond a certain point. Or at least, that Marco would never join him beyond the certain point which he had already passed.

Marco was quiet, frowning pensively. He looked as if he'd never considered that question before. "It's been so long, I don't know if I can say that," he replied finally. "I miss...I miss not being alone."

Daniele moved towards him and touched his hand. Marco looked at him and he swiftly moved away, but the angel grabbed his hand back and held it. They said nothing as they gazed over the grey water ahead of them.

## Chapter 23

Daniele's first task of the day was fixing a client's leaky shower. It was Saturday so really he shouldn't have been working, but the plumbers had the same idea, and the call of duty always needed to be picked up by someone. It was a small job anyway, taking only 90 minutes, plus another 90 to get home through weekend traffic.

He returned to find Marco bent over the coffee table, writing some kind of list. As soon as he heard the door close, the angel flipped the page to show its blank side.
"How was your morning?" he asked.
"I have never been so drenched."
Marco looked back at him and his shoulders rolled with contained laughter. Daniele's trousers were now several shades darker than they had been when he left, and his hair had dried at strange angles in the sun. His shoes had already been abandoned outside in hopes that the heat would perform the same magic on them.
"Do you need a shower?" Marco asked politely.
Daniele squinted at him, unimpressed. "I need a change of clothes," he replied. "And I need to ask you something."

Marco immediately looked wary. Ever since the day on the beach, he'd looked worried every time Daniele said that he wanted to ask a question. Aside from that, he was entirely normal, including his dramatics earlier in the week when Daniele decided to shave his beard.
"I'm actually going to cry," he had declared. "I'm so upset. How could you do this?"
He had made a deliberate effort not to look at Daniele, and if his gaze accidentally landed on the offending smooth skin, he pulled a face. Fortunately the hair had

grown back within a couple of days and Marco had made an equally big show of his relief to see it again. Daniele was already planning to repeat the experiment at another time. He hadn't originally intended to, but Marco's overblown reactions were too entertaining.

It felt odd that so little had changed between them since last weekend, but Daniele was content to let it go. He liked the balance they'd attained and under no circumstances would he jeopardise it. Nevertheless he sometimes found himself thinking about their conversation and was gripped by the need to do something, to let Marco know that he wasn't alone and if Daniele could help it, he never would be. Today he had a plan, and for the first Saturday in several weeks, it didn't involve lying around the house and watching the hours slip by.

"Are you busy today?" he asked, returning to the living room in a new dry outfit.
Marco was writing his list again and once again turned it over upon hearing Daniele's voice. "No," he said. "Are you doing something?"
"I might go to Ikea."
"Why?"
"It occurs to me that I haven't been a very good host to you."
Marco looked at him, squinting in confusion. "What are you talking about? You've been a great host."
Daniele smiled and shook his head. "No. It's been three months and you're still sleeping on a leather sofa."
"I don't mind."

Daniele folded his arms and leaned against the doorframe. "I never really thought about how long you would be here," he said. "I probably just took it day by day, and then one week at a time. If you're going to be with me for however many years I have left, then this needs to be your home too."

"So?" Marco queried warily.

"So we need to get you a proper bed," Daniele answered. "And while we're on the subject, you never lose an opportunity to tell me how much this room reminds you of...what was it, a lung?"

"I never said lung. I said liver, kidney..."

"I get your point."

"Although the purple is quite lung-like" Marco muttered quickly.

"I get your point," Daniele said again. "So if it really bothers you, we'll repaint it."

Marco turned his head sharply and stared at him. "Lele, you don't have to do that."

"I know," he shrugged. "But I will if you want me to."

Marco continued to look at him for a moment, and then unfolded himself from the sofa. "You're something special, you know that?" he said. "You're really something special. Come on then!" He suddenly bounced with excitement. "I'm going to paint it silver!"

"No, Marco, no garish colours."

"Oh, so you say it's my room and now you set conditions?"

"It's still my house."

Marco grinned brightly. "I know."

\*\*

Daniele hated Ikea. He recalled coming here with such high hopes to decorate his new flat, getting lost, and arriving home to find that simply eyeing a room wasn't the same as measuring it. He'd had to return half of his purchases, and the items he did keep gave him hours of sweat and frustrated swearing as he tried to assemble them.

Shopping with Marco was no more enjoyable, mainly because Daniele was a man with a budget and a mission, and the angel was neither of those things. He was constantly being distracted by items that Daniele had no intention of buying. A green and black draft excluder in the shape of a snake, a red lampshade designed like a disco ball, a water bed, framed photos of a beach or of New York at night, a miniature television…

When they finally made it to the futons, Marco nearly lost his mind. "When you said I was getting a futon, I thought you meant…!"
He was bouncing around so much that his sentence kept cutting off. "You know, some low quality fabric seat with the…back cushion that goes down! I've slept on those before! They're horrible! The cushions move and they scratch, but that…That's a sofa with a bed on it!"
He finally took a last leap and threw himself onto the bed, spread-eagling across the mattress.
"I guess you like it then" Daniele remarked mildly, smiling.
Marco lifted his head to answer. "It's brilliant. Look at how big this is. We could both fit on this. And look at the sofa." He turned onto his knees and crawled to the sofa portion, lifting his feet so that his shoes didn't touch the bed. "It's leather just like your old one."

Daniele admitted that it stung a bit to replace his old leather sofa, which was of a superior quality that probably wasn't manufactured anymore, but Marco was the one who used that seat more and so his needs were paramount. This particular futon was top of the line and he had to admit it looked great. As Marco had said, it was more of an actual double bed attached to a sofa than a sofa which turned itself into a bed.

A wicked part of his brain asked whether buying a futon was required at all, when there was a perfectly good bed already in the flat. It didn't have to mean anything. It could simply be sharing a bed for convenience and comfort. They could sleep top to tail if Marco preferred. He was too much of a coward to suggest the idea, however. It didn't feel right to offer Marco his own bed and then declare that he'd changed his mind and wanted Marco to move into his room instead, especially knowing how sensitive the angel was to perceived closeness. Besides, having a second bed would allow him to keep the kids overnight when they came for Christmas. That alone made the extra expense worth it.

One job was done and now only the paint was left. It took ten minutes of searching and one conversation with an employee to realise that the only paint Ikea stocked was for children's art sets, and so they were directed to another part of the retail park for their second purchase. Garish colours had been removed from contention, but Marco was very attached to the idea of blue walls, and kept pointing out lighter and lighter shades in an attempt to get Daniele's agreement. Daniele's suggestions of a more neutral cream were met with as much resistance.

For nearly half an hour, they were at a total impasse, unwilling to move for the other. It was Marco who bowed eventually. Having exhausted all of his blues, he pointed out something else, a very light green.

"How about that? It's still got some colour, but it's boring enough for you" he said, with his usual style of diplomacy.

The green was acceptable. As Marco said, it was incredibly light and straddled the line between neutral and coloured, in other words exactly what they both wanted.

They packed their purchases into the car and headed for home. Daniele suggested that they stop off at a café for lunch, and it was on the way back to the car after eating that Marco suddenly bolted ahead and plastered himself to the window of a nearby shop.

"Hey, Lele, what's your favourite colour?" he asked excitedly. Daniele arrived at his side and saw that they were outside a florist, with numerous bouquets displayed in the window. Red, yellow, orange and white seemed to be the fashionable colours of the moment.

"Purple" he answered.

Marco scanned the shop window and then hummed unhappily. "What's your second favourite colour?"

The true answer to that was black. In fact, black was probably his favourite colour overall, but there was no chance of finding black flowers if that was why Marco was asking. He looked at the angel and thought about the last time he'd brought flowers, as part of his ruse at the hospital, and how well the colour had suited him. His bright smile and sense of fun was like a little ray of sunshine, following Daniele around.

"Yellow" he said. Marco flashed a grin at him, and Daniele wondered if he'd realised the connection, but he simply turned and headed for the shop door.

"Where are you going?" Daniele asked.

"I'll just be a minute. Stay outside."

He did as instructed, leaning against the wall and opening his phone to check if there had been any new messages. It was a relief to see an empty inbox.

"Ta-da!"

He turned to find Marco had appeared beside him, holding a neat bouquet of small, round yellow flowers with a ribbon tying them together.

"Did you buy them?" Daniele asked.

"Of course."

"They're lovely."

"They're for you" the angel declared, pushing them into Daniele's hands.

"What for?"

"For being you."

Daniele blinked in surprise and Marco immediately looked away. "Forget I said that. That was too cheesy. They're to say thanks for...buying me a bed and stuff."

He nodded decisively and started walking away at speed. His escape was foiled by the need to share a car to get home, and since Daniele had never been good at expressing himself with words, the angel was mercilessly cuddled instead.

Now came the fun part - trying to put the damn sofa together.

"Alright, so the instructions are in Japanese. This is off to a very good start."

Daniele caught Marco's eye and the angel grinned at him, evidently amused by the situation. "I'm sure we can work it out with common sense," he said optimistically. "Okay, so this long piece has to be the back...or maybe this is what the mattress rests on. Huh..." He frowned at the stick in his hand, turning it around in search of clues. "Ah, it says F on it!" he declared triumphantly. "Look for E or G."

Daniele cast about and located the letters. E was a slightly shorter piece than F, and G was so much shorter than he almost couldn't find it. Marco took them both and tried to fit them against F, and then laid the three out on the floor and stared at them as if waiting for them to assemble themselves. Meanwhile Daniele took off his jacket, preparing for the amount of sweat he was about to give this project, and picked up another long piece entitled A. Experimentally he took F and screwed the two together. Marco's jaw dropped as he watched.
"Why does A go into F? That doesn't make sense!"
He sounded so infuriated that Daniele had to smile. Maybe this could be fun after all.

In total, the endeavour took an hour and a half. Marco was demoted to assistant after nearly exploding with frustration, and served his role well. He supervised, gave advice that was not always appreciated or helpful, brought lemonade and insisted on very welcome breaks, and made Daniele laugh by attempting to duel him with pieces of the futon. When it was done, he tested his new bed extensively - sitting, lying, experimenting with various sleep positions - and Daniele felt a warm glow that had nothing to do with his exertions, and everything to do with how happy Marco looked.

## Chapter 24

Daniele couldn't get to sleep that night. Summer was at its highest peak, and even though the air conditioning had been on for hours, the heat was building up again in its absence. He turned onto both sides and then lay on his back, wondering how comfortable Marco was out on his new bed.

"Hey Marco, are you sleeping?" he asked conversationally.

"No."

He smiled. "Do you want to make a midnight snack?"

"Yes."

They met in the kitchen, Daniele in the black shorts he normally slept in, Marco in a more modest T-shirt and pyjama bottoms. Daniele felt very underdressed by comparison.

"What are we going to make?" he asked. "I could bake us some brownies, maybe. I'm pretty good at cakes and stuff."

"Or we could take the easier option" Marco suggested, opening the cupboard and grabbing two bags of crisps. He tossed one to Daniele and opened the fridge, fetching a chocolate bar for each of them, and then concluded the feast by grabbing a box of biscuits from on top of the fridge.

"Yeah, or we could do that" Daniele conceded. There was no table in the kitchen and he didn't want to risk crumbs on the carpet, so they just sat on the cold tiled floor with the biscuit box placed between them.

"What kind of things do you normally bake?" Marco asked, unwrapping his chocolate bar.

"Mostly chocolate, to be honest," Daniele admitted. "I'm not a master baker by any stretch..."

Marco snorted and Daniele broke off, frowning, before he understood. "You..." He tapped his foot against the angel's leg and shook his head, trying to look disapproving. "I'm not a...an accomplished baker. I can do chocolate fudge cake, brownies and Rice Krispie buns. With two young kids, those are all the recipes I need."

"Have you ever tried torte, or red velvet buns?"

Daniele shook his head.

"They're still chocolate," Marco explained. "But chocolate for grown-ups."

"I'll check them out if you want."

"I'm not asking you for them. They make a huge mess, or maybe I'm not a master baker either." He grinned impishly and Daniele couldn't resist smiling back. He wondered how long it would take to live that one down.

"So do you have any other interesting skills I should know about?" the angel inquired, moving onto the crisps.

"I don't think so. What about you?"

"I can milk a cow" he replied immediately.

Daniele's eyebrows shot up. "That is interesting. Where did you learn to do that?"

"My grandparents lived on a farm. We used to go up there for the summer and they taught me how to milk the cows, brush the horse, collect the eggs from the chicken coop. I wasn't allowed to shear the sheep though. And I wasn't a great student. They'd try to teach me and I'd just chase the chickens around with a stick or try to ride the horse or play with the big dog. I did learn how to milk the cows though. That's one of the achievements I'm most proud of."

"Those summers sound like fun" Daniele remarked.

"They were," Marco nodded, smiling happily. "That farm was an oasis. My father never came with us so it was just me and my family up there. I had my first pet there. The big dog had puppies, and my grandmother sold them all except for one because I asked for it. I had to leave it on the farm at the end of the summer because my father would have killed it if I'd brought it home. I always remember that." He disappeared inside his head for a few seconds, and then re-emerged. "What about you? Did you have a pet when you were young?"

Daniele shook his head.
"Do your kids have a pet?" Marco asked.
He shook his head again. "It's a rite of passage," he explained. "Kids want pets, parents don't because they know who'll end up having to look after them."
"Okay, so no pets. Tell me something else. What about jobs? Have you worked anywhere other than the centre?"
Daniele started counting on his fingers. "Two weeks on a construction site, one day in a mechanic's shop, one month in an office, and three months as a motorcycle courier."
"Oh, so you were one of those people who zoom around the streets on their little mopeds? I bet you looked so cool."
Daniele chuckled and looked down, hoping the kitchen was dim enough to hide his embarrassment. "I doubt it. My recreational drug use was extending beyond the weekend at that point, so I was followed by more car horns than admiring glances."

He'd said it only to deflect the compliment. Modesty was a virtue, after all, and self-deprecation the highest form of it. The words were out before he really understood what he was saying and to whom, and by then it was too late to snatch them back. He was allowed one second of silence to comprehend the full horror of his mistake before Marco spoke.

"Is that why you didn't stay long?"

Daniele cautiously looked at him, but Marco was eating a biscuit and looking at him with mild curiosity. He didn't look like a dog slavering over a bone as so many did when Daniele let slip about his past, excitedly wanting to hear all the gory details. There was something distasteful about their interest. They reminded him of people who used to knit beside the guillotine.

"I got fired," he admitted. "They all fired me, and then they stopped hiring me altogether. I can't say I blame them."

Marco bit his lip. He looked like he wanted to say something, but was holding himself back. "Do you want to talk about it?"

Daniele shook his head. "I don't know what there is to say. I went to a party when I was seventeen and there was cocaine there," he said simply. "A lot of people I knew had been doing it from around fifteen. They said it would help me to loosen up and have fun, and it did. It made me...I thought it made me a better version of myself. I was so painfully shy, but when I was high, I could talk to people. I mean..." He pulled nervously at his hair. "I was incredibly loud. I only found out later that people thought I was insufferable when I thought I was being funny."

"Is that why you kept it a secret?" Marco asked. "I didn't want to push you, but I hoped you would tell me."

"Did you know?" Daniele asked, surprised.

"Not until recently. When you were talking to that guy Domenico, it was pretty clear." Marco reached out and briefly touched his hand. "It doesn't change anything," he said. "What happened in the past doesn't define who you are now."

"It's not something I'm proud of," Daniele said quietly. "I can see the way people's eyes change when they find out."

It happened all the time. People remained polite in their words and actions, but *drug addict* became the only thing on their minds. Wine bottles would be subtly moved out of reach and eyes would track him across a room. Even among his clients, especially the older ones, there was a loss of respect. He'd seen some of them check their medicine cabinets when they thought he wasn't looking. One of the old men had outright said that Daniele had no right to preach at him about how he should live.

"But you were able to get off them" Marco said simply.

"Yeah, I was..." He broke off and swallowed, reliving the memories and feeling his eyes sting. It was so painful that he didn't even want to speak about it. "One of my friends, Rico, overdosed in his bathroom when I was in the living room. I had to break down the door to get to him. And then...There was...I stole a car. A group of us stole a car and we did some joyriding through Rome. I was in the driver's seat when we crashed and the others left me. That was one of the worst feelings in the world, discovering that my friends weren't really my friends." He buried his face in his hands. "I know how awful this sounds."

"There is nothing you could say that would shock me," Marco said. "Did you set fire to a densely populated building for the glory? No, you did not. You made a mistake and you fixed it. Heaven loves atonement" he added, with the slightest hint of bitterness.

"They put me into a rehab programme in prison," Daniele said. "I know it worked out for the best, but it was terrible at the time. I felt like a child when I got out. No, I felt as if the world was empty and pitch black. That's the thing about addiction. It wasn't all about going mad and taking fits if I didn't have drugs every few hours. The drugs just became the centre of my world, and there were moments when I knew they weren't making me happy, but I couldn't stop because there was nothing else I enjoyed more. So when it was all gone…I didn't know what to do with my life."
"And what did you do?"
"I started looking for shards of light in the darkness," Daniele replied after a moment. "My kids, my friends, my job…" And Marco, he thought. Marco was one of those shards now. "Over time I gathered enough of them to create a column of light where I could live. I can still see the darkness all around me, but as long as I stay inside the area where the good things are, I'm okay."

Marco moved across the floor and hugged him.
"What is this for?" Daniele asked.
"I think you deserve it. You're a survivor. You won against an enemy that has defeated so many others and made a lot of people happy because of it. The least you can be given is a hug."
Daniele smiled and hugged him back. "You're sweet."
"Many people have said this. Well, a few people have said it many times." He pulled back and sat on the floor next to Daniele. "Are we going to paint the walls tomorrow?"

"I think so."

"Good," the angel declared. "I think it'll be fun. A nice busy weekend."

"How is your bed? Is it comfortable?"

"It's comfortable. It's so big, Daniele," he enthused. "I can roll around on it."

He chuckled. "Well, that's good."

"I was happy with the sofa," Marco continued. "I don't want you to think I wasn't, but it is nice to have my own bed. I know sleep isn't essential for me, but it's incredibly boring to be awake constantly. Once the clock hits 2am, nothing happens for hours. I hate it. Hey," He turned eagerly. "Now that there's a big comfy bed in there, we can watch movies in the living room."

Daniele smiled and lifted his arm, pulling the angel in for another hug. "That sounds great."

**Chapter 25**

The movie was reaching its climax now. The female lead had just been told by the ubiquitous 'other man who turned out to be an ass to make the first guy look like the best option' that her hero had departed with remarkable and barely believable speed. Now she was running through the streets in search of him.

"Why does no-one talk to each other?" Marco asked. His head was in its usual position on Daniele's shoulder, and every so often he'd shift a bit until he was almost nuzzling his neck. Daniele had been absentmindedly playing with the angel's hair for about twenty minutes, lulled by the repetitive motions and the feel of it between his fingers. "They're supposed to be in love. Why didn't he just tell her, this asshole is telling me stories, please confirm or deny?"

"Rule of drama" Daniele murmured.

"It's certainly very dramatic…"

"Oh, what are the chances of that happening?"

Daniele started at Marco's shout, looking around in confusion. What had happened? Why was the scene on the screen suddenly different? He looked at Marco for guidance and saw the angel grinning incredulously at him.

"You're falling asleep."

"Wha-? No, I'm no…" Daniele could hear his voice slurring, as badly as a man who'd downed eight glasses of wine. Marco's smile only widened.

"You are! Look, you're going right now."

Daniele quickly lifted his head and blinked his eyes open. "You…" he accused inelegantly.

Marco shook his head, on the point of laughter. "Not me, you're just weak."

"I'm weak" Daniele sighed.

"Go to bed, old man." Marco reached over and took his hand, rubbing his thumb over Daniele's knuckles, which was really no encouragement to get up and leave.

"Are you staying here?"

"Yeah, I'm going to finish watching."

"Tell me what happens." With regret, he disentangled their hands and stood up, stretching with a loud groan.

"Goodnight." Marco waved, and perhaps it was the lowered inhibitions as a result of being tired, but Daniele didn't wave back. He bent down and lightly kissed the other man's cheek.

"Goodnight."

He was sure that he didn't imagine the pink tinge in the angel's face, although what caused it was harder to ascertain. He nearly apologised for being so forward, but that would begin an awkward conversation that he didn't feel ready to face, so he let the moment be and went to bed.

As soon as he woke in the morning, he was skewered by regret. What had he been thinking? Marco had trusted him with sensitive information so that he would understand that they could never be more than a consultant and client. He'd clearly laid out why he didn't let himself get close to people and yet Daniele had forced himself on the angel, despite knowing he wouldn't want it. He needed to get a grip if he wanted to avoid ruining everything. That would never happen again, he swore. Never ever again.

It did happen again, and again. No matter how much he tried to honour his good intentions, Daniele's heart betrayed him every time. He found almost everything Marco did irresistible, and the poor angel was wholly innocent of the effect that simply being close to Daniele had on him. He seemed to have become more comfortable with affection - kissing Daniele's cheek when he was happy, cuddling up to him when they watched a movie, playing with his hands and tracing the tattoos when he was bored - trusting him to know that it meant nothing. Daniele found it difficult to cope. As time went on, his feelings were only growing stronger.

When they went to the supermarket and Marco tried to hide chocolate in the trolley, bickering gently with Daniele about how much milk they needed, and he couldn't shake the feeling of how nice and domestic it all was.

When they went for a walk in the park and Marco tried to snuggle every puppy they came across, while Daniele watched and quietly melted.

When they did housework together and Daniele found himself using it as an excuse to get closer to Marco, his heart rate going wild when their hands touched while passing something to the other.

When they would meet for their increasingly common late night snacks and talk until Daniele fell asleep mid-sentence, knowing Marco could go on for as long as necessary, not wanting to stop until he was incapable of continuing anymore.

When they washed the car and Marco would deliberately stand in the path of the hose, giggling hysterically when he was soaked, and the sound of his laugh was so wonderful that Daniele forgave him for being no help whatsoever.

When they spent a rainy weekend curled up on the futon, playing card games, eating reheated pasta because neither of them could be bothered to cook or go out, reading papers and books with Marco's feet on his lap like they belonged there. They watched cheesy black-and-white movies under a fuzzy blanket with hot chocolate, until Daniele fell asleep during *Roman Holiday*. He woke in darkness to find Marco sleeping next to him, and instead of doing the sensible thing and sneaking back to his bed, he closed his eyes and let himself fall back to sleep until morning.

When he was distracted, watching a football match so he could talk to Matteo about it or making a snack, and Marco would unexpectedly come up behind him and put his arms around him. The hugs were always brief and Marco would go about his normal business as if nothing unusual had happened, not even speaking to acknowledge it, but Daniele would be left frozen and very grateful that his face was hidden.

When Marco would look at him and suddenly giggle, not as if he'd noticed something funny, but simply as if he was happy. Or the moments when Daniele would turn and find Marco already looking at him, and the angel would smile shyly as if he'd been caught doing something he shouldn't have. Daniele never knew what to make of those moments, but his face would grow warm and he'd have to look away before Marco noticed.

This was getting worse on a daily basis, he accepted ruefully, and it needed to stop. It didn't matter how much he fantasised, it was never going to happen, and Marco might leave if Daniele continued to make him uncomfortable. It was strange to realise that only a few months ago, Marco leaving would have been a relief. Now it was more like a nightmare. Going back to the life he'd had before the angel arrived was unthinkable. And for that reason, he had to get over this ridiculous crush and appreciate that Marco was part of his life in any capacity.

He knew this, and yet why did he now find himself dialling the number of a well-known restaurant, keeping one ear on the phone and one ear on the sound of the shower running as he did so?

"Hello, La Locanda della Pizza" the chipper voice on the other end said.

"Hello," Daniele said quickly, almost sitting to attention. "Is it possible to reserve a table?"

"What time?"

"Uh…" He looked at the clock. "Say 9pm?"

"Inside or outside?"

He thought about for a second. "Inside."

Pasta cooled down too quickly outdoors, and he was hoping that the meal would involve more than shovelling food into their mouths before leaving.

"What name is the reservation under?" she asked.

"Caruso."

"That's on the system, sir."

"Hey, Lele, the bathroom is yours now."

He nearly dropped the phone, scrambling to hang up, and remembered too late that he hadn't said thank you. He turned quickly, hoping to compose himself and act normal, an ambition that was immediately ruined. Most people stepped out of the shower looking like the corpse of a drowning victim, but Marco looked ethereally beautiful with gently curled tendrils of damp hair framing his face. Daniele almost felt sick with desire.

"Thanks," he managed to say. "Marco, are you busy this evening? I was thinking we could go out for dinner, my treat."

The angel looked surprised, and then curious. "Where would you like to go?"

"How about La Locanda della Pizza?" Daniele suggested, as if he'd just pulled the name from the air.

"I don't know it."

"It's just a classic restaurant. They do great pizza and tagliatelle."

"Is it expensive? Do I need to wear a good shirt?"

"There's no dress code. You can go as you are," Daniele replied unthinkingly. Both of them glanced at Marco's pale blue bathrobe. "No, I mean..."

Marco smiled good-humouredly. "What are you going to wear? I don't want to look stupid either way."

He shrugged. "Probably jeans and a shirt."

"Okay," Marco nodded, looking almost shy as he backed towards the bathroom. "Um...I'm going to dry my hair properly then. Give me another half-hour."

Daniele had a decent selection of respectable shirts these days, thanks to Marco. Most of them were the same shirt in different colours, as Marco's style of shopping was to find a cut that suited and then clear the shop of every design he could find. The navy one would be his choice this evening. It wasn't too bold, it looked smart, and dark colours had always looked good on him. Obviously it didn't matter if he looked good considering it wasn't a date, but there was no harm in making an effort. Just like there was no harm in putting on some of the cologne that Marco said he liked every time Daniele wore it. And as for choosing to eat at La Locanda della Pizza, a cosy restaurant with soft lighting and an intimate atmosphere, that was only because he liked their food. It certainly wasn't a date, even if a large part of him wished it was.

Marco had gone in the opposite direction with his fashion, wearing a bright green shirt with a swirling pattern. He flashed a brilliant smile and Daniele wanted to kiss him, but he forced himself to stay still. This had been an awful idea, he realised. He'd placed himself in a situation that abounded with temptation, ignoring how difficult it was to stay cool around Marco under normal circumstances, and now he was condemned to spend this evening pretending that nothing was amiss. He was a moron, trying to bring dreams that should have stayed in his head to life, without thinking of how he would manage the consequences.

\*\*

Daniele rarely ate out at high-class restaurants, but when he did, it was always La Locanda della Pizza. The food was always good and the décor created a warm atmosphere. It was designed to make customers feel as if they were dining in a piazza with terracotta tiles and brick walls, plants and iron balconies. For those without reservations, there was always a queue for tables.

Daniele and Marco were able to bypass the crowd on the ground floor, and were brought directly to their table underneath one of the balconies. They were handed two crimson leather-bound menus. Daniele had no need to read it, being well-versed in the restaurant's selection and already knowing what he would order. While Marco studied the food, Daniele studied him. Was it the dim lighting that made him look so pretty, or something else? His hair was especially shiny and buoyant tonight, and his eyes looked darker and his smile brighter in the glow from the candles.

His hand was resting on the table beside the plate and Daniele couldn't help looking at it. Marco had beautiful hands. He was a little entranced by them. They were so smooth and delicate. He had held those hands before, but never in the way he now wanted to. That was the problem with them. They were already so familiar that there was no way to signal a changing level of interest.

The server came to take their orders. Daniele decided to have only water to drink, since he was driving, and a plate of spaghetti. Marco ordered fish and, after asking permission from Daniele, the house red. His eyes lit up when the drinks arrived.

"Look, water and wine," he declared, moving the glasses around the table as if performing a magic trick. "If I switch them very quickly, I'm performing a miracle."

"So you are. I'm very impressed" Daniele agreed.

The food arrived and he smiled at the server. "Thank you" he said. She smiled back and nodded. "Let me know if you need anything."

"We will…" Daniele trailed off as he turned and saw Marco lifting his fork, loaded with stolen spaghetti. "Are you serious?"

"I want to see how it tastes" the angel said unrepentantly, cramming the pasta into his mouth.

"How does it taste?" Daniele asked curiously.

"It's good."

He nodded. "Now I want to taste a bit of your fish."

"Absolutely."

Marco cut off a piece of fish and speared it on his fork, extending it across the table. The challenge in his face was unmistakeable and Daniele accepted it. Rather than take the fork, he leaned over and bit the fish straight off it.

"Good?" Marco asked.

"Good."

The tension could be cut with a knife. Daniele could almost feel the electricity between them, and for a few seconds, anything was possible. Marco abruptly sighed, drew up his shoulders and looked down at the plate. The spell was broken in an instant.

In another life, he imagined doing everything he was too cowardly to attempt. He thought of reaching out to hold Marco's hand, interlocking their fingers. He thought of speaking to him, making some smooth remark that would never actually survive the transition from his brain to his mouth, instead of grinning like a moron every time their eyes met and hoping the light was dim enough to hide the red in his cheeks.

When they got outside, he once again thought of holding his hand; not his wrist as if Marco was a child he didn't want to lose in a crowd, but his hand, feeling the warmth of another person's palm against his on a cold night. When they got home, he even thought about asking if Marco wanted to share the bed. Not to do anything, just to be there, just to let Daniele have him as close as he could ever be.

He attempted none of those things, of course. Instead, with the exception of their brief game, they stayed to their own sides of the table and passed a very pleasant meal together. Marco proved adept at napkin origami, making a swan from his own napkin and a flower from Daniele's, gifting both artworks to his dining companion. The decor of the restaurant reminded him of Romeo e Giulietta, and that began a talk on the play which lasted twenty minutes. Daniele couldn't follow everything, but he enjoyed listening to Marco's passion and knowledge more than what he was actually saying. They had gelato for dessert, which came in plastic cups shaped like monsters, causing Marco to light up with joy. He insisted on taking his cup home afterwards. For what purpose, Daniele couldn't ascertain, but he put the little orange gremlin on the coffee table in front of his futon like a prize statue.

As Daniele was heading for his room, Marco stopped him. "I had a great time, Lele. This was a great idea."

He hugged him, and Daniele had been coping well until then, but suddenly he was overcome with longing and had to force himself to let go. He put the origami figures on the bedside table and lay in bed, staring at the ceiling as music played above. This had been a great night. He'd had a lot of fun. There was no reason why his gut should be churning so much, or why his eyes should be stinging. There was no reason at all.

## Chapter 26

"Okay, help me out here. Have I got everything? My present, your present, change of clothes, pyjamas…"

"Toothbrush" Marco said.

"Yes," Daniele declared gratefully. "Phone, charger, keys…"

"Your pills."

"Right, I'd forgotten those."

"You are so bad about taking your pills," Marco complained. "They're supposed to be preventative, not a treatment."

"I know!" Daniele moaned. "Are you bringing anything?"

"I don't think so. I'll see what they wear in Milan and adjust accordingly."

He nodded and looked around the room again. His suitcase sat on the bed, half-packed with a selection of items piled around it, and Marco sat up against the headboard. He looked like an emperor watching proceedings with only vague interest.

"Is there anything else I need?" Daniele asked.

"An Italian phrasebook?"

"Why would I need that?"

"So you can be understood in Milan," Marco replied innocently. "No offence, but sometimes you speak in a language that is not Italian and I don't understand what you're saying. Even when you explain, I can't figure out how the words correlate."

"That's Roman dialect" he said.

"Hm, yes, I'm sure we will find lots of Romans wandering around Milan."

"We will find at least two, and they are the ones who matter."

Marco eyed him, smiling slightly, and then began speaking in an incomprehensible tongue. It sounded like Sardinian dialect, but when Daniele asked, Marco shook his head. Languages were not his strong suit and he shrugged, silently begging for help.
"It's Genoese" Marco said finally, taking pity.
"That's not a language I hear much of."
"Now the shoe is on the other foot" Marco said cheekily.
"Yes, but I have never been to Genoa. You, on the other hand, are in Rome" Daniele remarked.
"I suppose," the angel admitted. "I don't often stay anywhere long enough to pick up local slang."
"Have you been to a lot of places?"
Marco started counting on his fingers. The digits flew quickly up to twelve before slowing their progress. Daniele continued to pack his suitcase, occasionally looking over to see that another two or three fingers had been added to the tally.
"I'll presume that the answer is yes" he said at last.
"I'm up to twenty-five countries," Marco reported, returning his attention to the here and now. "And of course, I've been to a lot of those more than once."
"You really are a globetrotter," Daniele said admiringly. "So what's the best place you've ever visited?"
Marco thought for a moment. "I think Corsica," he said. "Rome comes second though."

**

They took the train up to Milan. TrenItalia helpfully provided a three hour express between the cities, which afforded Daniele the chance to sit back and relax, watching the countryside and even nodding off as they passed Florence. Marco watched the view as well, and then borrowed Daniele's phone to play *Angry Birds*, which he enjoyed so much that he handed the phone back with the battery at 38%.

The tannoy announced that they were arriving in Milan, waking Daniele. He kept his eyes closed and felt himself being shaken a few seconds later.

"Lele, wake up. We're nearly there."

"I know" he mumbled, sitting upright and rubbing his jaw.

They pulled into Milano Centrale, gathered up their belongings, and stepped into a shockingly large crowd of people on the platform. Daniele grabbed Marco's hand to keep them together and began to shuffle towards the building. He was afraid that his feet could be lifted from the ground at any moment, that he could fall and be trampled, or the crowd bottleneck and either suffocate him or stampede. Only knowing that Marco was still somewhere close behind kept him calm.

They made it into the building, where the air immediately cooled and became easier to breathe, and the crowd began to disperse. And then they were on the escalator, in their own piece of air, and into the spacious entrance hall. Daniele led the way to find a taxi rank. They were still holding hands and, wickedly, he decided to pretend he hadn't noticed. Apparently Marco had the same idea. Their hands split only when the taxi arrived, springing apart like two flipped magnets.

The hotel wasn't far from the station so the ride took only ten minutes. It was a basic, but comfortable three star establishment. Daniele would have saved money by booking into a simple B&B, but his angel's penchant for luxury had come to the fore and it had taken a while to talk him down from the five star palace he'd wanted. This was a compromise, and to give Marco his due, it was nice to walk into a room with working air conditioning and a bathroom clean enough to enter in bare feet. There was only one problem, an issue neither of them had thought about until they were looking at it.

"Maybe it's a..." Marco optimistically approached and pulled at the mattress. "No, it is not a twin." He looked at Daniele and grinned ruefully. "You don't snore, do you?"

The dormitory in the B&B had bunk beds. He'd seen it on the website. Why had he assumed that a hotel room would provide the same service? He cast his mind back and suddenly remembered that in the past, they had. When he went on holiday with his family, he would either get an apartment with two rooms or bunks for the kids. He had completely forgotten that those weren't standard in a normal hotel room.

"Do you want to be nearer to the window or the door?" he asked.

There was nothing he could do about it now, short of causing a scene and asking for a change of rooms, and this wasn't worth it. Besides, the room had a balcony with a view over the city and he didn't want to lose that.

"The window, I suppose, in case I want to stretch my wings in the night."

"Okay." Daniele dumped his suitcase on the other side, briefly thought about unpacking, and then decided that he couldn't be bothered. He would be here for only a few days. Living out of the case was easier.

"Do you need the bathroom?" Marco asked.

"Not at the moment."

"Okay, I'm going to wash my hair. Travelling always makes me feel dirty."

While Marco disappeared into the bathroom, Daniele dug his cigarettes out of his jacket and headed onto the balcony. The glittering yellow lights didn't fill him with a painful unnamed loneliness for once, because his kids were somewhere out there. He lit the cigarette and allowed his gaze to wander over the cityscape, wondering if one of those windows were theirs. He should have asked Cristina to put a brightly coloured lamp in the window so he could pick it out among the thousands. Were they in bed, resting for tomorrow's festivities? It was more likely in Sofia's case that she was fighting the sandman to stay up for midnight, and the thought made him smile. Last year she had run up to him on the morning of her birthday and declared with no small amount of disappointment that she didn't feel five. She looked so young in the photos now. It was unbelievable how much she'd grown in only twelve months.

He turned as the balcony door opened and Marco stepped out, clad in his omnipresent blue bathrobe. "Can I join you?" he requested.

"Sure, but watch you don't catch cold with your wet hair" Daniele said, touching the curls. They parted easily under his hand and he suddenly thought of how much fun it would be to play with them when they were wet, but that was a consideration for another time. He handed one of his cigarettes over and lit it, and they puffed in companionable silence for a moment.

"I wish you wouldn't smoke," Marco remarked suddenly. "Only because I'd miss you if you died of lung cancer."

Daniele glanced at him, grinning. "You'd miss me?"

The angel shrugged. "I'm used to you now."

"You sound like my son. If he sees my cigarettes, he'll steal them and put them in the bin. He thinks he can force me to quit that way."

"He's a wise boy."

Daniele shook his head, his sigh creating a large plume of smoke like dragon's breath. "No, he's too much like me. If there's an element of risk in anything, he takes it to its worst extreme. I tried to teach him about the dangers of throwing stones and now he's afraid of snowball fights in case there are stones in the snow. I've made him into a nervous wreck."

Marco leaned against the railings of the balcony and half-turned to face him. "So what are your kids like?" he queried.

"They're brilliant," Daniele said immediately. "I know I'm biased, but they really are. Teo is a bit quiet, but he's so clever and so kind. And Sofi is so much fun. I don't know where she came from. She has so much confidence and self-belief. Actually, remember when you told me about your sister, that she was like a little puppy chasing the big dogs? Sofi is a bit like that too."

"I can't believe you remember that," Marco flicked a bit of ash off his cigarette and took another drag, blowing the smoke in a long column. "I should like her then. And your son sounds just like you, so I'm sure I'll like him too."

Daniele looked away to prevent the infantile question from leaving his mouth. *Do you like me?* A question asked by shy children on the playground, trying to ascertain if they've found a new friend. *But do you like me, Marco? I like you so much.*

"You're a good father" the angel continued, and even though it was meant to be a compliment, it felt like a little stab to Daniele's chest.

"I'm not" he said quietly.

"You are. You love your children, you want the best for them, you teach them and take care of them..."

"Marco," he said sharply. "I'm not around enough to take care of them. I don't teach them well enough and I compensate by worrying. I love them, yes, but that doesn't make me special."

The angel turned away and rested his chin on his hands, staring out over Milan. Daniele was about to apologise for his harsh tone, knowing that Marco had only been trying to be kind, when the other man spoke.

"Maybe it's patronising of me to treat men who love their children as rare creatures who need to be paraded through the streets, but...I can't help myself. To me, they are."

Daniele moved towards him and gently put an arm around his shoulders, ready to move away if Marco rejected it. He didn't. He edged closer to Daniele and rested his head on his shoulder. Daniele tightened his hold and put a kiss in the angel's hair before he could stop himself. Marco wrapped one arm around his back and lifted his head. At first it seemed that he was only looking at Daniele, and then he kissed his cheek. It wasn't the first time, but this was softer and more lingering than all the others, and Daniele momentarily forgot how to breathe. Marco's head nestled in the crook of his neck, his curls tickling Daniele's jaw, and he pushed them back before holding onto the other man again. Something special was happening, he thought. They were in a place that they might never be again and his shoulder was stiff from trying not to move, not to do anything that might disturb this moment.

\*\*

Inevitably, of course, it had to end. The cigarettes burned out and the temperature dropped until it became uncomfortable. Even a never-ending hug couldn't stave off the chill and so they separated, seeking the warmth of the room and bed. Daniele went into the bathroom to change into pyjamas, and upon returning, found the angel staring at the bed and making no attempt to get into it. Somehow that moment of intimacy on the balcony made sharing seem like a bigger deal than it had been before, or at least that's how Marco seemed to see it.

"You know...I can sleep anywhere, if you'd prefer..." he said nervously.
"I don't mind sharing the bed," Daniele interjected. "Do you?"
"No."
"Then get in. Where else would you sleep anyway?" he asked as he lifted the covers. "Not on the floor?"
"Or sitting at the table" Marco said, gesturing to the small writing desk against the wall. Daniele got into the bed and forcefully patted the area next to him.
"Put your head on that pillow and get comfortable."
Marco smiled warmly at him. "It's like the times we fell asleep on the futon watching movies" he said, joining Daniele under the covers.

"It is just like that. So what do you like to do before sleep? Do you want to read or turn on the TV?"

"Okay, let's see what's on."

Their options were a late night re-run of a dog show, the South Korean stock exchange, or *Who Wants to be a Millionaire?* They settled on the quiz show, joining at the point where the 5,000 euro question was being asked. Marco answered quickly, Daniele chose another option soon after, and they both waited to see who was right.

The wait was longer than expected. Daniele had time to brush his teeth, and still the question hadn't moved on. Marco got frustrated and started directing remarks at the TV, until he got fed-up even of that and picked up a book. It took twenty minutes for a new question to be asked, by which point neither of them could remember who had been correct. The show played as background noise.

"How is your book?" Daniele asked.

"It's funny. I'll let you read it when I'm done."

"Sure."

"Just tell me when you want the lights turned off" the angel added.

"It's fine. I'm going to lie down. You can keep reading."

Daniele rolled over, away from Marco's lamp, and closed his eyes. Within thirty seconds the room had been plunged into darkness. "I hope that wasn't for my sake" he remarked into the abyss.

"It was."

This wasn't at all like watching a movie on the futon. There was an excuse to snuggle close then, in order to see the screen, and if he felt himself getting tired and chose not to move away... then that was simply due to a lack of energy and, if he was a little more honest, lack of inclination to leave a comfortable position. It seemed natural to roll over now and put his arms around Marco, but the centre of the bed had become an invisible wall between them, and so he lay there like a fish on a slab and waited to hear Marco's breathing change. It came sooner than expected. Only two or three minutes after the light went out, snores were heard in the darkness.

"Marco..." Daniele said quietly. The snores continued. He sighed quietly and tried to switch his mind off, allowing sleep to wash over him. When he found himself unable to hold onto any more thoughts, he knew it was almost time.

He was lying on his back, gazing up at an impossibly perfect sky. It was a deep blue and covered in bright yellow stars, with one brilliant white spot in the middle. It looked like the creation of a Renaissance painter, something that should belong on the roof of a cathedral, but there was no doubt that it was real. It was so beautiful. He could lie here and stare at it for hours.

Suddenly he saw Marco, or rather Marco's face, looming in the sky above him. His head was so enormous that Daniele could hardly focus on him.
"Roll onto your side," the giant Marco whispered. "You're snoring."
What a strange thing for his fantasy to say, but alright. "Uh-huh."
Daniele turned over, feeling something soft against his cheek, and his mind went dark.

He awoke to a room filled with sunlight, and a companion who was unusually still asleep. Daniele rolled over as carefully as he could to avoid disturbing him.

Marco hugged a piece of the duvet as if it was a teddy bear, and one of his fingers was twitching in response to a dream. Daniele had thought that nobody looked good in sleep - Matteo had sneakily taken a photo of him napping, as revenge for his father doing the same to him, and Daniele had been horrified by how old he looked - but Marco looked even younger than he usually did, with his face totally relaxed and free of the tension that was omnipresent when he was awake.

Daniele took a moment to admire those long fingers and smooth hands, the unlined face and the thick curls which shone in the morning sunlight. He couldn't quite believe how exceptionally bushy Marco's hair was in the morning. He wanted to sink both of his hands into it. Had he ever wanted anyone as much as this? Almost certainly, if he was being honest, but right now it felt as if Marco was the only one.

## Chapter 27

"What is Cristina like?" Marco asked. They were walking through Milan and had been for some time. Daniele had been unable to get Google Maps on his phone as he'd hoped, so they were following road signs. This was the first time Marco had spoken for almost twenty minutes.

"She's a lot like you, soft heart and sharp tongue," Daniele answered. "I think you'll like her. She finds it really easy to get along with people and she's very sociable. I don't know what she saw in me, but I was drunk when I met her, so maybe that fooled her."

"I have to hear this story now."

Daniele looked back at him, carrying two wrapped packages and wearing a thoroughly fed-up expression. "I saw her in a bar and I had to down a whole bottle of something before I had the courage to talk to her," he admitted, trying to sound dismissive to cover his embarrassment. "Apparently I tried to take my shirt off."

"Oh, I was wondering what impressed her, but now I understand. That would definitely work."

"Are you mocking me?" Daniele demanded, half-laughing.

"I'm not" Marco insisted.

"Why am I telling you this? You two are going to be exchanging stories about me all day. I'm not giving you any more ammo. Look, I know this street. The house isn't far."

"Good, otherwise I was just going to fly. This is exhausting!"

"Marco, if you think this is exhausting, you aren't going to last the day."

The house was an attractive semi-detached surrounded by neatly manicured lawns and unnaturally square hedges. There were two cars on the driveway, Cristina's white Fiat and a bold red Alfa Romeo.

"This is nice," Marco said, sounding surprised. "What does this guy do for a living?"

"Uh, I think he's a vet."

"Really? I wonder if the kids get to play with the cute puppies and kittens."

Daniele said nothing and started walking towards the building. "Sorry," he heard Marco mutter behind him. "That was insensitive."

He rang the bell and waited, crossing his arms and tapping his fingers anxiously. He felt a hand rub his shoulder and started to turn towards Marco, when he heard footsteps and looked forward as the main door opened. Cristina looked at Marco first and then Daniele.

"Hi, good to see you. You must be Marco" she added, looking at him again.

He stepped forward and extended his hand. "Nice to meet you."

"Likewise." Cristina shook it. "The kids are inside. We're leaving in ten minutes."

She led the way to the kitchen and knocked on the back window. "Matteo! Matteo, come in!"

Beyond her, Daniele could see his son kicking a football against the wall in the back garden.

"Sorry," Cristina shrugged. "It seems he's a little distracted."

Sofia was sitting at the table, doing a jigsaw puzzle with Lorenzo. She looked up as Daniele entered the kitchen and grinned, twitching as if she was about to jump out of her chair, and then settled down again.

"Hi Papa."

"Hello principessa. Happy birthday."

She kept smiling excitedly, but didn't move from the table.

"Can I have a hug?" Daniele requested, opening his arms. Sofia immediately rushed to him and he lifted her off the ground, encircling her in a warm embrace and squeezing as tightly as he could without causing pain.

"I missed you, Sofi."

She wrapped her arms around his neck and snuggled into him. "This is my birthday present" she declared.

"What is?" he asked. Sofia pulled back and gestured to herself, and Daniele noted her outfit, a red and white T-shirt with a cherry blossom motif and candy red jeans.

"Mama got it for me," she explained. "It's my birthday outfit. I'm wearing it today."

"You look lovely, sweetheart." He turned to introduce her to the other guest in the kitchen. "This is my friend Marco."

The angel lifted one hand in a wave.

"Hello," Sofia said. "What's my present?"

"Sofia, don't be rude. Your father has come a long way to see you" Cristina said.

"But it's my birthday" she protested.

"I think you'll like your present" Marco said, smiling. Sofia's mouth formed an O of anticipation and curiosity.

"Dad!"

At that moment, Matteo came running from the back garden and hurled himself at Daniele. His father squeezed him back. "Hello, little man. Good to see you."

"Good to see you too!"

His son looked up at him, smiling like he used to do when he was young and thought Daniele was the best person in the world. He'd grown out of that in the past few years, but apparently absence made the heart grow fonder.

"Are you Marco?" he asked, looking over Daniele's arm at the strange face in his kitchen.

"I am."

Matteo stepped towards him and held up his palm. The angel did the same and Matteo smacked his hand hard enough that the crack echoed around the kitchen.

"Gently" Daniele cautioned, wrapping an arm around Matteo's chest in a half-hug, half-restraining move. He pulled an apologetic face over his son's head. Marco returned a pained smile.

"Sorry." Matteo offered his palm again. Marco cautiously extended his other hand and received a light tap in greeting.

"Alright, have fun." Lorenzo unexpectedly announced, scraping his chair back and standing. Daniele had forgotten he was there. He looked at Cristina, but she didn't seem surprised.

"You're not coming?" he asked.

"No, twenty kids isn't my idea of fun, but I hope you guys have a good time. I'll see you later."

Lorenzo gave Cristina a kiss on the cheek and then left, taking his jacket from the coat stand. The front door closed and Sofia threw her arms around Daniele again.

"Can we go now? Is it time?" she asked excitedly.

Cristina looked at him. "Can you wait or do you want to eat something now?"

"I can wait" Daniele said immediately, knowing that Sofia would not be pleased if he delayed her departure.

\*\*

The table was a sugary feast for the senses; cups of lollipops, plates of cupcakes, and the centrepiece of it all, a chocolate cake. Six pink and white striped candles decorated the length of the cake, and a sparkly number *6* sat in the middle. The kids' eyes lit up with joy. Daniele caught Cristina's gaze and they shared a moment of mutual understanding, two soldiers preparing to enter the battlefield, knowing the chances of corralling twenty children on a sugar high without any injuries or tears were almost non-existent. He turned to Marco, to check whether the angel looked daunted by the task ahead, and saw a lollipop stick already protruding from the other man's mouth.

Sofia took her place at the head of the table, next to the cake, looking like a little queen with her family around her like servants and her friends seated around the long table like subjects at the banquet. They sang *Tanti Auguri* as Cristina lit the candles.
"Do you want to make a wish?" Daniele asked.
"Okay. I wish…"
"Don't say it out loud or it won't happen" Matteo interrupted.

Sofia snapped her mouth shut and closed her eyes, screwing her face up in concentration. Her wish lasted for almost ten silent seconds. Daniele wondered if she did the same thing he had as a child, repeating the wish in hopes that it would be more likely to happen. Finally she opened her eyes and blew on the candles. Four of the six were extinguished at once. Another breath took care of the survivors. The table clapped, and then Sofia's work was done. She joined the rest in excited chatter, interrupted only by brief "thank you"s when an adult handed them cake.

The adults swiftly became useless, silent guardians whose only function was to provide food and, in the case of Marco, entertainment. Daniele watched him go around the table, spending a bit of time with every single child. He pulled coins from behind their ears, made them disappear in his hands, asked them to guess a number and correctly predicted it. Sofia, as the birthday girl, got not only magic tricks, but also a short comedy show which Daniele recognised as word-for-word recitation of the cleaner jokes from a stand-up they'd watched a few weeks ago. His daughter found it hilarious and kept demanding more. It took Marco some time to escape her.

He came over to where Daniele and his son were sitting, and sat down on Matteo's other side. "Do you like magic tricks?" he asked.

"If they're good."

"Well, I'll see what I can do. I don't have any cards with me, but you know what they look like, right?"

Matteo nodded.

"Okay, so pick one and imagine it in your head. Don't tell me what it is."

"I've got one" Matteo reported.

"Okay. Is it...the 9 of Spades?"

"No."

"No? Then is it...the King of Hearts?"

"No." Matteo sighed wearily.

"Give me one more try. I almost have it. I've got it, the 3 of Clubs!"

"No, and you can't guess it. There are too many" Matteo said.

Daniele was torn between amusement at his son's logic and dying of embarrassment for Marco. The angel pulled a sad face and put his head on his hand.

"Maybe I was too ambitious," he admitted, sighing. "Daniele, will you check the time on your phone for me?"

Daniele frowned. "Sure." He pulled out his phone. "It's...What?"

His lockscreen, formerly a photo of Sofia, had turned into a 7 of Diamonds. He turned the phone to Matteo and his son's eyes grew as wide as saucers.

"That's my card!"

Marco grinned proudly. "How did you do that?" Matteo demanded.

"Luck" he replied.

"Marco," Sofia called. "Can I do your hair?"

The angel gave a resigned smile and stood up to go to her. Daniele turned back to his son. "How is it going?" he asked.

Matteo shrugged. "Fine" he said quietly.

"Have you thought about where you want to go tomorrow?"

"I don't know yet. I'll let you know."

"Okay," Clearly the exuberant greeting in the house had been the exception, not the rule. "I'm looking forward to it."

"Me too."

Daniele looked around the room and saw it through his son's eyes. A sea of children so much younger than him, with whom he had almost nothing in common. "We should have thought of inviting some of your friends to keep you company."

"It's okay. They wouldn't want to come, and I like this. I miss us being together," Matteo said, and then turned to meet Daniele's eye. "Dad, will you promise not to get a girlfriend?"

He felt his stomach drop at hearing that question. "I think it's very unlikely that I will" he replied lightly.

"But promise?" Matteo insisted, with unexpected gravity.

"Matteo, where is this coming from?"

His son looked down at the table again. "Teo?" Daniele put an arm around him, leaning in to speak quietly. "If something's bothering you, would you tell me?"

Matteo nodded without looking at him.

"So why are you worried about me getting a girlfriend?"

Matteo opened his mouth, closed it again, and then made another attempt to speak.

"You live so far away now and I'm afraid you'll forget us."

Daniele frowned, genuinely confused. "How could I do that?"

"You might get lonely and want another family."

"Matteo...That's not at all how this works. I can't just 'get another family' and I wouldn't want to. Why mess with perfection, huh?" he added, trying to lighten the mood. Fortunately he saw a smile break out on his son's face.

"Good. It's okay if you have a friend," Matteo added casually. "Just don't live with anyone else and don't have another family."

He didn't mean to look. He actively tried to stop himself, but somehow his eyes slid of their own accord towards the top of the table. Marco was sitting on the ground so Sofia could reach him, his hair pulled up in tufts and secured with sparkly butterfly clips. Daniele swiftly looked away before Matteo noticed.

"I won't," he said. "I promise. You're my family, you and Sofia. You always will be."

"And Mum. The four of us are a family. We always will be."

"You're absolutely right."

He agreed to keep the peace more than anything else. Cristina was a friend and co-parent, certainly. Anything beyond that was in a grey area.

After the food, it was time for presents. Chiara's gift was the first to be opened, and turned out to be a dark green T-shirt with an orange dinosaur on the front. Sofia was overjoyed with it. Other gifts included an orange bouncy ball, a cuddly rabbit and a remote control car. Most of the kids were as surprised as Sofia to see what they'd bought.

Matteo was the first member of the family to give a gift. Sofia took it and squeezed the package, shaking it next to her ear. "It's soft," she declared. "Is it socks?"

"No, it's not socks" Matteo assured her.

"Even if it was, you'd still be grateful, wouldn't you?" Cristina added. Sofia nodded quickly and pulled the paper off. She squealed for joy when the blue Tubby Teddy was revealed.

"It's Vincenzo! Thank you, Matteo!"

She jumped off the chair to hug her brother, who grinned as he returned the embrace. Daniele smiled at the sight, glancing at Cristina to see her looking as happy as he felt. He was so thankful that his children got along so well and hoped their bond would endure for many years. It was important that they would always have someone to rely on.

Cristina had already given her gift, so it was Daniele's turn next. He slid the hard, rectangular box across the table and caught Cristina's curious look. Sofia shook the gift next to her ear and pouted thoughtfully at the rattle within before opening it. She gasped aloud at the necklace and started to run to Daniele, and then doubled back to take it with her.

"It's so pretty," she declared, hugging him. "Papa, put it on."

"It goes over your head, love" he said, demonstrating.

She gripped the butterfly in her fist and grinned brightly up at him, and then launched into another hug which nearly strangled him. Fortunately the lure of presents drew her away swiftly, and she went through a few more before reaching a large box at the bottom of the pile. She knocked her fist gently on the top of it, looking for clues, before opening it.

"Oh. Shoes. Thank you," she declared, carefully putting them aside. "They're very nice."

Daniele glanced back at Marco. The angel smiled and shrugged, not looking offended by the comparative lack of enthusiasm.

After the food and gifts, the kids were brought downstairs to the jungle gym and left to go wild. In ten seconds, every one of them was out of sight, including Matteo. His son was growing up fast, but he wasn't too old yet for the simple joys of running and climbing. That left the adults to sit at a table outside the play area and wait until they were required.

"Love the new hairstyle" Daniele teased.

"Apparently I am as pretty as a princess," Marco replied with dignity. "She's not a bad hairdresser actually. I was surprised by how little it hurt."

They both turned as Cristina came towards them, having seen off the last of the kids.

"Don't worry," she said as she sat down. "The gifts that Sofia doesn't appreciate at first are the ones she ends up loving for the longest time. It always happens."

"It's okay. I know what kids are like."

"Do you have children?" she asked interestedly.

"No, but I have some nieces and nephews."

"That makes sense then. You're a real hit with the kids."

Marco beamed with pleasure. "Thank you."

"I'm sorry we haven't had a chance to talk much. How did you meet Daniele?"

Marco turned to look at him, silently requesting some clue as to the story they were going with. They probably should have discussed this before now, Daniele thought ruefully. Marco's presence was such a normal part of his life that he completely forgot about the need for cover stories until the very moment they were required.

"He moved in shortly after I was injured," he answered. "He took it upon himself to offer assistance and we became friends over time, didn't we?"

"Yes" Marco agreed, looking as if he could barely stop himself from laughing. Fortunately his face was turned away from Cristina and she remained none the wiser.

"I'm pleased he had you around" she said.

"We should probably take this opportunity to move the gifts into the car" Daniele suggested, keen to avoid any more questions.

"I'll help" Marco volunteered.

"Good idea. Let me just…" Cristina lifted her bag onto her lap and started rifling through for the car keys.

"Mum!" Matteo called, racing towards them. The panic on his face did not suggest good news. "One of the little kids fell down the slide."
"What do you mean, he fell?" Cristina asked frantically.
"He went down the Freefall and hit his head."
"Oh my God, you're too young for that slide. Where is he?"
She got up and walked after her son, abandoning the bag on a chair. Marco looked at it and then at Daniele. "Do we just take the keys or wait for her?"
"We'll wait in case she needs us. I hope that kid's okay."
Marco picked up the bag and closed the zip. "I'm sure he will be. Kids are tough. I was knocked out several times when I was young and I remember playing again within the hour."
He thought about asking and then decided not to. Marco's childhood stories were like a carpet which looked innocuous enough at first, but upon closer inspection revealed horrifying things beneath.
Fortunately a distraction was not far away.

"Papa!" Now Sofia was the one sprinting towards them. She rounded the table and climbed onto Daniele's lap.
"Hello piccola. What are you doing here?"
"Play with me" she ordered.
"What about your friends?"
She scowled. "They're not my friends anymore."
"What?" He felt a surge of panic. "Why not?"

"Chiara said you're a criminal and I said you're not, and then Luca said only criminals have tattoos and they wouldn't say sorry."

"Sofi," he sighed. He lifted her off his knee. "Don't fight with your friends over silly things like that. Go back to her."

"No!" Sofia folded her arms and refused to move. "I don't want to be friends with her. I want to stay with you."

"I'm too big to play with you" Daniele implored.

"You could take her to the arcade next door" Marco suggested. Daniele looked at him in disbelief. Whose side was he on?

"Yes!" Sofia grabbed his hand, looking at him with those bright eyes that he could never refuse.

"Are you sure you don't want to go and play with your friends?" he asked again.

She shook her head and started pulling his arm. "Alright then," he conceded. He stood and she grabbed his hand in a firm grip. "The birthday girl gets whatever she wants."

"I'll wait for Cristina to come back and then put those gifts in the car" Marco said. Daniele smiled gratefully. "Thanks."

The angel shrugged. "What are friends for?"

There were only a few people in the arcade, a group of boys at the basketball nets and some girls on the dance machine. Sofia directed him towards the air hockey table. When they got there, she could barely reach the paddle, and she certainly couldn't see over the table.

"I think you're too small for this game" he remarked unthinkingly. He should have known better. Telling Sofia that she was too young for something was a challenge.

"Let's play this!" she insisted.

Daniele sighed, preparing himself for the inevitable tears of frustration. "Alright."

Sofia lost the first game. She demanded another, and got one, which she lost again. Even with Daniele putting all of his effort into not scoring, his daughter was such a terrible goalkeeper that the puck still made it past her defences at least once per game. He attempted to score an own goal to help her, but she saw him and was furious. They were on their third game and Daniele was in danger of losing Sofia's affection for the rest of the day, when he saw Marco approaching in the corner of his eye.

"Cristina is back holding the fort. Can I join you?"

"Sure. Is the kid okay?" Daniele asked, breaking off from the game.

"He's fine. He just bumped his head and started crying. How are things in here?"

"Not good!" Sofia snapped.

Marco looked sympathetically at Daniele, and then returned his attention to the little girl, kneeling down to her height. "Hey, Sofia. Do you want to see a magic trick?"

"Okay."

"Give me your hands."

She presented her hands and Marco encased them in his, rubbing gently. "I'm going to take your papa's skill and give it to you for one game so you can beat him. Now the magic is done. Go and earn victory."

The puck fell on Daniele's side and he shunted it in a straight line across the board. Sofia swiped it aside easily, and when he returned the pass, she smacked it directly across the board and into his goal. Daniele looked down in shock. Sofia shrieked with delight.

"Papa, pick it up! Pick it up!"

He bent and grabbed the puck, firing it wildly towards her goal. She stopped it dead and then hit it in a zig-zag pattern that brought it straight into the corner of his goal. Her cry of joy was even louder now and she dropped her paddle in excitement. The delay allowed Daniele to aim at an empty goal, but he wasn't surprised when his strike misfired and slid behind the goal instead of into it. Marco picked up the paddle and returned it to Sofia. She moved the puck back into position with her hand, took aim and fired. Her shot misfired too, but Daniele's attempt to regain control failed. Somehow he missed it entirely and it slid into the centre of the table. Sofia stood on tiptoes and tried to reach it, her small arms falling well short.

Fortunately, the puck didn't stop, but continued a gentle trajectory until it was within her range and she hit it with the softest blow possible. It bounced off the corner of goal and Daniele sent it flying into her undefended slot. She let out a cry of rage and slammed the puck back on the table. Marco laughed and Daniele saw him quickly touch her hand. Perhaps it was the top-up of luck, or his momentary lapse in concentration at the sound of that delighted giggle, but the next shot sent the puck right into his goal and restored Sofia to triumphant happiness. He gasped and held his head in mock horror.

The final score was 7-2, a ridiculous margin of victory considering that Daniele had to sweat in order to get 4 or 5 goals in a normal game. Sofia didn't see fit to question her win. When the time ran out, she threw her arms up and jumped for joy.
"I beat you, Papa!" she declared, running around the table and into his arms.

"You certainly did, piccola."

"I'm happy now" she said, and he laughed.

"It's not about winning. It's about playing the game."

Sofia frowned at him. "What's the point of playing if you don't win?" she asked. Before Daniele could even attempt to answer that logic, she pulled away from him and scanned the area for a moment.

"Marco," She marched over to him. "Can you do your magic on the other games?"

"I can certainly try."

"I want the Pikachu in the claw machine, but it won't hold on. Come on." She took his hand and started to pull him away. Marco grinned over his shoulder at Daniele, who watched them go with a warm feeling in his heart.

**Chapter 28**

After the air hockey game, Sofia had decided that Marco was her new best friend, and even his failure to secure a Pikachu hadn't damaged his standing. His explanation that luck didn't extend to machines that were designed to fail had been accepted, and Sofia had held his hand on the way home. Daniele had to try not to stare at them too much. There was something so gorgeous about seeing the two halves of his world together that he thought his heart would break. He sorely wished that this could be normal life, instead of a special occasion.

Cristina had given them a bottle of wine as thanks for helping, as if Daniele needed some kind of repayment, but he wasn't going to say no to Tuscany's finest. Sofia had insisted on drawing a portrait of Marco before he left, which he had been delighted with and which now sat folded in his breast pocket. They were back at the hotel now, after the last of Sofia's friends had been collected from the house and Daniele's own children were preparing to go to bed.

He and Marco were sitting on the floor as they drank, just in case they accidentally spilled some and marked the bedsheet. "This has been a really great weekend" he said, lifting his plastic cup and toasting it against Marco's

"Yeah, it's been lots of fun, and this hotel is great. It's going to break my heart to leave it," Marco agreed. "It's not over yet though. You've still got your day out with Matteo."

Daniele nodded excitedly at the reminder. Matteo had chosen the science museum for tomorrow's excursion. His mother was going to bring him down and Daniele was charged with making sure he got home again at the end of the afternoon. It had all been arranged and he couldn't wait.

"Are you coming?" he asked.

Marco scoffed and shook his head. "You don't want me there. I'll go to the Duomo or something."

Daniele nodded, secretly pleased and grateful for the angel's consideration.

"What music do you want?" Marco asked, standing up and going to the radio. Daniele leaned back against the footboard and considered, gently sloshing his cup.

"How about a blast from the past?"

*Funiculi Funicula* began to play at full volume, and Daniele nearly choked on wine.

They spent the next few hours drinking, laughing and singing everything from *Nessun Dorma* to *I Will Always Love You*, which were sung about as well as could be expected by two men intoxicated by alcohol and high spirits.

"And IIIIIIIIIEEEIIIII will love always you!"

Daniele had to shush him, giggling uncontrollably, before another guest filed a noise complaint against them. Marco had pushed his hair back so that it framed his face like a lion's mane. Daniele had thought he couldn't get any more attractive, but apparently he was wrong. When he finally looked at the clock, it was a quarter to two.

"God, look at the time," he said. "I haven't partied like this for years."

"Wow, this is a party to you? I'm flattered" Marco said.

"One of the best parties I've ever been to," Daniele declared. "Are you having fun?"

"I always have fun with you."

He laughed, finding the sentence amusing without knowing why. "Well, all the credit goes to you. I wouldn't be so entertaining without your influence."

Marco took another draught of wine. Cristina's gift was long gone, the cups had gone missing somewhere, and they were now sharing their second bottle from room service. In the back of his mind, Daniele realised that he was quite drunk. Not unpleasantly so. Far from it.
"I hope you'll remember me fondly" he said.
Marco paused, looking thoughtful. "I don't know if I will."
"Why not? I thought things were going well."
"Oh, you're great," he said. "I'll just miss getting drunk and singing in a hotel room. It's going to be a bittersweet memory."
Daniele laughed. "I'm sure you can find someone else willing to do that."

He looked up and realised that Marco wasn't laughing. He studied the angel's expression, but it was difficult to make out, and his brain seemed reluctant to engage. All he felt able to focus on were parted lips and bright eyes. He felt a tidal wave of adrenalin rush through his body, blocking out all sound except his heartbeat thundering in his head.
"You're a nice person," Marco said. "That's why I like you, because you're so kind."
"Thank you. You're a nice person too."
"I'm not always," Marco said. "Sometimes people hate me and wish I would go away. They kind of stop when I come into the room, like 'oh no, it's him again, the nightmare is real'. Once I got into an argument with a client and he said I was driving him out of his own house."

He paused and looked at the floor. "I didn't mean to do that."

"They were stupid not to realise how great you are."

"No," Marco shook his head, lifting the bottle in order to better make his point. "I'm an asshole, deliberately an asshole so people don't like me and I don't like them."

"You're not an asshole to me" Daniele insisted. Marco grinned. "I can't be an asshole to someone who's more of an angel than I am" he said.

"Stop it," Daniele sighed. "I try to make people happy because I'm not."

"Oh? And I make people sad because I am."

"You can make people happy. You just have to try. You're doing it right now."

"Because I like you," Marco retorted. "I like you lots and do you know what will happen?" His voice broke and he stopped, as if he was waiting for an answer. When Daniele didn't give one, he continued. "You'll die and I'll be so sad. I'll cry so much, and then the next poor soul who gets me will find the biggest bastard they've ever met."

"So don't do that."

The angel shrugged and took a gulp of wine. "I probably will," he said casually. "I wish I hadn't met you and then I wouldn't feel like this."

"I wish I'd met you sooner."

Marco looked at him irritably. "Do you know what? Enough of this maudlin talk! You're not going to die because I'm not going to let you, now turn up the music!"

Daniele watched him march up to the radio and start fiddling with the dials, changing the music from piano to pop and then to electric guitar.

"What do you want to listen to?" he demanded.

Daniele smiled and leaned back against the footboard, undoing the first two buttons of his shirt. Marco turned to look at him, frowning at the lack of an answer, and his face lit up with amusement and fascination.

"Are you getting hot?" he asked.

"Now I can relax," Daniele explained. "It's like taking off a uniform at the end of a tough day."

He undid a few more buttons and Marco hurried across the room, putting out a hand to stop him. "Lele, don't. If you open any more buttons, you'll be naked."

He laughed and lifted his hands away. Marco didn't move his. Daniele could feel the warmth of his palm pressed against his skin. He looked at the angel and thought of how much he meant to him, how happy he was that they met, and then he placed his hand over Marco's.

"I'm so glad you were here with me" he said. Marco blinked slowly and then nodded.

"Thank you," Daniele continued earnestly. "For agreeing to come with me, for helping me, for being my friend..."

"Lele, are you drunk?" Marco cut him off, giggling.

"I'm not that drunk," Daniele retorted. "I'm happy. I was really scared about coming here and it turned out alright."

"Of course it was alright. Why were you scared?"

Daniele glanced down, playing with the neck of the wine bottle. "I was afraid that I wouldn't have a place here anymore and my children wouldn't want to spend time with me, and I thought...maybe you wouldn't have a good time and you'd feel alone surrounded by strangers. Thank you for being with me."

"Daniele...Lele..." Marco said quietly. Daniele's heart jumped, as it did every time he heard that name. "You're my favourite person. I couldn't feel lonely as long as you're around.

Daniele grinned joyfully and, careless of the position they were in, threw his arms around Marco and tried to hug him.

"No, no, not..." Marco attempted to protest, tried to push the weight off him, but Daniele was too slow to let go and they collapsed into a pile on the floor.

His first thought was that he'd landed on top of Marco, and if this were a movie, it would be the clichéd moment when they realised they were close enough to kiss. He should have lived long enough to realise that life wasn't a movie. Marco let out a winded grunt and shoved Daniele aside, and while he was still trying to recover from his undignified position on the carpet, the angel burst out laughing.

"Sorry, I'm stupid" Daniele mumbled.

"No," Marco insisted. "It's okay. It's really okay. There probably won't be an opportunity to do that again, so you might as well make the most of it."

When Daniele looked up, Marco was beside him, unexpectedly close. The words came before he could hold them back. "Can I kiss you?"

Marco's mouth opened and closed a couple of times, the man who always had a sharp answer momentarily rendered speechless. "Lele..."

There was a larger statement behind that simple word, but Daniele didn't know what it was and he couldn't risk getting it wrong. He shrugged and looked at the floor, waiting for Marco to fill in the silence. It seemed to last forever and finally he glanced up to find Marco in the same position, gazing at the carpet, deep in thought.

"Do you think that's a good idea?" he asked solemnly.

Daniele stared at him, thrown by the sudden change in demeanour. "I don't know" he said, at a loss for any other response. It seemed to be the wrong thing to say. Marco shifted away from him, curling into a ball and hugging his knees.

"I'm not saying I don't want to. I do, but this can't happen."

He stretched out his legs and stood up, grabbing the wine bottle by the neck. "Don't follow."

He walked out onto the balcony and closed the door behind him. Daniele remained on the floor, breathing heavily and feeling utterly confused.

\*\*

Sharing a bed had never been so awkward. Marco had stayed on the balcony for nearly three hours, and Daniele had wanted to go out to make sure he was still there, but the fear of scaring him away had forced him to stay in the room. He'd been lying in bed for fifteen minutes before the doors opened and one angel carefully stepped inside, moving quietly and standing on tiptoes over the bed.

"I'm still awake" Daniele said.

"Oh."

He felt the bed shake as he was joined under the covers and continued staring at the ceiling, watching the fan whir round and round. After about twenty seconds of silence, he turned his head and found Marco also fixated on the fan.

"I think we need to talk."

"There's nothing to talk about" the angel replied immediately, so quickly that he almost bit the end off his words.

"There is" Daniele insisted.

"No, there isn't. You were drunk and said something silly. It happens all the time. The sooner we put it behind us, the quicker everything will go back to normal."

His emotionless voice grated on Daniele's nerves. It sounded like he was reciting from a script that he'd written on the balcony. Well, if he thought Daniele would play his part, he was sorely mistaken.

"I think there's more to be said than that" he said.

"Lele, I don't!" The sudden explosion of anger took him by surprise. "We were drinking wine all evening and it made us stupid. We'll wake up sober tomorrow and this little drunken mistake will be nothing but an embarrassment. The worst thing we can do is make a big deal of it."

So saying, Marco turned to put his back to Daniele and tugged the covers up around his chin.

"It is a big deal."

"You will not let things lie, will you?" Marco turned and sat up so he was looking down on him. "I can't do this again, I really can't."

"If you feel something for me, denying it isn't going to change anything" Daniele retorted.

"Admitting it would make my job impossible."

"Marco, it wouldn't..."

"Of course it would. You know it would. I don't have to be here, Daniele. I can look after you from a distance and I will if I have to."

The threat in his tone was clear and Daniele had a horrible feeling that he was serious, that if he continued to push the issue, Marco would walk out of the room and never come back. He swallowed, and then nodded vigorously, rolling over in case Marco could see his face burning.

"Good decision," Marco said, and then coughed awkwardly. "I'd better go to sleep."

"Me too."

The night's sleep did nothing to dispel the awkwardness between them. As soon as he awoke, Marco marched to the bathroom and turned the shower on. Daniele remained sitting up in bed, waiting for him to finish. The angel returned fully clothed and immediately disappeared onto the balcony. Daniele took his turn to shower, dressed and had a light breakfast before poking his head out of the door. Marco was sitting on the ground, back pressed against the wall, and looked so forlorn that Daniele suddenly didn't want to leave him.

"I'm going now" he said.

"Have fun."

"Are you sure you don't want to come?"

"Do you think I can't last for a day without you?" Marco snapped. "I'll be fine. Enjoy your father-son bonding time."

Daniele knew he was trying to drive him away with unnecessarily harsh words, but that didn't mean the tactic wasn't effective. He turned to leave and then stopped.

"Marco," he said. "I know you don't want to talk about this, but let me say one thing. I have felt so lonely for the past year and, to be honest, very sad as well. I got stuck in a rut revolving around work, as if I could ignore how empty my life was by fixing other people's. Since you've been here, you have brought a lot of…a lot of happiness into my life. And I just think that there's no point in worrying about what will happen when that happiness is taken away. It won't change anything, except that we could enjoy the time we have together…"

He turned around. The balcony was empty.

**Chapter 29**

His temper hadn't quite settled even when he was standing outside the museum, smoking furiously, but then he saw Matteo running down the street towards him and the world instantly brightened.

"Hi Teo!" He extinguished the cigarette quickly to receive a hug.

"Hi Dad! Ready to go?" Matteo took his hand and looked up at him eagerly. Daniele smiled and nodded, and then turned his attention to Cristina as she approached.

"All good?" he asked, and got a thumbs-up.

"Your necklace has won present of the year," she informed him, and he felt a warm glow of pride. "Alright, bring him home any time up until 7pm. Lorenzo wants to take us out for dinner this evening…"

"Dad could come too" Matteo interrupted. He gazed hopefully at Daniele, and he thought that although his daughter's puppy eyes were famously lethal, his son's were just as good if he wanted to use them.

"Dad might have plans," Cristina said, saving him from having to disappoint. "His friend is here with him and they probably want to spend some time together."

Daniele swallowed and said nothing. "Okay," Matteo said. "Then let's go."

"Be good and have fun, darling. I'll see you later." Cristina gave him a squeeze goodbye, waved to Daniele, and walked away.

The first exhibit inside the museum was a large marble ball, spinning eternally in a pool of water. The placard challenged the visitor to stop the ball and then start it rolling again, and to see how much more difficult one was than the other. Matteo accepted the task and pressed both of his hands against the smooth wet surface, stopping the spin only to immediately send it rotating in the opposite direction. He went around the ball, changing its direction with one push from each side, and then gripped it tightly. With a monumental effort that took almost a full minute to achieve, he stopped the ball dead and then left it like that, looking at Daniele victoriously.

The only other exhibits on the ground floor were a broken fire tornado and some bubble machines, so they went upstairs, bypassing the younger children's play area to investigate a floor whose theme appeared to be physics. Matteo dragged his father over to a large tug-of-war set in the middle of the floor.

"You go over there" he ordered, grabbing the rope on the near side. Daniele did as instructed. As soon as he picked up the rope, Matteo pulled hard and rang the bell on his side.

"I wasn't ready."

"Tell me when you're ready" his son replied.

"Okay, go."

Both of them pulled as hard as they could, but Daniele couldn't move the beam even slightly towards him. It fell easily towards Matteo and rang the bell for victory.

"Best of three!" he called delightedly, and something about the way he giggled sparked a realisation. Once more, Daniele pulled so hard that he could see the veins in his arms, and once more his son's inferior strength nearly dragged him across the floor.

"I win!"

"One more time," Daniele said. "This time you come over here."

Matteo's grin disappeared at once. Daniele watched him try to think of a way to get out of it, come up empty, and submit to changing positions. When the game began again, Daniele did nothing, simply stood there as Matteo pulled the rope so hard that he ended up lying on the floor. The beam moved laboriously and at a certain point, stopped responding to the rope altogether. Daniele then took his rope and tugged it with one hand. The bell rang for victory.

Matteo stood up, sighing. "It took me ages to figure it out."

"It's a good idea. I like it" Daniele said, putting an arm around his shoulders as they moved on.

Strength was required again on the pulley system, which Matteo was apparently unable to work alone. Daniele could see why - the rope was so stiff that he had to pull it like he was ringing a bell to move the chair. Matteo's weight probably didn't help, but it was nevertheless sore in more ways than one to be defeated by a machine meant for children. Daniele's muscles ached by the time he'd got Matteo halfway up, and had to let him drift back to the ground because there was no way he could do any more. A series of videos were next, the purpose apparently being to speed up and slow down the images for comedic effect. At least that was how Matteo used them, grinning at starfish that sprinted across the seabed, at flowers that exploded into bloom, and at a misfortunate grizzly bear that fell through ice in humiliating slow-motion under his hand.

They continued on the next floor, putting small balls into the stream from wind tunnels and pretending to have powers of levitation. Matteo brought his father to his favourite part of the museum, and no wonder, as it was a VR goalkeeping game. With both of them standing in the computerised goal, those digital balls didn't have a chance. Daniele was also intrigued by a set of two wheelchairs, bolted to the floor and with a line of lights in front of each that was controlled by the wheels' rotation. The first to get to the big light at the top was the winner. Matteo was his first competitor, but the other kids around were enticed by the possibility of defeating a grown-up, and Daniele soon had a line of challengers. With Matteo's staunch support behind him, some of the kids came close, but none reached that light ahead of him.

Lunch was at McDonald's, Matteo's favourite and a treat he was sworn to secrecy about since Cristina frowned upon fast food. They concluded the afternoon at a gelato parlour, sitting on a bench outside with a view of the Duomo in front of them. It was a very pretty building, but a shame that it was impossible to walk in the square because of all the tourists.

"Dad, can we go shopping?" Matteo asked as they wandered through the streets.

"What for?"

"I need a new bag for school and a notebook because mine is full. And there's a video game I'd like, and new jeans, and maybe a football shirt. My old one is a bit faded now. And..."

He hesitated and Daniele realised that he was trying to think of items that he could conceivably need, just to stay out longer.

"And...Um..."

He pulled his son into a hug, right there on the street. As happy as he was that Matteo wanted to spend time with him, he was ten years old and shouldn't kids of that age be pulling away and regarding their parents as uncool, not behaving as if spending all day with them was the greatest of treats? He must be even more negligent than he'd thought. He checked his watch.

"It's 6pm, omino. Your mama wants you back in an hour. We can get your notebook and bag on the way home, okay?"

Matteo nodded and took hold of his hand again. "Are you staying in Milan for long?" he asked.

Daniele bit his lip at that question. "No, I'm sorry. I'm going home tomorrow."

"Tomorrow? Oh, okay…"

"I can look at my schedule and see if I can take a holiday next month, maybe?" he suggested, trying to salvage something.

"It's fine" Matteo sighed, kicking a stone viciously down the pavement.

"Teo, I'm sorry. I had a really good time today."

"Me too." Matteo was quiet for a moment, and then he spoke again. "There's a football match at San Siro in two days. It's going to be AC Milan versus Roma and I thought it'd be fun."

"It would be fun. I'll definitely watch and we can talk all about it afterwards" Daniele agreed eagerly.

Matteo sighed. "Yeah, I'll watch it, but I wanted to go. We've been here for months and I've never seen San Siro. I thought we could go together."

"Can't Lorenzo take you?"

"No, Lorenzo says that you get a better view on the TV and it's cheaper" his son replied. It wasn't cheaper, Daniele thought, if Cristina was paying for a season pass that Matteo wasn't using.

"Mum doesn't like football," he continued. "And Sofia asks questions all the time and it's distracting. You're the only one who…Anyway, it doesn't matter. I'll watch it on TV and we'll talk about it."

He sounded so defeated and Daniele loathed himself. Already he was calculating the price of an extra night in the hotel, the price of a ticket…God, it wasn't the price that would stop him, it was the waiting list. Two days was not enough time to get a ticket for such a big match. They would have been sold out months ago. Unless he could ask Marco for some angelic intervention…No, why was he even thinking that? Taking advantage of Marco was off the table anyway and after last night…Daniele couldn't even think about last night. Suffice to say that he couldn't possibly ask Marco for anything now.

\*\*

The door was opened by Lorenzo. "Hi guys, did you have a good day?"
"Yes, it was fun, wasn't it?" Daniele looked down at his son and Matteo looked back, raising a smile that didn't quite reach his eyes.
"Is Mum here?" he asked.
"She ran out for something. She'll be back in half an hour." Lorenzo stepped back to admit Matteo inside, but instead he turned and grabbed his father's hand.
"Dad, do you want to come in?"
"Well…" Daniele glanced at Lorenzo. "Do you mind?"
There was some element of territory here. He couldn't demand to come into Lorenzo's house and the other man was under no obligation to let him inside, since he'd already spent plenty of time with his children, so Daniele really had no power over the decision.
"Of course not, come in."

Sofia was sitting at the kitchen table, eating a bowl of fruit. She looked as the front door closed and her little face lit up with joy. "Papa!" She abandoned the table and half of her fruit to run to him.

"Piccola!"

He greeted her with as much enthusiasm and bent to hug her. It was adorable and a little flattering that she was so excited to see him, a mere twenty-four hours after their last meeting. "You're wearing your necklace, I see."

She nodded and touched the butterfly. "Yes, I love it very much."

"She would sleep with it if we let her" Lorenzo remarked good-humouredly as he passed them.

"I'm very happy you like it" Daniele said.

"And I love my shoes" Sofia added, pointing at her feet. Daniele looked down and regretted it. Seeing the gift reminded him of the person.

"Oh yes, they were a nice present, weren't they?"

"Uh-huh. They glow in the dark" she said proudly.

Daniele smiled brightly, even as he felt a stab in his gut at the realisation that he wouldn't get a chance to see that feature of the shoes. He'd have to ask Cristina to send him a picture. Once again, it was missing the small details of his children's lives which hurt most.

"Matteo, do you want to show your dad that new video game?" Lorenzo suggested, kindly sparing Daniele from having to sit at the kitchen table, hyper-conscious of his status as a guest. Matteo nodded and turned to his father.

"Dad, do you want to play Fifa?" he asked, as if he'd just come up with the idea himself.

"I'm coming too!" Sofia announced immediately.

Matteo looked at her irritably. "Okay, you can come, but only to watch."

He walked quickly and was setting up the TV when Daniele arrived, Sofia bringing up the rear and heading directly to the sofa. Matteo took advantage of her distance to pull his father closer.

"If Sofia's playing, I'll show you my flying game. She'll spoil my win record" he explained solemnly, and somewhat apologetically, as if it mattered what game they were playing. Daniele would be terrible at them all.

The game was set in the skies of World War 2, and as far as Daniele could see, the point was to courier supplies around the map without being shot. Matteo was an ace at it. He loved watching his son play video games, marvelling at how quickly he picked up the controls and how fast and nimble his fingers were. Daniele could barely open a menu. Sofia sat beside him, reaching for the controls every time Matteo finished a level. "My turn now" she said repeatedly, first as a question, and then as a demand.

"I want a go!"

"No, you can't play" Matteo retorted without looking at her.

"I can!" she insisted, and climbed over Daniele to get to the controls.

"Teo, will you let your sister have a turn?" he requested.

His son sighed and handed the controls over with the air of a martyr. As soon as the next level started, Sofia crashed the plane. The level restarted and it happened again. On the third time she was shot down. She growled in frustration and started stabbing buttons, which achieved nothing except sending her into another tailspin, this time sending a spiral of bullets into the air behind her.

Matteo attempted to assist, but she pushed him away. "I can do it!"

"She won't give the controls back until she's completed a level," Matteo explained to his father, dropping his voice to a whisper. "Will you distract her?"

Daniele turned to his daughter, stubbornly focused on the screen. "Your mama says you're going out for dinner tonight" he remarked.

"Yes" she replied without looking away.

"Are you going to wear your birthday outfit?"

"No. I'm wearing my dinosaur T-shirt."

She certainly would not if her mother had any say in the matter, he thought. He had been through this with Cristina a hundred times. Funny, if he'd been asked to describe his type, people with a very sharp eye for style would not have been on the list and yet it appeared to be a common theme.

"Are you coming with us?" Sofia asked hopefully, taking her attention off the game to look up at him. Matteo leaned over and quickly pressed a button on the controller.

"No, sweetheart, but you have fun." Daniele glanced over and spotted a yellow bar in the corner of the screen. *Autopilot Engaged*, it read, and he swiftly turned back to Sofia. "Would you like to draw a picture for me? I was very impressed with the portrait you made for Marco."

"I have to finish this first" she replied, sounding so harassed that it was almost amusing, and picked up the controls again. The level began once more and the plane took off smoothly, dodging attacks and turning with little regard for what buttons Sofia was pushing. The landing strip came into view and she guided it down for a perfect landing.

"I won!"

Matteo applauded gently and took the controls back.

"I'll do your picture now, Papa" Sofia declared, and ran off.

Daniele smiled and ruffled his son's hair. "Nice trick" he remarked. Matteo grinned victoriously.

Sofia returned with her pad and art set, and Daniele split his time between watching Matteo play the game and watching the picture take shape. She was still drawing when the front door opened. Her head lifted sharply and she scrambled to her feet.

"Mama!"

He heard Cristina laugh in the hallway and then she appeared in the living room, Sofia in her arms. She smiled at Daniele before turning to Matteo.

"Game off," she said. "Time to get ready."

He turned the game off immediately and left the room, like the good kid he was.

"Did everything go well?" Cristina asked. Daniele nodded and stood, ready to leave. Sofia started squirming at the sight.

"Wait, Papa, you need your picture" she insisted. Cristina let her down and she threw herself on the ground, scribbling frantically.

"Ten more minutes, baby, and then you have to get changed" Cristina ordered, and left the room. Daniele heard her enter the kitchen and greet Lorenzo. He knelt on the floor beside Sofia and watched admiringly as she carefully coloured inside the lines, selecting her colours with serious consideration. Her tongue was stuck out adorably as she worked.

"All done," she declared at last, pushing the page towards him. "Do you like it?"

It was a portrait of him in his favourite red shirt, albeit it was so long in this rendering that it could double for a dress, and two large circles around his eyes that were clearly meant to be glasses. His hair was thinner than the reality and his beard thicker, and Sofia had filled his mouth with teeth. The effect was a little terrifying, but to see that her image of him was smiling made his heart melt.

"Of course I do. It's lovely." He put an arm around her and pulled her into a hug. She giggled happily as he put a kiss in her hair, and moved to hug him back.

"Don't leave, Papa. Stay with us" she said.

He tightened his hold slightly. "I wish I could. We'll see each other at Christmas."

"Christmas is very far away" she complained.

Daniele could say nothing to that. He pulled out of the hug and held her in front of him.

"We'll talk all the time before then, I promise."

Sofia didn't appear comforted. Her lip wobbled dangerously and she hugged him again. "I want to come home with you."

"Sofi, sweetheart, come on," Cristina interrupted. "I've laid your clothes out on the bed."

His daughter looked at her mother and back at him, and then left a loud kiss on his cheek.

"Kiss" she ordered, presenting her own cheek.

Daniele pecked it. "Kiss. Love you."

"You too." She turned and ran off without another word. He got to his feet with some difficulty and tried to raise a smile. It came out a bit wobbly.

"Okay?" Cristina asked.

He nodded. "I'm fine. I'm always fine. Saying goodbye is always the hardest part. She didn't want me to go."

"I know."

There wasn't much more to be said. "Have a good night" Daniele said, heading for the door.

He stopped at the bottom of the stairs and called a goodbye, receiving two farewells from behind closed doors, and finally he was outside the house.

The warm yellow glow from the windows mocked him. *Everyone is safe and warm with their families*, they sneered. *And you are outside, alone and unloved.*

**Chapter 30**

He'd forgotten all about Marco until he unlocked the door of the hotel room, walked in, and found the angel sitting on the bed. The humiliation of this morning came rushing back at once. Marco's head snapped towards him and he leaped to his feet.

"Daniele! I need to talk to you!" he demanded.

He suddenly felt a desperate need for a cigarette and dug into his coat pocket. "Do you? I was begging to talk to you last night and you refused to listen, but by all means, let's talk if you're ready."

"What? What are you talking about?"

The box wasn't there. Matteo must have stolen them again. Why today of all days?

"I'm talking about this morning," he snapped, his anger erupting into full-blown fury. "It took a lot of courage to say all of that. I can't believe you didn't listen to a word."

Marco stared at him, apparently stunned into silence, but of course he rallied quickly. "Are you kidding? That's what's on your mind? This is far more important!"

"Oh, is it?" Daniele winced at the aggressive sarcasm in his tone. "I poured my heart out to you. God knows why I bother. I'm always the one trying to forge a connection with you and you're always running away like a skittish deer because you're so afraid of being vulnerable that you'd rather be miserable for eternity and put other people through hell while you're at it!"

He shouldn't have said that. He knew immediately that he shouldn't have. Marco looked devastated and Daniele wanted to apologise and take it all back, but the words got stuck in his throat. The anger took too long to leave.

"I didn't know what to do," the angel said quietly. "I didn't want to act until I'd spoken to you. Lorenzo hurt Sofia."

It was funny how the world could stop spinning for a moment and then restart on a slightly different axis, even more so that a few short words had the power to cause such an effect.

*I love you.*
*You're an addict.*
*Lorenzo hurt Sofia.*

"What?" he asked numbly. He could barely hear his own voice over the rush of blood in his ears. "What do you mean, he hurt her?"

"I went to the market to get some lunch and I saw Sofia with him. I don't know what happened. It doesn't even matter what happened!" Marco was getting more and more wound up, the reality of the situation apparently hitting him too. "I think she tried to sneak a chocolate bar into the basket and he went *mad*! He...He...He started screaming at her and she was terrified. She started crying and that made him yell more. I tried to intervene..."

He broke off and grabbed fistfuls of his hair, breathing heavily. "I'm so sorry," he whispered. "She ran to me and he dragged her away, and I was so afraid...I thought I would dislocate her shoulder if I held on, he was pulling so hard, but I should have held on. I should have done more. I shouldn't have let her go."

Daniele stared at him dumbly. Out of nowhere, he remembered the one and only occasion when anyone had raised a hand to his children. Matteo was two years old and had broken a vase at his grandparents' house. Salvatore Caruso was accustomed to old-fashioned discipline and had given him a few smacks as punishment, and Matteo had cried so long and hard that his grandfather had wound up on his knees, begging him to calm down and promising never to do it again. When Cristina found out, she'd gone in there like a raging bull and terrified his father in a way Daniele had never seen anyone do before. She would never allow Lorenzo to treat the children like that.

"I need to talk to Cristina" he said, already turning away.

"There's something else" Marco said. Daniele looked back impatiently.

"What is it then?"

Marco looked at him, fear and guilt written across his face, and reached into his jacket pocket. He proffered a smooth-edged silver phone on his palm.

"This is Lorenzo's phone" he said.

Daniele looked at him and then the phone in bemusement. "Where did you get that?"

"I took it from his back pocket. It was for a good cause though." Marco unlocked the screen and came forward, his thumb moving quickly. "I know that...I know that family affairs are complicated. When I was young, people turned a blind eye and it was better to lie and preserve the peace than try to seek help. I thought that if Sofia was coached or if she was too afraid to tell the truth, or if he has some tidy explanation tucked away, it would be better to have proof. I missed a lot of what he said to her" he added apologetically, and then handed the phone over.

Daniele looked at the screen as a video began to play. The rumble of a busy public place emitted from the receiver and he could see the bright red awnings of stalls, crates of food in red, green, black and brown, and the milling mass of the crowd as the camera moved amongst them. The screen was briefly filled with the white wall of an apartment building before it swivelled quickly to the right, and he caught sight of a tall, muscular man pulling a little girl along behind him. Daniele recognised the bright green soles of her shoes and lifted the phone closer to his face, as if he could cancel the distance and see them more clearly.

Lorenzo was looking down at her and even in profile, the anger on his face was clear to see. His mouth moved rapidly and he punctuated each sentence by tugging Sofia further forward. She was trying to pull out of his grip, digging her shoes into the ground and placing one small hand on his in an attempt to loosen his hold. Daniele could see that her little face was contorted with tears and felt his heart shatter. As he watched, Sofia went limp and dropped to her knees on the pavement. Lorenzo turned and with his face fully revealed to camera, he looked like a feral animal.

"Stop embarrassing me!" he yelled, so loudly that the phone's audio picked him up clearly. "You little bitch, get up!"

He lifted Sofia clean off the ground and let her dangle by one arm, her legs kicking frantically at empty air. Daniele threw the phone onto the bed and turned away, pressing his hands over his face as a sob crawled up his throat. He could Sofia screaming from the phone.

"Stop it, please, I've heard enough."

Marco grabbed the phone and pressed a button. The audio cut off and neither of them spoke or moved for several seconds.

"I left them for a job," Daniele whispered. "For a stupid job. I spend all my time and energy helping other people and I let down my own children."

"Lele, it's not something you could have imagined" Marco said quietly. Daniele waved the platitude away like it was a fly buzzing around his ear, turned and walked out onto the balcony. He leaned over the railings and swallowed huge mouthfuls of cold evening air to calm down.

"I'm sorry I didn't do more to help" Marco said, sounding on the verge of tears.

"We need to take this to Cristina."

"Now?"

Daniele looked back at him. "Yeah, now. I'm not leaving them in that house for another hour."

"Will I call a taxi?" Marco ventured after a moment.

"Taxi?" He turned around fully. "No. There's no time to mess around with traffic. I need you to take me there now."

\*\*

Flying was both exhilarating and terrifying. Daniele kept his eyes shut for most of the journey, missing out on a bird's eye view of Milan so that he wouldn't panic at the expanse of empty space beneath his feet.

"We're almost there. Open your eyes."

"How did you know they were closed?"

"Lucky guess."

He blinked against the wind and saw the top of tall white buildings only a few metres below. He drew his legs up to avoid kicking over a satellite dish or destroying any tiles, and then Marco swooped down into the street and deposited him on his feet next to a neatly trimmed hedge.

He gripped the wall and looked back to see the angel making an elegant landing behind him, folding his wings away and reaching a hand around to rub his back.

"You're heavier than I thought you'd be" he remarked.

Daniele almost smiled, and then turned towards the end of the street. Just around the corner was Lorenzo's house where he had so innocently, and foolishly, left his children a few hours ago. He suddenly remembered the way Matteo had stood up straight when Lorenzo answered the door, and how he'd quickly invited Daniele to come inside until their mother came home. Had the bastard hurt his son too? Or was Matteo aware of what had happened to his sister? Why hadn't he said anything? He'd had ample opportunity during the afternoon when it had only been the two of them. That question was going to kill him until he had an answer, but for now, there were more pressing matters to attend to.

"Do you want me to come?" Marco asked. Daniele felt a hand wrap around his and looked down, and back up at Marco. He looked so sad and guilty, and Daniele couldn't stand that. It wasn't his fault. He wasn't their parent, and he hadn't even met them until two days ago, and yet he had done more than either Daniele or Cristina.

"Yeah, I want you to come."

He squeezed Marco's hand in return. The events of last night and this morning seemed so long ago now, and so irrelevant in the scheme of things, but now he remembered the feeling of a bird thrashing in his chest whenever the angel touched him. When this was over, he was determined that they would talk. If he had to keep hold of Marco to stop him disappearing, he would. The problem was fear, not lack of feeling, and surely there had to be a way to solve that. This was too special not to fight for.

"I'm glad it was you" he said, surprised by his own words.

Marco looked confused. "What do you mean?"

"I'm glad that whatever powers are up there sent you to me."

Marco blinked and then a bright smile lit up his face. "So am I. I know I haven't been the best angel..."

"You have been the best. You've done so much for me, more than I ever asked for."

"You never asked for anything."

"And yet you still gave me everything."

Marco looked stunned. His breathing shook and he seemed unable to decide whether to laugh or cry, but in the end he did neither. He flung himself at Daniele and hugged him tightly, an embrace that was willingly returned. If this were any other moment, it would be perfect. Only 24 hours ago, the smell of warm skin and overly fruity hair from the hotel shampoo was all he could have asked for, the light kiss he felt next to his ear would have completed his happiness, but it wasn't the right time now. This wasn't the time to hold him close and admit that he loved him, that there was nothing he wouldn't do to make him happy if he was given a chance. They'd have to talk about it, but later. There would be time for it all later.

"Alright," Daniele stepped out of the hug, but kept hold of Marco's hand. "Let's go deal with this asshole."

## Chapter 31

It was Lorenzo who opened the door, and for a split second, Daniele caught him narrowing his eyes angrily at Marco. The angel stared back with burning hatred.

"Can I help you?" Lorenzo asked.

"We're here to speak to Cristina" Daniele said.

"She's putting the kids to bed."

"Call her, please."

The other man scoffed and shook his head. "Look, I'm guessing this guy has panicked you, but everything's okay. I've explained the situation to Cristina. You're only going to embarrass yourself."

"I've seen the video."

"What video?" Lorenzo asked, as a deep groove appeared in his forehead.

"I filmed you" Marco replied proudly, revealing the phone. Lorenzo stared incredulously and tried to grab it, but Marco stepped neatly out of his reach with impressive agility.

"I've been looking for that all day! You stole my phone?" he demanded.

"I think on balance, my crime is more easily forgiven than yours. Get Cristina for us, please" Marco ordered. Lorenzo looked at him like he was an insect.

"And what if I don't?"

Marco stepped forward so that he was almost nose-to-nose with Lorenzo. "Then I will take you up to the clouds and drop you."

His voice was so cold and calm that Daniele felt a shiver go through him, even though he wasn't the one in danger. Lorenzo did not seem to experience the same sense of dread. He squinted at Marco as if trying to figure out how serious he was, and then snorted derisively.

"Big words..."
"Big wings" Marco whispered.

Daniele couldn't help glancing over as the wings revealed themselves. He'd never seen them from this angle before; the bones which formed the support for the feathers, which started out as two thick plumes before they spread further and further from Marco's body, as he extended them to their full width until they nearly blocked the doorway entirely. They were beautiful. It was impossible to see them as anything else. Even the dark gleam in Marco's eyes and the smile that couldn't be classed as anything but demonic was stunning to Daniele. Marco looked like the perfect image of an avenging angel and he didn't know if his heart was thumping from fear or something else.

Lorenzo had gone as pale as a sheet. "What are you?" he gasped.
Marco's smile widened. "Get Cristina, please, or I won't ask again."
"C-Cristina!" He called behind him without taking his eyes off Marco. "Cristina, you need to come downstairs."
"Good boy."
The upstairs light turned on and Daniele felt breath on his cheek. "Too much?" Marco whispered, in an entirely different voice. He shook his head.
"No, it was good."
"Daniele, hi." Cristina appeared before them in her dressing gown. "What are you doing here? The kids are already in bed."
"Cristina, he's..." Lorenzo began, and then looked at them again. The wings were gone, of course.
"I need to talk you, preferably in private" Daniele said.

"Okay," She frowned, worried, and placed a hand on Lorenzo's shoulder. "I'll be up soon."

"Of course" Lorenzo said, leaving immediately. Cristina stepped outside and half-closed the door behind her.

"Lorenzo attacked Sofia at the market today" Daniele said, getting straight to the point.

"Attacked?" Cristina echoed. "No, there's been a mistake. Sofia tried to run in front of a car and he grabbed her. He explained this to me at dinner."

"He did more than that," Marco said immediately. "And I saw the whole thing clearly. She put a chocolate bar in his basket before he went to pay. He went ballistic about it, and from how frightened she was, that is not the first time he's done that."

She looked at him as she hadn't noticed his presence before, and then back at Daniele. "I'm not sure what you saw..."

"He twisted her arm. There should be a mark" Marco added.

Daniele nodded. "According to Marco, he pulled at her so hard that he was afraid her shoulder would be dislocated, and he suspended her by one arm after that so I'm honestly surprised if it wasn't."

Cristina looked between them again. "Lorenzo wouldn't do that."

"You don't want to believe he would do that," Marco retorted. He handed over the phone. "We have evidence."

"This is Lorenzo's phone. How did you get this?"

"I took it for a reason," Marco said. "I'm sorry. It's in the video recordings."

Cristina gave Daniele a curious look and, when he didn't respond, moved her thumb over the screen. "It needs a passcode" she said. Daniele sighed, and so did Marco, placing a hand over his forehead and rubbing at his temples. Cristina bit her lip as she looked at them, and then pushed the door open.

"Come inside. Let's see if we can sort this out."

Lorenzo was chopping tomatoes at the kitchen worktop. There was the smell of grilled cheese in the air and the sound of silence.

"Mr…" Cristina paused and looked at Marco. "I never caught your last name."

"De Laurentis."

"Mr De Laurentis claims that you were violent towards Sofia this afternoon."

Lorenzo looked astonished. "I don't understand. Where was this?"

"At a shop."

He swiftly set down the knife and hurried to Cristina, putting his arm around her and squeezing affectionately.

"I have no idea what they're talking about" he said. He smiled at her and then looked at the two men, the picture of wide-eyed innocence. Marco looked like he was about to bite him.

"Would you like me to repeat some of the things you said to her?" he asked, his eyes fixed on Lorenzo as if he was trying to burn a hole in his skull.

"What things?" Cristina asked.

"I panicked," Lorenzo said, to the surprise of Daniele, who had expected him to deny everything. "She suddenly pulled away from me and tried to run into the road. I shouldn't have done it, but in the heat of the moment, I used bad language. It just came out."

Cristina sighed and rolled her eyes. "For God's sake, Lorenzo, I don't care how panicked you were. You can't swear in front of the children."

"I am sorry."

"There was something else," Cristina said. "Did you twist her arm when you grabbed her?"

"I don't know," Lorenzo lowered his head sorrowfully. "I just reacted. I'd never forgive myself if something happened to them on my watch and if I was rougher than I intended, then it was an honest accident."

"Holding someone aloft by their arms used to be a tactic used for torture" Marco spat.

Lorenzo looked at him. "What? No, I...I didn't do..."

Cristina nodded and shrugged his arm off. "I need the passcode for your phone."

He reeled back in shock. "Cristina, you don't believe them, do you? This man doesn't have children. He saw me react on instinct to save Sofia's life and decided it was violence because he's never been in that situation. And your ex, I'm sure, was only too happy to believe him and discredit me because he wants you to move back to Rome."

"I don't care about that," Daniele interjected. "I just want my kids to be safe and happy."

"Lorenzo, the sooner I can see this video, the sooner we can sort this out" Cristina said calmly.

"If you don't want to give her the passcode, I can show you another of my tricks," Marco added. "But it's your choice."

Lorenzo had the audacity to roll his eyes. "1102."

Cristina entered the code and opened the recordings. Daniele thought about asking her to go into the living room. Not because he was afraid to hear the audio again, but because she was going to have to hear this in front of him, Lorenzo and a virtual stranger. This was something that required a semblance of privacy, but it was too late. She frowned, confused, for a few moments before her face brightened with recognition. A second later her eyes narrowed. She glanced at Lorenzo, still only curious, not upset or angry yet.

"Lorenzo, what...?"

She broke off before finishing the question, gasping audibly.

"You little bitch!" Lorenzo's tinny voice roared from the phone.

Cristina's back suddenly straightened and she looked away from the screen, glaring unseeingly beyond Daniele. He had rarely seen her look so angry. Slowly her eyes moved to focus on Lorenzo, and her mouth hung open with words that wouldn't come. The unintelligible noises of the video continued until Cristina moved her thumb and stabbed the button to leave the recordings, looking as if she would prefer that it was Lorenzo's eye.

"I appreciate you coming to tell me about this" she said. Her calmness was frightening. She looked and sounded capable of murder.

"I can explain..." Lorenzo began.

"Now would be a good time for you to be quiet," she said, without looking at him. "Go to the living room, please. We need to talk."

He glared at the other men. Marco bared his teeth in response, and whether it was because of that or Cristina's instruction, Lorenzo retired to the living room.

"Daniele, can I ask a favour?" Cristina asked. "I know it's a massive inconvenience, but could you stay and watch the kids tonight?"

He nodded quickly. "Yeah, I will. Are you going to be okay? I mean, he's a big guy..."

"I can handle him, don't worry."

When he looked at her eyes, he didn't doubt that she probably could.

## Chapter 32

As instructed, he went upstairs to make sure the kids were alright. He didn't dare to open their doors in case he woke them, but there was no light visible through the cracks and no sounds within. It reminded him of nights from long ago, back when Matteo was small and Daniele would read him bedtime stories about clever children defeating witches. His son always slept easier after such tales, safe in the knowledge that good would invariably triumph over evil. He had a blue night light with the shapes of moons and stars cut into the shade, he remembered. It cast hardly any light, but Matteo was determined that he wasn't scared of the dark.

Sofia had been. She used to have an orange lava lamp that cast far too much light, and between that and the hypnotising bubbles, had kept her awake long past bedtime. She hadn't been able to sleep alone for a while. Daniele blamed the nights when he would walk around the house with her, this tiny little thing resting against his shoulder, as a way to calm her when she was crying. She got used to sleeping in someone's arms and wouldn't let the parent putting her to bed leave. For months, Daniele had had to sit on her bed and wait for her to fall asleep before he could put her down.

How did she sleep now? He was sure there were no more cuddles before bed for his daughter, and for his son, less confidence in the ability of heroes to find out and overthrow villains. He realised that his thoughts were threatening to spiral and shook them out of his head before the pit opened and dragged him in. He turned and went back downstairs to see what was happening.

Marco was sitting on the bottom step, arms resting on his legs, staring at the living room door. He turned his head only when Daniele had sat down beside him.

"You don't have to stay."

"Maybe I want to" the angel replied, turning back to his vigil.

"How's it going down here?"

"I don't know. I can't hear very well, but I think the basis of his defence is that Sofia misbehaves a lot. Hang on..." Marco held up a finger, even though Daniele wasn't talking, and listened intently. "Yeah, he doesn't know how to cope with kids who aren't obedient robots."

"I don't buy that."

"I don't think Cristina does either. Can you hear her?"

"Not clearly."

"She's just yelling at him. I don't think any of that is a human language."

"Is he yelling back?" Daniele asked, ready to spring into action if Cristina showed any signs of being in trouble.

"No, he's pleading with her," Marco assured him. "How are the little ones?"

"They're sleeping."

Marco nodded and then looked down at his hands, nervously playing with his fingers. "Lele..." he said quietly. Daniele turned to him and the angel stared back, opening and closing his mouth twice, before looking at the ground. "Never mind."

"No, what is it?" Daniele put his hand on Marco's, unthinkingly rubbing his thumb against the skin.

"I just..."

"Mama! Mama!"

He turned immediately towards his daughter's distressed voice and saw her on the landing, dressed in green striped pyjamas and rubbing tears out of her eyes. He jumped to his feet and ran up to her.

"Hey, piccola. It's okay. Mama's downstairs."

She removed her hands and stared at him. "Papa? Why are you here, Papa?"

"I had to come over and speak to Mama. Why do you need her? Can I help?"

Sofia nodded. "I wet the bed again."

"Okay, sweetie. Marco and I are going to sort that out for you."

"Marco's here?" She looked beyond him and grinned happily when she saw him coming upstairs. "Hi Marco."

"Hello, darling," he said, kneeling down in front of her. "What's the problem?"

"My bed..." She turned and pointed towards her door, shifting uncomfortably and evidently unwilling to explain the problem fully.

"I'll get her some new pyjamas if you'd be willing to strip the sheets" Daniele said. Marco looked up at him and nodded.

"I can do that."

Daniele took his daughter's hand and brought her into the bathroom, fetching the first pair of new pyjamas that his hands found in the airing cupboard, and ran a shallow bath to let her get cleaned up. He instructed her to toss the old pyjamas onto the landing before leaving her to change. He had to venture into Cristina's room to put the soaked pair into the laundry basket, and it took him a minute to find because for some reason, it had been hidden in a small cupboard. When he came back, Sofia was waiting in a new pair of white pyjamas covered in colourful letters.

"There we are, all nice and cosy again" he said, picking her up.

"Yes!" she agreed cheerfully, and he couldn't resist putting a kiss on her cheek.

"Now let's fix your bed."

There was no need for that, however, as he brought Sofia into her room to find Marco arranging the pillows. A pile of bedclothes had been balled up in the corner. "Did you do it all yourself?" Daniele asked incredulously.

"I didn't see the point in waiting around. We don't want you staying awake all night, do we?" Marco asked fondly. He tickled under Sofia's chin and she giggled, lightly swiping at him.

"I want to" she declared.

"You can't," Daniele said. "You've got to go for a big sleep so you won't be tired tomorrow."

He put her down in bed and pulled the covers up. She immediately grabbed them and lifted them up to her neck, gazing up at him with her puppy eyes at full power. "Why are you here, Papa?" she asked again.

He sat down on the bed and stroked her hair. "Marco recorded what happened at the market" he said.

"Is Mama angry?" Sofia asked at once.

"Not at you, amore."

"At who?"

"At Lorenzo."

Sofia's lip started to wobble. "He'll be angry at me" she said tearfully.

"No, he won't," Daniele said, a little bit of his anger slipping out. "What happened today will never happen again, I promise."

"I'm sorry I didn't try to take you away" Marco added. Sofia turned to look at him and some understanding seemed to pass between them, a moment that Daniele wasn't privy to, before she raised a small smile.

"It's okay. He would hurt you too. He's bigger than you" she said. Marco looked away.

"Go to sleep, bambina," Daniele said quietly. He bent down and kissed her forehead. "Everything will be okay in the morning."

When he tried to move back, she gripped his hand. "Will you stay?"

"Sure."

She smiled and loosened her hold. "Marco, you stay too" she ordered. No request for him, Daniele noticed.

Marco smiled warmly at her and knelt down beside the bed, next to Daniele. "I'll stay if you want. Do you want me to sing a song to help you sleep?" he offered.

"Okay."

Marco took a deep breath. "Apologies if it's unfamiliar. I thought it up when I was bored" he said, and then started to sing in his beautiful, gentle voice.

"Tutte quelle piccole ali, che sbattono nell'aria
Il vento porta le loro canzoni
Il sole mi fa sentire felice…"

Daniele thought he might cry listening to him. Sofia's reaction was different. Her smile widened at first, and then her eyes began to grow heavy, closing three times before she forced them open to keep listening. On the fourth time, they fell shut and didn't reopen. Marco dropped his voice to a whisper to finish the song.

"Il mondo ora è caldo e bello
Ed io so di essere amato."

The only sound in the room was quiet, measured breathing. Sofia's hand was still in his. He looked at it as if he'd never seen it before, stunned by how small it was next to his. It brought back memories of sitting in the hospital after she was born, holding her and marvelling over what a little doll she was. There had been none of the nauseating fear over first-time fatherhood that had accompanied Matteo's birth, just overwhelmingly intense love. He had thought that he would never let any harm come to her. Such promises, it seemed, were easier to make than to keep.

He managed to lift his eyes and turn his head towards Marco. The angel had his fingers pressed against his mouth, looking lost in thought. He sensed Daniele looking at him and moved his eyes slightly, the corners of his mouth turning up briefly.

"Thank you" Daniele said. Marco shrugged.
"Will you give her a nice dream?"
The angel reached out to put a hand on Daniele's shoulder, and nodded silently.

**Chapter 33**

He awoke with a start, finding that he was on his knees next to his daughter's bed and sunlight was now creeping through the curtains. She was still sound asleep, hugging her plush dinosaur, and he smiled before slowly getting up and creeping out. His knees were absolutely killing him and he had to wait for the blood supply to return before he could proceed any further. He checked Matteo's room and found his son sleeping as well, apparently having missed the whole thing.

He went downstairs and found Cristina in the kitchen, still wearing her dressing gown and holding a mug of tea. She gave him a wan smile as he entered the room.
"How did you sleep?" she asked.
"Not well. What about you?"
"Not at all. I was up until nearly 4am trying to sort things out."
"And are things sorted?" Daniele probed cautiously. Cristina heaved a deep sigh and leaned against the counter, staring into her cup.
"He wouldn't accept that he'd done anything wrong," she said. "He kept saying that was how he was raised and it did no harm, and he didn't know how to handle misbehaviour in any other way. He wouldn't listen to me at all. So yeah, I'd say they're pretty sorted. He's gone to work now. I'd like to be gone before he gets back."
"I can book the hotel room for another night" Daniele offered immediately, and received another of those sad smiles he hated.
"You're very kind, but five of us wouldn't be able to squeeze into one room. I can keep the kids and myself in a hotel for a while until I've figured out the next step."

Cristina moved to the kitchen table, sat down and held her head in her hands. "I don't know how I'm going to explain this to them. Another upheaval and all because I'm a blind fool."

"Why don't we go out for lunch today?" Daniele suggested, sitting down across from her. "We can talk about it together, like we did before."

"Yeah...Yeah, I guess we can do that. There's a cafe nearby that the kids love."

"We'll go there."

Cristina lifted her head and smiled at him, a real smile now. "Marco's lucky to have someone like you" she remarked.

"No, it's...It's not like that," Daniele said, his attention suddenly becoming absorbed by the placemats. "He's...not interested."

"Oh. Are you sure?"

"Yes."

"That's a shame. The way you looked at each other, I thought…"

Daniele met her eye and he wondered what his expression said, if she read the discomfort and desperation on his face, because she waved the rest of the sentence away with a flick of her hand. They sat in silence, both lost in their own thoughts.

"I didn't ask enough questions," Cristina said finally. "What kind of mother am I?"

"One who went toe to toe with a guy twice her size and made him leave his own house."

She scoffed. "Yeah, a lot of good that did when I was the last to know. I don't even know how long this was going on for."

"We can talk about that at lunch too."

"I need to thank Marco. If it wasn't for him..." She shook her head. That sentence didn't need to be finished.

"Have you seen him this morning?" Daniele asked.

Cristina looked up in surprise. "No, I haven't seen him since last night."

Daniele nodded. He'd probably gone back to the hotel. He'd done good work yesterday, but there was nothing he could do now.

"Papa! You're not a dream!"

He turned and a smile split his face at the sight of Sofia, hair pressed flat on one side and wild on the other, racing towards him. "I certainly am not," he agreed, lifting her onto his knee. "How did you sleep, amore?"

"I dreamed I was riding a dinosaur!" she enthused. "It was a flying one and we were going over the sea, and then I fell in, but I could breathe and I went swimming, and then I found a big forest and there were loads of diplo...dip...big friendly dinosaurs with long necks in there."

"Sounds amazing, sweetheart."

She grinned happily, even giving a little bounce of joy, another reminder that she was growing up as it now hurt his poor old knees when she wriggled around like that. She looked across the table and the smile dimmed slightly.

"Mama, you look sad."

"I'm not sad, not really" Cristina assured her, reaching across to hold her hand.

"Is Lorenzo here?"

"No," Daniele found himself answering, even though she wasn't speaking to him. "We're all going out to eat now, the four of us."

Sofia's eyes grew wide with delight once more. "To the cafe?" she asked hopefully.

"Yes, baby, to the café," Cristina nodded. "Why don't you go and wake your brother so we can get there before the queue forms?"

\*\*

The café in question was only a short walk away from the house, and already filled with office workers and tourists. Cristina sent Daniele and the kids to save a table while she ordered their food, returning with soup, pasta, olives and bruschetta to share between them. Ten minutes of companionable eating and talking was allowed before the meeting was opened.

"Matteo, Sofia, there is something we need to discuss," Cristina said. Her serious tone immediately got the children's attention. "Lorenzo and I have decided that we will no longer be living together."

"Are you breaking up?" Matteo asked immediately.

"Yes."

"Does that mean we have to move?"

"It does, but..."

"Can we move back to Rome?"

Cristina glanced at Daniele and back at her son. "Is that what you want?" she queried.

"Yes," he said quickly. "I hate Milan."

"Can we stay with Papa?" Sofia piped up.

"No, piccola. My flat is too small."

"We can stay with Nonno and Nonna until you get a new house" Matteo said.

"Well, houses cost money and they take time to find..." Cristina replied.

"Hotels cost money too," he insisted. "Nonno and Nonna don't cost money."

Perhaps it shouldn't have come as a surprise that Matteo was so prepared for this, but it did. Daniele couldn't stand to think of how long he'd been waiting and hoping for this to happen.

"There's also the matter of my job..." Cristina began again.

Matteo cut her off once more, shouting loud enough for diners in neighbouring booths to hear. "You didn't care about moving your job before!"

"Matteo, come on," Daniele stood and gestured for his son to follow. "Let's go outside."

The boy stood and stormed towards the door like a teenager, Sofia watching wide-eyed, Cristina looking devastated. Daniele attempted to send her a supportive look, encouraging her that it would be okay, before following Matteo outside. He was pacing around in a tight circle on the pavement, stopping only when he saw his father. Daniele could see in his eyes that he was upset, on the point of crying, but his body language remained prickly and defensive, ready for a fight.

"Teo, hey, you can't talk to your mother like that" he said, trying to walk the line between firm and gentle.

"We only came here because that's what she wanted, and now she's trying to find excuses to stay!" Matteo retorted, his hands balling into fists even as his voice broke. He was trying so hard not to cry and it was impossible to be the hard disciplinarian in the face of that. Daniele hugged him and, even though they were on a public street, Matteo let him.

"That's not what's happening. She only wants to do the best thing for you and Sofia. She doesn't want to uproot you again."

"I just want to go home!" Matteo wailed into his chest. Daniele guided him to a nearby bench and sat down beside him, keeping an arm around his shoulders as he waited for his son to calm down. Once he was breathing normally again, Daniele spoke.

"Matteo, I need to ask you something and I want you to be honest."

His son nodded without looking at him.

"Did Lorenzo hurt you or Sofia?"

Matteo nodded. This didn't really come as a surprise, but it still boiled Daniele's blood to have it confirmed.

"She annoyed him," his son explained. "He thought she was too loud and if she didn't shush when he told her to, he'd smack her or put her outside. Mum was never around when he did it and he said if I told her, or anyone, we'd be taken away and never see her again."

Daniele heaved a sigh. "I wish you'd told me about all of this."

"I would have if I'd known how fast it would be fixed. I thought you were too far away to do anything."

That hurt, but what hurt more was admitting that he was right. The uselessness of his word alone had already been clearly demonstrated, and he would have been even more ineffective from Rome. Without that video, there was no guarantee that things would have changed even if Matteo had spoken up.

"Did he ever hurt you?"

"No, he just shouted sometimes. There was one time when he and Mum went out, and she said they'd be home for bedtime, but they weren't so I called her and Lorenzo yelled at me for making them come home even though I didn't. I just wanted to make sure they were okay. I'm sorry," Matteo added. "I tried to keep Sofi away from him and stop her crying."

"It's not your problem anymore, okay?" Daniele hugged him tighter. "It's important that you know that. Your mother and I are going to figure out what happens next. No more worrying about this, promise?"

"Promise," Matteo echoed with a faint smile. "Will you tell her to come back to Rome? She might listen to you."

He chuckled. "I'm not sure if you're right about that, but whatever she decides, it'll be what she believes is best for you two."

Matteo sighed and leaned his head on Daniele's arm. "I can't wait until I'm grown up so I can decide what's best for me."

"Don't wish to grow up too fast," he advised quietly, and then nudged Matteo's shoulder. "Do you want to go back inside? It must be nearly time for dessert."

His son looked up hopefully. "Can I have chocolate cake?"

"Do you have any money to pay for it?"

Matteo's face fell in horror and Daniele smiled. "Grown-ups have to buy their own desserts" he remarked.

"I'm not a grown-up yet" Matteo said quickly.

"No, you're not. Come on, omino."

## Chapter 34

Daniele stayed with his family throughout the afternoon, helping them pack and move their things to a B&B. He offered to stay for a few more days to help Cristina find a cheap flat - he was an expert at securing accommodation at short notice - but she'd insisted that she would be fine and he shouldn't change his plans.

"I need flexibility to decide what to do next," she said. "The kids don't want to stay in Milan and I'm not too keen on the idea either. It'll all depend on whether I can move my job and how difficult it is to find a new place."

She made no mention of Rome, but he quietly hoped that if her plan was to move, she wouldn't choose another brand new city. The original date of the planned Christmas visit was still intact and that was enough for now. He was going to send what money he could spare up to Milan to help with the cost of the B&B room. Cristina would have told him not to, so he wasn't going to tell her of his plan.

It was dusk and the sky was turning red when he returned to his hotel. He was starving and didn't think he could even go back out to find a restaurant. They might have to dine on room service tonight. He opened the door to his room and was greeted by eerie silence that sent a chill up his spine. The bathroom door was open and the bedroom was empty. Daniele went out to the balcony and found it devoid of life also.

For three hours, he sat in the room. Every now and then, he closed his eyes for a few seconds and then opened them in hopes that Marco would have appeared. He never had. Daniele would walk slowly up and down in case he might show up while his back was turned, but he didn't. Eventually he decided to go out. His stomach ached from hunger and perhaps Marco would prefer to join him in a public place where there was less chance of making a scene. Perhaps he would be back in the room when Daniele returned.

He wasn't.

Daniele walked out on the balcony, digging out the new box of cigarettes he'd bought after dinner, and lit one. He didn't know if he really wanted a cigarette, although the nicotine did calm him slightly. It was more something to do, a reason to stand on the balcony and look over the lights of Milan. It was a hypnotising view, beautiful and yet bleak, and he thought that there might be no lonelier feeling than to be far from home at night.

He felt the cold making the hair on his arms stand on end as he watched the orange lights twinkle in the distance, informing him that a whole city of people were safe and warm in their beds. The sight gave him a terrible feeling in his gut that made him want to sink to the ground and give up completely. He looked away from it and turned his eyes skywards, as if he had a chance to see bright feathered wings soaring overhead. All he could see were the stars. They were a little brighter here than in Rome, but he still had to squint to see the pinpricks of light above him.

*Where are you?*

He finished his cigarette and the cold drove him inside, into his bed. It felt too big to lie in alone. He could lie in the middle like a starfish without touching the edges, but he didn't. He stayed on his own side, because even if a part of him knew it was wishful thinking, he still wanted to give Marco the option to sneak in if he wanted to.

The sun woke him, streaming through the window and filling the room with warmth and light. Daniele blinked awake and then, remembering last night, was suddenly alert and looked around frantically. Marco was nowhere in sight. He could hear nothing to indicate the presence of another person. The balcony was his last spot of hope and he hurried out there, but he already knew what he would find.

The morning sun cast gentle warmth on his skin, but couldn't penetrate the cold inside. With a thunderclap of despair, he realised that Marco wasn't coming back.

It was possible to taste heartbreak. He'd never known that. It coated his tongue, wrapped itself around his neck, punched him in the stomach. He hadn't eaten anything for hours and now he was afraid to because of how sick he felt. Breathing required conscious effort and there was no medical reason for it, but his diaphragm felt like it had shut down and he had to pull air into his lungs. He kept looking down and feeling surprised to see his body intact, because the hollow feeling in his gut was so real that he couldn't believe there was no gaping hole to show for it. He'd never known it was possible to feel so sick from psychosomatic causes. He'd heard of it, he knew it was a real phenomenon, but he'd never experienced anything like this.

He stayed in the room until the maids came to throw him out, not wanting to walk the streets any longer than he had to, and then checked out and went straight to the railway station. There was nothing more he could do here, no more reason to stay. He dropped into the chemist at the station and bought some Pepto-Bismol, drank some as he waited for the train, and fell asleep before they'd even left Milano Centrale.

When he woke up, he felt desperately hungry, but his stomach was no longer churning. That was a relief. He looked around the passengers in the carriage in case Marco might be there, but of course he wasn't. What had happened? Maybe he had been taken away by whoever assigned him to missions. He remembered what Marco had said about how common it was for humans to lose their angels. Daniele didn't know what he'd done to deserve such measures. In the back of his mind, he worried that it had been his fault, that there was some rule against involvement between angels and their clients. But no, hadn't Marco said that he'd been involved with a client before and she'd died? It hadn't stopped him from carrying out the mission to its natural end in that case.

So what was the conclusion? That Marco had left of his own choice? In his heart, Daniele was certain that was the case. More than that, he had a horrible feeling that Marco would have disappeared on the day he took Matteo to the science museum, if it hadn't been for Sofia. Was this the price that had to be exacted? Love or family, but not both? If that was the case, it was an easy choice, but that didn't mean it didn't hurt like hell to be going home alone.

He watched the scenery for the rest of the journey, and then took a bus from Termini to the stop near his apartment. As he walked towards the building, he made a deal with himself. If Marco was there, all was forgiven. They would start afresh. He wouldn't mention what happened in Milan and wouldn't ask for anything. If Marco wasn't there, he would focus on his work and his family, and forget about that enjoyable but ultimately meaningless interlude in his life.

He opened the door and stepped inside. "Marco?"

There was no response. Daniele waited one, two, three seconds and then all hope deserted him. He sat down on the futon, picked up a cushion and pressed his face into it as he cried.

## Chapter 35

Daniele parked on the street outside his building and remained in the car for a few moments, resting his head on the steering wheel. He had returned from Milan only three days ago and already he felt permanently exhausted. His calf muscles hadn't recovered from the past two days of walking everywhere while his car was in the garage for its service, and they seized up whenever he sat still for any length of time. The only way to avoid the burning pain in his limbs and chest was to keep moving, and that was exactly what he'd been doing since his return to work.

He got out of the car, briefly bent double as his legs refused to work, and then compelled himself down the street. Someone was sitting on the steps outside his flat and stood up as he approached. Daniele felt his heart speed up briefly, and then felt ashamed for the flash of disappointment when the figure stepped under a street lamp.

"Where have you been?" Pietro demanded.

"Pietro, what are you doing here? It's late."

"It certainly is. You left the office at 8pm and it took you three hours to get home? I was about to call the police!"

Daniele stepped around him and took out his key. "How long have you been sitting here? And why?"

"Because I'm worried about you," Pietro leaned on the wall next to him and, even though the side door was now open, Daniele didn't step inside. "You haven't been the same since you came back from Milan. You're at work when I arrive and still there when I go home, and I don't want a return to the bad old days when you fell asleep at your desk. Will you tell me what's going on?"

Daniele shrugged. "I had to do a few jobs on the way home" he replied truthfully.

"Like what?"

"Paolo got out of hospital today so I brought him home, and I had to stop off at the bakery on the way for his favourite biscuits."

"Did you?" Pietro queried dryly.

"Well, he just got discharged," Daniele retorted. "It was a nice gesture."

"And that took you three hours?"

"No, I had to get some cat food for Rosa's kitten and pick it up from the vet."

"Excuse me?" Pietro stood up straight, looking shocked. "Who asked you to do that?"

"Rosa did. She's not having a good day," he explained. "She didn't feel able to leave the house, and the poor cat was the only animal left when I got there. It would have cost her money she doesn't have to leave it overnight."

Pietro sighed deeply and rubbed his forehead. "Daniele, your job is to help people learn to take care of themselves, not do everything for them. If Rosa was so worried about paying extra to leave her cat in the vet, it would have been an excellent incentive for her to go and get it herself."

"She was really upset, Pietro, and I don't mind."

"I know you don't," he snapped. "But I do. Daniele, what happened in Milan?"

"Nothing. I told you…"

"No, there's something else" Pietro insisted. Daniele looked at his front door, toying with the idea of simply stepping inside and locking Pietro out, but he couldn't face going into that dark abyss and isolating himself from the only people he had left.

"Do you remember Marco? The guy who helped me out after the incident?" he asked without meeting his friend's eye.

"Vaguely, yes."

"We were friends and I..." Daniele said hesitantly, playing with his keys as he spoke. "He came with me to Milan and I had...I told him I was interested in him and he said no, and he left."

"What do you mean?"

"He just vanished from the hotel room while I was with the kids."

There was silence from beside him and Daniele finally turned his head to see the reaction. Pietro's mouth was hanging open. "Bastard!" he declared finally. "I can't believe...Who would do that?"

He shook his head in disgust and took a step closer, placing his hand on Daniele's shoulder. "Lele, I can only imagine how you feel, but you can't let this undo all the progress you've made. You're not alone. If you need someone to talk to, we're here. I'm here."

Daniele suddenly felt like crying, but he quickly wiped a hand across his eyes to dispel that impulse. "I'm fine, I really am," he said, trying to raise a reassuring smile. "I just want to keep my mind off things."

Pietro answered his smile with a sympathetic one of his own. "This isn't the best way, my friend," he said gently. "Listen, we're going out paintballing this weekend and then Riccardo is hosting a barbecue. Would you be interested in joining us?"

"Who's going?"

"The barbecue is for the clients. The paintballing is for the usual suspects – me, Gianni, Carlo, Riccardo and you, if you're interested in coming."

He thought about it. It would be far better than staying in the house with his thoughts. It might even be fun. It had been a while since he'd spent some real time with his friends and he missed them. Right now they were the best thing in his life and he didn't want to neglect or risk losing them.

"Alright, sure."

"Great. Get some sleep," Pietro rubbed a hand over his back. "I'll see you in the morning."

Daniele waved him off as he walked away, and then stepped into the building. As soon as he opened the door to his apartment, he saw a brilliant white envelope lying on the mat, and felt his heart jump again. He hated this. He hated that he wondered whether every figure in the corner of his eye, every phone call and now every piece of post was a sign of Marco. He scoffed at his own stupidity and bent down to pick up the letter.

It was a wedding invite from Luca. Daniele was cordially invited to attend the reception on the last Saturday of the month, the week after next. There was a handwritten note from Luca, thanking Daniele for his help and saying that he would never have succeeded without him. He sat on the sofa and read it several times. After thirteen long months, Luca had come out the other side. A warm glow infused him. This was what it was all for. This was what made all the work worthwhile.

He looked at the invitation again and felt a chuckle rise in his throat. In the space of ten minutes, he had had two of his Saturdays filled with activity. Maybe Marco was still somewhere out there after all, watching from a distance as he'd promised.

"Is this your way of making sure I don't stay in the house?" he asked the air. Predictably there was no response.

\*\*

Daniele had never tried paintballing before and he had no intention of ever trying it again. That had been so painful, so unlike the soft splats of paint that he'd expected! The force of those pellets had stripped the bark from trees he'd tried to hide behind, and he'd nearly been crippled by three shots to the legs and one to the neck. As well as that, the camo gear was too hot and the mask steamed up and became impossible to see through. He couldn't remember the last time he felt so filthy. He would have stepped over his grandmother for a shower, but fortunately he had no such competition and for once was glad of his empty house.

Fifteen minutes later, he was blessedly clean and gave his hair a few quick rubs with a towel - no matter that he looked like he'd been electrocuted - before going out to retrieve the dirty clothes he'd discarded in a path leading to the bathroom door. He would throw these into the machine and then take a nap, he decided. After today's exercise, even the rumbling outside his bedroom wouldn't keep him awake. He bent down to grab his T-shirt and heard a knock at the side door.

"Just a minute!" he called. With more haste, he picked up his jeans and pulled them on. The door was knocked again.

"I said hang on! I'll be there in a second!"

He hauled the stinking pile to the washing machine, tossed it in and immediately opened the door. His heart nearly stopped at the sight in front of him.

"Marco?"

Marco looked awful. His hair was stuck to his head like a woollen helmet, parts of it split into sodden tendrils, other parts having lost their curl entirely. He looked like he'd been submerged. His arm shot out and Daniele saw a small, half-dead bunch of flowers in his hand. Most of the petals were drooping or turning brown.

"I picked them up from the side of the road" Marco said quickly.

Daniele could hardly speak. "Mar..." He moved forward to touch him, hug him, but Marco skittered back.

"Don't touch me, I'm sweaty."

"What happened?"

"They left me in Genoa. It took ages to get here. I've been walking all day. Can I come in?"

"Of course." Daniele stepped back quickly, gesturing for him to enter, and Marco stumbled straight into the living room. Daniele closed the door and followed, finding his surprise guest hovering over the sofa, and then turning to lie down on the floor.

"I'm too dirty for the futon," he explained. "Oh, my legs!"

"Do you want a shower?" Daniele asked.

"I can't stand up" Marco replied tearfully.

"Can I get you anything?"

"Water."

Daniele hurried to the kitchen and got water straight out of the tap, barely even waiting for it to turn cold in case he got back and Marco had disappeared again. He had not. He was still curled up on the floor where Daniele had left him, and even sitting up to receive the water seemed to pose some difficulty. Daniele watched as he drained half the glass in one gulp.

"Marco, where have you been?" he asked. "Who are they? Are you hurt?"

"I know I have a lot of things to explain, but can I rest first?"

"If you need to."

Marco put the glass on the coffee table, rolled over and closed his eyes. Daniele continued to watch him, noticed that he was shaking, and ran to get the blanket from the airing cupboard. He put it carefully around Marco's form and sat beside the angel on the floor, waiting for a sign that his body temperature was regulating. His skin was shining and his eyelids flickered constantly, chasing dreams. He was still breathing deeply, gasping even in slumber. Daniele carefully touched his forehead and felt how hot and damp it was, moved his hand into the curls – which were sticky and wiry now - and pushed a few off Marco's face. The sweat didn't bother him, he found, and he smiled when he rubbed his thumb over Marco's brow and the sleeping man's face relaxed.

After a few minutes, when he was sure that Marco was soundly asleep, he bent down and gently kissed his forehead. There were so many questions that he wanted to ask, but none of them seemed so important as knowing that Marco was here, that he'd come back for whatever reason, and perhaps there was an explanation after all.

\*\*

Marco slept for an hour, and Daniele was sitting in the armchair when he woke up, waiting for him.

"Hi" he said, sitting up.

"Hello," Daniele replied. He allowed a few seconds to go by and then spoke again. "This is a surprise."

"Yeah," Marco said quietly. "I hope you know…I didn't…I didn't deliberately vanish. I wasn't trying to run away. I don't want you to think that."

"I did. The timing is a little coincidental, don't you think?"

"That's what I was afraid of," Marco sighed. "But Lele, of course the timing is coincidental. That's the whole point."

"I have no idea what you're talking about."

Marco groaned and put his head in his hands, rubbing at his forehead, and then looked up. "They called me back," he explained. "Heaven, upstairs, the powers that be, whatever you want to call them."

"Why?" Daniele asked. He maintained the stony demeanour of an interrogator, although inside, every one of his senses went on alert.

"Do you remember when I told you about my need for atonement?"

Daniele nodded to indicate that he did.

"They said that I did it. They never actually told me what the terms of the deal were and there was a lot of discussion that I didn't follow, but I gather that it's something to do with helping someone that it's not my job to help. It makes me worthy or whatever, guardian angels are supposed to take an interest in all of humanity and not just the ones that they're told to look after, something like that. So what happened with Sofia somehow fulfilled what I had to do."

"Alright," Daniele nodded. "So what does that mean?"

"It means I don't have to do this job anymore. I can move on."

Daniele felt something like a death knell in his heart. Marco wasn't back after all, then. It was a courtesy call. He should be grateful for that. It would have been easy for the angel to just leave him, always wondering if he'd done something wrong, if things could have been different without that one stupid mistake. At least now he had closure, and most importantly, so did Marco. The angel was looking at him with wide eyes, like a puppy expecting to be scolded. Daniele could imagine how much he'd longed for this, how much this day meant to him. He certainly wouldn't let his bitterness get in the way, not when Marco had respected him by coming. He stood up and his legs felt weak for a reason that had nothing to do with muscles or bone.

"Well then, thank you for everything you've done, and thank you for coming to say goodbye. You didn't have to do that."

The words nearly choked him and he held out his hand, praying that Marco would shake it quickly and go before he fell apart. The angel didn't move.

"I told them I had unfinished business on Earth," he said. Daniele wasn't sure if he'd heard correctly. He must have looked dumbfounded because Marco carried on. "I asked if I could come back and finish the job, and then move on afterwards…with you."

Daniele realised that he was no longer breathing, and that his hand was still foolishly extended. His voice seemed to come from far away. "What did they say?"

It seemed like far too long before Marco replied. "They offered me a choice, move on now with my soul clean, or come back to Earth as a human. So I did a little thinking and I decided."

At that, Daniele felt a rush of hope and happiness, breathing easily for the first time in days. "You came back?"

He heard his voice break and earnestly wished that it hadn't. Marco stood up so that they were almost toe-to-toe. He put his hands in his pockets and looked at the floor.

"I thought about whether I should or not," he admitted, causing another painful crunch in Daniele's heart. "I was scared, but…then I remembered, someone once told me that when happiness makes a guest appearance in your life, it's better to enjoy it than spend all that time worrying about what will happen when the happiness is taken away."

He looked up and met Daniele's eye, who was now right on the brink of crying. "He sounds like a wise man" he remarked, barely able to choke up the words.

Marco smiled slightly and shrugged. "I wouldn't say that, but he has his moments."

Daniele laughed so unexpectedly that it choked him. "Stronzo!"

Marco grinned at him and God, he had missed that smile more than anything! "This was not how I expected this conversation to turn out" he said.

"Oh, I don't expect anything anymore," Daniele replied casually. "Nothing is ever simple with you. At this stage, I just go with the flow."

"What happened afterwards? Are the kids okay?"

"They're fine," Daniele nodded. "Cristina's going to decide the next step. I hope she'll bring them back, but I suppose the most important thing is that they're away from him."

Marco nodded. "So what now? I mean, you probably don't have any real need of me anymore."

"Marco, I never needed you. That doesn't mean I don't want you."

"Be careful with language like that."

Daniele laughed and hugged him, sweat be damned. "You need a shower," he said. "I'll make some food while you're in there."

## Chapter 36

Daniele hummed to himself as he prepared the food. He considered making a full meal, figuring that Marco could eat a lot after his great journey, but that would take too long and he just wanted to get food into his angel quickly. No, not his angel anymore, but still…His angel. How nice to think of him that way. In all this time, Marco had never felt like his. He'd been a temporary feature in Daniele's life, a gift that could be taken away at any time. Now everything was different.

The pasta was shared between two plates and he then grabbed the plastic carton of cheese sauce from the fridge, readying it in the microwave. Maybe they could eat outside. It was dusk now, but the communal garden had heat lamps. They could watch the sun go down and, if Marco wasn't too tired, see the stars. Daniele knew that drowsiness would be no issue for him. He felt wide awake, like he was having a sugar high. Speaking of sugar, why not make some hot chocolate too? It was the ideal drink for filling bellies and relaxing minds. He allowed his imagination to drift, creating an image of them sitting under the heat lamps, under the stars.
"Hi."
Marco's voice broke him out of his daydream and Daniele's heart melted at the sight of him hovering nervously in the hall, only his head poking around the doorframe. He had never seen Marco look so uncertain.
"Hi" he said. It was as if they'd just met and were shyly feeling their way through conversation.
"Do you need me to do anything?"
"I have it all under control. Do you want to go out and turn on the heat lamps? I was thinking of eating outside."

"Sounds fun," Marco nodded. "Lele...I don't have any clothes."

"Oh!" The disembodied head took on a new meaning. "Oh, of course. Grab whatever you want out of my drawers. I'm sorry, I didn't even think."

"Neither did I. There's a lot that I didn't think about."

Daniele averted his eyes and heard footsteps rush past, and his bedroom door firmly closed. He poured cocoa powder into two cups and stirred it together with boiling water and milk, took the sauce out of the microwave and poured it over the pasta. He took a moment to savour the delicious mix of cheese and chocolate that filled his kitchen, and then carefully carried the plates to the back door.

"Food is out here when you're ready" he called.

"Okay!"

He smiled fondly, imagining Marco rummaging through his drawers in search of something that he deemed stylish enough. He might be in desperate need of clothes, but some standards had to be maintained. Daniele could almost hear the words in Marco's voice. He set the plates down on the table and turned to go back for the mugs, in time to see the back door open. Marco was swamped by the monstrously large sweatshirt that Matteo had gifted him.

"You know, I have a lot of shirts in there if you prefer..."

"I know, they didn't fit me," Marco replied. "It's quite inconvenient being a human. Getting tired, getting hungry, having to get dressed manually, walking...It's very annoying. How do you find time to do anything?"

"I don't know why you're talking as if you've never been a human."

"That was ages ago," he said dismissively, taking a seat at the table. "I've forgotten what it was like."

"And you call me the old man."

Marco looked up at him and gave a small, sincere smile which Daniele couldn't help reciprocating. "I'll go get the drinks" he said, and hurried back into the house. He returned less than ten seconds later to find Marco, his mouth full, making a series of muffled sounds like a delighted baby.

"Lele," he declared before his mouth was quite empty. "Lele, I like cheese! It's got such a strong taste, but my tongue likes it! What about this?"

He grabbed a piece of bacon and stuffed it into his mouth. "It tastes like smoke, but it's good! What are the most disgusting foods you can think of? I need to try something horrible so I know my taste buds are working."

"Well, I don't think this is horrible, but maybe tomorrow…"

Marco had already taken a huge gulp from the mug, only to lunge forward and put a hand over his face to avoid spitting it out.

"Is it bad?" Daniele asked worriedly.

Marco shook his head. "My mouth!" he whined.

"Oh…" Daniele stroked his hair sympathetically. "Blow on it and drink slowly."

Following his instructions, Marco tried again and smiled warmly. "That's delicious" he said. Daniele nodded proudly. He sat on the chair beside Marco, sipped from his own mug and took a bite of cheesy pasta.

"I thought you weren't coming back" he said.

Marco turned to look at him. "But I did" he replied matter-of-factly.

"But I thought you wouldn't," Daniele insisted. "What happened? Why did they leave you in Genoa?"

"It was my home once," Marco explained. He laughed lightly. "They put me right back at the scene of the crime. There's another family living in my house now and there's a tyre swing on the tree. That was strange."

"How did you get back to Rome?" Daniele asked, sensing that he was about to get lost in memories.

"I thought the ferry would be quickest," Marco explained. "I had to walk to Savona and I snuck on because I didn't have any money. And I forgot that Corsica belongs to France now so they wouldn't let me in. It took another day to walk back to Genoa and I tried to get a train, but they threw me off in Pisa because I didn't have a ticket. So I had to walk the rest of the way."

Daniele stared at him in horror, his imagination conjuring images of Marco tramping the country roads during the heat of noon and the cold of midnight, exhausted and hungry. He should have been there. If he'd only known, he would have driven every road leading to Pisa to find him.

"Couldn't you have got a message to me?"

Marco gazed sadly into his mug. "I had no money, Lele, and I was panicking. I knew you would think I abandoned you. I was just trying to get back quickly and I was so scared..." He broke off, heaved a shaky breath, and dropped his face into his hands. "I was so scared you wouldn't forgive me for leaving."

Daniele stood up quickly. "How could I?" he asked, placing a hand on Marco's shoulder, but it was too late. The dam was broken and his lovely, happy angel was crying unstoppably. At a loss for what to do, Daniele wrapped him in a hug and rocked him gently. He caught the smell of his skin and only then realised how familiar it was. Somehow that indefinable scent had become synonymous with home.

"Shhh, it's okay," he murmured. "You've had a very stressful time, I know, but you're home now. You're home," he repeated, smiling as the words sank in. "And I'll take care of you."

"That's my job. That's supposed to be my job," Marco protested, resting his head on Daniele's shoulder nevertheless. "Lele, I don't know who I am anymore. How am I supposed to look after you if I'm not an angel?"

"You're Marco. That's all you need to be. And I don't want you to look after me anymore. I just want you here with me."

Marco pulled out of the hug and looked at him. Daniele could barely focus on his face, but he could feel light breaths ghosting past and the tips of their noses brushing together when one of them moved. He longed to close the distance and feel those lips against his, but with great difficulty, held back. His impulsiveness had nearly messed everything up before. This time Marco needed to take the lead.

He felt a brief peck against his lips, so fast and light that he could have imagined it, if not for the nervous look in Marco's face. "Was that okay?" he asked.

"Are you kidding? Of course it was" Daniele retorted, and was immediately embarrassed by his eagerness. Marco giggled and shook his head.

"Still, I should have asked for permission to…"

"It's okay," he replied quickly. He placed his hand over Marco's and gently squeezed. "Look," he said, lifting his other hand and pointing. "The moon."

Marco looked up at the round yellow circle in the dark sky, nodded admiringly, and turned his focus back to Daniele. "It's beautiful. Haven't you seen a full moon before?" he asked. Daniele smiled shyly.

"I know it's very cheesy, but I've always liked the idea of kissing below a full moon."

The confusion on Marco's face made way for a teasing grin. "Well, it is the moon," he said. "Cheesy seems appropriate."

"So if you wouldn't mind doing that again…"

Marco's arms wrapped around his neck, and Daniele put his hands on the angel's back, holding him tightly against his body. Soft lips pressed against his, gentle and confident, as a hand moved up the back of his head and grabbed a fistful of hair. His mind exploded into shards of colour. Every thought was wiped away and he was floating amongst the stars. When they finally stopped, it was only to let him breathe, and Marco put their foreheads together as he waited. One of his hands stroked Daniele's hair, smoothing it fondly.

"You have such lovely hair" he said.

"So do you."

"It's so soft and rebellious. I don't know how you can look good with bedhead, but you do. You should keep it like this."

"Most people would prefer it to look a bit neater."

"No, it suits you," Marco insisted. He thoughtfully ran his fingers through his hair, gently pulling it into spikes until Daniele was sure he looked like a porcupine. "Neat hair is for middle-aged people."

"I am middle-aged so that may be appropriate."

"No," he said again, grinning. "Any man who walks around in a leather jacket and band T-shirts is young at heart." His hand moved to gently touch Daniele's face. "I'm very envious of this beard."

"It's got grey in it" Daniele said ruefully.

"Let me give you a compliment. I love your little button nose..." His gaze automatically drifted to the lips below it and he swallowed before redirecting his gaze. "And your eyes..."

"They're not special."

"Let me give you a compliment," he hissed. "And I love your smile, especially that one."

"Your eyes are special," Daniele replied. "They're so clear."

"They can't decide whether to be blue or green. It's freaky."

"They're beautiful. And your smile is gorgeous."

Marco grinned and kissed him again. "I'm not used to getting a compliment, never mind so many at once."

"That's a pity. I should change that."

Their meal was finished within ten minutes, but they stayed out in the garden. The heat lamps were forgotten. When the temperature started to drop, Marco moved onto Daniele's seat. There really wasn't enough room for him there, but Daniele didn't mind the weight or the cold or Marco's ticklish hair. He kept his arms firmly wrapped around his beloved and left kisses on every part of him that he could reach.

At a certain point he became aware of how dark it was, and how many stars had appeared in the sky. They were a lot brighter than usual tonight and he squinted, amazed and confused, at how each one looked like a tiny diamond embedded in black velvet. It was a beautiful sight and he thought about staying out a little longer to watch, but then Marco suddenly shivered and that idea was discarded at once.

"Are you cold?" he asked.

"Maybe a bit," Marco conceded. His head rested on Daniele's shoulder as one hand played with his hair, and that hand was now pulling him closer in search of heat. "But you're warm so I'm happy to stay if you are."

"Shall I carry you inside to save your legs?"

Marco chuckled. "I don't think you can lift me."

"I'm sure I could if I tried. You aren't that heavy. Or I could roll you up in the duvet and drag you in."

"Are those my options?" Marco struggled to sound indignant while his eyes sparkled with amusement. "Thank you for affording me such dignity. I feel so loved."

"Good, because I do love you."

Marco pulled away, looking stunned. Daniele held onto his hand as if he could still disappear, hoping that wouldn't frighten him even more.

"You don't have to say it back. I just want you to know."

Marco's surprise started to become a smile. "Lele, of course I love you. Why would you ever doubt that?"

They went back into the house, still holding hands, and Marco started to turn towards the living room. Daniele gave his hand a light tug in the other direction.

"My bed is over there" Marco said, sounding confused.

"No," Daniele shook his head, smiling. "It's not."

## Chapter 37

He was woken by how hot the room was, unbearably so, too much to stay in bed for a moment longer. Something had happened last night, he thought as he flung the duvet from him. He couldn't remember what, but he was sure it had been important. The heat moved then, assuming a more solid shape, that of a head on his chest and an arm across his stomach. His heart lifted.

When he lifted his head to look, all he could see was auburn hair, and beyond that a now exposed back moving with long slow breaths. Had he really fallen asleep like that? No, the last thing Daniele remembered was watching Marco's face, trying to memorise every detail as if he might be gone tomorrow. Marco must have moved during the night. He gently traced his fingers over the smooth white skin, feeling Marco's breathing change as he did so.

"Are you asleep?" He gently stroked his hair, watching the tousled curls move under his hand and then spring back into position.
"Hmm…"
"I have to get up."
"No." There was a smile in his voice that promised mischief.
"Marco…" He pushed against the weight of Marco's head to sit up, and the arms immediately tightened their grip on him. Daniele attempted to pull free, but he succeeded only in dragging Marco across the bed, not in loosening his hold.
"Marco, I have to get up!" he insisted, laughing.

Finally green eyes blinked open and looked at him, brightly and alertly. "Do you want to know something weird?" Marco asked, letting go and sitting up. "I can't remember what day it is."

Daniele smiled. "It's Saturday."

Marco frowned at him and folded his arms petulantly. "Well, you could at least compliment me back by pretending not to remember" he remarked.

Daniele smiled and kissed the top of his head. "I only remember because Riccardo is having a barbecue today," he said. "I have no idea what the date is."

Marco grinned, satisfied. "That will do."

"By the way," Daniele called over his shoulder as he made for the bathroom. "I know it's a bit soon, but do you want to come?"

\*\*

"When you said your friend was hosting lunch, I thought it was going to be an occasion with chairs" Marco complained.

"We don't need chairs. We can sit on the wall" Daniele said, waving across the lawn towards the cohort gathered around the grill.

"I'm too overdressed. I need to go home and change."

Before Marco could make good his escape, however, Daniele's friends descended upon them. Hugs and exuberant greetings were exchanged before anyone even looked at Marco.

"And who's this?" Riccardo asked curiously.

"This is Marco. You already know Pietro and Gianni, right? This is Riccardo and this is Carlo."

"Nice to meet you," Marco reached forward and shook Carlo's hand, turning to Riccardo and immediately fixing his eyes on his chest. "Is that a suggestion or an instruction?"

Riccardo glanced down at the *Kiss the Cook* apron he was wearing and grinned. "It's an instruction. It's the only way you'll get any food" he said, clacking his barbecue tongs.

Daniele took a breath. This was his moment. He put an arm around Marco and pulled him closer. "Sorry, but this one's mine."

Riccardo, Carlo and Gianni's eyes widened in unison. It was quite funny to see.

"Oh!"

"Hang on a second..."

"How long has this been going on?"

"Riccardo," Pietro interrupted, smiling at his friends' dramatics. "Why don't you show Marco your wares?"

"Absolutely," Riccardo put his arm around Marco from the other side and led him away. "What are you in the mood for, burgers or hot dogs? Or are you a salad kind of man?"

Daniele watched their backs walking towards the barbecue, until Pietro stepped into his line of sight and he refocused. "You sorted things out then?" his friend asked.

"We did."

"I'm glad. If he messes you around again..."

"I know I can depend on you to rally the troops, but that won't be necessary" Daniele assured him. He looked beyond Pietro towards the barbecue. Riccardo was piling cheese, tomatoes and lettuce atop a burger until he could hardly close the bread, while Marco watched in alarm. The sight brought a small smile to his face.

"You love him, don't you?" Pietro said.

"Yeah."

"I hope you'll be very happy together."

His friend's support filled his heart with joy. "Thank you."

"And thank you for earning me 20 euros," Pietro replied. "Gianni said it would take over a week before you got back together, but I had a feeling romance would win the day. What can I say?" he asked, noting Daniele's scandalised expression. "Sometimes I know you better than you know yourself."

\*\*

The next people to be informed were the most important. Cristina expressed no surprise at all when he explained the reason for his call. She dropped her voice to a whisper and told him how happy she was for him, and she hoped everything worked out well for them, before passing the phone to the kids. He crossed his fingers before speaking. His kids' blessings meant the world to him, but nevertheless he hoped they wouldn't kick up a fuss about this.

"Is he going to live with you?" Matteo asked as soon as Daniele had finished delivering the news. His son had a gift for getting to the heart of a matter, and he'd done it again.

"He is, but he doesn't have to be there during visits if you prefer."

"It's okay. He can't replace Mum and he seems cool," Matteo said thoughtfully. "He's nice to the good people and nasty to the bad ones."

"That's not necessarily a good thing" Daniele said.

"Of course it is. I like him."

Daniele released the breath he'd been holding. He'd been preparing himself for a far more difficult interrogation.

"Sofia?" he queried. "Do you want to say anything?"

There was an ominous silence before his daughter replied. "I don't want you to date him."

Daniele felt his heart sink. He had thought that the friendship Sofia had struck up with Marco would make her amenable to the idea of having him around, but of course she would be suspicious of this development.

"Can you tell me why you feel that way?" he probed gently.

"Because if you fall out, he won't be my friend anymore."

Daniele was lost for words. He'd tried to predict what issues might arise and think of a good answer for them, but he hadn't thought of this.

"Just stay friends" Sofia ordered.

"I hope you know that no matter what happens, Marco will always be my friend and yours. You won't lose contact with him if that's what worries you."

"Oh," Sofia said. "Okay then. Papa, can I wear my blue dress if you get married?"

"We'll discuss that at the time, love."

\*\*

Finally, on the tail of that delightfully successful conversation was what felt like the most difficult. He and Marco went to visit his parents on a Thursday night. They sat in the living room, like the points of a compass, the elder two listening in total silence as their son explained the situation.

His mother was the first to break the silence. "Marco, would you like to help me serve the tea?" she asked, standing up.

Daniele watched in alarm. He hadn't expected his mother to celebrate, but he'd thought she would acknowledge the news in some way. To be ignored hurt more than he expected. He turned to Marco, who looked just as worried as he stood to answer his summons. That left only Daniele and his father alone in the living room.

"I thought..." his father began. Daniele leaned forward, hanging on his every word, fervently hoping for a positive or at least neutral response. "Well, I don't know what I thought. I'm confused. You have children so you can't be gay..."

"I'm not gay. I'm bisexual" he explained.

His father looked blank. "Does that mean you like everyone?"

"No, not everyone. I like men and women, but that doesn't mean I like everyone."

"Right," he nodded, none the wiser, but pretending to be. "But you like Marco now?"

"I love him."

"Right," he said again, shifting uncomfortably. He didn't know how to handle sentimental displays and would have reacted in the same way if Daniele had been speaking about a woman. "That's good. I'm happy for you. I hope you're happy," he muttered, speaking to the arm of his chair, and then suddenly looked up. "One question though...This wasn't happening when he was helping you in a professional capacity, right? He didn't breach any ethical codes?"

"No, no," Daniele shook his head, inexpressibly happy that this was the issue. "That stopped months ago."

"That's alright then. And you are happy?"

"Very happy."

He smiled and his father tentatively returned the gesture. They both looked up, thankful to break the silence that could quickly have become awkward, as his mother returned to the room. She was beaming from ear to ear.

"Bring him to the family dinner on Sunday, won't you?" she said. It was more of an order than a suggestion, and so the date was made for Marco's baptism of fire.

\*\*

Daniele went to the back of the car to grab the bottle of wine he'd brought along - chosen after an intense discussion about price versus quality in the supermarket aisle - and came back to find Marco staring at the building as if he was preparing to launch an assault on a heavily defended castle.

"I hope they like me" he said.

"Of course they will. They've met you before."

"Yeah…" He chuckled nervously and took hold of Daniele's hand. "They're nice. It'll be fine."

His parents' apartment was a wall of sound as soon as he opened the door, still holding Marco's hand. His niece and a couple of his cousins' kids came sprinting out of the living room to see who was there, greeted him and tried to pull him to join their game, and then accepted Marco's offer instead. Daniele continued towards the kitchen as his boyfriend was ferried away on a tide of children. His mother and siblings were already moving fluidly around the room.

"Sorry I'm late..." he began, approaching his mother as she laid the table. She turned, gave him a kiss on the cheek and took the wine with a thank-you, and then carried on her work. Daniele, seeking to be useful, approached one of the boiling pots and picked up the wooden spoon. Stefania promptly appeared by his side and shook her head sternly.

"That's my job," she said, removing the implement and gently nudging him aside. "You're helping Antonio."

He moved around the table to where his brother was cutting vegetables with all the flair of a sous-chef, even if not quite with their precision. "You're serving" he advised, pushing thin and thick slices alike towards him. Daniele swiftly set to work depositing them on the lines of plates, trying to make sure everything was distributed equally. Nothing could cause a fight quicker than the cry of, "They have more than me!"

Stefania appeared with her pot and started delivering pieces of meat from its seemingly bottomless depths. Daniele finished the line and circled the table to start again from the top, bringing plates two at a time over to the places as his mother went into the living room to call everyone for food. Antonio quickly grabbed a chair before the stampede began. Daniele managed to get a good seat, near the bottom of the table on the left hand side, and thought about putting his hand on the neighbouring chair like a kid in elementary school. But no, Marco was among the first responders and headed straight for the seat beside him.

It was a completely normal, natural scene. The combat for resources had begun in earnest, but Daniele sat back and watched for a moment. His siblings were talking and laughing with their neighbours. His mother was doting on her granddaughter. His father was calling for someone to pass the pesto. There were so many people here, relatives he barely knew and plus ones who might never appear again. Marco was just another one of them. If he showed up repeatedly, there might be a little more interest in him, but no more than was given to any new partner. Daniele had worried that this dinner might be difficult, but to see Marco accepted into the fold so easily filled him with a wonderful feeling of warmth.

**Chapter 38**

If the first few days of the relationship could be summed up as a series of nerve-wracking conversations, the first two months were encapsulated as a time of extraordinary changes in Daniele's life.

The first of these was the creation of a 5pm rota for the first time since he'd started working at the centre. It had never been questioned that he would cover the graveyard shift, but he had learned his lesson about neglecting a work-life balance and the end of his loneliness had also removed the desire to do extreme amounts of overtime. Pietro seemed pleased with the development, although Gianni was accustomed to leaving early whenever he chose and took some time to adjust.

The centre also had a new volunteer in the form of Marco, who took one week to realise that the opportunity to spend more time with Daniele and make sure his soul was kept squeaky-clean was right in front of him. His previous employment made him well qualified for the role and Gianni had already said that when he inevitably burned out of this job, he knew his desk would be in safe hands. Pietro had jokingly begged not to be left alone with the lovebirds, but he'd smiled nevertheless and said it was a possibility.

In addition, the new rota meant that Daniele had more energy to enjoy his evenings. The once silent house was now filled with conversation and a light-hearted atmosphere pervaded every inch of it. Sometimes they cooked together and sometimes, if they didn't feel like it, they simply went to a restaurant or a food van. There was a truck selling pasta around the corner from Daniele's building that he'd never noticed before, and their carbonara was worthy of a Michelin-starred restaurant. One of the side-effects of being in love, apparently, was a certain reluctance to behave as a sensible middle-aged person should. There were better things to do, and none of them involved YouTube.

Marco called the assistant manager of La Baia at the end of September. The man was surprised to hear from him, and even more surprised that Marco wanted employment and not a date, but apparently the response to his playing hadn't been entirely due to heavenly trickery. Marco was now paid to play on Monday and Tuesday nights, when prices were cheaper and there were fewer people around, in the hopes of enticing more people into the bar. Daniele started leaving work early on those days to join the crowd for a drink and a show at his workplace, much to the delight of Gianni who was once again able to leave early on Fridays.

La Baia became a regular haunt at the weekend too. He and Marco would go out on a Saturday night, get drunk and have a karaoke session before swaying home and falling into bed. Domenico was delighted to see them and over the course of time and regular visits to his workplace, he became something close to a friend. They'd been to see a few movies on his recommendation, he sometimes brought coffee on Sunday mornings when they couldn't be bothered to get out of bed, and he had the honour of pushing Marco into attending the cooking class that he'd enjoyed so much. Ironically Marco's culinary skills hadn't improved all that much since, but he'd discovered a great talent for baking.

One night, Daniele came home from work to find his boyfriend cooking dinner, or rather poking at a saucepan with a wooden spoon while he peered suspiciously at the pasta within. Daniele took his place at the cooker and, as he stirred, Marco's head landed on his shoulder.

"Lele," He used that imploring tone of voice which meant he was about to ask for something. "You know that you love me?"

"I do."

"And you know that everything I do is to help you?"

"This is sounding very ominous."

"I just want you to remember that you love me."

"Is there a reason I would forget that?"

Marco heaved a breath, blowing hot air over Daniele's neck, and then stepped back. "I called a surveyor to look at the flat."

Daniele turned to face him. "When? Why?"

"This afternoon. She came this afternoon. The report's on the coffee table." He turned away and Daniele saw him gnawing nervously on his finger. He abandoned the pasta and hurried into the living room. The report was seven pages long and his eyes danced over the words, able to focus less and less as he read further.

"Jesus Christ, Marco!" He burst back into the kitchen, waving the paper. "Look at this! They're saying the house is barely inhabitable!"

"To be fair, surveyors pick up every tiny fault so they can't be blamed for missing things," Marco said. "Obviously it's inhabitable, you've lived here for ages, but it's a good report to take to the housing authority."

"Is that why you did this? Are you trying to help me move?" He came up behind Marco and wrapped his arms around him. "It's a lovely thing to try, sweetheart, and thank you, but this place is convenient for work and the housing authority aren't going to put me in a better flat."

"You can hide it in a drawer if you want, but there's something else."

Daniele lifted his head and put his chin on his boyfriend's shoulder. "Please say there's no more" he requested.

"There is a small community of mobile homes opening in Ostia. Pietro did his ambush thing, writing the owners a letter to say how much you deserve it. It must have been good because they called to say you can view one before it goes on the market."

"And how do you know about this?"

"They put a brochure through the door. It's on the bed."

Daniele sighed and pressed his forehead into Marco's back. "There's not enough water for the pasta in there" he said, gesturing to the saucepan. He turned on the kettle and headed to the bedroom. Once again, he found a neatly presented stack of papers awaiting him in the centre of the duvet. He sat down and started to read. He had to admit, the glossy photos and information booklet painted a pretty picture. There were twenty homes spread out across the sea with two entrances, one for pedestrians and one for cars, each of which had a security booth to ensure unauthorised personnel couldn't enter.

The homes themselves were more like bungalows. According to the booklet, they each had a spacious open-plan kitchen and living room, two bedrooms and a bathroom. In other words, they were the size of an apartment. A good apartment judging by the photos.

There was a covered wooden porch and a small piece of lawn outside which formed a garden for each family. It wasn't enclosed, sure, but it was still more private than a communal courtyard. There was also a children's playground somewhere in the complex and the Pontile Di Ostia was a mere five minute walk away.

A quick search on Google Maps revealed that Ostia was an hour's drive away, only a little less convenient than Fiumicino would have been, and had the added bonus of no planes roaring overhead. Daniele's mind conjured images of playing on the beach with the kids, making dinner on the barbecue, sitting on the porch at night with Marco and a cold refreshing beer. It seemed ideal.

"What do you think?"
When his daydream faded and his eyes refocused, the dreariness of his bedroom was almost a surprise. Marco was standing in the doorway, still holding his wooden spoon. Daniele smiled at him.
"I think that in some ways, you haven't changed at all" he answered.
"Is that a bad thing?"
He smiled, but the concern in his eyes was clear. Daniele stood, crossed the room and gently sandwiched Marco's face in his hands. "I wouldn't want you to be any different. You wouldn't be my Marco otherwise."

Marco gave a relieved smile. Daniele left a kiss on his nose and turned to pick up the brochure. "Alright," he declared. "So when are we going to look at this place?"

\*\*

In mid-October, nine months and one week after the shooting, Stelis Ornata had come to play in Rome. Marco had approached him shyly with the tickets.

"I like them, so I'm going," he said. "You can come if you want, only if you want. It's okay if you don't like them or you're not...happy about going to a venue."

The seats weren't in the stalls, he added. "I don't know if that makes a difference. I bought a box so there won't be people around us. It'll just be you and me."

Daniele had agreed to go, and Marco's delight when he did seemed to indicate that he'd made the right choice. He'd come a long way since the attack. When he thought of attending another concert, there was only a mild nervousness, soon quelled by his logical side. The chances of being shot in the same place twice were miniscule. He would be fine.

It was a shame that real life often didn't turn out like the movies. If Daniele had lived inside a film, this would have been the last part of a triumphant recovery before the credits rolled. Instead, one hour before they were due to leave, he was struck down by debilitating fear and almost couldn't leave the house. By the time they reached the venue, he felt like he was going to die, and was in the box for only five minutes before having to run to the bathroom to be sick. For almost the entire concert, he was in and out of the bathroom, needing to purge even when there was nothing left in his stomach. He thought about simply not returning and allowing Marco to have his fun, but his angel came looking for him and missed about four songs in doing so. Daniele stayed in the box after that, solely because he worried about getting both of them thrown out if he kept acting like a plague victim, barely focusing on the music and concentrating entirely on keeping his panic from spiking anymore.

   The one thing which stopped the night from being a total failure, aside from Marco singing and dancing through every number and fortunately having a wonderful time despite his companion, was when Daniele forced himself to rally for the second-last song. It was the only one he knew, the *Enter Sandman* cover that he'd played at random on Marco's first night in his home, and it caught his attention even through the fog of pain. Once he was standing, singing and concentrating on anything else other than where he was, the panic lifted. He wondered if he would have had a better time if he'd battled the fear and forced himself to move before, but it didn't matter. For those two songs, he had fun. Marco was buzzing with joy as they walked home, and inside Daniele was a small nugget of happiness that hope wasn't lost, and one day he might be completely alright again.

**

   At the end of October, they took their first holiday as a couple to Kythira. The decision was made partly because Cristina had let it be known that she and the kids were returning to Rome in November, and as overwhelmed with happiness as Daniele was, he knew that meant the freedom and the giddy early days of the love affair were going to dissipate to make room for the responsibilities of parenting. Even knowing that Marco was fond of his children, Daniele had worried about how he would respond. After all, they were used to giving each other their undivided attention and now that was no longer an option.

"The kids are coming back next month" he said, after hanging up the phone.

"They are? That's brilliant news! You must be so happy!"

Marco hugged him and Daniele grinned. "I am, but I think we should take a holiday before they're here. We'll probably end up going to Disneyland next summer" he said lightly. Marco's face had lit up like a child's.

"I can't wait for an excuse to go to Disneyland!" he declared, and Daniele fell a little more in love with him in that moment. It still amazed him that he'd managed to find someone whom his heart was so well made for.

Before Disneyland, however, there was Greece. They stayed in a guest house directly above the beach and it had been incredible. They had lived on the sand or under the cypress trees at the top of the cliff, swimming in the sea or hiring a boat to explore the caves. Marco had been in his element out on the water. There were days when they left in the morning and didn't come back to shore until evening, and only concern that the taverna would close and send them to bed hungry had persuaded them to return.

Daniele still had his tan when, ten days after returning to Rome, he once again stood in Fiumicino Airport. This time he was in the Arrivals lounge, watching the crowd of disembarking passengers. They were near the back of the throng, and he caught sight of them only an instant before he was spotted.

"Papa!" Sofia pulled free from her mother's grip and bolted for him, ignoring the barrier set up to divide passengers from those awaiting their arrival, and ducked underneath to reach him. He swung her up and set her on his hip, putting a kiss in her hair. "And Marco! Marco, you're here!"

Daniele chuckled and put her down, turning to the other two arrivals. Cristina was laden down with a large suitcase and a holdall slung across her chest. Matteo had a backpack for his luggage and was pulling a second, smaller suitcase with both hands. By contrast, Sofia carried only a tiny handbag. Daniele felt a stab of sympathy for his ex and son, having to drag all of that through train stations and airports without assistance.

"Let me take one."
He reached out and Cristina willingly yielded the holdall, exhaling wearily. Daniele picked it up and put the strap over his shoulder. Marco stepped in and took Matteo's suitcase, freeing him to go to his father and hug him around the middle. Daniele ruffled his hair and returned the embrace, trying not to let relief overwhelm him or squeeze too tightly.
"Hi, Marco."
Marco lifted his palm in greeting as Matteo took a step towards him, starting to lift his own hand to give the high five, before dropping it and hugging Marco too. It lasted only a second before he moved away and reattached himself to Daniele.

Cristina and Marco led the way towards the exit. Daniele held a child's hand in each of his and delighted in the simple pleasure of it. "How was your journey?" he asked as they followed their luggage.
"We got lost" Sofia answered.

"We couldn't find the train station" Matteo agreed.

"And then we had to run to catch our flight," Sofia added. "Mama got upset because the security lady took her water."

"A tough day overall then? It's nearly over" Daniele said in an attempt to be reassuring.

"I can't wait to see Nonna," his daughter remarked cheerfully. "Papa, I was thinking. I know you love Marco, but I don't want another dad. Can he be my uncle instead?"

"You'd have to ask, but I don't think…"

"Marco, will you be my uncle?" she called, as Matteo sighed. Marco looked over his shoulder and beamed at her.

"I'd love to be your uncle!"

Sofia fell asleep in the car on the way to her grandparents', rousing only as Daniele carried her into the building. She was able to give a tired hello and a hug to Nonna as hoped, and then draped herself across the armchair and fell back to sleep. Daniele brought her to the spare room, where the old double bed was already freshly made up, and left Cristina to coax her into pyjamas.

When he returned to the living room, his father held a red plastic sack with Santa on the front, and was showing its contents to Matteo. Inside was an apparently endless stream of sweets and toys. Daniele knew the culprit at once.

"Mama, you shouldn't have bought so much."

"I wanted to welcome them home properly" she replied unrepentantly.

"Thank you Nonna. Thanks Nonno" Matteo said, and then sat down on the floor to figure out the mechanics of a remote control car.

Cristina returned to the room, looked at the sack, and sighed. "Eleonora, that wasn't necessary."

"I know, but I love seeing the children happy," she declared and stood up. "Can I offer you some biscuits?"

Daniele sat on the sofa, cradling a mug of tea, letting the quiet conversation drift over him. There had been a small dispute about whether Matteo was allowed a biscuit before bed, in which Cristina had gotten her way over the indulgent grandparents, and his son was now finishing up his glass of warm milk.

"Alright, Teo, time for bed" Cristina ordered as soon as the last dregs were gone.

"Night Nonno." He stood and hugged his grandfather. "Thanks for letting us stay. Night Nonna. Thanks for the presents."

She chuckled as she hugged him goodnight, and then he was gone. Daniele heard the creak of the kitchen door as he went in to return his milk glass, the soft murmur of voices, and then footsteps heading up the hall towards the bedrooms. He drained the last of his tea and stood.

"Does anyone want more biscuits?"

Marco was standing at the kitchen sink, washing dishes. Daniele left his mug on the draining board and hugged him from behind. "You don't have to hide in here."

"I'm being useful."

"You don't have to be useful," Daniele kissed his cheek. "You can come and sit with us."

"I don't know..." Marco picked up his mug and dunked it in the basin.

Daniele sighed and released his hold. "Well, Matteo's gone to bed now so we don't have to stay much longer."

"Only if you don't want to. I wouldn't drag you away from your parents."

"By all means, do. I only wanted to make sure the kids were settled and they are. Now I just want to go home and cuddle with you."

Marco turned around, smiling. "I'll finish the dishes first. Oh, did you know Matteo came to say goodnight to me."

"I heard that" Daniele said, smiling at his beloved's enthusiasm.

Marco shrugged, failing to conceal his delight, and turned back to the dishes. "It was nice of him to do that," he remarked faux-casually. "I'll see you out there."

Daniele nodded and left him to it, sticking his head into the living room to say his goodbyes. "Hey, Marco and I are going to head out. We'll talk tomorrow."

"Will we see you on Sunday?" his mother asked. "Please say you'll come. It will be so nice to have the whole family together again."

Daniele chewed those words over in his mind and liked the sound of them. *The whole family*. "You're right," he said, nodding. "We wouldn't miss it."

## Chapter 39

No less than three locks clicked before the front door opened, and Isabella's wrinkled face creased into a smile at the sight of him. "What a surprise! How have you been?" she asked, already shuffling aside to let him in. "I didn't know you were coming today."

"It's just a flying visit to see how you are. Sorry it's been so long."

She waved away his apologies and showed him to the living room, directing him to sit in front of a piece of clapboard set on four milk trays. "There's a spare cushion there."

"I didn't realise you didn't have a table" Daniele remarked, attempting to fold his legs under him.

"I do have a table," Isabella protested. "It's like the Japanese tables, ikimatsu or whatever they're called."

She walked towards the kitchen, one of her legs dragging noticeably.

"How's your hip?" Daniele asked.

"It's fine. I have pills for it. How are you?"

"Good."

"I'm pleased."

He heard an alarming rattle and a high-pitched whistle from the kitchen, and stood to look around the dividing wall. Isabella was making tea in a tin pot, using the ring on the stove to heat it up. The curtains were lopsided, hanging off the window with a few rings missing.

While Isabella was distracted, he turned and wandered down the hall. There were several buckets in the bathroom to catch a leak from the ceiling. The heater in her bedroom was the orange three-bar variety, not a proper radiator. The walls could use repainting as well.

Whatever colour they originally were, it had faded to dull brown.

Alright, so his tasks were to call a plumber to fix the ceiling and install a radiator, and meanwhile Daniele could buy a kettle, a table and some paint for...He stopped. It wasn't good to get caught up in this trap again. The urge to fix things was overwhelming, but he forced himself to think again. The leak and radiator were the most important things. It would be the New Year before a plumber could come in, but Isabella could cope with her makeshift tools until then. With his new work-life balance, Daniele wouldn't have time to sort out her walls, but he could call a professional for that too and hand over responsibility. And while he couldn't provide clients with every small luxury these days, he could certainly stretch to a kettle. It could be framed as a late Christmas present.

He returned to the kitchen and helped Isabella carry the tea into the living room. They sat down on either side of her Japanese table and drank their tea. Daniele noticed the small tree in the corner, decorated with the silver foil from cigarette packets, and smiled.
"Oh yes," Isabella said, observing his gaze. "I thought I'd make some small gesture to the season, even if I'm not celebrating."
"Not at all?"
"I have been writing Christmas cards," she said. "I sit by the window and watch the lights while I'm working. It really gets me in the mood. Christmas is such a beautiful time. It's so nice to see everyone having fun. In fact," She struggled to her feet. "I wrote one for you too. I was planning to post it, but since you're here..."
"You didn't have to..." Daniele protested.

"After all you've done for me, why wouldn't I? Besides, who else am I going to write to? I wouldn't say I have a great social life," she said, still smiling. The card she handed him bore a red-breasted robin on the front, and simple festive wishes inside. "Why are you working on Christmas Eve anyway?"

"I'm not. I came over to see you, but officially I'm off work until 6th January" he declared proudly.

"Make sure that you are," Isabella replied, a warning very similar to the one Pietro had delivered on Daniele's last day. "Have you any plans for the season?"

Daniele smiled as he thought about his plans. Matteo wanted to get reacquainted with the museums in Rome as well as with the new laser tag facility he'd seen advertised. Sofia had recently discovered a love for stargazing, thanks to Marco's influence, and he had no hope of keeping her away from the Christmas funfair. Marco, of course, wanted to see a play at the theatre or a band at one of the local bars. His own plans were more sedentary; watching movies under a blanket fort with his son, challenging his daughter to a drawing competition, sharing music with his boyfriend. He couldn't care less what he did as long as his favourite people were with him.

"Tomorrow we're having a big Christmas dinner at my parents' house, and then between Christmas and New Year will be spent with my partner. No concrete plans for after that."

"Go out for New Year. It's a lot of fun for couples" Isabella advised.

Daniele grinned. "I'm fairly sure that we will."

\*\*

For once the warm glow from the kitchen windows didn't sadden him. He was no longer alone on the street, glancing into other people's homes in a futile attempt to absorb their warmth. He had his own home waiting for him.

He loved his new home. His living room was open-plan, spacious and airy with honey yellow walls that radiated happiness and warmth. Marco had got his way on the paint this time and, with the benefit of distance, Daniele could see how prison-like and cramped the old living room had been. The futon had come with them to Ostia and it remained the best place to relax of an evening, as well as gaining a new purpose as a jungle gym and sleepover centre whenever the kids were with them. The hallway to the bedrooms was lined with bright canvases and framed photographs, meticulously compiled by Marco.
"I think they're beautiful. What do you think?" he had asked, holding the images up to the wall. He had looked so hopeful and Daniele had realised that he wasn't the only one for whom this house represented a fresh start.
"I think you're a brilliant interior designer" he had said, and revelled in Marco's overjoyed smile.

He could see the Christmas tree in the corner as he approached, every inch of it covered in multi-coloured baubles and lights. The four of them had decorated it at three weekends ago and a strange feeling had come over Daniele as he sat carefully disentangling the bauble strings, watching Matteo help Marco with the lights and Sofia making a ball out of silver tinsel, demanding to be lifted so she could put it atop the tree. He had given up hope of being able to experience such moments again, of feeling like he was part of a family.

He opened the front door and was struck by a wall of heat and the smell of melted chocolate.

"Papa's back!" Sofia shouted.

"Oh no, hide the evidence" Marco replied.

"Evidence of what?" he asked, removing his hat, scarf and coat. "What are you up to?"

He walked over to the kitchen and felt his mouth fall open when he saw the origin of the smell. A chocolate cake stood on the counter, decorated with strawberries which in turn had been coated in dark chocolate on both sides and a lace of white chocolate across the middle. There was also a plate of four cupcakes, two coated in red icing with red glitter on top, the other two decorated to look like footballs.

"You made this?" he asked, looking awestruck at Marco, and once again thought about ringing the Vatican and arranging for Domenico to be made a saint for suggesting that cooking class.

"I helped!" Sofia piped up. "I did the strawberries!"

"It turned out well, didn't it?" Marco said proudly. "Do you want to try it?"

"I'd love to. I'm getting hungry just looking at it."

"You can't eat it," Sofia declared, aghast. "That's my art."

The two men glanced at each other and shared a smile.

"We're going to put it in the fridge until tomorrow," Marco explained. "This is going to be dessert for the Christmas dinner. The cupcakes are free to try though."

"I'll take whatever the kids leave" Daniele said. He picked up his daughter and brought her over to the sofa to join Matteo.

"How was your day?" he asked, putting an arm around both of them.

"Really good," Sofia enthused. "We had pasta for lunch and Marco took us to the market and let us all buy one thing. I got a ring."

She proudly waved a fluorescent pink band under his nose. "Matteo got a notebook and Marco got a jacket for you," she added. "It's black and really smooth. He put it in a box under the bed."

"Sofi," Matteo scolded. "It was supposed to be a surprise! You didn't have to say everything."

His daughter turned slightly red. "Well, I'm not allowed to lie. Am I, Papa?" she demanded. He couldn't help smiling. Sofia truly was a master at adapting every situation to her benefit. God knew how he'd cope when she was a teenager, but that was a worry for another time.

"No, you're not allowed to lie" he replied. She smiled triumphantly, and then climbed off the sofa and ran back to the kitchen.

He turned to greet Matteo. "Were you at work?" his son asked quietly.

"No, I went to see an old woman who's alone, but I'm on holiday for the next two weeks so we can spend lots of time together."

"Really?" Matteo's eyes briefly lit up before he attempted to replace his poker face.

"Really." Daniele ruffled his hair and pulled him into a hug.

"Can you help me paint my solar system then?"

That was how the rest of the day was spent, sitting on the floor and Googling planets to find out what colour they were supposed to be, Daniele assisting with Jupiter and Saturn while Matteo took charge of the smaller and more delicate ones. Marco distracted Sofia from employing her creative flair on her brother's school project, suggesting that she write down what she wanted to do over the holidays instead. She was delighted to have a project of her own to attend to.

"Sweetheart, what does this mean?" Marco asked, pointing over her shoulder.

"I'm going to play video games with Matteo" she answered innocently.

"Okay, then maybe you should say that. I think your teacher might be surprised to read that you were shooting planes over Christmas."

Cristina arrived to pick them up in the evening, as Matteo was carefully painting Neptune, and Sofia was watching *L'eredita* with a cupcake in her hand.

"Can we stay for a few more minutes? I only have one planet to do" Matteo protested.

"Okay, finish your planet" his mother agreed.

Daniele took the opportunity to draw her into the corner and lowered his voice. "My parents are doing Christmas dinner tomorrow. Would you be interested in coming?"

"Hmm, it's always a fight between the grandparents at this time of year" Cristina murmured thoughtfully.

"You could go to your mother's on St Stephen's," he suggested. "I'd like to see the kids opening their presents so if you even came for the morning?"

She bit her lip and then nodded. "I'll talk to my mother. I think St Stephen's should be fine for her. It's less pressure. She'll want us to stay until New Year though."

"That's fine. Marco and I have plans."

"Really?" Cristina's voice rose a little in surprise. Daniele held a finger to his lips and she nodded in understanding.

"I'm finished!" Matteo announced. Sofia looked at him and then at her mother.
"We can't go yet. The show isn't finished" she complained.
"We have to head off to beat the traffic. Say goodbye" Cristina ordered. Sofia pouted and then shoved the rest of her cupcake into her mouth.
"Hope I haven't spoiled her dinner" Daniele remarked.
"It's fine, I'll probably just get a takeaway at this point. It's funny how their hunger levels change when they see what's on the plate" Cristina said good-humouredly.

Sofia walked over to Marco and tugged his hand. "Kiss" she demanded. He bent down to her level and let her kiss his cheek, and then did the same back. It never failed to give Daniele a warm feeling when he saw them perform that ritual so naturally.
"Need some help or are you okay carrying it on your own?" Marco asked, as Matteo carefully lifted his completed project.
"I'm fine, thanks. Bye Marco."
Daniele hugged the kids goodbye and went to the door to wave them off. Once he couldn't see them anymore, he came back inside to find Marco already washing the dishes.

"Did you have a good day?" Daniele asked. It had only been two months since his family expanded and he was still trying to find the perfect balance between considering Marco and his children. It was clear that they got along well and Marco didn't seem burdened by them at all – he had read four bedtime stories in a row last weekend without complaint – but Daniele still felt bad about leaving them in his care all afternoon.

"I had a great day," Marco replied, leaving the last plate aside for Daniele to dry. "Use the bathroom now if you need to. I'm taking a shower."
"Do you want some company?" he offered hopefully.
"No," Marco shot him that impish smirk he loved and hated so much. "Why, did you miss me today? I missed you, walking around for two and a half hours with no offer of a piggyback."
"I'm afraid Sofia is the only one who'll ever get a piggyback from me."
"Then we shall both suffer alone." Marco blew him a kiss before disappearing around the corner, and Daniele shook his head in amusement.

He dried and put away the dishes, before heading down to his bedroom to prepare for slumber. As he opened his drawer to select a T-shirt for bed, his eyes fell upon a royal blue book with a hardback cover and a gold ribbon tied around it for privacy, and he lifted it out. He'd bought it because he now had too many photos to frame and keep on a table, and he knew that once he started looking through the album, he could be here for hours. Nevertheless he opened the front page.

The first photo was the trip to the beach when Sofia was a baby, and then her first and second birthdays, a football match with Matteo, holidays and Christmases, and then a time jump from one page to the other. Suddenly there was Sofia's first day at school, Matteo with the trophy his team had won, Marco sitting on a roundabout as both children tried to make it spin, Sofia wearing his sunglasses and looking like a cross between a blues singer and a bumblebee, a photo that the tavern owner had taken in Kythira...

"Why are you looking at pictures when I'm here?"
Daniele looked up and smiled at the sight of Marco in a white T-shirt and a pair of red checked pyjama pants, with his hair in one big fluffy mass.
"You look good."
Marco frowned inquisitively. "Like this?"
Daniele nodded, reaching out to take his hand and pull him onto the bed. "You look very soft and cuddly."
"I am so insulted," Marco declared, snuggling into him. "I spend ages trying to look nice and you say this is what you like? How dare you?"
He rested his head on Daniele's shoulder and left a light kiss on his neck, a clear indication of what grave offence had been caused. Daniele put an arm around him and played with the hair at the back of his head.
"You always look so sharp and smart. I like this side of you."
"Well, enjoy it. It's nocturnal."

An arm looped around Daniele's neck and he gladly returned the hug, laughing quietly. He loved how cuddly Marco got when he was tired or bored. It had been added to the list of amusements he made for himself when nothing else was happening. Read, play games, hug Daniele, and it didn't matter where they were or what they were doing. Last week, they'd been in the supermarket and Daniele had been trying to choose between spaghetti Bolognese and roast beef for dinner, when Marco had decided to start cuddling him in the middle of the aisle like a particularly affectionate cat. If anyone had looked at them, Daniele hadn't noticed. He'd felt so happy and cared for that the public arena truly hadn't mattered, and that was a revelation in its own right.

"Be careful or I'll think you like me" he said now.
"Oh, I wouldn't want you to get that impression," Marco squeezed him tightly and then lifted his head to kiss him on the lips. "Come on, you said you wanted an early night so you weren't tired tomorrow."
Daniele quickly pulled on a T-shirt and a pair of shorts, and hurried to join Marco under the covers. "Cold night" he remarked, pulling the duvet over his shoulders with relief. Marco hummed in agreement and started efficiently rubbing Daniele's arms and shoulders.
"Better?"
"Very much so."
Marco shifted closer, hugged him around the middle and pecked his lips. "Do you want to know what happened today?" he asked.
"Yes, of course."
"Matteo called me Uncle Marco. It's the first time he's done that."
"You're part of the family" Daniele said simply. Marco blinked and bit his lip, and then laughed and put a hand over his face.
"Are you okay?" Daniele sat up anxiously.
"I'm just happy."
Daniele would have pulled him into a hug immediately, except he didn't think Marco would appreciate that when he was fighting so hard not to cry. He watched until Marco

lowered his hand, blinking suspiciously fast, and then smiled.

"Sofia was quizzing me today" he said.

"About what?"

"About us. She asked if I was your prince."

Daniele threw his head back and laughed. "Oh, she's so sweet," he said fondly. "Yes, she's very much into the whole prince and princess thing right now. She loves the idea that a prince will come for her on a white horse."

Marco nodded thoughtfully. The familiar spark of mischief was back in his eyes. "Yes…Well, it's wonderful if a prince comes for you," he said, smiling softly at Daniele. "It's even better if you come for each other."

Daniele choked and then descended into unstoppable laughter. He had to hide his face in his hands because he just knew from the heat in his cheeks that he was turning red. He could hear Marco's dry, wicked cackle spurring him on.

"Tell me…" he managed to gasp. "Please tell me you did not say that to my child."

Marco giggled again. "Why? Is there a meaning I didn't catch?" he teased, but then shook his head. "No, I told her that I wasn't your prince. You were mine. It fits. You saved me."

Daniele shook his head. "I don't think I did."

"You gave me a second chance, Lele" Marco insisted.

He sighed and lay back on the pillow. "You say that I saved you, but the way I see it, you gave me everything."

"I haven't given you everything yet" Marco said solemnly.

Daniele frowned, confused and a little concerned. "What more is there to give?"

"The leather jacket that is no longer a surprise."

He chuckled with relief and pulled gently on a curl, and then immediately undid the punishment with a kiss.

"Speaking of that..." He brushed his hand along Marco's arm. "How much did you spend on my Christmas present?"

"Um...not a lot" Marco murmured, losing the ability to make eye contact.

"We set a budget of a hundred euros. Did you remember?"

"Lele, the money doesn't matter," Marco said piously. "Your smile is worth any price."

Daniele looked at him, unimpressed. "I will not be smiling if I see three digits on our bank statement."

"Oh, shush. Christmas is a time for being generous" Marco retorted, rolling over.

Daniele grinned and hugged him from behind, planting a few kisses on his cheek and neck. "We really need to stay within our budget, Marco. Your present wasn't cheap either."

"Now I'm intrigued."

"I hoped you would be."

He rolled away and reached into the drawer beside his bed, lifting out the long white envelope he'd secreted in there. "As your surprise was ruined, there's no harm in evening the field," he said. "I know we've already had a holiday, but it's for the New Year so technically I'm not being extravagant."

He handed over the envelope. Marco looked at it curiously, turning it over in a way so reminiscent of Sofia, and then carefully unstuck the glue from one side. He pulled out a rectangular piece of paper, read the words inked across it, and let out a small gasp.

"Is it a good present?" Daniele asked, suddenly panicked that Marco might not be as excited by this surprise as he was. "I don't know, maybe you don't want to..."

Marco hugged him with enough force to knock him onto his back, and left a trail of kisses from his mouth to his ear.

"Are you serious?" he cried. There were other words as well, muffled beyond comprehension in Daniele's neck, but the barely contained sobs of joy were all he needed to hear.

"I don't know how often you've been, but you clearly loved Corsica so I think I'd like to see it" he said casually.

"Ti amo" Marco whispered. Daniele thought his heart might split with joy.

"Anch'io," he said. "I chose Bastia because the ferry goes from there. I'd like to see all the places that are special to you."

Marco kissed his cheek and sat up, looking down at him. "I got you a jacket and you got me this?"

"You gave me a home, a family, a life and a jacket," Daniele corrected. "This is the most equivalent thing I can offer."

"You have no idea how much this means to me. I can show you where I used to live."

"I can't wait."

Marco kissed him again, soft and a bit saltier than usual, and put the tickets carefully back in the envelope. He reached over Daniele to replace them in the drawer and then lay down. Daniele reached for his hand and caressed the knuckles with his thumb.

"This has been the best Christmas of my life already" Marco remarked happily.

"Let's see if you still say that tomorrow. It'll be mayhem."

"Good," he replied. "Thank you again. Now sleep. You're tired, I can see it."

Daniele held Marco's hand over his heart and closed his eyes, ready to welcome dreams that couldn't be better than reality.

Printed in Great Britain
by Amazon